Mysteries

Mysteries

KNUT HAMSUN

NEWLY TRANSLATED FROM THE NORWEGIAN BY
GERRY BOTHMER

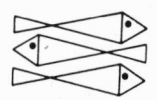

Farrar, Straus and Giroux

NEW YORK

Mysteries

1

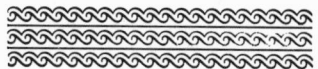

I N the middle of the summer of 1891 the most extraordinary things began happening in a small Norwegian coastal town. A stranger by the name of Nagel appeared, a singular character who shook the town by his eccentric behavior and then vanished as suddenly as he had come. At one point he had a visitor: a mysterious young lady who came for God knows what reason and dared stay only a few hours. But let me begin at the beginning . . .

It all started at six one evening when a steamer landed at the dock and three passengers appeared on deck. One of them was a man wearing a loud yellow suit and an outsized corduroy cap.

It was the evening of the twelfth of June; flags were flying all over town in honor of Miss Kielland's engagement, which had been announced that day. The porter from the Central Hotel went aboard and the man in the yellow suit handed him his baggage. At the same time he surrendered his ticket to one of the ship's officers, but made no move to go ashore, and began pacing up and down the deck. He seemed extremely agitated, and when the ship's bell rang the third time, he hadn't even paid the steward his bill.

While he was taking care of his bill, he suddenly became aware that the ship was pulling out. Startled, he shouted over the railing to the porter below: "It's all right. Take my baggage to the hotel and reserve a room for me."

With that, the ship carried him out into the fjord.

This man was Johan Nilsen Nagel.

The porter took his baggage away on a cart. It consisted of only two small trunks, a fur coat (although it was the middle of summer), a satchel, and a violin case. None of them had any identification tags.

Around noon the following day Johan Nagel came driving down the road to the hotel in a carriage drawn by two horses. It would have been easier to make the journey by boat, but still he came by carriage. He had some more baggage with him; on the front seat was a suitcase, a coat, and a small bag with the initials J.N.N. set in pearls.

Before getting out of the carriage, he asked the hotel-keeper about his room, and later, on being taken up to the second floor, he began to examine the walls to determine how thick they were and whether any sounds could come through from the adjoining rooms. Suddenly he turned to the chambermaid and asked: "What is your name?"

"Sara."

"Sara." And without pausing: "Can you get me something to eat? Well, so your name's Sara. Tell me," he went on, "was there ever a pharmacy on these premises?"

Surprised, Sara answered: "Yes, but that was many years ago."

"Oh, many years ago? I knew it the minute I came in; it wasn't so much the smell, but somehow I sensed it."

When he came down for dinner, he didn't say a word during the entire meal. His fellow passengers from the day before—the two men at the other end of the table—made signs to each other when he came in, and made no effort to hide their amusement at his previous evening's misfortune, but he took no notice of them. He ate quickly, declined dessert, and left the table abruptly by sliding backwards off the bench, lit a cigar, and disappeared down the street.

He stayed out until long after midnight and didn't return till a few minutes before the clock struck three. Where had he been? Only later did it become known that he had walked to the next town and back—along the same long road he had driven over that morning. He must have had some very urgent business there. When Sara opened the door for him, he was wet with perspiration, but he smiled at her and seemed to be in excellent spirits.

"My God, girl, what a lovely neck you have!" he said. "Did any letters come for me while I was out—for Nagel, Johan Nagel? Three telegrams! Oh, would you do me the favor of taking away that picture on the wall, would you? I don't like to have it staring at me. It would really annoy me to lie in bed and have to look at it! Besides, Napoleon III didn't have such a bushy beard, anyway! Thank you."

When Sara had gone, Nagel remained standing in the middle of the room. He stood absolutely motionless, staring fixedly at a spot on the wall, and except that his head slumped more and more to one side, he didn't move.

He was below average in height; his face was dark-complexioned, with deep brown eyes which had a strange expression, and a soft, rather feminine mouth. On one finger he wore a plain ring of lead or iron. His shoulders were very broad; he was between twenty-eight and thirty, but definitely not older, although his hair was beginning to turn gray at the temples.

He awoke from his thoughts with a violent start, so exaggerated that it didn't seem genuine; it was as if the gesture had been made for effect, even though he was alone in the room. Then he took some keys, small change, and what looked like a lifesaver's medal on a crumpled ribbon out of his pocket and put them on a table next to the bed. He stuck his wallet under the pillow, and from his vest pocket he pulled out a watch and a small vial labeled "poison." He held the watch in his hand for a moment before putting it down, but immediately put the vial back in his pocket. Then he removed his ring and washed, smoothing his hair back with his fingers, never once looking in the mirror.

He was already in bed when he suddenly missed his ring, which he had left lying on the washbasin, and as though unable to be separated from this perfectly ordinary ring, he got up and put it on again. Then he began opening the three telegrams, but before he had finished the first one, he uttered a short, muffled laugh.

He lay there laughing to himself; his teeth were exceptionally fine. Then his face became serious again and a moment later he nonchalantly tossed the telegrams aside. Yet they all apparently dealt with a matter of great importance; they referred to an offer of 62,000 crowns for a country estate, the money to be paid in cash if the deal were concluded at once. They were brief, matter-of-fact business telegrams, definitely not sent as a hoax, although they were unsigned. A few minutes later Nagel fell asleep. The two candles on the table, which he had forgotten to put out, illuminated his clean-shaven face and his chest and quietly flickered on the telegrams, which lay wide-open on the table.

The next morning Johan Nagel sent a messenger to the post office, who returned with some newspapers—several of them foreign—but no letters. He put his violin case on a chair in the middle of the room, as if he wanted to show it off, but he didn't open it, and simply left it there.

All he did that morning was to write a couple of letters and walk up and down his room reading a book. He also went to a shop and bought a pair of gloves, and then wandered over to the marketplace, where he bought a little reddish-brown puppy for ten crowns which he im-mediately presented to the hotelkeeper. Everyone thought it very amusing that he named the puppy Jacobsen, al-though it was a female.

He managed to do nothing the rest of the day as well. He had no business to attend to in town, no offices to contact, and no calls to make, as he didn't know a soul. The people in the hotel were baffled by his strange apathy toward everything, including his own affairs. The three telegrams lay open on the table in his room for everyone to read; he hadn't looked at them again since the night they arrived. And sometimes, when asked a direct ques-tion, he didn't even answer. Twice the hotelkeeper had tried to engage him in conservation to find out who he was and what had brought him to town, but both times

Nagel had avoided the issue. Another instance of strange behavior occurred during the course of the day. Although he didn't have a single acquaintance in town and had made no effort to get in touch with anybody, he had nevertheless stopped all of a sudden in front of one of the young ladies of the town at the entrance to the cemetery, fixed his eyes on her, and then bowed deeply, without a word of explanation. The young woman blushed to the roots of her hair, deeply embarrassed, whereupon the impudent fellow walked out of town on the main road, as far as the parsonage, and beyond. He did this several days in a row, always returning to the hotel after closing time, so that the front door had to be opened for him.

On the third morning, as Nagel was leaving his room, he ran into the hotelkeeper, who greeted him with a few pleasant remarks. They went out on the veranda and sat down; by way of making conversation, the hotelkeeper asked him about the shipment of a crate of fresh fish. "Do you have any idea how I should go about it?" he asked.

Nagel looked at the crate, smiled, and shook his head. "I don't know anything about those things," he said.

"You don't? Well, I thought perhaps you had traveled a lot and had seen how they did it in other places."

"No, as a matter of fact, I haven't traveled much."

Pause.

"Well, you've probably been busy with other things. Are you a businessman, by any chance?"

"No, I'm not a businessman."

"Then you didn't come here on business?"

Nagel didn't answer, but lit a cigar, inhaled deeply, and assumed an absentminded air.

The hotelkeeper was observing him out of the corner of

his eye. "Won't you play for us sometime? I see that you have a violin with you."

"Oh, no, I've given that up," Nagel replied in an offhand manner.

He got up and walked away rather abruptly, but a moment later he came back and said: "By the way, it just occurred to me, you can give me the bill any time you like. It makes no difference to me when I pay."

"Thank you," said the hotelkeeper, "but there's no hurry. If you stay with us for any length of time, there will be a discount. Are you planning to stay for some time?"

Nagel suddenly seemed to come to life. His face flushed for no apparent reason and he quickly answered: "Yes, I may stay on here for some time; it all depends. Perhaps I didn't tell you; I'm an agronomist—a farmer. I've just returned from abroad and I might decide to settle down here for a while. But perhaps I even forgot to—my name is Nagel, Johan Nilsen Nagel."

He then heartily shook the hotelkeeper's hand and apologized for not having introduced himself sooner. There was not the slightest trace of irony in his expression.

"I've been thinking that we might be able to find you a better room, a quieter one," said the hotelkeeper. "You're close to the stairs now, and that can be rather noisy."

"Thank you, but there's no need for that. My room is quite satisfactory. Besides, I can see the entire town square from my window, and that is very pleasant."

After a slight pause, the hotelkeeper continued: "So you are taking a brief holiday now? Then you'll probably be here through the summer?"

"Two or three months, perhaps longer," Nagel replied. "I don't know for sure. It all depends. I'll make up my mind when the time comes."

At that moment a man walked by and bowed to the hotelkeeper. He was an insignificant-looking man, rather short and very badly dressed. He obviously moved with difficulty, but in spite of his handicap he was surprisingly agile. Although he bowed deeply, the hotelkeeper ignored him, but Nagel made a polite gesture and doffed his corduroy cap.

The hotelkeeper turned to him and said: "That's a man we call The Midget. He's not quite right in the head, but I feel sorry for him; he's a good fellow."

Nothing further was said about The Midget.

"A few days ago I saw something in the papers about a man who was found dead in the woods somewhere around here," Nagel said suddenly. "What kind of a man was he—Karlsen, I think his name was. Did he come from here?"

"Yes," said the hotelkeeper. "His mother was a leech-healer. You can see her house from here—the one with the red tiles. He had only come home for the holidays and then ended his life while he was at it. It was especially tragic since he was a talented boy, and about to be ordained. The whole thing is very strange. Since the arteries on both wrists were severed, it could hardly have been an accident, could it? And now they've found the knife—a small penknife with a white handle; the police found it late last night. The whole thing seems to point to some love affair."

"That's interesting. But is there really any question as to whether he committed suicide?"

"Everyone hopes the matter will be cleared up—I mean

some people think that he may have been walking with the knife in his hand and stumbled so awkwardly that he cut both wrists at once. But that seems highly improbable. Nevertheless, he will be buried in consecrated ground. But I for one don't believe he stumbled!"

"You say they didn't find the knife until last night? But wasn't it lying next to him?"

"No, it was lying several feet away. After using it he threw it into the woods; they found it quite by chance."

"But why would he throw the knife away when he was lying there cut and bleeding? It certainly must have been clear to everyone that he had used a knife?"

"God knows what was in his mind, but, as I said, there is probably a woman mixed up in it somehow. It's strange; the more I think about it, the more complicated it gets."

"What makes you think that a woman is involved?"

"Several things. But I'd rather not go into it."

"But don't you think the fall could have been an accident? He was lying in such an awkward position—wasn't he lying on his stomach with his face in the mud?"

"Yes, and he was covered with it. But maybe he arranged it that way on purpose to hide the final death agony. Who knows?"

"Did he leave a note of any sort?"

"He seems to have been writing something, but apparently he was in the habit of making notes while taking his walks. Some people think that he might have been using the knife to sharpen his pencil when he stumbled and fell, and jabbed a hole in one wrist and then in the other—all in the same fall. But he did leave something in writing. He was clutching a piece of paper in his hand with the words: 'Would that thy knife were as sharp as thy final no.'"

"What rubbish. Was the knife dull?"

"Yes."

"Why didn't he sharpen it first?"

"It wasn't his knife."

"Whose knife was it?"

The hotelkeeper hesitated for a moment: "It was Miss Kielland's knife."

"Miss Kielland's knife?" repeated Nagel, and after a slight pause: "Well, and who is Miss Kielland?"

"Dagny Kielland. She is the minister's daughter."

"That's very strange—very odd. Was the young man so madly in love with her?"

"He must have been. But they're all mad about her. He wasn't the only one."

Nagel seemed to drift away, lost in his thoughts.

The hotelkeeper finally broke the silence by saying: "What I just told you is confidential, so I must ask you to . . ."

"I understand," Nagel replied. "You don't have to worry."

When Nagel went down to lunch a while later, the hotelkeeper was already in the kitchen announcing that at last he had had a real talk with the man in yellow in Room 7. "He's an agronomist, and he's just returned from abroad. He says he'll be here for several months. Hard to figure him out."

2

THAT night Nagel suddenly found himself face to face with the fellow everyone called The Midget. Their meeting resulted in a tedious and endless conversation which went on for the better part of three hours.

The entire episode, from beginning to end, went like this: Johan Nagel was in the hotel café reading a newspaper when The Midget came in. There were a few people sitting around the tables, among them a stout peasant woman with a black and red knitted shawl over her shoulders. They all seemed to know The Midget. He bowed politely right and left as he entered, but his greeting elicited only shouts and derisive laughter. The peasant woman even got up and wanted to dance with him.

"Not today, not today," he mumbled, trying to get away from the woman, and walked straight up to the hotelkeeper and with his cap in his hand said: "I've brought the coal up to the kitchen. Is there anything else you want me to do today?"

"No," said the hotelkeeper. "What more could there be?"

"Nothing," said The Midget, and meekly withdrew.

The Midget was extremely ugly. He had serene blue eyes but grotesquely protruding front teeth, and his gait was contorted due to an injury. His hair was quite gray; his beard was darker than his hair but so scraggly that his skin showed through. He had once been a sailor but was now living with a relative who had a small coal business down on the docks. When he talked to anyone, he hardly ever raised his eyes from the floor.

Someone called to him from one of the tables—a man in a gray suit who was excitedly beckoning to him and pointing to a bottle of beer.

"Come and have a glass of mother's milk!" he said, then added: "I also want to see what you look like without your beard."

Respectfully bowing, his cap still in his hand, The Midget approached the table. As he passed Nagel he gave him a special bow, moving his lips slightly. He stopped in front of the man in gray and whispered: "Please, sir, not so loud. There are strangers present."

The young man, who was the magistrate's deputy, cried out: "Good Lord, I only wanted to offer you a glass of beer, and here you come accusing me of talking too loud!"

"I didn't mean it that way; I beg your pardon. But with strangers present I'd rather not make a fool of myself. And I can't drink beer—not now."

"What? You can't drink beer?"

"No, thank you. Not now."

"So you thank me, but not now? When will you thank me then? And you the son of a parson! You ought to be more careful how you express yourself."

"You didn't understand what I was trying to say, but it doesn't matter."

"Don't be silly. What's wrong with you, anyway?"

The deputy forced The Midget down on a chair; The Midget sat there for a moment but then got up again.

"Leave me alone," he said. "I can't stand drink. I can't take as much as I used to; I don't know why. I get drunk before I know it and become all confused."

The deputy got up, fixed his eyes on The Midget, and said: "Drink!"

Pause.

The Midget looked up, pushed his hair from his forehead, but said nothing.

"Well, only a little, just to please you and have the honor of drinking your health."

"Drink up!" roared the deputy, and had to turn away to keep from exploding into laughter.

"No, I can't drink it all. Why should I when it doesn't agree with me? Please don't be offended and don't look at me like that; I'll do it this once if you really insist. I only hope it won't go to my head. It's ridiculous, but I can take so little! To your health."

"Bottoms up!" shouted the deputy again. "All the way! That's fine! Now we'll sit down and make some funny faces. First you'll gnash your teeth for a while, and then I'll take your beard off and make you look ten years younger. But first you have to gnash your teeth!"

"No, I won't—not in the presence of these strangers.

Don't insist, because I won't do it," said The Midget, and made an attempt to leave. "Besides, I don't have time," he added.

"No time either? That's bad. Not even time?"

"No, not now."

"Suppose I told you that I have been thinking of getting a new coat for you! Let's have a look at the one you're wearing—it's completely worn out. It goes to pieces when you so much as touch it." The deputy found a small hole and punched his finger through it, which broke the threads. "Just look at this . . ."

"Leave me alone! For God's sake, what harm have I done you? Don't touch my coat!"

"But, good Lord, I promise to get you another coat tomorrow, in the presence of—let's see—two, four, seven witnesses. What's the matter with you tonight? You flare up, and become insulting, and try to bully all of us—yes, you do! Just because I touched your coat."

"I'm sorry. I didn't mean to be rude. I'll do anything to please you, but . . ."

"Then please me by sitting down."

The Midget pushed his gray hair from his forehead and sat down.

"Good. Now you can please me further by gnashing your teeth."

"No, I won't!"

"So you won't? We'll see about that! Yes or no!"

"Dear God in heaven, what harm have I done you? Can't you leave me in peace? Why should I play the fool in front of everyone? I see that stranger over there looking at us. He keeps glancing in our direction and I suppose he's laughing too. That's always the way it is; the very first day you came here as deputy, Dr. Stenersen cornered me and taught you to make a fool of me, and now you're encouraging the man over there to do the same. One passes it down to the other."

"Well, is it yes or no?"

"I said no!" cried The Midget, and jumped from his chair. But suddenly struck by the feeling that he had gone too far, he sat down again and said: "I just can't gnash my teeth. You must believe me!"

"You *can't*? Of course you can! You gnash your teeth beautifully."

"I swear to God, I can't!"

"But you've done it before."

"Yes, but I was drunk. I don't remember; my head was spinning. I was sick for two days afterwards."

"That's right," said the deputy. "I admit that you were drunk at the time. But why do you sit there blabbering about it in the presence of all these people? That's a stupid thing to do."

At this point the hotelkeeper left the café. The Midget didn't say a word; the deputy fixed his eyes on him and said: "Well, what have you decided? The coat—you remember?"

"I remember," said The Midget. "But I can't and I won't drink any more, and that's final."

"You can and you will! Did you hear what I said? You can and you will! Even if I have to pour it down your throat . . ." The deputy got up with The Midget's glass in his hand. "Now, open your mouth!"

"No, by God in heaven, I won't drink another drop!" cried The Midget, pale and trembling. "Nothing can make me do it! You must excuse me, but it makes me sick. You have no idea what it does to me. I beg you, don't be so cruel! I'd rather—rather grind my teeth a little without any beer!"

"Well, that's another matter. If you want to do it without beer, it's all right with me."

"Yes, I'd rather do it without beer."

To the accompaniment of roaring laughter from the spectators, The Midget began gnashing his horrible teeth together. Nagel seemed to be absorbed in his paper and was sitting quietly at his place by the window.

"Louder, louder!" shouted the deputy. "Gnash them louder; we can't hear you."

The Midget sat rigid in his chair, desperately holding on with both hands as if he were afraid of falling, and gnashing his teeth until his head shook. Everybody laughed, and the peasant woman laughed so hard that she had to wipe her eyes. She was almost hysterical and so carried away that she twice spat on the floor in sheer delight.

"Oh God, what a sight!" she shrieked, beside herself. "Oh, that deputy!"

"I can't do it any louder," said The Midget. "I really can't, as God is my witness—it's the truth; I can't any more."

"Well then, have a little rest and start all over. But you're going to gnash your teeth! Then we'll take off your beard. Now, have a sip of your beer—you have to. Here it is."

The Midget shook his head but said nothing. The deputy took a twenty-five-øre coin from his change purse and put it on the table, saying: "You used to do it for ten, but I don't mind giving you twenty-five. I'm raising your wages. Now, let's proceed!"

"Don't torment me any longer; I won't do it."

"You won't? You refuse?"

"In God's name, stop it! Leave me alone! I'm not going to let you make a fool of me any longer for the sake of a coat. I'm a human being, after all. What do you want from me?"

"Watch me! You see me flipping this bit of cigar ash into your glass—right? And I'm taking this piece of match here and that piece of match there and dropping them into the same glass while you watch. And now you're going to drink that glass down to the last drop. That I promise you!"

The Midget jumped up. He was shaking all over. His gray hair had again fallen over his forehead. He looked the deputy straight in the eyes, holding his gaze for a few seconds.

"No, you're going too far," the peasant woman cried. "Don't do it! God save me from the likes of you."

"So you won't do it? That means you refuse?" said the deputy. He too rose to his feet.

The Midget tried to say something but couldn't get a word out. All eyes were on him.

Then suddenly Nagel got up from his table by the window, put his paper down, and walked slowly and quietly across the room, as all eyes shifted to him. He stopped in front of The Midget, put his hand on his shoulder, and said in a loud, distinct voice: "If you'll pick up your glass and fling it at that bastard over there, I'll give you ten crowns and offer you my protection besides. I mean that one," he said, pointing straight at the deputy's face.

There was dead silence. Terrified, The Midget looked from one to the other, stammering, "But . . . No, but . . . ?" He didn't get any further but kept on repeating the words over and over in a trembling voice as if they were a question. No one else uttered a sound. Confused, the deputy took a step backwards, groping for his chair. He had turned pale and didn't say a word either, although his mouth was wide open.

"I repeat," said Nagel in a loud voice, emphasizing each word, "I'll give you ten crowns if you throw your glass at that bastard's head. Here is the money—and you needn't be afraid of the consequences." And Nagel produced the ten-crown note for The Midget to see.

The Midget's reaction was odd. With his short crooked gait, he shuffled off to a corner of the café and sat down without answering. His head was bent but his eyes were darting in all directions, and several times he jerked his knees up in a gesture of terror.

The door opened and the hotelkeeper came back in. He began to busy himself at the desk and paid no attention to what was going on until the deputy suddenly jumped up and faced Nagel, flailing his arms about, almost choking with rage, whereupon the hotelkeeper looked around and exclaimed: "What on earth . . . ?"

No one said anything. The deputy twice lashed out wildly at Nagel but each time he was blocked by Nagel's fists. His frustration at not being able to get at Nagel made him all the wilder, and he foolishly kept on punching the air as if trying to fight off the world. Finally he retreated sideways through the tables, stumbled over a stool, and fell on his knees. He was panting loudly and his whole body was twisted with rage. And on top of all that, his arms were bruised black and blue from the encounter with Nagel's clenched fists, which blocked his every blow. The café was now in a state of turmoil; the peasant woman and her party made for the door, while the rest all shouted at once, trying to explain to each other what had happened. Then the deputy got to his feet, made his way toward Nagel, stopped and screamed at him, furious at not being able to find the right words: "Go to hell, you damned fop!"

Nagel looked at him and smiled, walked over to the table, picked up the deputy's hat, and handed it to him with a bow. The deputy snatched the hat from Nagel and made a movement as if about to fling it back furiously, but then apparently changed his mind and, exploding with rage, he smacked it on his head and stormed out. It was bashed in on two sides and made him look like a clown.

The hotelkeeper forced his way through the crowd and demanded an explanation. He grabbed Nagel by the arm and cried: "What's been going on here? What's the meaning of this?"

"Let go of my arm," said Nagel. "I'm not going to run away. Besides, nothing is going on here. I made some remarks to the man who just left and he sought to defend himself. That's all there is to it; everything is settled."

But the hotelkeeper was furious and stamped his foot: "I won't tolerate any brawls here. If you want to fight, go out into the street, but not in here! Everyone seems to have gone berserk!"

Several of the customers interrupted him: "But we saw the whole thing!" they cried. And with the tendency of people to side with the victor of the moment, they were completely on Nagel's side and set about to explain the altercation.

Nagel shrugged his shoulders and walked up to The Midget. Bluntly, he asked the little gray jester: "What have you to do with the deputy that he can treat you that way?"

"Nothing. I don't even know him. I only danced for him

once in the square, for ten øre. Since then he's always making fun of me."

"So you dance for people and take money for it?"

"Sometimes—not often—only when I need ten øre and can't get it any other way."

"What do you spend the money on?"

"I need it for a lot of things. In the first place, I'm stupid. I'm no good at anything and I have a hard time making ends meet. When I was a sailor and earned my living, I was much better off. But then I had an accident—I fell from the rigging and got a hernia—and since then it hasn't been easy. I get my food and everything I need from my uncle. I live with him and am well taken care of; we have plenty of everything—my uncle has a coal business which earns him a living. But I contribute something toward my room and board, especially now during the summer months when we don't sell much coal. Every word I'm telling you is true! There are some days when I can use ten øre. I always spend it on something to take home. But as for the deputy—it amuses him to see me dance because with my hernia I move so clumsily."

"Does your uncle want you to dance in the square for money?"

"No, no, you musn't think that! He keeps on saying, 'Don't take that clown money,' and scolds me for letting people make a fool of me."

"Well, that was the first thing. How about the second?"

"What do you mean?"

"The second reason?"

"I don't understand."

"You said that *in the first place* you were stupid. Well, what comes in the second place?"

"If I said that, I shouldn't have."

"So you're only stupid?"

"Please, I beg you to excuse me."

"Was your father a parson?"

"Yes, he was."

Pause.

"Listen. If you have nothing else to do, how about coming up to my room for a while? Do you smoke? Fine! My room is upstairs. I shall be very pleased if you will pay me a visit."

To the amazement of everyone, Nagel and The Midget went up to the second floor and spent the rest of the evening together.

3

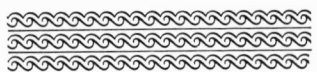

THE Midget sat down and lit a cigar.

"Don't you drink at all?" asked Nagel.

"No, not much. I get dizzy and begin to see double in no time at all."

"Have you ever had champagne? Yes, of course you must have."

"Yes, many years ago at my parents' silver wedding anniversary."

"Did you like it?"

"Yes, very much."

Nagel rang and had some champagne brought up.

As they were smoking and sipping champagne, Nagel suddenly looked intently at The Midget and said: "This is only a question, and you'll probably think it absurd, but would you, for a certain sum, be willing to assume the paternity of a child that wasn't yours? It was just an idea that passed through my head."

The Midget stared at him but said nothing.

"For a modest sum—fifty crowns, or let's say up to two hundred?" Nagel asked. "Money is no problem."

The Midget shook his head but was silent for a long while.

"No," he said at last.

"You couldn't do it? I would pay you cash."

"No, I can't do it; I'm sorry I can't be of service to you."

"Why not?"

"Please don't ask me. I'm a human being, after all."

"Well, maybe I was asking too much. Why should you do a service like that for anyone? But I would like to ask you something else: would you be willing—for five crowns—to go around town with a newspaper or a paper bag on your back—starting from the hotel and walking through the square and along the docks? Would you do that—for five crowns?"

The Midget lowered his head in shame and mumbled: "Five crowns." But he didn't answer.

"Oh well, let's make it ten crowns—we'll make it ten crowns. Would you do it for ten crowns?"

The Midget pushed his hair from his forehead. "I can't understand why everyone who comes here seems to feel that they can make a fool of me," he said.

"As you can see for yourself, I have the money right here," Nagel repeated. "It's up to you."

The Midget stared at the bill, with a helpless and forlorn expression, but suddenly wetting his lips in anticipation, he mumbled: "Well, I . . ."

"Just a moment," Nagel interjected quickly. "Excuse me for interrupting you," he went on, to keep The Midget from saying anything. "What's your real name? I don't believe you told me."

"My name is Grøgaard."

"Grøgaard. Are you related to the Grøgaard who was one of the authors of the constitution?"

"Yes, I am."

"What were we talking about? Oh yes, Grøgaard, since that is the case, you certainly don't want to earn ten crowns that way?"

"No," whispered The Midget, confused.

"Now listen to me," said Nagel, speaking very slowly. "It will give me pleasure to give you the ten crowns because you *didn't* agree to my proposition. And I will give you another ten crowns if you will give me the further pleasure of accepting it. Don't get up; this trifling amount means nothing to me." He took out the money and said: "Here you are. You will be doing me a favor by accepting it."

The Midget just sat there, speechless. But the unexpected windfall had gone to his head and he struggled to hold back the tears. He blinked his eyes and swallowed hard.

Nagel said: "You must be about forty?"

"Forty-three—past forty-three."

"Put the money in your pocket. You're most welcome to it. What is the name of the deputy with whom we were talking in the café?"

"I don't know. We just call him the deputy. He's from the magistrate's office."

"Well, it doesn't matter—but tell me . . ."

"Excuse me," said The Midget, unable to control himself any longer. Overcome with emotion, he tried to say something, but stuttered like a child. "Please forgive me," he said, and for a long time he couldn't utter another word.

"What did you want to say?"

"Thank you. From the bottom of my heart . . ."

Pause.

"Forget it."

"No, wait," cried The Midget. "Excuse me, but we can't forget it. You thought I didn't *want* to do you the favor, that it was unwillingness on my part, and that I was just being stubborn, but as God is my witness . . . How can we forget it if you got the impression that my only concern was the money, and that I wouldn't do it for five crowns? That's all I wanted to say."

"That's all right. A man with your name and breeding shouldn't let himself be talked into doing a foolish thing like that. Incidentally, you know this town well, don't you? I've been thinking of settling down here for a while during the summer. What do you think about that? You're from here, aren't you?"

"Yes, I was born in this town. My father was a parson here, and I've lived here for the last thirteen years—ever since I had my accident."

"Do you deliver coal?"

"Yes, I take coal around to the houses. It doesn't bother me, if that's why you're asking. I'm used to it and it doesn't hurt if I'm careful when I climb stairs. But last year I fell, and for a while I was in such bad shape that I had to use a cane."

"You did? What happened?"

"It was on the steps of the bank. They were a bit icy. I started climbing them carrying a sack that was very heavy. When I had gotten about half way up, I noticed that Consul Andresen was on his way down. I wanted to turn around and go down so that he could get by. He told me not to, but it was the right thing to do and I did it without being asked. But unfortunately I slipped on the steps and landed on my right shoulder. 'What's the matter?' the consul asked. 'You haven't hurt yourself, have you?' 'No,' I said. 'I guess I was lucky.' But five minutes later I fainted twice in a row. I began to swell where I had been hurt before. By the way, the consul was most kind to me afterwards, although it hadn't been his fault."

"Was there no other injury? Wasn't your head hurt?"

"Yes, I did hurt my head, and for a while I was spitting blood."

"And the consul helped you the whole time you were ill?"

"Yes, and most generously. He sent me all kinds of things; he never forgot me. But the nicest thing of all happened the day I was up and around again: I went to thank him, and he already had the flag hoisted. He had given orders to fly the flag in my honor, though it was also Miss Fredrikke's birthday."

"Who is Miss Fredrikke?"

"She's the consul's daughter."

"Oh—well, that was very nice of him. Incidentally, do you know why the flags were flying a few days ago?"

"A few days ago? About a week ago? That must have been for Miss Kielland's engagement—Dagny Kielland. They all get engaged, married, and leave town, one after the other. I've got friends and acquaintances all over the country—and I would be glad to see all of them again. I've watched them play, go to school, get confirmed, and grow up. Dagny is only twenty-three and she is everybody's darling. She's pretty, too. She became engaged to Lieutenant Hansen, who gave me the cap I'm wearing. He's also from here."

"Is Miss Kielland blond?"

"Yes, and very beautiful. Everyone is extremely fond of her."

"I think I must have seen her on the way to the parsonage. Does she usually carry a red parasol?"

"That's right! And there isn't another red parasol in town, as far as I know. She wears her hair in a long, blond braid. If you've seen her, you couldn't forget. She is different from everyone else around here. But perhaps you haven't had a chance to talk to her yet?"

"I may have." And Nagel added pensively to himself: Could *that* have been Miss Kielland?

"But maybe you haven't had a chance to have a real talk with her? That's something to look forward to. She laughs out loud when something amuses her—she is so gay. Often she laughs at just about anything. When you talk to her, you'll notice how attentively she listens to what you have to say, before replying. And while talking, she often blushes. She becomes very animated, and even more beautiful. But with me it's different; she chats quite casually when we happen to meet. When I walk up to her, she stops and shakes my hand even if she's in a hurry. If you don't believe me, you'll see for yourself one day."

"But I do believe you. So Miss Kielland is a good friend of yours?"

"What I mean is that she has always been very kind to me; that's all. Sometimes I go to the parsonage when I'm invited, but even when I'm not, I never have the feeling that I am unwelcome. Miss Dagny also lent me books when I was ill—she even brought them herself, carrying them all that way under her arm."

"What kind of books?"

"What you mean is what kind of books would I be able to read and understand?"

"No, now you misunderstand *me*. Your question is shrewd and to the point, but that wasn't what I meant. You are an interesting man! I meant, what kind of books does the young lady herself own and read? That is what I really wanted to know."

"Once, I remember, she brought me a copy of Garborg's *Peasant Students*, and two others—I think one of them was Turgenev's *Rudin*. And once she read aloud to me from Garborg's *Irreconcilables*."

"Were they her own books?"

"Well, no, they belonged to her father. His name was written in them."

"By the way, you started to tell me about the time you went to Consul Andresen to thank him . . ."

"Yes, I wanted to thank him for all he had done for me."

"I understand. And the flag was already hoisted when you arrived?"

"Yes, he was flying it in my honor. He told me so himself."

"I see. But couldn't it have been in honor of his daughter's birthday?"

"Yes, I suppose it was. Quite likely, as a matter of fact. It would have been a shame not to raise the flag on Miss Fredrikke's birthday."

"You're right again. By the way, how old is your uncle?"

"He must be about seventy—perhaps not that old, but certainly over sixty. He is active for his age and he can still read without glasses if he has to."

"What's his name?"

"Grøgaard also. We're both Grøgaards."

"Does your uncle own the house he lives in or does he rent it?"

"He rents the room in which we live, but the coal shed belongs to him. We have no trouble paying the rent, if that's what you're thinking. We pay our bills in coal and sometimes I contribute a bit by doing odd jobs."

"But your uncle doesn't carry coal?"

"Oh no, that's my job. He weighs it and handles the business details, and I do the delivering. I'm better at that because I'm stronger."

"Of course. I presume you have a woman to cook for you?"

Pause.

"Please don't be offended, but I'm ready to leave whenever you wish. Maybe you asked me here out of kindness, although I can't see how my affairs could be of interest to you. Or perhaps you're talking to me for some reason which escapes me—if so, I don't mind. But you mustn't think that someone will bother me when I leave here. I never really have trouble with unkind people. The deputy won't be waiting outside the door to take revenge if that's what's worrying you—and even if he were there, I don't think he would do me any harm."

"It would give me pleasure if you stayed, but you don't have to feel obliged to tell me anything just because I gave you a couple of crowns for tobacco. But of course it's up to you."

"I'll stay!" cried The Midget. "God bless you! I'm glad I can please you in some way, although I'm ashamed of both myself and my clothes. I could have been a bit more presentable if I'd had time to change. This is one of my uncle's old coats and it's almost falling apart—just a

touch would make it fall to shreds. That's where the
deputy tore it—I hope you'll pardon my appearance . . .
No, we don't have a woman to cook for us. We do all our
own cooking and cleaning. It's no problem, but then we do
only the essentials. When we have coffee in the morning,
we drink what's left from the evening before without re-
heating it, and we do the same with our dinner. We cook
when we have a chance, the rest of the time we eat left-
overs. My job is the washing. It helps pass the time when I
have nothing else to do."

A bell rang and guests could be heard going down the
stairs to supper.

"That's the supper bell," said The Midget.

"Yes," Nagel said. But he didn't get up, nor did he show
any sign of impatience. On the contrary, he settled back in
his chair and asked: "Did you know this man named
Karlsen who was found dead in the woods the other day?
An awful business, wasn't it?"

"Yes, a terrible tragedy. I certainly did know him. He
was a wonderful person—a noble character. Do you know
what he said to me once? He sent for me early one Sunday morning—over a year ago—last May, as a matter of
fact. He wanted me to deliver a letter for him. 'Yes,' I said,
'I'll do it, but I can't let people see me in these shoes. If it's
all right with you, I'll go home and borrow another pair.'
'No, don't bother,' he said. 'That is, unless you'll get your
feet wet in those.' He even thought of that—that I might
get my feet wet in those shoes! Then he slipped a crown
into my hand and gave me the letter. When I was outside,
he opened the door again and came after me. His face was
all aglow when I stopped to look at him, and I saw that he
had tears in his eyes. Then he drew me close to him, put
his arm around my waist, and said: 'Deliver the letter, old

friend. I'll make it worth your while. When I'm ordained and have a parish, you'll come and live with me. Well, on your way, and good luck!' Unfortunately, he never got his parish, but had he lived, he would have kept his promise. I'm sure of that."

"You delivered the letter?"

"Yes."

"And was Miss Kielland happy to get it?"

"How do you know that it was for Miss Kielland?"

"How do I know? You said so yourself."

"*I* did? That's not true."

"It isn't true? Are you accusing me of lying?"

"I beg your pardon. Perhaps you're right; but I shouldn't have said it; it just slipped out. But did I *really* say it?"

"Why shouldn't you? Did he forbid you to mention it?"

"No, *he* didn't."

"Did she?"

"Yes."

"Don't worry. The secret will be safe with me. But can you understand why he should pick this time to die?"

"No, I can't. It was fate, I guess."

"When will he be buried?"

"Tomorrow at noon."

Nothing more was said on that subject, and for a while neither of them spoke. Sara stuck her head inside the door to announce that supper was being served. A moment later Nagel said: "So Miss Kielland is engaged. What is her fiancé like?"

"Lieutenant Hansen is a fine, upstanding man. She'll be well off with him."

"Does he have money?"

"Yes, his father is extremely wealthy."

"Is he a businessman?"

"No, he's a shipowner. He lives a few houses from here. It isn't a big house, but he doesn't need a bigger one. When the son is away, the two old people are left alone. They also have a daughter, but she is married and lives in England."

"And how much do you think old Hansen is worth?"

"Perhaps a million. Nobody knows."

"The wealth of this world is badly distributed. How would you like to have a little of that money, Grøgaard?"

"In the name of God, why? We must be satisfied with what we have."

"That's what they say. But I would like to ask you something. Carrying all that coal around can't leave you much time for other work? Yet, didn't I hear you asking the hotelkeeper whether he had anything else for you to do today?"

"No," said The Midget, shaking his head.

"It was down in the café. You said you had brought the coal into the kitchen and you asked whether there was anything more for you to do today?"

"There was a reason for that. So you heard me? The reason was that I had hoped to be paid for the coal right away but I didn't dare ask for the payment straight out. That's all. We are in a tight spot just now and were hoping to be paid."

"How much would you need to get out of your predicament?" Nagel asked.

"Good God, no!" cried The Midget. Don't even mention that again. You have already been more than generous. We only needed six crowns, and now I have your twenty crowns in my pocket. God bless you! We owed the grocer money for potatoes and some other things. He sent us a bill; it weighed on our minds and we didn't know what we were going to do. But now that the problem is solved, we can sleep with an easy conscience and face tomorrow with good cheer."

Pause.

"Well, perhaps we'd better drink up and say good night," said Nagel, getting up. "Your health! I hope this isn't the last time we'll meet. You must come back and see me! The room number is 7. Thank you for your company."

Nagel's words had an air of sincerity as he shook The Midget's hand. He escorted his guest down the stairs and to the front door, and bowed deeply, doffing his corduroy cap as he had done once before.

The Midget took his leave, bowing repeatedly as he backed into the street; he kept trying to say something, but the words wouldn't come.

When Nagel came into the dining room, he made effusive apologies to Sara for being late for supper.

4

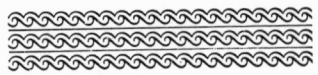

THE next morning Johan Nagel was awakened by Sara knocking on the door to bring him the papers. He glanced quickly through them, throwing them on the floor as he finished them. He burst into laughter after twice reading the bulletin on Gladstone's health—he had been confined to his bed two days with a cold but was now on his feet again. Then he crossed his arms behind his head and began talking out loud to himself:

It's dangerous to walk through the woods with an open penknife in your hand. How easy it would be to stumble and fall awkwardly enough for the blade to slash both wrists! Look what happened to Karlsen. But it's also dangerous to walk around with a medicine vial in your vest pocket. You could stumble, break the glass, the splinters would penetrate your body, and the poison would enter the bloodstream. Danger lurks around every corner.

We're all aware of it. But there is one safe road—the one Gladstone is taking. I can just picture Gladstone cautiously walking down that road, how he avoids taking a false step, how Providence and he join forces in protecting him. Now he has gotten over his cold and will live until he dies a natural death from too much comfort.

Pastor Karlsen, why did you hide your face in a puddle? Was it to conceal your final agony, or did the death throes distort your face, forcing your head downwards? In broad daylight, you chose to bury your head, like a child afraid of the dark, and you lay there with a farewell note in your hand. Poor Karlsen, how I pity you!

And why did you go into the woods for this rendezvous with death? Were you fond of these woods, and did they mean more to you than a field, a road, or a lake? The little boy walked there the whole livelong day, la la la la.

Imagine the Vardal woods on the way from Gjøvik— you lie there and leave the world behind. Look straight up into heaven and you almost hear what they're saying about you up there. "If he comes here," says my blessed mother, "I'll leave," and she really makes a big issue of it. "Ha, ha, don't worry," I answer, "I won't disturb you." And I say this so loud that I attract the attention of two female angels, the Jari girl and Svava Bjørnson.

Anyway, what the devil am I doing, lying here laughing? Am I trying to show my superiority? Only children and young girls should be allowed to laugh like this. Laughter originated in .our monkey days—a revolting sound coming out of the windpipe. It's expelled from wherever it happens to be in my body when I'm tickled under the chin. What was it Hauge, the butcher, who had an uproarious laugh of his own, said to me once? He said that no one who had all his five senses . . .

And what a delightful child he had! The day I met her

on the street, it was raining. She was on her way to the soup kitchen with a pail and was in tears because she had lost the money. Blessed Mama, could you see me from your heaven—did you realize that I didn't have a single shilling to console the child with? Did you see me tearing my hair on the street because I didn't have an øre to give her? At that moment the band marched by; the pretty girl who works at the parish turned and smiled at me; then she walked home, subdued, with head bowed, probably regretting the glance she had given me. Suddenly at that moment a bearded man in a soft felt hat grabbed me by the arm and saved me from being run over. God knows what would have happened if he hadn't been there.

Quiet! One . . . two . . . three; how slowly it strikes! Four . . . five . . . six . . . seven . . . eight . . . is it already eight o'clock? Nine . . . ten. Ten o'clock? I must get up. Where was that clock? Could it have been the one in the café? Well, it makes no difference, no difference at all. But that was really an amusing scene in the café last night, wasn't it? The Midget was shaking all over and I came at precisely the right moment. He would have ended up drinking that beer—cigar ashes, matches, and all. Well, so what? What right do you have to meddle in other people's business? Why did you come here in the first place? Was it because of some universal catastrophe —Gladstone's cold, for instance? God help you if you told it the way it really was; that you were really on your way home but were intrigued by this town despite the fact that it looked so small and insignificant—that you almost wept with an inexplicable joy when you saw the flags flying. By the way, it was June 12 and it was in honor of Miss Kielland's engagement that the flags were hoisted. Two days later I met her.

Why did I have to meet her just that evening when I was so confused and wasn't really functioning? Whenever I think of it, I feel so terribly ashamed.

"Good evening, miss. I'm a stranger here. Excuse me, but I'm out for a walk and I've lost my way."

The Midget was right. She blushes on being spoken to, and when she answers, she blushes even more.

"Where do you want to go?" she said, giving me a penetrating look.

I took off my cap, and standing there bareheaded, I found myself saying: "Could you tell me how far it is to town—the exact distance?"

"I can't tell you exactly," she said. "Not from here. But the first house you come to is the parsonage and from there it's a mile and a half to town." Then she turned abruptly and began to walk away.

"Thank you very much," I said, "but if the parsonage is on the other side of the woods, do let me walk with you if that's where you are going—or even farther, for that matter. The sun has gone down; let me carry your parasol. I promise not to bother you; I won't even talk, if you prefer that. All I want is to walk by your side and listen to the birds singing. No, please don't go! Why are you running away?"

When she went on running and wouldn't listen to me, I ran after her, to apologize: "Forgive me, I couldn't help it, I was carried away by your beautiful face!"

She now began to run in such panic that she was out of sight in no time. As she ran, she held her heavy blond braid in her hand. It was something to see.

That is exactly what happened. I wasn't going to molest her—I had no bad intentions. I'm sure she's in love with her lieutenant; I never would have dreamed of forcing myself on her. But that's all right. Maybe the lieutenant will challenge me. He'll join forces with the magistrate's deputy and they'll both come after me.

Incidentally, I'd be curious to know if that deputy intends to give The Midget a new coat. We're willing to wait a day, even two, but if he hasn't come across with it by that time, we'll remind him. Period. Nagel.

There is a poor woman here who looks at me in great embarrassment, as though she wanted to ask for something but couldn't bring herself to it. I'm fascinated by her eyes—though her hair is white. I've gone out of my way four times to avoid meeting her. She isn't old, but prematurely gray. Her eyelashes are still black—jet black—and give a smoldering look to her eyes. She almost always carries a basket concealed under her apron, which is probably what she is ashamed of. When she has passed me, I turn and watch her go down to the market. She takes a few eggs out of her basket, and she sells these two or three eggs to anyone willing to buy them, whereupon she goes back home with the basket under her apron, as before. She lives in a tiny house down at the dock; it's a one-story house and unpainted. Once I caught a glimpse of her at the window. There were no curtains, but there were white flowers on the windowsill. She stood far back in the room staring at me as I walked by. What kind of a woman she is, God only knows, but her hands are quite small. I could give you alms, my white beauty, but I would rather give you help.

I know why I'm obsessed by your eyes; I knew it instantly. Strange how a love affair from one's youth can linger on and make itself keenly felt at the oddest times. But you don't have her beloved face, and you are much older than she. She ended up marrying a telegraph operator and moving to Kabelvåg! Well, everyone to his own taste. I couldn't expect her to love me, and she didn't. There was nothing to be done about that. The clock is striking eleven . . . But if you only knew how constantly you've been in my thoughts these ten, twelve years. I've never gotten you out of my mind—but that's my fault. You can't help that. After a year, people usually forget; my feelings are still the same after ten years.

I'll help the egg woman, yes, I'll give her both alms and help for the sake of her eyes. I've got lots of money— 62,000 crowns from an estate—in cash! And lying there on the table are those important telegrams. What a clever move that was! I'm a capitalist as well as an agronomist and I don't sell at the first offer; I sleep on it and think it over, yes, I think it over, and carefully. But my stratagem didn't arouse any attention, although I made it as bold and blatant as I possibly could. Man is certainly an ass. You can lead him by the nose wherever you want him to go.

Over there, for instance, sticking out of my vest pocket is the neck of a vial. It contains "medicine"—prussic acid. I carry it because I'm curious by nature, but I don't have the courage to take it. But why do I carry it around, and why did I get it in the first place? Hypocrisy again, nothing but a sham; the decadence, phoniness, self-adulation, and snobbery of our times! To hell with all of it! She's as white and delicate as china: she's my morbid Melesina . . .

Or let's take an innocuous object such as my lifesaver's medal. I earned it honestly, as they say. One plays around with all kinds of things like saving people's lives. But whether I really deserve any credit for that, God only knows. Judge for yourselves, ladies and gentlemen. A young man is standing at the ship's railing. He is sobbing so violently that his shoulders shake. When I speak to him, he gives me a frantic look and suddenly darts down to the lounge. I follow, but he has already disappeared into his cabin. I scan the passenger list, find his name, and note that his destination is Hamburg. It's our first night out. From that moment I keep my eye on him. I come upon him in unexpected places and confront him. Why? Ladies and gentlemen, judge for yourselves! I see him cry; something is tormenting him and he stares into the sea with a crazed and frenzied expression. What concern is that of mine? None whatsoever, of course, and, therefore, do judge for yourselves—don't hold back! A couple of days go by; we have a head wind and the sea is stormy. At two o'clock in the morning he comes aft. I'm already hiding out there, waiting for him; the light of the moon gives his face a yellow tinge. He looks in all directions, flings his arms up in the air, and jumps overboard, feet first. A scream escapes from his lungs. Did he regret his impulse? Did he panic at the last moment? Is that why he cried out? Ladies and gentlemen, what would you have done in my place? I leave it entirely in your hands. Perhaps you would have respected the genuine though wavering courage of the poor unfortunate soul and remained in your hiding place. But I shout to the captain on the bridge and, without thinking, leap overboard, head first. I splash around madly, striking out in all directions, churning the water around me. On board, voices are roaring commands. Suddenly I hit against one of his arms, outspread, fingers rigid. His legs are moving slightly, thank God! I grab him by the neck; he gets heavier and heavier; he goes limp and doesn't move his legs any more. Then he tries to wrest free. I struggle with him; the heavy sea knocks our foreheads together, and I feel myself beginning to lose consciousness. What next? I gnash my teeth, curse to high heaven, and keep a firm grip on the fellow's neck until the boat finally arrives. What would you have done? Saving him was like fighting a bear.

But was there any merit in it? Well, I've left that up to you, ladies and gentlemen! Judge me without emotion. What difference could it make to me? But let us suppose that the man found it utterly impossible to go ashore in Hamburg for some reason? Perhaps he was supposed to meet someone he just couldn't face? Yet the medal is in recognition of an act of valor; I carry it in my pocket, and I don't cast it before swine. This, too, is for you to judge. Judge all you want to—what the hell do I care? It's of so little concern to me that I don't even remember the poor fellow's name, though no doubt he is still alive. Why did he do it? Perhaps in despair over a hopeless love affair— maybe there really was a woman involved; I have no idea. But it's all the same to me. Period.

Ah, women, these women! Take Kamma, for instance, my little Danish Kamma. God bless you! Gentle as a dove, full of tenderness and devotion, but still quite capable of luring the last shilling out of you, cleaning you out, just by putting her head coquettishly to one side and whispering: "Simonsen, darling Simonsen!" Well, God bless you, Kamma, you were so devoted; now, as far as I'm concerned, you can go to blazes; we're even.

It's time I got up.

No, one has to steer clear of that type. A great writer says: "My son, when a woman offers you her favors, beware,"—or whatever it is a great writer says. Karlsen was a weakling, an idealist who died because of his violent emotions; that is to say, because of his shattered nerves, which in turn is to say because of improper diet and lack of outdoor exercise. "Would that thy knife were as sharp as thy final no!" He spoiled his posthumous fame by quoting a poet! Let's suppose that I had met Karlsen in time—the last day, or even half an hour before the tragedy—and he had told me that he would quote someone in his dying moments; I would probably have said: Look at me, I'm a sane and sensible man, and I ask you for the sake of mankind not to ruin your last hour by quoting a so-called great poet. Do you know what constitutes a great poet? He is a person without shame, incapable of blushing. Ordinary fools have moments when they go off by themselves and blush with shame; not so the great poet. Look at me again. If you really have to quote someone, quote a geographer; that way you won't give yourself away. Victor Hugo—do you like a good laugh? One day Baron Lesdain was talking to Victor Hugo. During the course of the conversation, the crafty baron asked: "Who, in your opinion, is the greatest French poet?" Victor Hugo smiled, bit his lip, and after a moment's reflection said: "Alfred de Musset is the second greatest." But maybe you don't get the joke? Do you know what Victor Hugo did in 1870? He wrote a proclamation addressed to the people of this planet in which he strictly forbade the German troops to besiege and bombard Paris. "I have grandsons and other members of my family here, and I don't want them to be hit by shells," he said.

I still don't have my shoes. What has Sara done with my shoes? It's nearly eleven and she still hasn't brought them.

So let's quote a geographer . . . By the way, that Sara has a beautiful figure. The way her hips sway when she walks—like the hindquarters of a well-fed mare! She is a marvelous creature—I wonder if she has ever been married? Anyway, she doesn't seem to mind being poked in the ribs; she's probably game for anything. I've observed one marriage in my life, and at close range. Ladies and gentlemen, it was on a Sunday evening at a railroad station in Sweden—Kungsbacka station. Let me stress that it was a Sunday evening. Her hands were large and white; he was wearing a brand-new cadet's uniform and looked as if he didn't even shave yet. They were on the way from Gothenburg—she was very young, too—they were both children. I sat there peering at them from behind my newspaper. My presence made them uncomfortable and they kept looking at each other. The girl's eyes sparkled; she couldn't sit still. Then there was the whistle announcing Kungsbacka; he took her hand; they exchanged a look, and when the train stopped, they quickly got off. She dashed off to the ladies' room with him at her heels. My God! He made a mistake and went in the same door! They quickly shut the door behind them. At that moment the church bells in town started to ring—it was Sunday. They stayed in there throughout the chiming of the bells. Three, four, five minutes pass. What's become of them? They're still in there and the church bells keep ringing. Are they going to miss the train? Finally he opens the door and looks around cautiously. He is bareheaded; she is standing right behind him and puts his cap on; he turns and smiles at her. He runs down the steps, she follows him, still fumbling with her dress. They get on the train and resume their places without anyone paying the slightest attention to them; that is, no one except me. The girl's eyes were radiant as she looked at me, and her small breasts were heaving up and down, up and down. A few minutes later they were both asleep, dead asleep, blissfully asleep.

Well, how do you feel about that? Ladies and gentlemen, this is the end of my story. I pass over the respectable lady over there, the one with the lorgnette and the mannish collar—I mean the bluestocking. I am addressing myself to the two or three among you who don't go through life with clenched teeth while performing their acts of social welfare. I'm sorry if I've offended anyone. My special apologies go to the bluestocking lady with the lorgnette. She's getting up! Either she is leaving or she is about to quote somebody. And if she is about to quote someone it will be in order to challenge me, and she'll say something like this: "This man has the crudest masculine ideas about life I've ever heard. Is *that* life? Maybe he is unaware of what one of the world's greatest minds has said on the subject. 'Life is a war with the trolls in the vaults of the heart and brain,' he says."

Yes, life is a war with the trolls in the vaults of the heart and brain; that is certainly true. Ladies and gentlemen, one day Per Skysskaffer was chauffeuring a great writer. As they were driving, the simple-minded Per Skysskaffer said: "Please, could you explain to me what a poet really is?"

Tight-lipped and puffing up his frail chest, the great writer made the following pronouncement: "By writing poetry, the poet brings down the Day of Judgment on himself." At this, the Norseman Per Skysskaffer was visibly shaken.

Eleven o'clock. Where the devil are my shoes? Well, speaking about being against everything and everybody . . .

A tall, pale lady, dressed in black and with a bright red smile, grabs my arm in a friendly way and tries to stop me. "If you can say something as challenging as the writer," she says, "you are entitled to speak your piece."

"I who have never even known a poet or an author, and never even talked to one! I'm an agronomist; I've lived with guano and bran mash since childhood. I can't even make up a rhyme about an umbrella, let alone death and life and eternal peace."

"Well then, what about any other great man?" she says. "You go around bolstering your ego by denigrating all great men. But great men remain so and will endure— time will prove their worth."

"Madame," I say, bowing respectfully, "you can't imagine how ignorant and shallow your remarks sound to me. Forgive me for being so outspoken, but if you were a man instead of a woman, I would be willing to bet that you were a liberal. I don't castigate all men who have become famous, but the publicity that surrounds him fails to impress me. I judge him by my own standards, within the framework of my limited mind and intellect. In other words, I judge him by the taste his work leaves in my mouth. This is not being superior; it's merely being subjective; it is the logic in my blood expressing itself. The important thing at this moment is unobtrusively to get Kingo's hymnal replaced by Landstad's in Høivåg parish in Lillesand. It isn't a question of stirring up a lot of lawyers, newspapermen, or Galilean fishermen, or of publishing a book about Napoleon *le petit*. The point is to bring pressure to bear upon those in control, the chosen few, the elite, the masters, Caiaphas, Pilate, Caesar. What do I accomplish by stirring up the mob if I must still be crucified? You can collect large crowds and incite them to grasp at power with their nails. You can put a butcher's knife in their hands and incite them to stab and slash, and you can whip them into winning an election. But to achieve a true victory, a moral victory, progress for their fellow man, is something the mob can't manage. Men of letters make good conversation, but the tycoons of intellect, the supermen, the spiritual leaders on horseback, have to stop and search their minds when the name of a 'truly' great man is mentioned. So the 'truly' great man is left behind with the crowd, the rabble; in other words, the majority—the lawyer, the teacher, the newspaperman, and the Emperor of Brazil, all of whom make up his flock of admirers."

"Ah," says the lady in a voice sharp with irony. The chairman raps his gavel and asks for silence, but the lady persists: "Well then, since you claim you don't excoriate all great men, perhaps you can mention some, or at least one, who may meet with your approval. That would be most interesting."

"I'll be glad to. But unfortunately you have taken my remarks too literally. If I were to mention one, two, or ten, you would assume that this was the end of my list. Why should I? If, for instance, I asked you to choose between Leo Tolstoy, Jesus Christ, and Immanuel Kant, you would have a hard time deciding. You would make a general statement to the effect that they were all great men in their way, and the liberal and progressive press would agree with you . . ."

"But, in your opinion, who is the greatest?" she asks.

"In my opinion, madame, those who make the most money are not the greatest, although they always make the loudest noise. My blood speaks out and tells me that the greatest of them all is he who has brought us the basic values, and that is, after all, the greatest gift to the human race. The man of influence, the wielder of supreme power, the mighty one who turns the switch that revolutionizes the world . . ."

"But, of the three you mentioned, it must be Christ who . . ."

"Yes, of course it's Christ," I say quickly. "You are right, madame, and I'm glad we agree, at least on this point. I have no respect for merchants and preachers; as far as I'm concerned, their only talent is coming up with the right word at the right time. What is a professional preacher, really? He is a kind of middleman who for the wrong reasons tries to make people buy his goods. The more he sells, the more his stock rises. The louder he hawks his wares, the larger his business grows. But what is the point of preaching Faust's philosophy of life to my good neighbor, Ola Nordistuen? How could that possibly influence thinking in the next century?"

"But what will become of Ola Nordistuen if nobody . . ."

"Ola Nordistuen can go to hell," I say brusquely. "He has no other mission in this world except to walk around waiting for death until he's blue in the face—and the sooner he's out of the way, the better. Ola Nordistuen has been put on this earth to fertilize the soil; it's Ola Nordistuen that Napoleon tramples under his horse's hoofs; that just about sums up Ola Nordistuen. Ola Nordistuen isn't even the beginning of something, and therefore he can't be the result of anything. He isn't even a comma in the Great Book, but only a blot on the paper. And there we have Ola Nordistuen."

"For heaven's sake, be quiet," says the lady, looking in alarm at the chairman to see if he is about to throw me out.

"All right, I won't say any more." But focusing my eyes on her lovely mouth, I say: "I'm sorry I talked on at such length. But thank you for your kind attention. Your mouth is beautiful when you smile. Goodby."

She turns crimson and invites me home—she actually invites me to her house! She gives me her address and says she would like to pursue this conversation a bit further. She doesn't agree with me on a lot of points. Tomorrow evening she will be alone if I would like to come. Tomorrow evening? Fine. Goodby until then.

And all she wanted to show me was a new rug from Hallingdal, woven in folk-art style!

Deia, and the sun is shining on heia . . .

He jumped out of bed, pulled up the shades, and looked out. It was a calm day without wind and the square was bathed in sunlight. He rang, intending to use Sara's neglect of his shoes to get on more familiar terms with her. Let's see what she's made of, this Trondhjem girl with the alluring eyes. Her sexy look is probably only a come-on.

Without preliminaries, he put his arm around her waist.

"Leave me alone," she said angrily, and pushed him away.

"Why didn't you bring me my shoes sooner?" he said, feigning a cold tone.

"I'm sorry about the shoes," she said. "But it's washday and we're very busy."

He stayed in his room until twelve and then went to the cemetery for Karlsen's funeral. As usual, he wore his bright yellow suit.

5

WHEN Nagel got to the cemetery, he found himself alone. He went up to the grave and looked down into it; two white flowers were lying there. Who had thrown them down there, and why? He had the feeling that he had seen those flowers before. Suddenly it occurred to him that he needed a shave. He looked at his watch, and after a moment's reflection, he quickly made his way back to town. When he got to the middle of the square, he saw the deputy coming toward him. Nagel kept on walking; they stared at each other but neither of them spoke, nor did they exchange greetings. Just as Nagel entered the barbershop, the church bells began ringing for the funeral.

He appeared very casual, spoke to no one, but spent several minutes examining the pictures on the walls,

going from one to another, looking at them intently. Then his turn came, and he settled down into the chair.

When he was through and went out into the street, he again saw the deputy, who seemed to have retraced his steps and appeared to be waiting for something. He was carrying a stick in his left hand, but as soon as he caught sight of Nagel he shifted it to his right hand and began swinging it around. The two slowly approached each other. He didn't have a stick when I saw him a while ago, Nagel said to himself. It isn't new; he hasn't bought it but borrowed it. As he got closer, he saw that it was a cane.

When they were side by side, the deputy stopped, and so did Nagel. Nagel pushed his corduroy cap forward, as if to scratch the back of his head, and then straightened it again. The deputy banged the cane hard against the cobblestones and then leaned back on it. For a few seconds he held this pose. Then suddenly he straightened up, turned his back on Nagel, and walked away. Nagel watched him disappear around the corner of the barbershop.

This pantomime took place with several people looking on. Among them was a man who was selling lottery tickets from a revolving cylinder. A bit farther down, there was a man selling plaster figurines. He, too, had seen the whole thing. Nagel recognized him as one of the clients in the café who had witnessed the scene of the previous night and who had afterwards sided with the hotelkeeper.

When Nagel arrived at the cemetery the second time, the minister was already delivering his eulogy. The place was literally black with people. Nagel started to walk toward the grave but stopped and sat down on a large, new marble slab on which was inscribed: "Vilhelmine

Meek. Born 20th May 1873. Died 16th February 1891."
That was all. The slab had just been placed there, and the
sod around it was freshly laid.

Nagel beckoned to a little boy. "Do you see the man
over there—the one in the brown coat?" he asked.

"The one with the visor cap? That's The Midget."

"Go and ask him to come over here."

The boy did as he was told.

When The Midget approached, Nagel stretched out his
hand and said: "Hello there. I'm glad to see you again. Did
you get the coat?"

"The coat? No, not yet, but I'm sure I will," The Midget
replied. "Thank you very much for last night—and thank
you for everything. Well, today we're burying Karlsen. I
guess it's God's will."

They sat down on the new marble slab and began to
talk. Nagel took a pencil out of his pocket and wrote
something on the slab.

"Who is buried here?" he asked.

"Vilhelmine Meek. We used to call her Mina Meek for
short. She was just a child; I don't think she was even
twenty."

"She wasn't even eighteen, according to the epitaph.
But was she also a 'good' girl?"

"That's such a strange way of putting it, but . . ."

"It's because I notice the way you have of saying only
good things about people, no matter who they are."

"If you had known Mina Meek, I'm sure you would have
felt the same way. She was an unusually fine human
being. If there are such things as angels, she is one of
them."

"Was she engaged?"

"Engaged? No, definitely not. That is, not that I know

of. She was always reading the Bible and talking aloud to God, often in the middle of the street where everyone could hear her. People would stop and listen. Everyone was fond of Mina Meek."

Nagel stuck his pencil back in his pocket. There was something written on the stone—lines of verse that looked ugly on the clean white marble.

The Midget said: "You are attracting a lot of attention. As I was standing over there listening to the sermon, I noticed that at least half the people were watching you."

"Me?"

"Yes, some of them were whispering among themselves, wondering who you were. Now they are looking this way."

"Who is the lady with the big black feather in her hat?"

"The one holding the parasol with the white handle? That's Fredrikke Andresen, the Miss Fredrikke I was telling you about. And the lady standing next to her, looking in our direction just now, is the daughter of the chief constable—Miss Olsen, Gudrun Olsen. Oh, I know all of them. Dagny Kielland is also here; she is wearing a black dress, and it's almost more becoming than anything else I've ever seen her wear. Have you noticed her? Well, of course they are all in black today, so how could you pick her out? Do you see the gentleman with the blue spring coat, wearing glasses? That's Dr. Stenersen. He's not the doctor in charge of the district; he's in private practice; he was married last year. His wife is standing farther away; I don't know whether you can spot the short, dark-haired lady wearing a coat with a silk border? That's his wife. She is rather fragile and always has to be warmly dressed. And there we have the deputy . . ."

"Can you point out Miss Kielland's fiancé to me?"

"No, Lieutenant Hansen isn't here; he's on maneuvers. He left a few days ago, right after the engagement."

After a moment's silence, Nagel said: "Two flowers were lying at the bottom of the grave, two white flowers. I don't suppose you know who they were from?"

"Yes—that is, do you really want to know? Do I have to answer? I'm ashamed to tell you—maybe they would have let me place them on the coffin if I had asked, instead of throwing them down like that. But two flowers seemed so meager, and wherever I put them, it would still be only two flowers. So I got up a little past three this morning— or last night, rather—and threw them into the grave. I even went down into it and arranged them, and said goodby to him there aloud—twice. I was so grief-stricken that I went into the woods and covered my face with my hands to hide my sorrow. It's such a strange feeling to say goodby to someone forever, and although Jens Karlsen was so superior to me in every way, he was still a good friend."

"So those flowers were from you?"

"Yes, but I didn't do it to attract attention, as God is my witness. Besides, it's of no importance. I bought them last night after I left you. When I gave my uncle your money, he gave me a half-crown to do with as I liked. He was so happy that he almost knocked me down! One of these days he'll come to thank you in person—I'm sure he will. But when he gave me the half-crown I suddenly remembered that I didn't have any flowers for the funeral, so I went down to the dock . . ."

"You went down to the dock?"

"Yes, to see a lady who lives there."

"In a one-story house?"

"Yes."

"Does the lady have white hair?"

"Yes, snow-white hair. Have you seen her? She is the daughter of a sea captain, but still she is very poor. At first she wouldn't take my half-crown, but I left it on a chair—though she kept protesting. She is terribly shy and it seemed to make her very uncomfortable."

"What's her name?"

"Martha Gude."

"Martha Gude." Nagel took out his notebook, wrote down her name, and said: "Has she been married? Is she a widow?"

"No. She used to go to sea with her father, but since he died she has been living here."

"Doesn't she have any relatives?"

"I don't know, but I don't think so."

"But how does she live?"

"God knows. But she must be getting something from the parish."

"Since you've visited this lady, Martha Gude, maybe you can tell me what her house looks like inside?"

"How would an old, miserable shack like that look? She has a bed, a table, and a couple of chairs; now I think of it, there must be three chairs, because one is standing in the corner next to the bed. It's upholstered in red plush, but it's leaning against the wall—apparently one of the legs is broken. I don't remember seeing anything else."

"Are you sure there's nothing else? Isn't there a clock on the wall, an old painting, or something like that?"

"No. Why do you ask?"

"The chair that's broken—the one covered in red plush—what's it like? Is it very old? Why is it standing by the bed? Is it unusable? Does it have a high back?"

"Yes, I think it has a high back, but I don't remember exactly."

They were singing the final hymn at the grave; the ceremony was at an end. When the hymn was over, there was a moment of complete silence, after which the crowd dispersed. Most of the mourners walked toward the main gate; others remained, talking in hushed voices. A small group came toward The Midget and Nagel—they were all young, and the ladies looked at the two in astonishment. Dagny Kielland turned crimson, but she kept her eyes straight ahead, looking neither to the right nor to the left. The deputy also kept his eyes averted while he quietly conversed with one of the ladies.

As they were passing, Dr. Stenersen, who was with the group, stopped. He waved to The Midget, who got up, while Nagel remained behind.

"Would you ask the gentleman . . ." he heard the doctor say; he didn't get the rest. But a moment later he distinctly heard his name mentioned. He got up too, took off his cap, and made a respectful bow.

The doctor apologized; a lady had asked him to perform the unpleasant duty of asking the gentleman to be more respectful of the gravestone and not to sit on it. It had just been laid, the base was not quite dry, the sod around it was soft, and it might easily sink. The request came from the deceased's sister.

Nagel begged pardon profusely; it was careless and thoughtless on his part, and he completely understood the lady's concern. He expressed his thanks to the doctor.

The group kept moving. When they reached the gate, The Midget said goodby, and the doctor and Nagel found themselves alone and they introduced themselves.

"Do you intend to stay on here for a while?" the doctor asked.

"Yes," said Nagel. "One has to follow the fashion—have a summer vacation in the country, gather strength for the winter months, and start out fresh . . . This is a delightful little town."

"Where do you come from? I've been trying to place your accent."

"I came from Finnmark originally—I'm a Finn, but I've lived in many places."

"Have you just come from abroad?"

"Only from Helsingfors."

At first their conversation was general, but they soon got on to other things—the elections, the crop failure in Russia, literature, and Karlsen's death.

"What is your opinion? Did you bury a suicide today?" Nagel asked.

The doctor couldn't say, and wouldn't say. It didn't concern him, and he wasn't going to get involved. There was a lot of talk. But why shouldn't he have committed suicide? All theologians ought to do away with themselves.

"Why?"

"Why? Because they fulfill no further function in our century. People have begun to think for themselves and their religious convictions are gradually fading away."

A liberal, Nagel thought to himself. But what did man have to gain by robbing life of all its symbolism, all its poetry? Besides, it was open to question whether this era had really made theologians superfluous, since religion was by no means dead.

"Perhaps religion survives among the lower classes—

although even there its influence seems to be on the wane. But among educated people it is definitely on the way out.

"However, let's not talk about that," the doctor broke off rather brusquely. "Our thinking is too far apart."

The doctor was a so-called free thinker; he had been through this kind of discussion countless times before. And had it made him alter his opinions? He had held on to the same ideas for the past twenty years. As a physician, he had assisted in scooping out people's "souls" by the spoonful! No, he was beyond superstition . . . "How do you feel about the elections?"

"The elections?" Nagel smiled. "I hope for the best," he said.

"Yes, so do I," said Dr. Stenersen. "It would be a terrible disgrace if the government didn't win a majority on such a far-reaching democratic platform." The doctor professed to be a liberal, even a radical, ever since he'd had a mind of his own. He was afraid of Buskerud, and Smålene was out of the question. "The fact of the matter is, we don't have enough money on our side," he said. "You and others like you who have the money ought to support us. The future of the whole country hangs in the balance."

"I? Do I have money?" exclaimed Nagel. "I'm afraid you're wrong."

"Well, maybe you're not exactly a millionaire. But I've heard that you have money—that you had property worth sixty-two thousand crowns."

"That's utter nonsense. It so happens that I've recently inherited a few thousand crowns from my mother. But I don't own any property. Where that rumor came from is a mystery to me."

They had reached the doctor's house—a two-story yellow house with a veranda. The place needed painting, the gutters were in bad shape, a pane of glass was missing from one of the upstairs windows, and the curtains were far from clean. The shabby appearance of the house was so depressing that Nagel wanted to get away as soon as possible, but the doctor said: "Won't you come in? No? Well, then, I hope you'll come back another time. My wife and I would be pleased if you would pay us a visit. Are you sure you can't come in and say hello to my wife now?"

"Wasn't Mrs. Stenersen at the cemetery? She can't be home yet."

"Yes, of course; she went with the others. Well, do stop in some time when you're passing by."

Nagel wandered off in the direction of the hotel, but just as he was about to go in, a thought flashed through his mind. He snapped his fingers, chuckled, and said out loud: "It would be amusing to see whether the lines of verse are still there!" And he turned around and went back to the cemetery. He stopped at Mina Meek's tombstone; there was nobody around, but the lines had been rubbed out.

Who had done it? Not a trace of his writing remained.

6

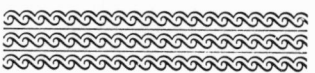

THE next morning Nagel was in unusually good spirits. While still in bed, he had felt strangely exhilarated. It was as if the ceiling of his room kept on floating upward toward infinity and became one with the firmament. Suddenly he felt a soft, fragrant breeze sweep over him as if he were lying with the sky as his ceiling on a bed of green grass. It was a warm summer morning; flies were buzzing around the room.

He quickly dressed, left the hotel without breakfast, and took a stroll through the town. By then it was eleven o'clock. Everyone who had a piano seemed to be playing it; a cacophony floated out through the open windows, and a rattled dog responded from the street with protracted howls. Nagel was filled with a sense of well-being. He began singing softly to himself, and as he passed an old man who greeted him, he slipped a shilling into his hand.

He found himself in front of a big white house. On the second floor a window was opened, and a slender, white hand secured it with a hook. The curtain stirred, the hand was still resting on the hook, and Nagel had the distinct feeling that someone was watching him. He stood there looking up for a few moments, but saw no one. The sign on the door read: F. M. Andresen, Danish Consulate.

Nagel was just about to leave when Miss Fredrikke's long, aristocratic face appeared at the window. A look of surprise crossed her face; their eyes met and she blushed, but assuming a defiant air, she pushed up her sleeves and leaned her elbows on the windowsill. She remained in this position for a long time, but made no move, so finally Nagel felt impelled to walk on. Then a strange thought occurred to him. Was the young lady kneeling at the window? If that was so, the ceilings in the consul's house must be quite low: the window could hardly be more than six feet high, which meant that the top of it was only about a foot below the eaves. He had to laugh at himself for indulging in this flight of fancy. What the devil did he care what kind of house Consul Andresen had?

And he kept walking. Warehouse employees, customs people, and fishermen were scurrying about, getting in each other's way. Capstans creaked; two steamers blew their sirens and pulled out almost simultaneously. The sun beat down on the water and transformed it into a glistening sheet of gold with ships and small craft set in it. From a big, three-master in the distance came the plaintive sound of a hurdy-gurdy, and when steam whistles and capstans let up for a moment, the wistful melody sounded like the quavering voice of a girl drawing her last breath.

The men on board the three-master got into the spirit and began dancing a polka to its melancholy strains.

Nagel caught sight of a child, a small girl, holding a cat in her arms; the cat was in a vertical position, patient and immobile, its legs almost touching the ground.

Nagel stroked the girl's cheek and asked: "Is that your cat?"

"Yes. Two—four—six—seven."

"So you already know how to count?"

"Yes. Seven—eight—eleven—two—four—six—seven."

He walked on. When he got close to the parsonage, he saw a white dove, frenzied by the sun, like a shining silver arrow zooming downward, descending sideways and disappearing behind the treetops. Then there was the sound of a muffled shot, and shortly thereafter a cloud of blue smoke rose from the woods on the other side of the fjord.

When he came to the last pier, which was deserted, he strolled up and down several times and then walked up the hill and without thinking headed toward the woods.

He walked for a half hour or so, getting deeper and deeper into the woods, and at last came to a halt at a narrow path. There wasn't a sound; there wasn't even a bird to be heard, and not a cloud in the sky. He walked a few steps off the path, found a dry spot, and lay down on his back. To the right was the parsonage, to the left the town, and above, an endless sea of blue sky.

What would it be like to be floating around up there among the planets, feeling the tails of the comets brushing against one's forehead? What a tiny speck the earth was, and how insignificant its inhabitants—Norway had two million bumpkins supported by mortgages and bank loans. What was the point of living, anyway? You fight your way ahead with blood and sweat for a few miserable years, only to turn into dust! Nagel put his head in his hands. He would finally get out of it all—end it! Would he ever be capable of carrying it off? Yes, by God, he wouldn't falter! He felt euphoric at the idea of having this escape hatch in reserve. Tears of rapture came into his eyes, and the intense emotion made his breathing heavy. He was already rocking on the seas of the heavens, singing as he fished with a silver hook. His boat was made of scented wood, and the oars gleamed like white wings; the sail was of light blue silk and shaped like a half moon . . .

A tremor of ecstasy ran through him. He felt himself carried away and engulfed by the magic rays of the sun. The stillness filled him with an intoxicating sense of wellbeing; he was free from worry; the only sound was a soft murmur from above, the hum of the universal machinery —God turning his treadmill.

Not a leaf stirred in the trees—not a pine needle dropped. Nagel hugged his knees in sheer delight; he felt exhilarated because life was good. It beckoned to him and he responded. He raised himself on his elbow and looked around him. There wasn't a soul in sight. He said yes to life once more and listened, but no one came. Again he said yes, but there was no answer.

Strange; he had distinctly heard someone calling him. But he dismissed the thought; perhaps he had imagined the whole thing. But nothing was going to shatter his joyful mood. He was in a strange, euphoric state of mind; his every nerve vibrated; music surged through his blood; he was part of nature, of the sun, the mountains; he was omniscient; the trees, the earth, the moss, spoke to him alone. His soul went into a crescendo, like an organ with all the stops pulled out. Never would he forget how this heavenly music seemed to pulsate through his blood.

For quite a while he lay there, enjoying the feeling of being completely alone. Then he heard footsteps on the path; they were real footsteps; there was no mistake about it. He raised his head and saw a man coming from the direction of town. He was carrying a long loaf of bread under his arm and leading a cow behind him on a rope. It was a warm day. He was wearing only a shirt and kept wiping the perspiration off his face. But, despite the heat, he wore a thick wool scarf wound twice around his neck.

Nagel lay quietly watching the peasant. There he was —the Norwegian country bumpkin with bread under his arm and leading a cow on a rope! What a sight he made! God help you, bold Norse Viking! Pull your pants down and let the lice out! But that would do you in; the fresh air would kill you. And the newspapers would mourn your untimely death and make a big thing of it. And to prevent a tragedy like that from ever happening again, the liberal representative Vetle Vetelsen would introduce a bill in Parliament dealing with the conservation of our national vermin.

Nagel's mind produced one bitter sally after another. He got up, angry and despondent, and headed back toward the hotel. He was right, after all; there was nothing but lice, peasant cheese, and Luther's catechism. And the people were middle-sized burghers living in three-story houses, eating and drinking to survive, filling their leisure with alcohol and politics, earning their living from laundry soap, metal combs, and fish. And at night when there was thunder and lightning, they lay abed trembling and read Johann Arndt. I'd like someone to find me a single exception—if there is one! For instance, I'd like to see a carefully planned crime, something to make one sit up and take notice! But none of your ridiculous minor transgressions! It would have to be an extraordinarily vicious and terrifying piece of villainy, a superb instance of depravity, with all the raw splendors of hell. It was all empty, useless talk. And what is your opinion of the elections, sir? Buskerud chills me to the bone . . .

But when he came back to the docks and saw the bustling activity all around him, his spirits gradually brightened and he again began singing to himself. The weather was glorious, a beautiful June day, no reason to feel depressed. The little town, shimmering in the sunshine, looked like an enchanted city.

When he entered the hotel, his caustic and bitter mood was gone. His heart was free of rancor, and in his mind's eye he again saw the boat of scented wood, with a light blue silk sail in the shape of a half moon.

This state of euphoria lasted for the rest of the day. Toward evening he again went out. He took the road leading toward the sea, and again found himself enchanted by a thousand small wonders. The sun was going down. Its harsh glare faded into a soft, diffused glow which spread over the water. Even the noise from the ships was muted. Nagel noticed flags flying here and there all around the fjord; several houses in town also had flags hoisted, and gradually all work came to a standstill on the docks.

He didn't attach any particular importance to this, but wandered off into the woods again; he went as far as the outbuildings of the parsonage and looked around the grounds. Then he went back into the woods in search of the darkest place he could find and sat down on a rock. He supported his head with one hand while tapping his knee with the other. He remained in this position for a long time, an hour perhaps, and when he finally got up to leave, the sun had sunk below the horizon and dusk was settling over the town.

When he emerged from the woods, he was surprised to see quite a few bonfires on the surrounding hills. There were perhaps twenty of them, burning like miniature suns. The fjord was full of boats, and people in them were lighting sparklers, which gave off green and red flares. From one of the boats, where a quartet was singing, they were sending up fireworks. Everyone seemed to be out of doors; the pier was crowded with people strolling and sitting around.

With an exclamation of surprise, Nagel turned to a man standing nearby and asked the reason for the flags and the bonfires. The man looked at him and spat and looked at him again before answering; it was June 23, Midsummer Eve! So it was Midsummer Eve! That was it, of course!

There had been one pleasant surprise after another today, and now this, too, into the bargain! Nagel, happy as a child, joined the crowd on the pier, delighted at his good fortune.

At a distance, he spotted Dagny Kielland's blood-red parasol in the middle of a group of people. When he noticed that Dr. Stenersen was among them, he walked up to him without hesitating. He bowed, shook the doctor's hand, and remained standing, cap in hand, for quite a while. The doctor introduced him to the group. Mrs. Stenersen also shook hands with him, and he sat down beside her. She had a pale, grayish complexion which gave her a sickly look, although she was very young— scarcely twenty. She was warmly dressed.

Nagel put his cap back on and addressed himself to the whole group: "I hope you'll excuse my intruding in this way, uninvited . . ."

"Not at all, it is a pleasure to see you," Mrs. Stenersen broke in amiably. "Maybe you'll sing something for us?"

"No, I'm afraid I can't," he replied. "I couldn't be more unmusical."

"I'm glad you came over," the doctor interjected. "We were just talking about you. You play the violin, don't you?"

"No, I don't," said Nagel again, smiling and shaking his head. Then suddenly, impulsively, he jumped to his feet, and with eyes that sparkled he said: "I'm so happy today. It's been a wonderful day from the moment I woke up this morning. For ten hours I've been walking around in a most exquisite trance. I feel as if I were in a boat of scented wood with a crescent-shaped, pale-blue silk sail. Isn't that a beautiful reverie? I couldn't possibly describe the fragrance of that boat, no matter how I tried. I have the feeling that I'm out fishing—fishing with a silver hook. But, ladies, don't you think that it's . . . ? Well, I don't know."

None of the ladies made any reply; rather, they looked at each other in embarrassment; they seemed to be silently consulting each other as to what to do. Then, one after the other, they began to laugh. They showed no mercy; they even laughed out loud.

Nagel looked from one to the other. His eyes were still shining, and in his mind's eye he was obviously still seeing the boat with the blue sail. But his hands trembled, although his expression was serene.

The doctor came to the rescue, saying: "That is a kind of hallucination . . ."

"No, it isn't," Nagel retorted. "Well, if you like, why not? It doesn't matter what you call it. I've been living in an enchanted world all day, whether it's hallucination or not. It all began this morning while I was still in bed. I heard a fly buzzing; this was the first sound I heard upon awakening. The next thing, I saw the sun seeping in through a hole in the curtain, and suddenly I felt extraordinarily happy. Summer was in my soul. The wind was stirring gently through the grass, and through my whole being. Hallucination—perhaps; I don't know. But I do know that my mind was in tune even with the buzzing of that fly; and to make it perfect, there was that ray of sunlight that I needed just at that moment, filtering through the hole in the curtain.

"When I got up and went out, the first thing I saw was a beauitful lady at a window—" He looked at Miss Andresen, who lowered her eyes. "Then I saw a lot of boats and a little girl holding a cat in her arms—one impression was superimposed on the other, but each made its separate impact on me. Then I went into the woods and it was there that I had the vision of the boat and the crescent sail; it came to me as I lay on my back, looking up into the sky."

The ladies were still laughing, and the doctor seemed about to burst. "So you were fishing with a silver hook?" he said, smiling.

"Yes, a silver hook."

"Ha ha ha!"

Then Dagny Kielland flushed and said: "I can well imagine having a daydream like that. I can see the boat clearly, with its sail, a blue crescent, and then the silver hook shimmering in the water. I think it's beautiful."

She was unable to continue, but stood there stammering, her eyes fixed on the ground.

Nagel immediately helped her out: "Yes, isn't it? And I said to myself: Heed it, it's a white dream, a warning; a reminder to fish with clean hooks—clean hooks! You were asking, Doctor, if I played the violin. No, I don't. I carry a violin case around with me, but there is no violin in it, only a lot of soiled linen, unfortunately. But I thought it would look good to have a violin case as part of my baggage; that's why I got it. Perhaps you won't think too highly of me for this, but it can't be helped, though I'm sorry about it. It's all because of the silver hook, you see."

The ladies were so taken aback that they stopped laughing. Even the doctor, Reinert the magistrate's deputy, and Holtan the schoolmaster sat there gaping in astonishment. Everyone was staring at Nagel. The doctor was obviously ill at ease. What on earth was the matter with this oddly behaved stranger? Nagel quietly sat down and didn't seem to have anything further to say. An agonizing and seemingly endless silence followed. But then Mrs. Stenersen came to the rescue. She was charm personified and like a mother tried to smooth things over and make everyone feel at ease. It seemed as if she were frowning on purpose, to make herself look older than she was and so lend more authority to her words.

"You come from abroad, Mr. Nagel?"

"Yes, madame."

"From Helsingfors, I believe my husband said?"

"Yes, that is, Helsingfors was the last place I lived in. I'm an agronomist, and I studied there for a while."

Pause.

"And how do you like the town?" Mrs. Stenersen asked.

"You mean Helsingfors?"

"No, *our* town."

"Oh, it's delightful—charming! I don't ever want to leave, honestly. But don't be alarmed. Some day I'll probably have to, though it all depends on circumstances. By the way," he said, getting up again, "if I intruded, please forgive me. But it would give me so much pleasure to sit here with you. I'm a stranger and don't know many people, so I've gotten into the habit of talking to myself far too much. You would do me a favor by ignoring my presence and picking up your conversation where you left off when I came."

"But you certainly did divert the conversation," Reinert said with a distinct undertone of anger.

Nagel replied: "I owe you an apology, sir, and I'm ready to give you any satisfaction you demand, but not now— you don't want it now?"

"No, this is hardly the time," Reinert said.

"Besides, I feel happy today," Nagel continued with a smile that lit up his face, so that for a moment there was a childlike radiance about him. "It's a glorious evening, and soon the stars will appear. There are bonfires on the hills, and people are singing on the fjord. Listen! Isn't it lovely? I know nothing about music, but it sounds beautiful to me. It reminds me of a night on the Mediterranean, off the coast of Tunis. There were about a hundred passengers on board—a choral group from Sardinia. Since I couldn't join in, I sat and listened to their voices coming from the saloon below. They sang most of the night. I'll never forget the sound of their voices floating on the sultry night air. I quietly closed the doors to the saloon, and that made the voices sound as if they were coming from the bottom of the sea; as if the ship were sailing into eternity to the strains of ethereal music. Try to imagine a sea filled with song—a subterranean choir!"

Miss Andresen, who was sitting next to Nagel, exclaimed: "God, it must have been lovely!"

"Only once have I heard anything to surpass it, and it

was in a dream. I was a child; it was a long time ago. Adults don't have beautiful dreams like that."

"You don't think so?" asked Miss Andresen.

"Definitely not—well, maybe that's an exaggeration, but . . . I still remember my last dream so vividly. I saw a swamp, but forgive me, here I keep on talking and I'm being a bore; I usually don't talk this much."

Then Dagny Kielland broke in: "I'm sure we would rather listen to you than talk." And leaning toward Mrs. Stenersen, she whispered: "Can't you persuade him? Please try! Just listen to that voice!"

Nagel smiled. "I don't mind talking. I'm just in the mood tonight; God knows what's come over me. Well, the dream I mentioned wasn't important. As I was saying, I saw a swamp, without trees, but with a myriad of roots sprawled in all directions like a mass of writhing serpents. Then I saw a madman walking among all those twisted roots. I can still see him; he was pale and had a dark beard, but it was so scraggly that his skin showed through. His eyes were full of suffering and he looked around distractedly. I was hiding behind a rock and I called out to him. He turned in my direction and wasn't at all surprised at the sound of my voice. He seemed to know where I was, although I wasn't visible. He kept on staring at the rock. He won't find me, I thought, and if he does, I can make a dash for it. And although it made me uneasy to have him standing there staring, I shouted again, just to provoke him. He took a couple of steps toward me; his mouth was open as if he were about to bite, but he couldn't get through the maze of roots. I cried out again, many times, to get him really worked up, and he began tugging at the roots to clear a path. He ripped them up by the armful and threw them aside in his struggle to reach

me, but he got nowhere. He began groaning, too, and his
eyes were bulging with pain and exertion. When I realized
that I was safe, I got up, revealed myself to him in my full
height and waved my cap, and drove him into a frenzy by
stamping my feet and shouting hello over and over again.
I even moved closer to him to rile him even more. I
pointed my finger at him, yelling hello close to his ear to
get him even more worked up. Then I crawled back behind my rock to taunt him and show him how close I was.
But he hadn't given up; he was still struggling with the
roots, struggling stubbornly and wildly to rip them out of
his path; they tore at him until he bled, his face was all
scratched, but he raised himself on tiptoe and shouted at
me. His face was distorted and steaming with sweat and
rage because he couldn't get at me. I wanted to egg him on
even farther, so I edged closer still, snapped my fingers
and jeered at him. I threw a root at him, which hit him
right in the mouth. The blow almost knocked him down,
but he spat out the blood, put his hand to his mouth, and
went on fighting the roots. Then I decided to be daring
and touch him; I wanted to poke my finger at his forehead
and then pull away. But at that moment he grabbed me.
Good God, did I panic! He lurched forward and grabbed my
hand. I screamed, but all he did was to hold my hand and
follow me. We made our way out of the swamp. The roots
didn't seem to bother him, now that he had a grip on my
hand, and we reached the rock which had been my hiding
place. He threw himself down and kissed the ground I had
walked on. He knelt there before me, bloody and bruised,
and thanked me for being so good to him. He blessed me
too, and prayed to God to bless me for what I had done for
him. His eyes were wide open and filled with supplications
to God on my behalf. He didn't kiss my hand or even my

shoe but the earth my shoes had touched. 'Why do you kiss the ground I have walked on?' I asked. 'Because my mouth is bleeding and I don't want to soil your shoes,' he said. 'But why do you thank me when I've only hurt you and made you suffer?' I persisted. 'I thank you,' he said, 'for not causing me more suffering, because you were kind enough to torture me no further.' 'Yes, but why did you scream at me and open your mouth as if to bite me?' 'I wasn't going to bite you,' he said. 'I opened my mouth to ask you for help, but the words wouldn't come and you didn't understand. And then I screamed in desperation.' 'Is that what made you scream?' I asked. 'Yes, that was the reason.' I looked at the crazed man, who was still spitting blood and still praying to God for me. Suddenly I realized that I had seen him before and that I knew him—a middle-aged man with gray hair and a scraggly beard: it was The Midget."

Nagel stopped. His listeners were stunned. Reinert lowered his eyes and stared at the ground.

"Was it really The Midget?" Mrs. Stenersen asked.

"Yes."

"Ugh, how creepy!"

"I knew it!" Dagny Kielland burst out. "I knew it the moment you said he knelt down and kissed the ground. I knew immediately who it was. Have you had a chance to talk to him?"

"No, I've only met him a couple of times. But I'm afraid I've ruined your evening. Mrs. Stenersen, you're quite pale. It was only a dream, you know."

"This is ridiculous," the doctor joined in. "What the devil do we care if The Midget . . . Let him kiss every root of every tree in Norway if he wants to. Look, Miss Andresen is crying!"

"I am not," she responded. "Why should I? But I do admit that this dream made an impression on me—and I think you were moved by it too."

"I?" cried the doctor. "Not in the slightest. I think you've all gone mad. Let's take a walk. Get moving, everybody! It's getting chilly. Are you cold, Jetta?"

"No, I'm not. Let's stay here," said his wife.

But the doctor was determined to take a walk; as a matter of fact, he was quite insistent on it. It was getting chilly, he said again, and he wanted to walk even if he had to go by himself. Nagel got up and joined him.

They strolled up and down the dock several times, making their way through the crowd, chatting and greeting people. About half an hour later Mrs. Stenersen called down to them: "Come back right away! Guess what we've decided while you were gone? We're going to have a big party at our house tomorrow night. You must come, Mr. Nagel! But I must warn you, at our parties there's only a minimum of food and drink."

"And a maximum of gossip," the doctor said laughingly. "But it's not a bad idea at all; you've had far worse notions, Jetta." The doctor's good humor had returned and he laughed gaily in anticipation of the party. "Don't come too late," he said. "Here's hoping I won't have any calls."

"But may I come in these clothes?" Nagel asked. "I don't have anything else to wear."

Everyone laughed, and Mrs. Stenersen replied: "Of course; it's very informal."

On the way home Nagel found himself walking next to Dagny Kielland. He hadn't maneuvered it; it had happened quite by accident, but she had made no effort to avoid him. She had just said how much she was looking forward to tomorrow night; everything was always so

pleasant and relaxed at the Stenersens'; they were delightful hosts and knew how to make their guests feel at ease.
Nagel suddenly interrupted her in a low voice: "I hope
you've forgiven my indiscretion in the woods the other
day?"

His words were so intense as he spoke them, almost in
a whisper, that she was touched. "Yes, I think I understand your behavior the other evening. You're different
from other people."

"Thank you," he murmured. "I'm more grateful to you
than I've ever been to anyone in my life. But why am I not
like others? I want you to know that all evening I've made
an effort to change that first impression you must have
had of me. Every word I spoke was meant for you. Do you
realize that? I know I had offended you terribly, and I had
to make amends. It's true that I have been in a strange
mood all day long, but I have made myself appear a good
deal worse than I really am, and I've been playing a
devious game most of the time. You see, I had to make you
think that I am unpredictable, that I am in the habit of
doing outrageous things, so that you would understand
and forgive me more easily. That is why I forced my
dreams on you at the most awkward time and place, and
why I exposed myself even further by mentioning the
violin case voluntarily—I wouldn't have had to do that."

"Excuse me," she broke in hastily, "but why are you
telling me all this and spoiling everything all over again?"

"I'm not spoiling anything. If I tell you that when I ran
after you in the woods I yielded to a momentary spiteful
impulse, you will understand. I had a sudden urge to
frighten you because you ran away. But I didn't know you
then. Now if I tell you that I'm no different from other
people, you'll understand that too. Tonight I made a fool

of myself and shocked everyone by my eccentric behavior in order to get you into a kinder frame of mind so that you would at least listen to me when I tried to explain. I succeeded; you listened to me and you understood."

"No, I'm sorry; I haven't completely understood—but let's leave it at that. I'm certainly not going to waste my time worrying about . . ."

"Of course not; why should you give it another thought? But am I not right in assuming that the idea of the party tomorrow night came about because you all thought I was an odd character who might provide some amusement? But maybe I'll disappoint you. Perhaps I'll only say 'Hm' and 'Yes,' and maybe I won't come at all. Who knows?"

"But you have to come!"

"I do?" he said, and looked at her.

She didn't answer and they continued walking.

When they reached the road leading to the parsonage, Miss Kielland stopped. She burst into laughter and, shaking her head, she exclaimed: "I've never met anyone like you!" She stopped and waited for the rest of the party to catch up with them. He had just mustered enough courage to ask if he could walk her home, but at that moment she turned around and called to the schoolmaster: "Come on, Mr. Holtan, you're trailing behind!" And she eagerly waved at him to hurry.

7

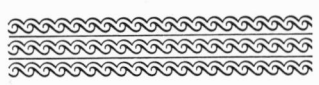

A T six o'clock the following evening Nagel arrived at
the Stenersens' house. For a moment he thought
he was too early, but the party of the previous evening
was already there. There were also two other people
whom he didn't know—a lawyer and a young blond student. They were already drinking brandy and soda at
two tables. At a third table the ladies, Reinert, and the
student were engaged in conversation. Holtan, the schoolmaster, who hardly ever opened his mouth, was already
quite drunk. His face was flushed and he was flitting
from one subject to another in a loud, excited voice. Take
Serbia, where eighty percent of the population was illiterate. Did they think those people were well off? That
is what he would like to know. And Holtan looked around
belligerently, though no one had contradicted him.

The hostess called Nagel and asked him to join her at the ladies' table. What would he like to drink? They had just been talking about Christiania. What an odd idea of Nagel's to come settle in a small town when he had a free choice and could even make his home in Christiania!

But Nagel didn't find this odd at all! He had come to the country for a holiday. Besides, under no circumstances would he live in Christiania—that would be one of the last places he would ever choose.

Really? But it was the capital, after all. It was the place where the great men and the celebrities of the country gathered, and it was the center of the arts, the theater— everything.

Yes, and it was also the meeting place of all foreigners, Miss Andresen added—actors, singers, musicians, and all kinds of people in the world of the arts.

Dagny Kielland listened but said nothing.

That was certainly true, Nagel admitted. He didn't know why, but every time Christiania was mentioned, he thought of the old part of town and the smell of unaired clothing. He couldn't help it; that's the way he felt. To him it was a stuffy little town with illusions of grandeur, with a couple of churches, a couple of newspapers, a hotel, and a community water pump, and with the most arrogant people in the world. He had never seen people put on such airs as in that place, and when he had lived there, good God how he had wished himself far away!

Reinert couldn't fathom how anyone could conceive such a strong dislike, not for a person, but for a whole town, the capital of a country. Christiania wasn't really a small town any more; it was taking its place among the important cities of the world. And the Grand Café was nothing to sneer at!

Nagel didn't comment immediately, but a moment later he frowned, and addressing himself to everyone, he remarked: "The Grand is a very unusual café."

"You don't sound as though you mean that."

Oh yes. The Grand was the gathering place for everyone of any importance. There sat the world's greatest painters, the world's most promising young men, the world's most well-dressed ladies, the world's most able editors, and the world's greatest writers. There they sat putting on airs for each other's benefit—each one basking in the other's recognition. "I've seen nobodies sitting there elated because other nobodies acknowledged them."

His remarks shocked everybody. Reinert leaned over Miss Kielland's chair and said in a stage whisper: "I've never heard such pompous nonsense."

She quickly glanced at Nagel. He must have heard what Reinert said, but he did not seem to be offended. On the contrary. He was drinking with the student Øien and, looking very unconcerned, he began to talk about something else. In fact, his air of superiority irritated her too. God only knows what he must think of them if he felt he could take the liberty of being so insolent! What conceit—what arrogance! When Reinert asked her what her opinion was, she answered in a voice that was intentionally loud: "My opinion of Christiania? Why, it's good enough for me!"

Even this didn't seem to bother Nagel. On hearing this remark, obviously half addressed to him, he looked at her in a puzzled way, as if trying to think how he might have offended her. For a long moment he stared at her with a pained and pensive expression.

By now Holtan had gotten into the discussion and protested against Christiania's being considered smaller than, say, Belgrade. Christiania wasn't smaller than any other medium-sized capital . . .

Everyone laughed. The schoolmaster looked too funny with his flushed cheeks and pugnacious air. Hansen, the lawyer, small and fat, with gold-rimmed glasses and a bald pate, was doubled up with laughter and kept on slapping his knees.

"Medium-sized, medium-sized," he shrieked. "Christiania is no smaller than other capitals of the same size— of exactly the same size. Not much smaller. That's a good one! Here's to you!"

Nagel again struck up a conversation with Øien. In his youth he, Nagel, had also loved music, especially Wagner. But with the years, he had gradually lost interest. And he had never progressed beyond learning to read notes and play a simple tune.

"The piano?" said Øien. That was his instrument.

"No—mine was the violin. But, as I said, I didn't get very far and soon dropped it."

He happened to look in the direction of Miss Andresen, who had been chatting with Reinert in the corner next to the glazed-tile stove for the past quarter of an hour. Her eyes chanced to meet his—quite unintentionally, but it made her squirm uneasily in her chair, and she couldn't seem to remember what she had been about to say.

Dagny was absentmindedly tapping her hand with a folded newspaper. She wore no rings on her slender, white fingers. Nagel stole a glance at her. How beautiful she was this evening! In this light, against the dark wall, her thick, blond braid seemed even fairer than usual. When she was seated, there was a suggestion of roundness about her which disappeared when she stood up. She walked as gracefully as a skater, with a slight undulating movement.

Nagel got up and walked over to her. For an instant she focused her dark-blue eyes on him, and without thinking, he exclaimed: "God, how beautiful you are!"

She was completely flabbergasted by his outburst. With her mouth wide open, she stared at him in utter confusion, and then whispered: "You don't know what you're saying!"

Then she got up, went over to the piano, and stood thumbing through some sheets of music, her cheeks flaming.

The doctor, who was dying to talk politics, broached the subject by saying: "Have you seen today's papers? But, damn it all, I can't help feeling that *Morgenbladet* is going a bit far these days. They don't seem to aim at the educated classes any longer; they report nothing but gossip and slander."

But, since no one answered, the doctor got nowhere. Hansen stepped in and said ingratiatingly: "Couldn't we assume that there are faults on both sides?"

"Now wait a minute," said the doctor, jumping to his feet. "You don't mean to tell me . . ."

Supper was ready; the guests moved into the dining room while Dr. Stenersen went on talking, and the conversation continued at the table. Nagel, who was sitting between his hostess and Miss Olsen, the daughter of the chief of police, took no part in it. By the time they left the table, they were deeply involved in European politics. They had discussed the Tsar, Constans, Parnell, and when they finally got to the Balkan question, the schoolmaster, who was already in his cups, had another go at

Serbia. He had just finished reading *Statistische Monatschrift;* things were in a terrible state; education had gone down the drain, it seemed . . .

"But there is one thing that makes me very happy," said Dr. Stenersen with tears in his eyes. "Gladstone is still alive. Fill your glasses, gentlemen, and we'll drink to Gladstone—a great democrat, a man of the present and of the future."

"Let's all join in," cried his wife. In her excitement she filled the ladies' glasses to overflowing, and her hands shook as she passed the tray around.

They all drank.

"There's a real man for you," exclaimed the doctor. "Poor fellow, he's been down with a cold the past few days, but let's hope he's better. Gladstone is the statesman I personally feel we could least afford to lose. To me, he is like a lighthouse sending beams of light all over the world. You seem so far away, Mr. Nagel—don't you agree?"

"I'm sorry. Of course I am in complete agreement with you. There are many things that impress me about Bismarck too—but Gladstone!"

Still no one would contradict the doctor. They were all used to his rambling. But after a while the conversation came to a standstill, and Dr. Stenersen suggested a game of cards to keep the party going. Who wanted to play?

At that point Mrs. Stenersen called out to Nagel from the other end of the room: "You know what Mr. Øien has just been telling me?—that you haven't always thought as highly of Mr. Gladstone as you seem to this evening. Mr. Øien once heard you speak at a union meeting where you really came down on Gladstone. You're a fine one! Are you going to deny it? Ha, you just try!"

Mrs. Stenersen smiled as she said this and gaily pointed at Nagel with her forefinger, repeating her challenge.

Nagel was a bit taken aback and insisted that there must be some mistake.

"I'm not saying that you deliberately maligned him," said Øien. "But you were violently opposed to him. I remember, for instance, your saying that Gladstone was a bigot."

"A bigot! Gladstone a bigot!" cried the doctor. "You must have been drunk!"

Nagel laughed.

"I most certainly was not—well, perhaps I was—I don't know. But it sounds like it."

"It certainly does," said the doctor, somewhat mollified.

Nagel obviously wanted to drop the subject, but Dagny Kielland pleaded with her hostess: "Please do make him tell us what he meant. It would be such fun!"

"Well, what did you really mean?" asked Mrs. Stenersen. "You must have a reason for being against him. Do tell us! You'll be doing us a favor, because if you men start playing cards, we'll be ever so bored."

"If it will amuse you, that's someting else," Nagel replied. Was he laughing at himself and the role he was playing?

In the first place, he didn't remember the incident Øien was alluding to. "Have any of you heard Gladstone speak in person? One comes away with a definite impression: his sincerity and his strong sense of justice. It's as though his motives could never be questioned. How could this man ever be accused of evil—of sin against God? He is so imbued with purity that he takes it as a matter of course that his audience is equally pure—that his listeners are as noble as he."

"But isn't this a laudable trait? It certainly proves his honesty and his love of humanity," the doctor interjected. "I've never heard such nonsense!"

"That's exactly what I mean. I only bring it up to point up a fine trait in his character. An incident comes to mind; I'd like to tell you about it. Well, I needn't go into details, I'll just mention the name Carey. I don't know whether you remember how Gladstone as prime minister made use of information passed on to him by Carey, who was a traitor? Subsequently, he helped Carey to get to Africa to escape the vengeance of the Fenians. But that's another story.

"I don't consider the affair particularly important. It's the kind of petty intrigue a minister may be forced into now and then.

"But let's come back to what we were discussing. Gladstone, when speaking, projects only the noblest ideas. If you had seen or heard Gladstone speak, I would only need to remind you of the expression on his face during his performance. He is so convinced of his righteousness that it marks every one of his gestures, colors his whole image —shines in his eyes and echoes in his voice. He speaks simply, slowly, and distinctly—and unendingly: his flow of words never seems to give out. You should see how he addresses his remarks in turn to all segments of the audience—a few to the ironmonger here, a few to that furrier over there—and he is so confident of his words that one would think he valued them at a crown apiece! It's an amusing spectacle! Gladstone is the champion of inalienable rights—that is his specialty. He would never for a moment admit that he could possibly be wrong. Since he is convinced that justice is on his side, he uses it ruthlessly, expounds on it, brandishes it like a banner in front of his audience to embarrass his opponents. His principles are noble and unshakable; he works on behalf of Christianity, the furthering of human ideals, and for civilization in general. If someone offered that man thousands of pounds to save an innocent woman from the scaffold, he would save the woman, indignantly refuse the money, and never take any credit for it. He would never dream of using it to his advantage—he's not that kind of man. He is a tenacious fighter for good causes, daily assumes personal responsibility for justice, truth, and God. How could he possibly fail? Two and two is four, truth has conquered, glory be to God! Now Gladstone can go beyond two and two. I have heard him claim, in a budget debate, that seventeen times twenty-three is three hundred ninety-one, and he came off with a smashing, enormous victory. Again, right was on his side, which made his eyes sparkle with righteousness, put a tremor in his voice, and filled him with elation. But at that point I had to stop, look, query. I didn't doubt his sincerity, but I still felt that I had to get up. I stood there checking his arithmetic—three hundred ninety-one—and it was correct, yet I turned it over and over in my mind, saying to myself: Wait a minute. Seventeen times twenty-three is three hundred ninety-*seven*! I knew very well that it was ninety-one, but against all logic I decided on ninety-seven, just to oppose this man, this man who makes it his business to be in the right. Something in me cried: Speak up against this arrogant righteousness! And I got up and said 'Ninety-seven' from a burning need to preserve my conviction of what is right from the onslaught of this man who was so unquestionably on the 'right' side."

"Good God, I've never heard such nonsense," cried the doctor. "Does the fact that Gladstone is always right upset you?"

Nagel smiled. Whether he was accepting the point made or was striking a pose was hard to tell. "It doesn't upset me in the least, nor does it destroy my conviction," he retorted. "I don't really expect anyone to understand what I'm trying to say, but it doesn't matter. Gladstone is a dealer in honesty and justice; his mind is filled with virtuous thoughts, rigid with praise received for his accomplishments. That two and two is four is his premise —to him it is the greatest truth under the sun. Can we deny that two and two is four? Of course not! I merely mention it to show that Gladstone's logic always wins out. The question is whether one is crazy enough about truth to accept it; whether one's sensitivity has become so blunted by truth that one can be struck down by it. That is the point I'm trying to make. Gladstone is so right and so sincere that he would never give up his good works in this world. He is always active, and always in demand. So he hammers away at his principles in Birmingham and re-peats them in Glasgow. He fights valiantly for his convic-tions, converts a cork-cutter and a lawyer to the same political views, and bellows at the top of his resilient old lungs so that not one of his precious words should be lost on his listeners. And when the performance is over and the people have cheered and applauded, and Gladstone has taken his bow, he goes home, folds his hands and prays, and goes to sleep, without the slightest flicker of doubt, without the slightest feeling of shame at having filled the halls of Birmingham and Glasgow—with what? He is convinced that he has done his duty toward his fellow men and that he has been true to himself, and so he falls into the deep sleep of the righteous. He wouldn't be capable of self-criticism to the point of saying: Today you didn't come across; the two cotton spinners in the first row were bored to death—one of them yawned in your face. But he couldn't admit that, and so he would say to himself that he wasn't actually sure that the man *did* yawn! And yet he wasn't going to lie, because lying is a sin, and Gladstone doesn't sin. He would say to himself: I had the impression the man was yawning, but I must have been mistaken.

"Perhaps I said something in this vein in Christiania, but it doesn't matter. At any rate, I must admit that Gladstone's intellectual acrobatics have never impressed me."

"Poor Gladstone!" said Reinert.

Nagel made no reply.

"But that wasn't what you said in Christiania," cried Øien. "You attacked Gladstone because of the Irish and Parnell, and you said, among other things, that he was no great intellect. I distinctly remember your saying that. He was an important and powerful force, you said, but mediocre to an extreme when it came down to it—no more than Beaconsfield's terrible little finger."

"Now I remember: they put me out for that. But I'll admit to that too, and why not? It can't make things any worse. But do judge me compassionately!"

Dr. Stenersen asked Nagel: "Are you a conservative?"

Nagel looked at him in astonishment. Then he burst into laughter and asked: "What do you think?"

At that moment the doctor's office doorbell rang. Mrs. Stenersen got up; it was always like this; the doctor would have to go out on a call. But no one was to leave, under no circumstances; well, not until midnight anyway. Anna would bring more hot water—lots of it; it was only ten o'clock.

"Mr. Reinert, you aren't drinking anything!"

Mr. Reinert said he was well able to look after himself.

"But none of you must leave. You have to stay. Dagny, you're being very quiet."

But Dagny was no more quiet than usual.

The doctor came back from his office and asked to be excused. He had an emergency—a hemorrhage. It wasn't too far away; he would be back in two or three hours and hoped to find his guests still there: "Goodby, everyone; goodby, Jetta."

And the doctor left in a great hurry. He was joined by another man, and they both ran toward the landing.

"Now let's think of something to do!" Mrs. Stenersen exclaimed. "It's a terrible bore to be stuck here alone when my husband has to go on a call—especially on winter nights when I'm not even sure he can get back."

"You don't have any children?" Nagel asked.

"No, but I'm beginning to get used to these endless nights. At first it was ghastly. I was so frightened, worried—and afraid of the dark, too—that sometimes I even got up and went and slept with the maid. Now, Dagny, you have to say something! What are you thinking about? Your fiancé, of course!"

Dagny blushed, and answered laughingly: "Yes, of course. That's only natural. But why don't you ferret out Mr. Reinert's thoughts? He hasn't opened his mouth all evening."

Reinert protested; he had been chatting with Miss Olsen and Miss Andresen; he had been engaged in conversation, had listened attentively, had followed the political discussion . . .

"Miss Kielland's fiancé has just gone to sea again," said the hostess, addressing herself to Nagel. "He's a naval officer; he went to Malta—wasn't it Malta?"

"Yes," said Dagny.

"Well, it doesn't take long for fellows like that to become engaged! He comes home on leave for two or three weeks, and then one night—oh, those lieutenants!"

"They're the best," said Nagel, "usually handsome, weatherbeaten men, with a brisk, straightforward manner." Their uniforms were good-looking and most becoming, too. As a matter of fact, he had always been fascinated by naval officers.

Smiling, Miss Kielland turned to Øien: "That is what Mr. Nagel says now. But what did he say in Christiania?"

There was a burst of laughter. Hansen cried out in a shrill, drunken voice: "Well, what did he say in Christiania? What did he actually say in Christiania? Cheers!"

Nagel clinked glasses with him and they both drank. Then Nagel resumed his train of thought: He had always been intrigued by naval officers. As a matter of fact, he would go so far as to say that if he were a girl, it would be a naval officer or nothing.

This brought forth another sally of laughter. Hansen gaily clinked all the glasses on the table and drank. Suddenly Dagny remarked: "They say all naval officers are clods. You don't agree?"

Of course not! But even if it were true, he'd still prefer a handsome man to an intelligent one, if he were a girl. No question about it! And especially if he were a *young* girl! What good was a brain without a body? But you could of course turn it around—what good is a body without a brain? Ah, but there was a hell of a difference! Shakespeare's parents were illiterate. It seems that Shakespeare himself couldn't read very well, but still he achieved everlasting fame. But to come back to the point: a girl would get tired of an ugly intellectual sooner than she would of a handsome dunce. If he, Nagel, were a young girl and had the choice, he would choose the handsome man, without question. And the man's opinions on Norwegian politics and the philosophy of Nietzsche—let the ravens take them.

"Let me show you a picture of Miss Kielland's fiancé," said Mrs. Stenersen, going to fetch an album.

Dagny sprang to her feet and cried, "Oh no!" But she regained her composure and sat down again. "It's a bad picture," she said. "He is much better-looking than that."

Nagel found himself looking at a handsome young man with a beard, sitting at a table in an erect, yet graceful posture, his hand on his sword. His rather thin hair was parted in the middle. There was something very English about his looks.

"Yes, I do agree, he is much better-looking than that," Mrs. Stenersen chimed in. "Before I was married, I was in love with him myself. The man next to him is the young theology student who died recently—Karlsen. It happened a week or so ago—a terrible tragedy. No, it hasn't been that long—his funeral was the day before yesterday."

The photo showed a sickly-looking man with hollow cheeks and lips so pinched and thin that they looked like a streak across his face. His eyes were dark and large, and his forehead unusually high, but his chest was sunken and his shoulders no broader than a woman's.

So this was Karlsen! Nagel thought: those veined hands and an interest in theology were suited to a face like this. He was just about to say that there was something very sad about Karlsen's countenance when he noticed that Reinert moved his chair closer to Dagny and began talking to her. Nagel withdrew and went on thumbing through the album.

"Since you've all been complaining of my silence," said

Reinert, "maybe you'll allow me to tell you what happened during the Kaiser's visit. It's a true story, and it just happened to come to mind."

But Dagny interrupted him, saying in a low voice: "What have you been talking about the whole evening over in that corner? I'd much rather hear about that. I only wanted you to know that I was aware of your private conversation. But of course you were gossiping as usual. You're downright mean to be always laughing at people. I know it's ridiculous the way he shows off that iron ring on his pinkie—the way he holds it up, rubs it, looks at it. But it's probably only an absentminded gesture.

"And he didn't make as much of a spectacle of himself as you seemed to insinuate, although he is so conceited and batty that he has it coming to him. Gudrun, you went too far, laughing at him like that. He certainly must have noticed that he was being laughed at."

Gudrun defended herself by saying it was Reinert's fault—he had been so terribly funny—it was the way he said: "Gladstone's intellectual acrobatics have never impressed me"—*me!*

"Gudrun, you're talking too loud again. I'm sure he heard you, because he turned around. But did you happen to notice that when he was interrupted he didn't show the least sign of impatience? He just looked sad. You know, I'm beginning to feel rather ashamed of sitting here talking about him this way. Do tell your story about the Kaiser's visit, Mr. Reinert."

Reinert told the story. Since it was no secret but a harmless tale about a woman with a bouquet of flowers, he raised his voice little by little until at last he had everyone's attention. It was an involved story and it took him several minutes to tell it.

When he finished, Miss Andresen said: "Mr. Nagel, do you remember the story you told us last night about the choir on the Mediterranean?"

Nagel abruptly closed the album with a startled look. Was he acting or was it real? In a quiet voice he allowed that he might have been mistaken in some of the details but that that wasn't intentional. He hadn't invented the story—it had really happened.

"Good heavens, I never meant to imply that you had made it up," she said, with laughter in her voice. "But do you remember what you said when I told you it was beautiful? You said that only once before had you heard anything more beautiful, and that was in a dream."

He nodded silently.

"Won't you tell us about that dream? Please! You're such a marvelous raconteur! We all beg you!"

But he refused, with several excuses: it was a dream without beginning or end, an ephemeral fantasy that had come to him during the night. It just couldn't be put into words. Everyone must at one time or another experience these flights of fancy that flash through the mind as quickly as lightning and fade just as quickly. The whole thing seemed all the more foolish since it took place in a white silver forest . . .

"A silver forest—and then what?"

He said no, shaking his head.

He would do anything for her; she had only to put him to the test. But he couldn't talk about that dream; she must believe him.

"All right. But do tell us another story. Please."

He didn't feel up to it, not tonight. They must excuse him.

There was some casual conversation then, a few

bantering remarks, whereupon Dagny said: "You say you would do anything for Miss Andresen. What, for instance?"

This caprice of Dagny's brought forth general merriment, and Dagny herself had to laugh. After a moment's reflection, Nagel retorted: "I would be capable of doing something really terrible for your sake."

"Something terrible? Do tell. A murder, perhaps?"

"Yes, I assure you, I could kill an Eskimo, skin him, and make a blotter for you."

"Well, that's impressive! But what about Miss Andresen? What could you do for her? Something extremely noble?"

"Perhaps—I don't know. By the way, the bit about the Eskimo I've read somewhere. It isn't original."

Pause.

"You're all terribly kind," he said. "You keep on trying to draw me out, just because I'm a stranger."

Holtan stole a glance at his watch.

"You might as well know right now," said Mrs. Stenersen. "You won't be allowed to leave until my husband gets home. Absolutely out of the question. You may do anything you like, but you can't leave."

Coffee was brought in and the group came to life once again. Hansen, who had been deep in conversation with Øien, jumped to his feet, light as a feather despite his weight, and enthusiastically clapped his hands together; Øien massaged his fingers, went over to the piano, and played a few chords.

"How stupid of me," cried the hostess. "How could I have forgotten that you played the piano. Please go on!"

Øien would be happy to oblige. He wasn't too accomplished, but if they had no objection to Chopin, or a Lanner waltz . . .

Nagel applauded enthusiastically and, turning to Dagny, said: "When you hear that kind of music, don't you feel you'd like to be a little distance away, in the next room perhaps, holding your beloved's hand, without speaking? I've always thought of that as a moment of great beauty."

She gave him a long, scrutinizing look. Was he serious? There didn't seem to be the slightest trace of irony on his face, and she resumed her bantering tone: "But you wouldn't want too much light, and the chairs ought to be low and soft. And it would have to be rainy and dark outside."

This evening she was more beautiful than usual. Her dark-blue eyes contrasted strikingly with her fair skin. Though her teeth weren't perfect, her smile was uninhibited; she would laugh at practically anything and then one couldn't help noticing her voluptuous red mouth. But perhaps the most enthralling thing about her was the blush which spread over her face as she talked and then faded just as fast.

"Now Holtan has disappeared again!" cried Mrs. Stenersen. "As usual. It's impossible to keep track of him—it always ends up the same way. At least, Mr. Reinert, I hope I can count on you to say good night before you leave!"

The schoolmaster had left by the kitchen door, slipping out quietly as always, depressed and exhausted after his carousing, and pale from lack of sleep. He had not returned, and when Nagel heard this, the expression on his face changed completely. The thought struck him that he might dare ask Dagny if he instead of Holtan could accompany her through the woods. He lost no time in asking her, and with beseeching eyes and head bowed, he added: "And I promise to behave."

Laughingly, she said: "In that case, all right."

He felt obliged to wait until the doctor returned. But the thought of walking with Dagny through the woods stimulated him; he talked incessantly, made everyone laugh, and was most affable. Elated as he was, he agreed to take a look at Mrs. Stenersen's garden, since he considered himself something of an expert—particularly the corner where bugs had gotten at the currant bushes. He would get rid of them even if he had to exorcize them!

Was he also versed in witchcraft?

Oh, he played around with all kinds of things. For instance, he wore a ring—they might have noticed it—an ordinary iron ring, but it had magic powers. No one would believe it by looking at it! But if he should lose the ring— at ten o'clock, say—he would have to find it by midnight, or something dreadful would happen. He had gotten it from an old Greek—a merchant in Piraeus. Of course he had reciprocated the kindness and given the man some tobacco in return.

But did he actually believe in the magic powers of the ring?

Yes, to a certain extent. It had cured him once.

A dog was barking on the road leading to the fjord. Mrs. Stenersen looked at the clock; yes, the doctor must be coming home, she recognized the dog's bark. How marvelous! Midnight, and he was already back. She rang for more coffee.

"So this ring has extraordinary powers, Mr. Nagel, and you have faith in it?"

"Yes, more or less." That is to say, he had good reasons not to doubt it. Well, did one's professed beliefs really matter—or was it what one really believed in one's heart? The ring had cured him of nervous tension and given him renewed strength and confidence.

At first Mrs. Stenersen laughed, but then she began to raise objections. No, she couldn't take that kind of nonsense—he must excuse her—but she was sure he didn't mean a word of it. When educated people talked like that, what could be expected of the man in the street? Where would it lead to—and, besides, wouldn't the doctors have to close up shop?

Nagel came to his own defense. One cure was as good as another. The important thing was the will, the faith, the character of the patient. But there was certainly no reason for doctors to close up shop. They had a faithful following. Their patients were educated people and they were cured by drugs, while heretics and peasants were cured by iron rings, charred human bones and mold from graveyards. Weren't there instances of patients being healed by ordinary water because they were persuaded that water was an especially effective remedy? Weren't there many such cases among morphine addicts, for example? On the strength of these remarkable cures, people who believed in non-scientific healing could tell medical science to go to the devil, and ignore its teachings. He hoped he wasn't giving the impression that he thought he was an expert on these matters. He was not a professional and didn't have the facts to back up his ideas. Besides, he was in a very good mood and didn't want to depress anyone else by talking about unpleasant things. Mrs. Stenersen, and everyone, must forgive him.

He kept glancing at the clock and was in fact already buttoning his jacket.

The doctor's arrival interrupted the conversation. He was obviously nervous and in a bad mood, greeted his guests with forced joviality and thanked them for having stayed. Well, of course there had been no holding the schoolmaster—peace be with him—but otherwise the party was still going strong. Ah, well, the world was certainly full of struggle!

As he always did, he began to tell about the sick call. He was despondent, he felt he'd been let down by his patients, who had behaved like idiots—they ought to be put behind bars. What a place he had just come from! The woman was ill, her father was ill, her son was ill—and the stench! Yet the rest of the family was healthy and rosy-cheeked, and the little ones were flourishing. The whole thing was incredible—it was beyond him! There was the old man, the woman's father; he was lying there with a gash that big. So they sent for a leech-healer and her remedies. She stopped the bleeding, all right, but the way she did it! It was revolting and criminal. He couldn't even talk about it, but the smell was enough to kill you! And then of course gangrene set in. If he hadn't been called this evening, God only knows what the outcome would have been. They ought to make the laws against quackery more stringent and really get after these people. Well, the bleeding was stopped. Then in came the son, a tall, loutish-looking fellow with pimples all over his face. "The other day I gave him some ointments, with specific instructions to apply the yellow salve for one—*one*—hour a day, and the white salve, the zinc ointment, the rest of the time. And what did he do? He did exactly the opposite, of course. He put on the white salve for an hour, and the yellow one, which draws and burns like hell, that one he left on round the clock. And he kept this up for two weeks! The amazing thing is that his skin did heal—in spite of his stupidity! That oaf manages to get cured no matter what he does! Tonight he showed me a cheek and snout without a blemish. Just luck! He could have done serious damage to his face for a long time to come, but that didn't bother him a bit! Then there's the boy's mother. She is ill, weak, exhausted, nervous, has no appetite, and feels dizzy because of a buzzing in her ears. 'You have to take baths,' I tell her. 'Baths! Get some water on your body, damn it! Wash yourself! Kill a calf, eat and get some meat on your bones; open your windows and let in some fresh air; don't walk around in wet clothes; stay outdoors as much as possible—and that book over there, that book by Johann Arndt, throw it away, throw it in the fire! But the most important thing: baths, rubdowns, and more baths; otherwise, my medicine won't do you any good.' Well, she couldn't afford a calf, true—unfortunately—but she did bathe and got some of the filth off. But she claims it makes her sensitive to the cold, all this cleanliness makes her shiver, makes her teeth chatter, so she's stopped using water. She couldn't stand it any longer! Then what does she do? She gets hold of a chain, supposedly an antidote for rheumatic fever, a Volta cross, or whatever they call it, and hangs it around her neck. I asked to see it: a zinc disk, a rag, a couple of hooks of varying sizes—that's all there was to it. 'What the devil is this for?' I ask her. But it really has done her some good, made her feel a little better. The pains in her head are gone and she doesn't feel the cold so much. The zinc disk and those hooks cured her—what can you do with someone like that! I could spit on a stick and hand it to her, and the effect would be the same. But try to tell her that! 'Take it off,' I say. 'Otherwise I won't touch you—I won't treat you!' And what do you think she does? She holds on to her zinc disk and sends me away, sends me packing! Jesus Christ! I shouldn't be a physician—I should be a witch doctor!"

He sat down and began drinking his coffee, obviously

very much shaken. His wife and Nagel exchanged glances, whereupon she said in a laughing voice: "Mr. Nagel here would have done exactly the same thing as that woman. We were just talking about that when you arrived. Mr. Nagel doesn't believe in your science."

"Oh, he doesn't, does he," remarked the doctor dryly. "Well, that's entirely up to Mr. Nagel."

Angry and hurt, and fed up with neglectful patients who ignored his advice, the doctor sipped his coffee, morose and silent. The way the others kept looking at him merely added to his irritation. "Do something, don't just sit there!" he exclaimed. But then, after he finished his coffee, he was his usual cheerful self again, talked to Dagny, and joked about the boatman who had rowed him to his patients. Then his professional problems overwhelmed him once more and he again lapsed into an irritable mood. He couldn't get over that business with the ointments; wherever he went, he ran into stupidity, loutish behavior, and superstition. The ignorance of those people was terrifying!

"But the man was cured, wasn't he?"

This remark of Dagny's made him want to sink his teeth into her; he stiffened. The man got well, yes, but what did that prove? The ignorance of most people is enough to make one's hair stand on end.

The man got well, that's right; but what if he had burned off his face? Was she really defending such abysmal ignorance?

This maddening confrontation with a country bumpkin who had done exactly the opposite of what he had been told, who had in effect cured himself, was unendurably irritating to the doctor, and his usually kind eyes flashed with indignation behind his glasses. He had been humiliated beyond words, made a fool of because of a zinc disk, and it took a stiff toddy on top of the coffee to calm him down.

Then suddenly, out of the blue, he said: "Jetta, listen, I gave the boatman five crowns—I just want you to know. He was an odd character! The seat of his pants was all worn, but that didn't seem to bother him in the least. He was the very devil, and strong as an ox. He sang the whole way and assured me that he could reach right up to heaven with a fishing rod if he stood at the top of Etje Mountain. 'I guess you'd have to stand on tiptoe, though,' I said. But he took me seriously and assured me that he could stand on tiptoe as well as anyone. He was certainly an odd character, and very amusing."

Finally Miss Andresen got up to leave, and so did everyone else. When Nagel said good night, he expressed his thanks so warmly and so sincerely that the doctor, who had been annoyed with him the last quarter of an hour, was quite disarmed.

"Come back soon," he said. "Do you have a cigar? Have one of mine!" And he insisted that Nagel have another cigar.

Dagny was already standing at the door, with her wrap on, waiting for him.

8
White Nights

IT was a beautiful night. The few people who were still on the streets looked gay and animated. In the cemetery a man was pushing a wheelbarrow and singing to himself, despite the hour. Everything was so still that his voice was the only sound to be heard. The town lay sprawled below the doctor's house like a strange, monstrous insect, flat on its belly with its tentacles stretched out in all directions. Here and there it would extend a leg or draw in a feeler, as now down on the fjord, where a small steamer glided along seemingly without a sound, leaving a black furrow behind it.

The smoke from Nagel's cigar rose in a blue spiral. He was already inhaling the fragrance of the woods and the grass, and he was filled with a sense of contentment. It was a feeling of intense joy, which brought tears to his eyes and choked him. He was walking next to Dagny; she still hadn't said a word. As they passed the cemetery, he made a few complimentary remarks about the Stenersens, but she made no reply. The beauty and the stillness of the night filled him with such elation that his breath came in gasps and his eyes welled with tears. What magic in these white nights!

In a loud voice, he exclaimed: "Just look how clearly one can see the ridges over there! Forgive me, but tonight I'm so happy, I would be capable of doing something insane out of pure joy. Look at those firs and crags, and the tufts of grass, and the juniper bushes! In this light they look like persons sitting down! And the night is so fresh and cool; it's open and clear and doesn't weigh down one's spirit with strange forebodings—one isn't filled with ominous feelings. Don't you agree? Please forgive me if it sounds odd, but I feel as though angels were soaring through my soul. Do I frighten you?"

She had stopped short, which is what had prompted his question. Her blue eyes smiled at him. Then, suddenly becoming serious, she said: "I've been trying to figure out what kind of a man you are."

As she said this, she stood absolutely still and looked at him. When they began walking again, her voice was clear but had a slight tremor, as if she were afraid and happy at the same time.

They began talking, and they talked during the entire walk through the woods, touching on one topic after another, going from one mood to another, both filled with the same agitation and restlessness.

"Have you really thought about me? But, I assure you, I've thought much, much more about you. I knew about you even before I met you; I overheard some people mention your name on the boat. I arrived here on the twelfth of June—June 12!"

"Did you? June 12, of all days."

"Yes, and all the flags were flying—the town impressed me with its charm; that's why I decided to come ashore. And then I kept hearing about you . . ."

She smiled, and said: "I suppose you've been talking to The Midget?"

"No, but I heard how you were loved and admired by the whole town . . ." And Nagel suddenly thought of Karlsen, the theology student, who had taken his life because of her.

"Tell me," she said, "did you really mean what you said about naval officers?"

"Yes. Why?"

"Because I completely agree with you."

"Why shouldn't I mean it? I've always admired them, their freedom, their uniforms, their health and utter fearlessness—they are usually fine, upstanding characters besides."

"But let's talk about you. What happened between you and Mr. Reinert?"

"Nothing. Mr. Reinert, did you say?"

"Last night you apologized to him for something, and tonight you hardly spoke to him. Do you always offend people and then ask their forgiveness?"

He laughed and lowered his eyes. "I really shouldn't have offended Mr. Reinert," he said. "But I'm sure I can straighten it out when I have a chance to talk to him. I do admit I'm impulsive and outspoken; the whole thing started when he jostled me going through a door. It was nothing, really; I just felt he was being somewhat impolite. But like an idiot I jumped up, called him names, shook a beer mug under his nose, and bashed in his hat—whereupon he walked out. As a gentleman, there was nothing else he could do. But afterwards I was sorry for the way I'd behaved, and decided to make amends. Though I do have something to say in my defense. I was on edge that day, several things had happened which annoyed me immensely. But of course no one could possibly have known that. Those are things you can't explain; so I prefer to take the blame."

His words had a spontaneous and sincere ring, as if he were trying to be fair to both sides. His expression, too, was open and candid.

But Dagny stopped abruptly, looked him straight in the eyes, and said, utterly astonished: "But that isn't the way it happened! I heard an entirely different story."

"The Midget is lying!" cried Nagel, turning red.

"But I didn't hear it from The Midget! Why do you talk yourself down like that? I heard it from the man in the marketplace who sells plaster figurines—he told me the whole story, he saw everything."

Pause.

"I can't understand why you're belittling yourself," she went on, her eyes fixed on him. "I heard all about it today, and I was so happy—I mean, I thought you had acted with such sensitivity and nobility of spirit. It seemed so in character. If I hadn't heard the story this morning, I don't think I would have dared to walk with you now. I mean it, really."

Pause.

"And you admire me for that?" he said at last.

"I don't know," she replied.

"Oh yes, you do. Look," he continued, "all this was only a farce. You are an honest person and I can't lie to you. I want you to know exactly what happened."

And brazenly looking her straight in the eyes, he proceeded to tell her how he had planned the whole thing: "You will see that when I gave you my version of the incident with Reinert, perhaps distorting the facts slightly, perhaps even talking myself down a bit, it was purely for my own benefit; I want to get all I can out of this. I'm being honest with you because I assume that one day somebody will tell you the true story, and since I have already demeaned myself as much as I possibly can in front of you, I stand only to gain by it—to be richly rewarded. I would rise in stature, acquire a reputation for magnanimity and nobility of spirit which I could not easily earn otherwise. Am I not right? But I can only attain this by being so lowly and so crude that I thoroughly disgust you. I have to confess all this to you, because you deserve complete honesty. But of course I know what will happen: I'll drive you a thousand miles away from me."

She kept looking at him, completely baffled by this man and what he had just said, trying to sort it all out in her mind. What was behind it all? What was his purpose in revealing himself to her in this way? Again she stopped abruptly, clapped her hands together, and burst out into loud, ringing laughter: "You're the most shameless person I've ever met! Imagine, going around saying all those ghastly things about yourself with a straight face—it's so self-destructive! What can you possibly hope to achieve by it? I've never heard of anything so insane! How could you be sure that I would ever find out what really happened? Tell me—no, don't—it would only be another lie! What horrible things you've been saying! When you make such careful calculations and fabricate your story to suit your ends, and then undo everything by confessing your deviousness—or deceit, as you call it—what am I to think! Last night you did more or less the same thing. I just don't understand. Why do you plan your moves so carefully and then fail to realize that you are exposing yourself—your own lies?"

He was silent for a moment, and then he said, without wavering: "But, on the contrary, it's part of my scheme. I'll try to make you understand what I mean. I'm risking nothing if I reveal myself to you, as I just did—at least, not very much. I can't be sure that the person I open up to will believe me. At the moment you don't believe me, but even so, in the end I will gain doubly, enormously; I will reap rich rewards and my soul will soar to the mountain tops. Even if you did believe me, I would come out on top. You shake your head in disbelief? I assure you, I've operated this way quite a number of times, and it always works. Even if you believed what I just confessed to you, you would still be taken aback by my candor. You would say to yourself: 'He deceived me, but he confessed afterwards, though there was no reason for him to do so. His audacity mystifies me; his self-abasement confounds me!' What it really amounts to is that I force you to notice me; I arouse your curiosity and make you pay attention to me; I shock you into taking notice. A minute ago, you said you couldn't figure me out. You said it because you were *thinking* about me, which thrills and delights me. I do have a lot to gain, whether you believe me or not."

Pause.

"And you are trying to make me believe," she said, "that you have cunningly laid out all these plans, step by step, that you have foreseen every turn of events, anticipated every difficulty? But by now nothing you could say would surprise me. After this, I can expect only the worst from you. You are really not a bad liar, though. As a matter of fact, you're quite clever."

He retorted that her remarks only confirmed his convictions. He was grateful to her, because now he had attained his goal. But she had been much too kind—far more than he deserved . . .

"That's enough," she exclaimed, abruptly cutting him off.

Now it was his turn to be taken aback: "But I'm telling you again that I've been deceiving you," he said, looking intently at her.

For a moment they stared at each other; her heart began to pound and she turned pale. Why was he so anxious to make her believe the most degrading things about himself? He seemed ready and willing enough to give in on other points, but on this he absolutely refused to yield. What an absurd obsession he had! Beside herself with anger, she cried out: "I can't understand why you keep turning yourself inside out for me. You did promise to behave."

Her anger was spontaneous and genuine. His blind, unshakable convictions so unnerved her that she momentarily lost her self-control. She was thoroughly irritated at having been shaken up like this, and showed it by thumping her parasol on the ground as she walked.

He seemed crestfallen and made several droll and disarming remarks about it. Finally she had to laugh again and assured him that she hadn't taken him seriously. He was incorrigible, and that was that. If he thought it was funny, he could go ahead and laugh, but not another word about this crazy obsession . . .

Pause.

"Perhaps you remember," he mused. "This is where I met you for the first time. I will never forget the way you looked as you ran away—a vision, a fairy princess.

"But I'd like to tell you about a true adventure I once had." It was brief and unimportant, really, and there wasn't much to tell. One night he was sitting in his room—it was in a small town—not Norway—but that doesn't matter. It was a night in autumn, 1883—eight years ago. He was sitting with his back to the door, reading a book.

"Were you reading by lamplight?"

"Yes, it was pitch-black outside. I was sitting there reading when I heard, I distinctly heard footsteps on the stairs and then a knock on my door. I said, 'Come in!' but there was no response. Then I opened the door, but there was no one there. I rang for the maid: Had anyone come upstairs? No, no one. 'Thank you,' I said. 'Good night.' And the maid left.

"I sat down again and began to read. Suddenly I felt someone breathing close to me and I heard a whisper, 'Come!' I turned around but saw no one. I went on reading, but in my irritation I said, 'Damn!' Then before me appeared a tiny, pale man with a red beard and dry, stiff, bristly hair. He was standing to the left of me. He winked at me and I winked back; we had never seen each other before, but we kept this up for a few moments. I closed the book with my right hand; the man moved toward the door and vanished. I actually saw him disappear—with my own eyes. I got up and walked to the door, and again I heard that exhortation, 'Come!' I put on my coat, slipped into my galoshes, and went out. But then I thought I would have a cigar, and I returned to the room to get one. I stuffed a few into my pocket, God knows why, but I did. and went out again.

"It was pitch-black, as I said, and I couldn't see a thing, but I felt the presence of the little man at my side. I groped around trying to get hold of him. I made up my mind not to go another step if he wouldn't identify himself, but he wasn't to be seen. I then tried to wink at him here and there in the dark, but there was no response. 'Never mind,' I said. 'I didn't come out because of you; I do hope you realize that. I just wanted to take a walk.' I talked in a loud voice so he would hear me. I walked for several hours; I found myself in the country, then in the woods. Dew-drenched branches, twigs, and leaves slapped against my face. Then I took out my watch as if to look at it, and said: 'Well, I guess I'll go back home!' I didn't go home, though; something kept me from turning back and drove me on. 'Since the weather is so marvelous,' I said to myself, 'you can keep wandering for a night or two, as you have nothing else to do.' I said that, though I was tired, and drenched with dew. I lit another cigar. The little man was still at my side; I could feel him breathing alongside. I walked in all directions but never back toward town. My feet were beginning to ache, I was soaked to my knees, and my face was raw from the lashing of the wet branches. 'It may seem strange for me to be wandering around like this at this time of night,' I said, 'but since childhood I've been in the habit of exploring forests by night.' And I walked on, gritting my teeth. The town clock struck twelve: one, two, three, four—I counted the strokes. I was cheered by the familiar sound, although it irked me that we hadn't gotten farther away from town after all that walking. As I was saying, the town clock was striking, and at the twelfth stroke the little man appeared before me and laughed. I'll never forget it; he was as alive as I was. He had two front teeth missing and he held his hands behind his back . . ."

"But how could you see him in the dark?"

"He radiated a light of his own. There was a strange glow about him that seemed to come from behind him and which made him transparent. Even his clothes were luminous. His trousers were worn and much too short. I saw it all in a flash. Stunned, I blinked my eyes and took a step backwards. When I looked up, the man was gone . . ."

"Oh!"

"But there's more. I saw a tower ahead of me. As it came into focus, I saw that it was a dark, octagonal tower; it looked like the Tower of the Winds in Athens, if you've seen a picture of that. I had never heard of a tower in this forest, but there it was. As I stood in front of it, I again heard 'Come!' and I went in. The door was left open behind me, to my great relief.

"I stepped inside under the arched roof, and there was the little man again. A lamp was burning on one of the walls, and I could see him clearly. He came toward me as if he had been standing there the whole time, and laughed silently as he stared at me. I looked into his eyes, and they seemed to reflect all the horrors he had seen in his life. Again he winked at me, but I didn't wink back and I backed away as he approached me. Suddenly I heard light footsteps behind me. I turned and saw a young woman come in.

"I looked at her and a happy feeling came over me. She had red hair and black eyes, but she was shabbily dressed and walked barefoot on the stone floor. Her arms were bare and smooth, without a blemish.

"She looked at us both; then bowing to me, she walked up to the little man. Without a word she began unbuttoning his clothes and feeling him all over as if she were looking for something. Then she pulled a small, faintly glowing lantern out of the lining of his coat and hung it on her finger. The lantern was now so bright that it outshone the lamp hanging on the wall. The man was standing absolutely still and laughed silently as before, while being searched. 'Good night,' said the woman, pointing to the door, and this strange, terrifying being, who was half man, half monster, left. And I was alone with the woman.

"She came toward me, bowed again, and without smiling or raising her voice, she said: 'Where do you come from?'

" 'From town, my pretty one,' I replied. 'I've come all the way from town.'

" 'Please, stranger, forgive my father's behavior!' she cried. 'Don't hold it against him. He is ill—out of his mind—you could see that from his eyes.'

" 'Yes, I saw his eyes; they cast a spell over me; they hypnotized me.'

" 'Where did you meet him?' she asked.

" 'In my room. I was sitting there reading when he came.'

"She shook her head and lowered her eyes.

" 'Don't give it another thought, my pretty one,' I said. 'I enjoyed the walk and I enjoyed meeting you. Look at me, I'm happy and feel very much at ease, and you must smile too!'

"She didn't smile, but said: 'Take off your shoes. You're not leaving here tonight. I'm going to dry your clothes.'

"She looked at my sodden clothing; water was oozing out of my shoes. I did as I was told: took my shoes off and gave them to her. As I did so, she blew out the lamp and said: 'Come!'

" 'Just a minute,' I said. 'Since I'm not going to sleep here, why are you making me take my shoes off?'

" 'I can't tell you,' she said. She led me through the door and into a dark room. There was a sound behind us, as of someone breathing. I felt a soft hand on my mouth, and the girl said out loud: 'It is I, Father. The stranger is gone!'

"Again I felt the presence of the dwarfed madman. We walked up a flight of stairs, and neither of us spoke. We went into a room with a vaulted ceiling; not a ray of light penetrated the inky blackness.

" 'Shh,' she whispered. 'This is my bed.' And I groped around and found it.

" 'Now take off the rest of your clothes,' she whispered.

"I took them off and handed them to her.

" 'Good night,' she said.

"I pulled her back and begged her to stay. 'Don't go yet! I know why you made me take off my shoes downstairs. I'll be very quiet; your father didn't hear me. Come.'

"But she wouldn't. She said good night and left."

Pause.

Dagny had turned crimson, her bosom heaved, her nostrils quivered. "And did she really leave?" she blurted out.

Pause.

"Now my night turned into a fairy tale, a lovely, golden memory. Imagine a pale, white night. I was alone. The night was as thick and heavy as velvet. I was exhausted, my knees were shaking, I was in a daze. That lunatic had led me around in circles for hours in the wet grass, like an animal, beckoning to me and saying, 'Come, come!' If he comes near me, I'll take his lantern and hit him on the jaw with it, I said to myself. I was terribly upset, and in order to calm down, I lit a cigar and went to bed. For a while I lay there, watching the glow of the ashes. Then I heard the door shut down below, and all became still.

"About ten minutes passed. Now this is important: I was lying wide awake in bed smoking a cigar. All of a sudden I heard a murmur that came from the vaulted ceiling; it was as though the roof had been lifted. I leaned on my elbow, let my cigar go out, and stared into the darkness, but saw nothing. Again I lay down and listened, and this time I heard sounds that seemed to come from a distance; marvelous music—a choir of a thousand voices, somewhere outside me, perhaps from the sky, singing softly. The music kept coming closer and closer, until finally it was just above me, over the tower. Again I raised myself on my elbow, and I experienced something which fills me with supernatural rapture whenever I think of it: a myriad of tiny, luminous figures, dazzlingly white, appeared. Angels in countless numbers seemed to be descending on a diagonal beam of light. There were perhaps a million of them, floating about in waves from floor to roof as they sang, naked and white. I held my breath and listened. They brushed my eyelids, touched my hair, and the whole vault seemed to be filled with the fragrant breath from their tiny open mouths.

"I put out my hand to them; a few of them wafted down and settled on it. It was like having the twinkling Pleiades on my hand. I bent over, looked into their eyes, and realized that those eyes were unseeing. I released the seven blind ones and caught seven others, but they were also blind. They were all blind—the whole tower was filled with blind angels singing.

"I lay there motionless; this vision left me breathless and my soul was in torment over those blind eyes.

"After a moment or so, I heard a muted, metallic sound from afar which reverberated with cruel distinctness for a long time; it was the town clock again—this time striking the hour of one.

"Suddenly the angels stopped singing. I saw them arrange themselves in formation and fly off. They soared up to the roof, swarming around the opening, eager to get out, riding on a broad beam of light, turning toward me as they floated away. The last one turned once more, gazing at me with its blind eyes before it departed.

"That's the last thing I remember—the blind angel turning to look at me. Then everything became black again. I lay back on the bed and fell asleep . . .

"When I awoke, it was broad daylight. I was alone in the vaulted room. My clothes were lying on the floor next to me. They were still damp, but I put them on just the same. Then the door opened and the girl from the night before appeared in front of me.

"She walked right up to me, and I said: 'Where do you come from? Where were you last night?'

" 'Up there,' she replied, pointing to the roof of the tower.

" 'Didn't you sleep?'

" 'No, I kept watch.'

" 'But didn't you hear singing during the night?' I asked. 'I heard the most heavenly music.'

" 'Oh, it was I who was playing and singing,' she answered.

" 'You? Tell me honestly, my dear, was it you?'

" 'Yes.' She gave me her hand and said: 'Come, I'll show you the way.'

"We left the tower and walked hand in hand through the forest. The sun shone on her golden hair and her black eyes were afire.

"I took her in my arms and kissed her twice on the forehead, and I got on my knees before her. With trembling fingers she loosened a black ribbon from her dress and tied it to my wrist. She cried as she did so; she was overcome with emotion.

" 'Why are you crying?' I asked. 'Forgive me if I've done anything to hurt you.'

"But all she said was: 'Can you see the town from here?'

" 'No,' I said. 'Can you?'

" 'Get up and let's go on,' she said, taking my hand. Again I stopped, took her in my arms, and said: 'You make me very happy. I can't help loving you.'

"She trembled in my arms, and said: 'I have to go back now. Can you see the town?'

" 'Yes,' I said, 'but you can see it too?'

" 'No,' she said.

" 'Why not?' I asked.

"She pulled away from me and looked at me with those enormous eyes of hers, and then she left, her head bowed. When she had walked a few steps, she turned and looked at me once more.

"Then I realized that she, too, was blind.

"The next twelve hours are a complete blank to me. They're wiped out, and I keep telling myself that those twelve hours must be accounted for somehow; they are lost and I must find them. But I don't have a clue as to where they've gone.

"Again it's night—a dark, mellow autumn evening. There I was in my room with a book in my hand. I looked down at my legs, which were still damp. I looked at my wrist—there was a black ribbon tied around it. Everything fits into the story.

"I rang for the maid and asked her if there was a dark, octagonal tower in the forest, not too far from town. She nodded and said yes, there was a tower. 'And does anyone live there?' 'Yes, a man lives in it, but there is something wrong with him; they say he's possessed by evil spirits; people call him the lantern man. He has a daughter who also lives there.'

"She said good night and I went to bed. The next morning I again set out for the forest. I took the same path; I saw the same trees, and also the tower. When I reached the door, I saw a sight which froze my heart. Lying on the ground was the mangled body of the blind girl; she had obviously fallen; her bruised body showed that all too clearly. She lay there, her mouth wide open, the sun shining on her red hair. On the edge of the roof, a shred of her dress that had got caught was still flapping in the breeze. And there on the gravel path below, the little man, the father, stood looking at the corpse. His body was heaving and he was howling out loud. He kept walking around the corpse, overcome with grief. When he espied me, I shuddered at the sight of those terrible eyes. Horrified, I ran all the way back to town. That was the last time I saw him . . .

"So there you have my fairy tale."

Dagny didn't say a word; she walked slowly, her eyes fixed on the ground. After a long pause she said: "That was certainly a strange tale!"

There was another long silence, and Nagel tried to

break it by saying something about the profound feeling of peace in the forest. "Can you smell the wonderful fragrance here? Do let's sit down for a minute!"

She sat down, engrossed in her own thoughts, and he sat down opposite her.

He had the feeling that he ought to try to cheer her up. It was no tragedy—really, it had all been quite an adventure. When you compare it with the fairy tales of India—now, they can really chill your blood! There are two kinds: first, supernatural tales about caves filled with diamonds, princes who come down from the mountains, beautiful creatures from the sea, spirits of the earth and air, palaces of pearl, castles beyond the horizon, flying horses, forests of silver and gold. Then there are stories dealing with mysticism—things fantastic, strange, and marvelous. The Orientals, fired by fevered minds, invented fabulous and magnificent tales, never to be surpassed. From the very beginning, these people lived in a fantastic world, a world of unreality, and it was just as natural for them to talk about fairy-like palaces beyond the mountains as it is for us to discuss the Great Silent Power of the sky that putters around in space, chewing stars. The basic difference was that these people lived under another sun and ate fruit instead of meat.

"But don't you think we have a rich mythology of our own?" said Dagny.

"Our myths are marvelous, but they're different. We can't conceive of a sun that would shine and burn mercilessly. Our fairy tales deal with the earth and what is beneath it; they are the product of the imagination of peasants in leather breeches, they come out of dark winter nights spent in log cabins with smoke vents in the roof." Had she ever read *The Arabian Nights*? So different from the truly rustic, earthbound poetry of the tales from Gudbrandsdal—these were our creation, a reflection of our genius. Our fairy tales don't make us shudder; they are fanciful and amusing; they make us laugh. Our hero was no handsome prince but a wily village bumpkin. What did you say? Weren't our tales from the North just as fantastic? Hadn't we created something out of the mystery and the wild beauty of the sea? Well, a Nordland fishing sloop would indeed seem to an Oriental like a fabulous phantom ship right out of a fairy tale. Had she ever seen one of those sloops? No? It looked like a great big female animal, her belly bulging with unborn young, and with a flat bottom to sit on. Its nose protruded like a horn to summon the four winds . . . We live much too far north. Well, at any rate, that was the modest opinion of an agronomist about a geographical fact.

She must be growing tired of his chatter by this time. There was a hint of mockery in her blue eyes as she asked: "What time is it?"

"The time?" he said, as if lost in thought. "It must be about one—but it's still early."

Pause.

"How do you feel about Tolstoy?" she asked.

"I don't care for him very much," he said, eager to seize a chance to continue the conversation. "I liked *Anna Karenina, War and Peace,* and . . ."

Smiling, she asked: "And what is your opinion about the possibility of a lasting peace?"

That was a good one! He lost his self-assurance and couldn't think of anything to say.

"What do you mean? Oh, I must have been boring you."

"No, honestly, it was just a thought that came to me," she said quickly, blushing. "Don't be offended. What made me think of it was that we are organizing a bazaar for the benefit of the Defense Fund."

Pause.

Suddenly he looked at her, his eyes full of animation. "I have a confession to make. I feel happy tonight, and perhaps that's why I've talked so much. Everything is wonderful, but most of all the fact that I'm walking here with you. Tonight is the most beautiful night I've ever known. I can't explain it, but it's as if I were a part of the forest, a part of nature—the branch of a fir, or a stone, yes, even a stone, but one permeated with the exquisite fragrance and the feeling of peace that surrounds us. Look over there; it's almost dawn. See that silver streak?"

They both looked at it for a moment.

"I, too, am happy tonight," she said.

She said it impulsively, spontaneously, as if she had a need to express herself.

Nagel looked at her intently and again began talking. Nervously, he launched headlong into a monologue about Midsummer Eve; he said the trees were swaying and murmuring; that the coming of dawn was doing something strange to him, bringing him under the spell of magic powers. As Grundtvig expressed it in song: "We are children of light, and now for us the night is over!" But, instead of talking so much, maybe he could show her a trick with a straw and a twig, to prove that the straw was stronger than the twig. There wasn't anything he wouldn't do for her . . .

"Look over there at that lonely juniper bush—sometimes the most insignificant thing catches my fancy. It seems to be bowing to us so friendlily. And the spider spins its web from tree to tree. It looks like a Chinese design, like suns spun out of water. You're not cold, are you? I'm sure we're surrounded by warm and smiling dancing elves at this very moment—but if you're cold, I'll make a fire. Incidentally, it just occurred to me—wasn't Karlsen found somewhere near here?"

Was he trying to get back at her? He seemed capable of just about anything.

She sprang to her feet, aghast, crying: "Leave him be, please! What a horrible thing to say!"

"I'm sorry," he said contritely. "But they say he was in love with you, I can't blame him for that . . ."

"In love with me? And don't they also say he killed himself because of me—with my penknife? Let's go now."

There was sadness in her voice but no trace of embarrassment or affectation in her manner. He was amazed at her reaction. Knowing that she had been the cause of the death of one of her admirers seemed to have made no impression on her. She wasn't indignant; neither did she try to use it to her advantage. She merely alluded to it as a tragic incident and let it go at that. Her long, blond hair fell down over the collar of her dress, and her cheeks had a warm, fresh glow, now moistened by dew. As she walked, her hips swayed slightly.

They had come out of the forest and into a clearing. A dog barked, and Nagel remarked: "We're already at the parsonage. Those large white buildings look so inviting—and the garden, the doghouse, the flagpole—right in the middle of the forest! Miss Kielland, don't you think you'll be homesick for this place after you've left—I mean, when you're married? Well, of course that depends on where you're going to live."

"I really haven't thought about it," she said, adding: "Sufficient unto the day . . ."

". . . is the joy thereof!"

Pause.

She seemed to be thinking over what he had said.

"Incidentally," she said, "I hope you're not surprised at my being out at this hour. But we're night owls around here. We're country people, children of nature. Mr. Holtan and I have often walked along this road talking until broad daylight."

"Mr. Holtan? He didn't strike me as being very talkative."

"Well, I guess I did most of the talking; that is, I asked questions and he answered. What are you going to do now when you get home?"

"Now? I'll go to bed and sleep until about noon, like a log, like the dead, without waking up once and without dreaming. What are you going to do?"

"Don't you lie awake thinking about all kinds of things? Do you always fall asleep right away?"

"The minute my head hits the pillow. And you?"

"Listen! A bird! It must be later than you say. Let me see your watch. Good God, it's past three—almost four! Why did you say just now that it was only one o'clock?"

"I'm sorry," he said.

She looked at him, but without the slightest trace of annoyance, and said: "You didn't need to be so devious. Honestly, I would have stayed out this late, even if I had known. I hope you won't misunderstand me. There aren't too many things I care for, and when I do, I grasp them with both hands. That is the way I've lived since we came here, and to my knowledge I haven't shocked anyone. Come to think of it, I'm not so sure about that, but it doesn't matter. Anyway, Papa doesn't object, and he's the one that counts. Let's walk a little farther."

They passed the parsonage and entered the woods on

the other side. The birds were singing, and the white streak of daylight in the east kept widening. The conversation ebbed; they talked of nothing in particular. After a while they turned and came back to the parsonage gate.

"Hello, old boy," she said to the watchdog, who was pulling at his chain. "Thank you for bringing me home, Mr. Nagel. It's been a wonderful evening. Now I'll have something to write to my fiancé about. I'll tell him that you are the kind of man who is at odds with everybody and everything. He won't know what to make of it. I can see him now, rereading the letter with a puzzled look on his face. He is such a kind man—you can't imagine how good he is! He never says anything to hurt anyone's feelings. It's a shame you won't meet him while you're here. Good night."

"Good night," said Nagel, not taking his eyes off her until she had disappeared into the house.

Nagel removed his cap as he walked through the woods. He was preoccupied with his thoughts. He stopped several times, looked up and stared straight ahead for a moment or so, and then walked on at the same slow pace. What a beautiful voice she had! He'd never heard anything like it before—her every word was music.

9

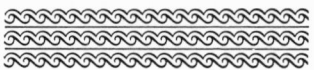

IT was the following day, about noon.

Nagel had got up and left the hotel without having breakfast. He had already walked through most of the town, lured on by the marvelous weather and the animated life of the docks. As if on a sudden impulse, he turned to a man and inquired how to get to the magistrate's office. The man gave him directions and Nagel was on his way.

He knocked and walked in, passed several clerks busy at their desks, went up to Mr. Reinert, the deputy, and asked to speak to him for a few minutes—it wouldn't take long. Rather reluctantly, Reinert got up and ushered Nagel into a private office.

Nagel began by saying: "Please forgive me for coming

back to this affair once again—I'm referring to The Midget. I hope you'll accept my profound apology."

"I considered the affair closed after your apology in the presence of everyone on Midsummer Eve."

"That's very kind of you," said Nagel. "But I'm not very happy about the way we settled it, Mr. Reinert. As far as I'm concerned, yes, but I'm thinking of The Midget. I would hope you'd feel that The Midget deserves an apology and that you are the one to straighten things out with him."

"Are you saying that I ought to go and apologize to that fool for a mere prank? Is that what you mean? Wouldn't you do better to mind your own business and not . . ."

"Yes, we've been through that before! But to get back to the point: you tore The Midget's coat to shreds, and you did promise him a new one, didn't you?"

"Look here. You are in a public office and you keep talking about a private matter which doesn't even concern you. This is *my* office. You don't have to go back through the main office; you may leave through this door."

And the deputy opened the side door for Nagel.

"Thank you. But I still feel that you ought to send The Midget the coat you promised him, immediately. He needs it, and he took you at your word."

At this, Reinert flung the door wide open, crying: "This way!"

"The Midget took you for an honest man," Nagel went on, "and you mustn't disappoint him."

Now the deputy opened the door to the outer office and summoned the two clerks. Nagel tipped his cap and left without another word.

This had really gone badly. It would have been much

wiser to stay out of the whole thing. Nagel went home, had lunch, read the papers, and played with the puppy, Jacobsen.

That afternoon, looking out of his window, Nagel saw The Midget struggling along the gravel road from the dock, carrying a sack of coal. The weight of it made him stoop so low that he couldn't see where he was going. His legs were so shaky and he walked so crookedly that his trousers were worn to shreds on the inside. Nagel went out and overtook him at the post office, where The Midget had put down his sack to rest for a minute.

They bowed to each other. As The Midget straightened up, it was obvious that his left shoulder was the lopsided one. Nagel grabbed it, and without relaxing his grip, he whispered fiercely: "Have you been telling anyone about the money I gave you? Did you breathe a word about it to anybody?"

Taken aback, The Midget answered: "No, I haven't, not a word!"

"Just let me tell you," said Nagel, white with fury. "If you ever breathe a word about those few shillings, I'll kill you! Kill you! Do you understand? And, by God, you'd better tell your uncle to keep quiet too!"

The Midget stood there with his mouth wide open, stuttering incoherently; he wouldn't say anything, not a word, he promised . . . he swore . . .

Almost as if to apologize for his violent outburst, Nagel added: "This is a hole, a rotten little backwoods town. I can't move without people staring at me. I won't put up with this constant spying! To hell with them all! Consider yourself warned. Also, I have reason to believe that this Miss Kielland from the parsonage, for one, is clever at drawing you out and making you talk. But I'm on to her, and I will not have any of her spying. I happened to meet her last night. She is a great flirt, but that's beside the point. Again I must insist that you not mention our little transaction. I'm glad I met you. I wanted to ask you about the day before yesterday, when we were sitting together on the tombstone up in the cemetery."

"Yes."

"I wrote some lines of verse on that stone. I admit that they were salacious and inappropriate, but the fact is, I did write them. When I left, they were still there, but when I came back a few minutes later, someone had wiped them off. Was that you?"

The Midget looked down and said: "Yes."

Shaken at having been caught out doing such a bold thing on his own initiative, The Midget stutteringly tried to explain: "I wanted to prevent . . . You didn't know Mina Meek, otherwise you could never have done it . . . you couldn't have written those words. I said to myself that you must be excused because you were a stranger, and since I live here it was easy for me to undo what you had done—so, I thought, why shouldn't I. I wiped the words off—no one had seen them."

"How do you know?"

"Not a soul had seen them. After going with you and Dr. Stenersen to the gate, I immediately went back and wiped them off. I had been away only a few minutes."

Nagel looked at him, grasped his hand, and squeezed it without a word. They looked at each other; Nagel's lips trembled slightly.

"Goodby," he said. "Incidentally, did you get the coat?"

"No, but I'm sure I'll have it by the time I need it. In three weeks . . ."

Just then the egg woman with the white hair walked

by—Martha Gude. She was carrying her basket under her apron, her black eyes downcast. The Midget greeted her, and Nagel also bowed, but she scarcely looked up at them. She hurried along to the market, where she sold her two or three eggs, and left again with her coins in her hand. She was wearing a green dress of light material. Nagel, his eyes fixed on the dress, said: "So you need the coat in three weeks? What is the occasion?"

"A bazaar, a big gala affair. Haven't you heard about it? I'm going to play a part in the tableaux—Miss Dagny has given me a part."

"I see," said Nagel slowly. "Well, you'll have a coat to replace the old one. Mr. Reinert said so himself today. He's not really so bad. But remember, and remember well: you must never thank him! Not ever! You must never mention that coat to him—he doesn't want any gratitude. It would offend him deeply. Besides, you realize that he wouldn't like to be reminded of the day when he got drunk and stormed out of the hotel looking so foolish, with his hat all bashed in."

"Yes."

"You're not to tell your uncle where you got the coat either; no one must know. Mr. Reinert insists on that. You realize, of course, that he would look very foolish if word got around that he had been rude and disorderly and then had to make up for it with a coat."

"Yes, I understand."

"Tell me, why don't you use a wheelbarrow to deliver your coal?"

"I can't because of my injury. I can carry a lot of weight if I'm careful, but I can't push or pull anything. If I do, I strain myself and fall flat on my face in great pain. But carrying one sack isn't so bad."

"That's good. Come and see me again. No. 7—remember? Just walk right in."

As he said this, he slipped a bill into The Midget's hand and quickly walked down the street toward the dock. His eyes had been on the green dress the whole time, and now he was in pursuit of it.

When he reached Martha Gude's little house, he stopped for a moment to look around. No one was watching him. He knocked on the door, but there was no answer. He had knocked twice before without getting any response, but this time he had seen her coming home from the market and he was determined not to leave before he had been inside. Boldly he opened the door and walked in.

She was standing in the middle of the room, looking at him. She turned white and was so terrified that she just stood there holding her hands outstretched, not knowing what to do.

"Please forgive my barging in like this," said Nagel, making an unusually respectful bow. "I would appreciate it very much if you would let me talk to you for a moment. I promise it won't take long. I have already called on you twice but did not find you at home, unfortunately. My name is Nagel, I'm a stranger in town and I'm staying at the Central."

She still hadn't said a word, but pushed a chair toward him and started walking in the direction of the kitchen door. She was in a state of utter confusion, and as she looked at him, she kept fussing with her apron.

The room was the way he had pictured it—a table, a couple of chairs, and a bed were about the only furnishings. At the windows were some plants yielding white blossoms, but there were no curtains and the floor wasn't clean. Nagel noticed the shabby, high-backed chair in the corner next to the bed. It had only two legs and was balanced against the wall: a sad-looking sight. The seat was covered in red plush.

"Please, I would like to assure you that you have nothing to worry about," said Nagel. "I usually don't frighten people when I come to call. This isn't the first time I've called on people here in town, so you aren't the only one. I go from house to house and try my luck everywhere—perhaps you've heard about me? No? Well, it's true. It's part of my job—I'm a collector—I buy all kinds of old things and pay whatever they might be worth. Don't be alarmed! I'm not a thief—I assure you I'm not in the habit of walking off with other people's belongings. You are quite safe with me. If I can't bargain in a friendly way and buy what I want to the satisfaction of both parties, I'm not interested."

"But I don't have any old things," she said at last, looking desperate and quite bewildered.

"Everyone says the same thing," he replied. "Lots of people have things to which they have become attached, objects they're reluctant to part with—things that have played a role in their lives, perhaps an heirloom from parents or grandparents. But all these discarded objects are standing around and are of no use whatsoever! Why should they take up space when they could be turned into money? Some of these useless family antiques are quite valuable, but they end up falling to pieces and being relegated to the attic. So why not sell them while they can still serve a purpose? Simple people are annoyed when I call on them, and tell me they don't keep old things around. Fine; that's their prerogative. There is nothing to be done, so I bow and leave. Then there are those who are embarrassed and balk at showing me a cooking utensil with a hole in it. They just don't understand the value of things. They're unsophisticated people who just have no idea what a popular craze collecting has become these days. I say craze advisedly; I confess it's a real mania that impells me and I therefore call it by its right name. I might as well be honest about it. But that of course is a very personal matter. What I wanted to say was that it's stupid and ridiculous of these people to be so reticent about showing an antique. Look at the state of disintegration of the weapons and rings that are being dug up from the ancient burial mounds! Does that mean they have no value? You should see my collection of cowbells! I have one—a plain iron bell—that was considered sacred by an Indian tribe. Imagine—for ages it hung on a tent pole in their settlement, the object of prayers and sacrifices. Just think of that! But to get back to the point—when I get on the subject of my cowbells, I get carried away."

"But I really don't have any old things like that," Martha said again.

Nagel assumed the air of a connoisseur and said slowly: "Would you permit me to have a look at the chair over there? Of course I wouldn't make a move without your permission, but I've had my eye on it from the moment I walked in the door."

Flustered, Martha said: "That chair . . . of course . . . but two legs are broken . . ."

"Yes, the legs are broken. But what difference does that make? On the contrary, that may even enhance its value. May I ask where you got it?"

Nagel was examining the chair, turning it around and carefully looking over every detail. The gilding was gone, and the only decoration was a sort of crown on the backrest, carved in mahogany. Someone had hacked at it with a knife, and the woodwork around the seat bore marks of having been used for cutting tobacco.

"We got it from somewhere abroad—I don't remember where. My grandfather once brought home several of these chairs, and this is the only one left. He was a sailor."

"Was your father also a sailor?"

"Yes."

"Did you go along on his voyages? Excuse my asking."

"Yes, I sailed with him for many years."

"How interesting! You must have visited many countries, plowing the salty brine, as the saying goes. And then you came back here to settle down? Well, there's no place like home, is there? You really have no idea where your grandfather got that chair? I attach great importance to knowing the provenance of an object—everything I can find out about it."

"No, I don't know where he got it. Holland maybe. I don't know."

He noticed with pleasure that she was responding to him and becoming increasingly more lively. She had moved toward him and stood quite close as he continued to inspect every detail of the chair, as if he couldn't take his eyes off it. He kept remarking on the details and the workmanship; he talked incessantly. He was delighted to discover a small disk on the back, with another one superimposed on it—a crude piece of carving, sloppily done. The chair was falling apart and he handled it with great care.

"Well," she said, "if you really want it, if it will give you pleasure, you may have it. I'll bring it to the hotel if you wish. It's of no use to me." And suddenly she had to laugh at his eagerness to possess this worm-eaten chair. "It's only got one good leg," she said.

He looked at her. Although her hair was white, her smile was the bright smile of a young woman, and her teeth were exquisite. When she smiled, her eyes glistened. What a stunning, dark-eyed spinster! Nagel's expression did not change.

"I'm glad that you're willing to part with the chair," he said casually. "Now let's discuss the price—no, please let me finish. I won't let you set the price; I always do that myself. I evaluate the object, offer a price, and that's it! Otherwise you might ask far too much and try to force me to accept your terms—and why shouldn't you? You might insist that your price is not excessive. That's true enough, but still, I have to deal with all kinds of people, and I prefer to set the prices myself, to feel in control. It's a question of principle. If it were up to you, what would prevent you from asking three hundred crowns for that chair? You would be justified since you know we are discussing a rare and valuable piece. But I couldn't pay a fantastic price like that—I'm telling you this in all honesty, since I wouldn't want you to have any false illusions. I'm not going to ruin myself financially; I would be out of my mind if I paid you three hundred crowns for that chair! I'll give you two hundred for it and not a shilling more. I'm willing to pay what I consider an object to be worth, but I won't go higher than that."

She stared at him wide-eyed with astonishment but didn't say a word. Then in a flash it came to her that he must be joking, and she smiled her hesitant, embarrassed smile.

With studied deliberation Nagel took the red banknotes

out of his wallet and waved them about, never once taking his eyes off the chair.

"It's possible that someone else might give you a bit more—I'll admit that quite honestly. But I've estimated the value of this piece at two hundred, and I don't feel that I can go beyond that. It's your decision, but do think it over. Two hundred crowns isn't a bad price, you know."

"No," she answered with her timid smile, "but I don't want your money."

"You don't want my money? What do you mean? What's wrong with my money? Do you think it's counterfeit? Surely you couldn't think that I've come by it dishonestly?"

She was no longer smiling. He seemed to be serious and she was turning it over in her mind. Was this eccentric man trying to get something out of her? He had shifty eyes—he might be capable of anything. He seemed to have an ulterior motive; it was almost as if he were setting a trap for her. Why should he come to her, of all people, offering money? She apparently came to a decision and said: "If you insist on giving me a crown or two for the chair, I'll appreciate it. But I don't want anything more."

He seemed a bit agitated and moved closer to her. Then he started to laugh: "This is the first time in all my years of collecting that anything like this has happened to me! Well, I can take a joke!"

"But it isn't a joke! I've never heard anything so ridiculous! I don't want anything. If you want the chair, take it!"

Nagel laughed heartily. "No one appreciates a good joke better than I. I laugh myself sick over a good joke. But now let's get down to business. Don't you think we ought to settle this while we're in a good mood? In a minute you might put the chair back in its corner and insist on five hundred!"

"But take it! I . . . I don't understand."

They stood there staring intently at each other.

"If you have any idea that I'm thinking of anything but getting the chair at a reasonable price, you're mistaken," he said.

"But, for heaven's sake, take it—it's yours!" she cried.

"I'm most grateful for your kindness. But whether you believe it or not, we collectors have a code of honor, although it might not always be too evident, and it would make itself felt, rear on its hind legs, so to speak, if I ever tried to procure a valuable object by other than honest means. My whole collection would diminish in my—in the collector's estimation—if I were to acquire an object in such a way. It would reflect on the whole collection. But how incongruous—here I am standing arguing your case instead of looking out for my own interests! But it seems that I'm being cornered."

She wouldn't yield, and he got nowhere with her. She was adamant; he would either take the chair for a few crowns or forget about it. Unable to break her down, he finally said, to save face: "All right. We'll let it go for the moment. But will you promise not to sell that chair to anyone else without letting me know? Because I won't let it go, even if the price goes up a bit. At any rate, I'm willing to match anyone else's price, and remember, I was first!"

On leaving, Nagel furiously stalked up the street. What a stubborn creature she was—poor and suspicious! And that bed! Not even a straw mattress, not even a sheet, only those two petticoats—she probably had to wear them both in the daytime to protect herself against the cold! Yet she was so terrified of getting involved that she even refused a good offer! But what the devil did he care? He didn't give a damn. But she really was the limit! Suppose he sent a man over to bid on the chair in order to drive the price up, would that also arouse her suspicions? What a stupid, stubborn creature! But why had he gone there and exposed himself to such a rebuff?

He was so engrossed in his own anger and irritation that, before he knew it, he found himself outside the hotel. He stopped abruptly, still furious, and went back down the street to J. Hansen's tailor shop. He asked to speak to the proprietor in private, ordered a coat, selecting the style and the material, and insisted that the order be kept confidential. As soon as it was ready, it was to be sent to The Midget, Grøgaard, the crippled coal delivery man who . . .

Was the coat for The Midget?

Yes, what of it? Why did he want to know? What business was it of his?

Well, there were the measurements . . .

Oh! Yes, it was for The Midget. He would certainly come and be measured—why not? But there was no reason to discuss anything that wasn't absolutely to the point—was that understood? When would the coat be ready? In a couple of days? Fine!

Nagel counted out the money, said goodby, and left. His irritation had gone, and he contentedly rubbed his hands together, humming to himself. Yes, he'd pull it off after all! Just wait and see! When he reached the hotel, he ran up to his room and rang the bell. His hands trembled with impatience, and the second the door opened, he cried: "Telegram blanks, Sara!"

He had opened his violin case as she entered, and to her

amazement she saw that this case which she had always handled so carefully contained only some soiled linen and some papers and writing materials, but no violin. She stood transfixed, staring at it.

"Telegram blanks," he shouted, louder still. "I asked for telegram blanks!"

When he finally got the forms, he drafted a message instructing someone in Christiania to send two hundred crowns to Miss Martha Gude, residing in this town. To be sent anonymously, without a word. Johan Nagel.

But it wouldn't work. After thinking it over, he decided against it. Wouldn't it be better to explain and to send along the money, to be sure that it was forwarded? He tore up the telegram, burned it, and quickly dashed off a letter. Yes, that would be better; a letter conveyed more information; this way his plan had a far better chance of working. He would show her—make her understand!

But after he had put the money in the envelope and sealed it, he began thinking it over once again. She might still be suspicious—two hundred crowns; it was what he had waved in front of her. No, that was no good. He pulled a ten-crown note out of his pocket and made the amount two hundred ten. Then he resealed the envelope and mailed it.

For the next hour he was very pleased with his scheme. The money would fall on her like manna from heaven, be wafted down to her by unseen hands—a miracle. What would be her reaction when all this money rained down on her! But the more he thought about it, the more despondent he became. The idea was crazy and much too risky; he had acted too hastily. When the money came, she would become confused and panicky and would turn it over to others. She would spread it out over the counter at the post office so that the whole town would be in on it. Or perhaps she would become obstinate and say: "Keep your money!" Whereupon the clerk would put his finger to his nose and say: "Wait a second. I've got an idea." And he would thumb through the ledger and find that the same sum had been sent from here a few days ago—exactly the same amount, maybe even the same bills—two hundred and ten crowns to a Christiania address. The sender would turn out to be Johan Nagel, a stranger staying at the Central. Those post-office clerks were snoopy characters . . .

Nagel rang again and got the porter to retrieve the letter.

He had been in a state of nervous tension all day and was thoroughly sick of the whole business. He didn't give a damn what happened. What business was it of his that the Good Lord had brought about a fatal collision on the Erie Railway in far-away America? None whatsoever. And he had just as little to do with Martha Gude, the respectable town spinster.

For the next two days he didn't leave the hotel.

10

O<small>N</small> Saturday evening The Midget visited Nagel in his hotel room. He was wearing his new coat and beaming.

"I met Deputy Reinert," he said. "He asked me point-blank who had given me the coat. He's a sly one—he just wanted to test me."

"And what did you say?"

"I laughed and said I wouldn't tell—not anyone—and he'd have to excuse me, goodby! Oh, I knew how to handle him! Well, I thought about it and came to the conclusion that it must be about thirteen years since I've had a new coat. I want to thank you for the money you gave me last time. It was far too much for someone like me. What am I going to do with all that money? You overwhelm me with kindness; I'm all mixed up inside. But I'm being very childish—I knew I would get the coat some day—I told you so, didn't I? It sometimes takes time, but I'm never disappointed in the end. Lieutenant Hansen once promised me two wool shirts that he didn't wear any more. That was two years ago, but I'm just as sure of getting them as if I were already wearing them. It's always like that; people eventually remember, and give me what I need in due time. Don't you think I look like a new man in decent clothes?"

"It's been a long time since your last visit."

"Well, I was waiting for the coat. I didn't want to come in the old one. Maybe I'm being foolish, but I feel uncomfortable turning up in a shabby coat. I don't know why, but it takes away my self-respect. Forgive me for talking about my self-respect as if it were of any importance. It isn't in the slightest, but I do feel it now and then."

"May I offer you some wine? No? How about a cigar?"

Nagel rang for wine and cigars. He immediately poured himself a drink while The Midget smoked and talked incessantly. It seemed as if he would never stop.

"It just occurred to me," said Nagel, suddenly interrupting him. "Maybe you need a couple of shirts? I hope you don't mind my asking."

The Midget hastily objected: "That isn't why I mentioned the two shirts. As sure as I'm sitting here, I didn't have that in mind."

"Of course not. But why are you shouting? If you have no objection, I would like to see what you're wearing under that coat."

"Gladly. You can see this side, and the other isn't any worse . . ."

"Wait a minute! The other side does happen to look worse!"

"What's wrong with it?" cried The Midget. "I assure you that I don't need any shirts at the moment. As a matter of fact, this one is far too good for me. Do you know who gave it to me? Dr. Stenersen—he gave it to me himself. I don't think his wife knew about it, although she is extremely generous. I got it for Christmas."

"For Christmas?"

"Does that seem like a long time ago to you? I wouldn't mistreat a fine shirt like this. I'm very careful with it and that's why I take it off at night and sleep naked, so as not to give it needless wear and tear. That way it lasts much longer and I can feel respectable, and not ashamed because I don't have a decent shirt. But I'm very pleased to have it to wear at the bazaar; Miss Dagny still insists that I have to appear in the tableaux. I met her at the church yesterday. She also mentioned you . . ."

"And I'll get you a pair of trousers. It will be worth the money to see you perform in front of an audience. If Mr. Reinert can give you a coat, I can offer you a pair of trousers—but only on the same condition—that you keep quiet about it."

"Yes, of course."

"I think you ought to have some wine. Well, it's up to you. I need something, though. I'm feeling nervous and a bit depressed tonight. I'd like to ask you something that may be somewhat indiscreet. Do you know that you have a nickname? Did you know that people around town call you The Midget?"

"Yes, I'm aware of it. In the beginning, it hurt very much, and I prayed to God about it. I spent a whole Sunday in the woods, kneeling in three places I found where it was dry—it was spring and the snow was melting. But that was many years ago, and now no one calls me anything but The Midget, and I suppose I've come to accept it. What made you ask? Even knowing, what could I possibly do about it?"

"Do you know how you happened to get such a silly name?"

"Yes. It was a long time ago, before I became a cripple, but I remember it distinctly. It was one night at a stag party. Maybe you've noticed the yellow house down by the Customs House—on the right as you go down? In those days it was white and was the mayor's residence. His name was Sørensen, he was a bachelor and a gay blade. It was a spring night and I was coming from the dock, where I had been strolling around looking at the ships. When I got to the yellow house, I could hear that a party was going on; there was a lot of noise and laughter. As I passed by, they caught sight of me and knocked at the window. I went in, and there were Dr. Kolbye, Captain William Prante, Folkedahl, the customs official, and many others. All of them have left town or died since. Anyway, there were seven or eight of them and they were all drunk. They had smashed all the chairs just for laughs. The mayor seemed to enjoy that thoroughly, and we had to drink out of the bottles because they had broken all the glasses. And my getting as drunk as the rest seemed to add to the bedlam: the gentlemen took off their clothes and ran around the room stark-naked, although the curtains hadn't been drawn, and when I wouldn't go along with them, they grabbed me and stripped me. I tried to fight them off as best I could, but there was nothing to be done, so I begged their pardon—I took them by the hand and begged their pardon."

"For what?"

"I thought I might have said something that made them

jump on me. I asked their forgiveness so that they would hurt me as little as possible. But it didn't help—they still stripped me completely. The doctor found a letter in my pocket and began reading it out loud. That sobered me a little, because it was a letter from my mother, who used to write to me when I was at sea. Well, I ended up calling the doctor a sot, because everyone knew how much he drank. 'You're a sot!' I cried, at which the doctor went wild and tried to grab me by the throat, but the others stopped him. 'Let's get some liquor into him instead,' the mayor said—as if I hadn't had enough already. And then they began pouring it into me from all kinds of bottles. After that, two gentlemen—I don't remember which ones they were—came in with a tub of water. They put the tub down in the center of the room and announced that they were going to baptize me. Well, they all thought this was a great idea, and let out terrific yells to show their approval. Then they proceeded to put all kinds of filth into the water; they spat into it, emptied liquor into it, and even went into the bedroom for the worst they could find and dumped it into the water. And, on top of it all, they poured two shovelfuls of cinders from the stove to make it still filthier. Then they were ready to begin the ceremony. 'Why can't you baptize one of the others?' I asked, grabbing the mayor by the knees. 'We've already been baptized,' he said, 'and in the same way!' And I believed him because he always wanted the people he caroused with to be baptized.

"'Come here,' the mayor demanded, but I wouldn't yield, I just stood there hanging on to the doorknob for dear life.

"'Come right over here this minute!' he cried, but I still refused. But he didn't say 'minute'; it sounded more like 'midget,' because he came from Gudbrandsdal and that's the way they talk. But still I wouldn't move. Then Captain Prante roared: 'The Midget, The Midget, that's it. We have to baptize him The Midget!' And everyone agreed to that, because I'm so small. Two of them grabbed me and dragged me off to the mayor, and I was such a lightweight the mayor lifted me all by himself and dunked me in the tub. He put my head under, rubbed my nose against the bottom of the tub, which was full of ashes and broken glass, whereupon he pulled me up and said prayers over me. Then the godfathers had to get into the act. Each of them lifted me up in the air and then dropped me, and when they got bored with that, they lined up on either side and tossed me from one to the other, like a ball. They said they were doing this to dry me off, and kept that game up until they tired of it. Then the mayor ordered them to stop, so they dropped me and called me The Midget, all of them; they all shook hands with me and called me The Midget to make the baptism official. Then they threw me into the tub again—this time it was Dr. Kolbye, and he was so violent that he hurt me badly on the side—apparently he couldn't forget that I had called him a sot. Since that night my nickname has stuck. The next day the whole town knew that I had been at the mayor's house and that I had been baptized."

"So you were hurt on one side. But you didn't receive any head injury?"

Pause.

"This is the second time you've asked me if I've had a head injury—I don't understand what you're getting at. My head wasn't hurt at that time—there was no concussion of any kind, if that is what you are implying. But I was banged so hard against the tub that I had a fractured rib. But it's all right now. Dr. Kolbye treated me, free of charge, and I've had no trouble with it since."

While The Midget talked, Nagel had been drinking steadily. He rang for more wine and poured himself another glass. Then suddenly he said: "Would you consider me a good judge of people? Don't gape at me like that—it's only a friendly question. What I want to know is: do you think I can see through the person I'm talking to?"

The Midget looked at him in bewilderment, not knowing what to say. Nagel went on: "Please forgive me; the last time I had the pleasure of your visit, I seemed to have upset you by asking some indiscreet questions. You may remember that at that time I offered you some money to assume the paternity of a child—legally. Since I didn't know you, I didn't know how to express myself. But I seem to be offending you again, despite the fact that I now know you and have great respect for you. But I guess it's because I'm nervous today and quite drunk. That's all I can say in my defense. Of course you can see that for yourself. You can—why deny it? But what was I saying? Oh, yes: I wanted to know to what extent you consider me capable of judging human beings? I think I can detect undertones in the voice of the person I'm speaking with —I have a very sensitive ear. When I'm talking to someone, I don't have to look at him to follow his thinking. I can sense immediately if he is lying or trying to put something over on me. The voice is a dangerous instrument. I don't mean the timbre of the voice, which may be high or low, melodious or grating. I'm not talking about the *sound* but about the inner world from which it springs—the underlying mysteries. Oh, to hell with what lies behind the voice! What the devil do I care?"

Nagel drank some more wine and went on talking: "Why are you being so quiet? Don't let my sounding off about how good a judge of character I am frighten you. Then I would really have made a mess of things! But again I've forgotten what I was about to say. Well, I'll go on talking until it comes back to me. Good God, how I rattle on! Tell me, what do you think of Miss Kielland? I'd very much like to know. In my opinion, Miss Kielland is such a flirt that she would be extremely flattered if more men—the more the better—myself included, would lay down their lives for her sake. Anyway, that's my impression. She is a lovely creature, and it must be an exquisite pain to be trampled on by her—perhaps I'll even ask her to do it to me one day—by God, that's an experience I'd like to have! Not now, though; I'm biding my time. But I'm scaring you out of your wits with my ranting tonight! Have I said something to offend you—personally, I mean?"

"If you only knew how kindly Miss Kielland speaks of you! I met her yesterday, and we talked for quite a while . . ."

"Tell me, excuse me for interrupting you, but perhaps you are also sensitive enough to sense the undertones, the vibrations, in Miss Kielland's voice? Now I'm talking nonsense, and I'm sure you're aware of it, aren't you? But I would be glad if I felt I had an ally in you—that you were also able to size up people. Then we could shake hands, have a sort of pact, and never betray each other. Do you understand what I mean? In other words, I would never use what I know about you, although I read you like a book. Now you have that harried and confused look again! Don't take me seriously; I've had far too much to drink. But now I suddenly remember what I was going to say about Miss Kielland, and it couldn't matter less. But then, why should I volunteer my opinion when you haven't even asked me? I'm sorry if I've said something to displease you.

"When you came here an hour ago, you were in such high spirits. All this talk comes from drinking too much wine. But I must try to stick to what I was trying to say. You were talking about the stag party at the mayor's—you remember—when you were baptized. That suddenly gave me the idea that *I* would like to give a stag party. Just a few friends—and you must come too—I'm counting on you. Don't worry—you won't be baptized again. I'll see to it that you're treated with courtesy and respect. This time there won't be any smashing of tables and chairs—I promise you! But I would like to get a few friends together here some evening—soon—over the weekend. How do you feel about that?"

Nagel downed two glasses, one after another. The Midget still said nothing, his childlike exuberance was gone, and he seemed to listen to Nagel's talk only out of politeness. He stubbornly refused to drink anything.

"You're being terribly quiet all of a sudden," said Nagel. "You look as if you were shocked by something—a word, an allusion—as if you had suddenly been struck down by something. Did I see you give a little start just now? Well, maybe I was mistaken. Have you ever thought about how a forger would feel if one day an officer of the law put his hand on his shoulder without a word, looking him straight in the eyes? But what am I going to do with you? You're withdrawing more and more and getting more morose by the minute. I'm on edge today and making you ill at ease, but I have to talk—I always do when I'm drunk. You mustn't leave—then I would have to talk to that maid,

Sara, and that wouldn't be proper—besides, it would bore me. Would you let me tell you of an experience I had? It's of no importance whatsoever, but maybe it will amuse you, and at the same time I can prove to you that I am a judge of character. Ha ha! But I must tell you that if there is someone who can't read people, it is *I!* Maybe this little confession of mine will bolster your ego. Well, to make a long story short—I was in London about three years ago—I met a young and fascinating woman, the daughter of a man with whom I had some business. I got to know the young lady well; we were together every day for three weeks and became very good friends. One afternoon she wanted to show me London, and off we went, visiting museums and art collections, looking at architecture, strolling around the parks, and before we knew it, hours had gone by; it was evening. I felt the call of nature—to put it bluntly, I found myself in a situation one may very well find oneself in after spending an afternoon walking. What was I to do? I couldn't disappear, and I couldn't excuse myself. Well, I just had to let go, and got soaking wet all the way down to my shoes. But what the hell could I do? Fortunately, I was wearing a long coat which hid my embarrassing state. We passed a café on a brightly lit street, and what do you think the lady did? She stopped and asked if we could have something to eat! Ordinarily this would have been a reasonable request—we had walked for hours and were dead tired—but I had to say no. I knew she thought I was being rude by the way she looked at me and said: 'Why not?' The excuse I gave her was that I didn't have any money on me—not a penny! It was a good one, and as it happened, the lady didn't have any money either. We stood there looking at each other, laughing at our predicament. Then she looked around and was struck by an idea: 'I have a friend in that house—on the second floor—she'll give us some money.' And with that she darted off. She was gone for several minutes and I was in a panic. What in God's name was I to do when she came back with the money? I just couldn't go into that brightly lit café with all those people! I would be thrown out and that would be worse still. I would just have to grit my teeth and ask her to go in alone, saying that I would wait outside. After a few minutes she came back. She seemed in high spirits, reported that her friend wasn't in but that it didn't matter—she could hold out a little longer—she'd be home in fifteen minutes. She also apologized for having made me wait. I was the one who was immensely relieved, although I was sopping wet and uncomfortable. But now comes the best part—perhaps you've already guessed? I'm sure you know, but I'd still like to tell you. Not until this year—1891—did it occur to me how stupid I was. I thought the whole thing through, and suddenly all sorts of things which seemed insignificant at the time fitted together. The lady didn't walk up any stairs at all! What she did was open the back door and slip through it. I also have the feeling that she came out by the same door. What does that prove? Nothing, of course. But isn't it odd that she didn't go up the stairs but used the back entrance? Ha ha. I see that you get the picture, but I didn't put it together until 1891—three years later. I hope you don't suspect me of having planned the whole thing in advance in order to create this situation. I just couldn't tear myself away from the hyenas in the zoo, and I went back three times, all the while keeping my eye on the lady so that she couldn't possibly get out of my sight for a single moment. You certainly couldn't think me guilty of something like *that*? But of course it is possible that a man, out of sheer perversity, would suffer and even wet himself all the way down, rather than forgo the exquisite pleasure of watching a young, beautiful girl writhing in agony. But, as I said, it just occurred to me this year, three years after it happened. Well—ha ha—what do you think?"

Pause.

Nagel drank some more wine and went on talking: "You may ask what this story has to do with you and me and the stag party. Nothing whatever, my friend. But I felt like telling it to you anyway to prove how dense I am when it comes to human behavior. Oh, that human psyche! What do you think I, Johan Nilsen Nagel, caught myself doing the other morning? I found myself pacing up and down in front of Consul Andresen's house on the hill, trying to estimate the height of the ceiling in his living room! Isn't that bizarre? But there you have the psyche rearing up its head again! It records the most insignificant detail; there isn't anything that isn't absorbed. How would you feel, for instance, if on your way home one night from work or from a meeting you suddenly came upon a man standing on a corner staring at you in silence and turning to follow you with his gaze as you walk by? And suppose that the man, to confound things further, is dressed in black, and all you can see are his face and eyes? Ah, the vagaries of human behavior! One evening you go to a party; there are twelve of you, let's say, plus a thirteenth—it might be the girl in the telegraph office, an impoverished law student, a clerk, or even the captain of a steamer—in other words, someone of no importance. This person sits in a corner and doesn't participate in the conversation but still makes his presence felt and, despite his silence, plays a distinct role in the group. It's because he is dressed in a certain way, because he is so uncommunicative, because he looks at the others with such an empty and indifferent expression, and because he is a nobody, that he contributes to the gathering just by his presence. It's precisely because he contributes nothing that he constitutes a negative force and creates the gloomy atmosphere that makes the other guests talk in muted voices. Don't you agree? In this way, the person in question can become, paradoxically, the center of attraction. As I told you, I'm no judge of character, but it's amusing to observe the importance of apparently insignificant things.

"I was once present when an engineer, a complete stranger in the crowd, who didn't even open his mouth. . . . But that's another story and has nothing to do with what we're talking about, except that it made a vivid impression on me. But to come back to the trend of thought that brought this on: maybe it's your stony silence this evening that has given a different slant to my words—apart from the fact that I'm drunk. Or could it be your expression—that half-shy, half-innocent look in your eyes that makes me talk this way? It's perfectly natural. You listen to me—to what a drunken man says—and now and then something hits home—I repeat—hits home. And I feel tempted to go still further and fling another dozen words in your face. I mention this again to emphasize the value of insignificant things. Don't overlook trifles, my friend—they are of the utmost importance.

"Come in!"

It was Sara, who announced that supper was ready. The Midget got up immediately. By now Nagel was really drunk and could not even enunciate properly. He kept contradicting himself and was increasingly incoherent.

The brooding expression in his eyes and the protruding veins in his forehead seemed to reflect the confused thoughts that were pounding through his head.

"Well, I'm not surprised that you take advantage of this interruption to take your leave," he said, "after all the rambling you've had to listen to this evening. But there are several other things I would have liked to ask your opinion about. For one, you never answered my question about how you really feel about Miss Kielland. To me, she is an exotic, unattainable creature full of loveliness and white as snow—imagine an utterly pure, deep, silky snow. That is how I see her. If I gave you a different impression a while ago, I didn't mean to. Now I'd like to drink my last glass with you. Cheers! But something just came to mind —if you have the patience to listen to me for another minute or so, I would be most grateful. Come a little closer—the walls in this hotel have ears—the truth is that I'm hopelessly in love with Miss Kielland. So there—I've said it! These simple words can't express my feelings, but God in heaven knows how madly I love her. Well, I'm in love and I'm suffering the tortures of the damned, but that's beside the point. I do hope that you will respect my confidence—will you promise me that? Thank you, my dear friend. But you are probably asking yourself how I can be in love with her when just now I called her a flirt. In the first place, there is nothing to prevent one's falling in love with a flirt. That's irrelevant. But there is something else. But did you admit to being a good judge of people or not? Because if you are a judge of character, you will also understand what I'm going to say: I couldn't possibly believe that Miss Kielland was a flirt—not seriously—quite the opposite. She has such an unaffected manner! Have you noticed how spontaneously she laughs, and in such a completely uninhibited way, though her teeth are not the whitest? But that doesn't prevent me from spreading the rumor that Miss Kielland is a flirt. I'm not doing it to hurt her or to take revenge but to protect my ego; she's a goddess, and unattainable; she won't accept my attentions or declarations because she is already engaged. She is lost to me; it's hopeless. Here again, with your permission, we have a new aberration of human behavior. I might walk up to her in the street, within earshot of several people, with the obvious intention of hurting and humiliating her, and say in dead earnest: 'Good morning, Miss Kielland! I congratulate you on your clean undergarment!' It seems an outrageous thing to say, but I would be capable of doing it. What would be my next move? Would I head for home and sob into my handkerchief, or take a couple of drops from the vial I carry in my vest pocket—who knows? Or I might walk into church one Sunday while her father, Pastor Kielland, is giving a sermon, walk right up the center aisle, stop in front of Miss Kielland, and say: 'Would you like me to pinch your puff?' By puff I wouldn't mean anything in particular—it would just be a word to make her blush. 'Please let me touch the puff of your sleeve,' I would implore her. Then I might throw myself at her feet and beg her to give me the supreme joy of having her spit on me. Now you're really terrified. I admit that I'm being obscene, especially since I'm talking about a parson's daughter to a parson's son. Forgive me, dear friend—I'm not being malicious—at least, that's not my intention; but I'm drunk as a lord. Listen! I once knew a young man who stole a gaslight, sold it for scrap metal, and used the money to go on a wild spree. It's true! He is a relative of the late Pastor Haerem, and I knew him fairly well. But you're right again. What does that have to do with Miss Kielland and me? You're still not saying anything, but I can see that you're bursting to say what you're thinking, and you're perfectly right. But Miss Kielland is beyond my reach, and it's not her loss but mine. And you standing there, cold sober, with your ability to see through people, will understand if one day I let it be known around town that Miss Kielland sat on my knee, that I met her three nights in a row at a certain spot in the woods, and that she accepted gifts from me. You would be able to understand that, wouldn't you? You are such a shrewd judge of people—yes, you are, don't deny it! Have you ever walked along the street, absorbed in your own thoughts, and then suddenly become aware that people are staring at you? It's terribly disconcerting. You begin nervously brushing yourself front and back, you surreptitiously look down to see if any buttons are undone; you become so self-conscious that you even take off your hat to check whether the price tag is still there, though the hat is old. But you can't find anything wrong, you have to grit your teeth and tolerate the stares of every errand boy and every lieutenant. And, my friend, if this puts you through hell, how would you feel if you were summoned to appear in court? Now I've shocked you again, haven't I? I saw you jump! Well, to be summoned by a cunning police bastard, be cross-examined, and after endless questioning be brought right back to the starting point—what a delightful treat for a man who is detached, uninvolved, just sitting there listening, taking it all in. Do you follow me? Maybe if I squeeze the bottle I can get another glass out of it . . ."

He poured the last drop down his throat and continued: "I'm sorry about the way I keep flitting from one thing to another. But my mind keeps wandering, partly because

I'm so drunk, but also because I know there's something basically wrong with me. I'm just a simple agronomist—you know that—a student from a cow-dung academy. I'm a philosopher who has never learned to think. Well, let's not go into details, they're of no interest to you, and because they're part of my past, I find them repugnant. Do you know, it often gets to the point where I sit down here trying to come to terms with myself and then suddenly call myself Rochefort in a loud voice? I tap myself on the head and call myself Rochefort! Do you know once I actually ordered a signet ring with a hedgehog engraved on it? . . . That reminds me of a man I once knew—he was a respectable man, a philology student at a German university; nothing at all unusual about him. But he began to go to pieces; in two years he became an alcoholic, and a novelist to boot! When he met people who tried to ask him about himself, he merely answered that he was a fact. 'I'm a fact!' he would exclaim, his mouth drawn tight in arrogance. Well, this doesn't concern you. You mentioned a philosopher who had never learned to think—or was it I who was talking about him? I'm sorry—by now I'm really drunk, but so what? Don't let that bother you. But I'd like to explain about the philosopher who couldn't think. If I understood you correctly, you wanted to attack the man. Your reaction was so violent that I really got that impression; you spoke of him so scornfully. But that man deserves to be judged more objectively. In the first place, he was crazy—I still insist he was crazy. He always wore a long, red tie and smiled his stupid smile. In fact, he was such a fool that he always had his nose buried in a book when anyone approached him, though he never read. And another thing: he never wore any socks, so he could afford a rose for his buttonhole. That's the way he was.

But the best part of all was that he had a collection of photographs of simple though decent-looking working-class girls on which he inscribed fancy-sounding names, to give the impression that he was moving in important circles. On one of the photos he had written 'Miss Stang,' to suggest that she was related to the prime minister, though the girl's family name was probably only a Lie, or a Haug at the most. He he! What do you make of such phoniness! He imagined that people were talking about him behind his back—maligning him, he said. He he, do you think that anyone would ever even bother? Then one day he walked into a jewelry shop smoking two cigars—two cigars! He had one in his hand and one in his mouth; both were lit. Perhaps he wasn't aware that he had two cigars going at one time, but since he was a thinker who hadn't learned to think, he didn't ask why . . ."

"I really must leave," said The Midget finally in a subdued voice.

Nagel immediately got up.

"Must you go?" he said. "Do you really have to leave me now? Well, I must admit it would take me rather long to put the man in his proper perspective. Well, it will have to wait until another time. So you really insist on leaving now? Thank you very much for coming by to see me this evening! I seem to be drunker than usual—I'm just wondering how I must look. Take your thumb, put it under a magnifying glass, and what do you see? I can read your expression; you're an unusually clever man, Mr. Grøgaard, and to look into your eyes does something to me—they are so innocent. Do have another cigar before you leave! When will you come to see me again? Yes, of course, you must come to my stag party! I promise you that this time not a hair on your head will be touched. I promise you it will only be a small social get-together, a cigar, a drink, and nine times nine cheers for our Fatherland—to please Dr. Stenersen. Don't you agree? I think it will be an amusing party. It should be amusing. And I'll see to it that you get those trousers we were talking about, I'll be damned if you don't. But on the usual conditions, of course. Thank you for your patience this evening. Let's shake hands. Do light another cigar! One more thing: isn't there anything you would like to ask of me? If so, don't hesitate! All right, as you wish. Good night, good night."

11

THEN came the twenty-ninth of June. It was a Monday, and a number of unusual things happened that day: for instance, a strange, veiled woman turned up in town, went to the hotel, where she stayed for a couple of hours, and then disappeared.

Early that morning Johan Nagel had been contentedly humming and whistling in his room. As he dressed, he whistled gay little snatches, and seemed to be in a very happy frame of mind. The previous day he had been silent and uncommunicative after having drunk himself sodden Saturday night in the presence of The Midget. He had paced up and down the room, drinking great quantities of water. When he left the hotel Monday morning, he was still humming and looked very pleased with himself. His jovial mood even prompted him to speak to a woman who was standing at the bottom of the stairs, and he gave her a few coins.

"Would you know where I could borrow a violin?" he asked. "Do you know if anyone in town plays the violin?"

"No, I don't," said the woman, looking bewildered. Although she was of no help to him, he gave her the coins anyway and quickly walked away. He had just caught sight of Dagny Kielland coming out of a shop carrying her red parasol, and he hurried toward her. She was alone. Bowing deeply, he spoke to her. She flushed as usual, and tried to hide her face behind her parasol.

At first they talked about their walk through the woods. She had caught cold, though it was a warm night. She still hadn't quite got over it. She spoke matter-of-factly, as though she were talking to an old acquaintance.

"But you don't regret it, do you?" he asked, coming straight to the point.

"No," she said, looking surprised. "I don't regret it. What would make you say a thing like that? On the contrary, it was a very interesting evening, though I was terrified by that story you told me about the lantern man. I even dreamed about him—it was ghastly!"

For a while they talked about the lantern man. Nagel was in an expansive mood. He admitted that he too would suddenly become scared stiff for no reason at all, and feel like a fool. For instance, when walking up a flight of stairs, he sometimes caught himself looking around to see if someone was following him. Why? Perhaps because he sensed a mysterious essence which so-called science was too obtuse and too insensitive to perceive, an essence emanating from an invisible power—the supernatural making itself manifest.

"Do you know," he said, "at this moment I feel as if I

would like to get off this street and take another route: the houses, the curbstones on the left, and those three pear trees in the magistrate's garden depress me. When I'm alone I never come this way but go along another road, even if it takes me out of my way."

Dagny laughed. "I have a feeling Dr. Stenersen would attribute that to nerves and superstition."

"That's exactly what he would say! What conceit, what stupidity! Let's suppose that one evening you arrive in a strange town—this one, for instance—why not? The next day you walk around the streets to see what the place is like. Some houses, some streets make a bad impression on you, and other streets, other houses you find charming and aesthetically pleasing. Is that a sign of nerves? But now I'm assuming that you have nerves of steel, that you don't know what it is to be nervous. Well, you go on wandering through the streets. You see hundreds of people, and they make absolutely no impression on you. But on your way to the docks you suddenly stop in front of a shabby little one-story house with no curtains but with white flowers in the window. A man approaches you, and somehow you are struck by him. You look at him and he looks at you. There is nothing strange about him except that he is shabbily dressed and walks with a slight stoop. It's the first time you've ever laid eyes on him, but suddenly you have a flash of intuition and you know his name is Johannes. The name comes through clearly. What makes you so sure his name is Johannes? You have no rational explanation, but you can read it in his eyes, know it by the way he moves his arms, by the sound of his footsteps. It can't possibly be an association; you've never seen anyone who remotely resembles him and whose name is Johannes. So that's not the case. But there you are, confronted by this enigma and this almost mystical intuition for which there is no reasonable explanation."

"Have you met a man like that here in town?"

"No, no," he replied quickly. "The man, the town, and the one-story house are purely fictitious. But it's strange, isn't it? Then another odd thing happens: you arrive in a strange town, walk into a strange house—a hotel, let's say. You've never been there before in your life. But suddenly you have the distinct feeling that once, many years ago maybe, there was a pharmacy in the place. Now, what could possibly have given you that sensation? There are no indications whatsoever that this was so. You've talked to no one, there is no medicinal smell, no marks of shelves on the walls, no traces on the floor where a counter might have been. Yet you are dead-sure that many years ago there was a pharmacy in that place! There is no doubt whatsoever. You suddenly have extra-sensory perception. How else can it be explained? Has it ever happened to you?"

"I've never thought about it. But now that you mention it, I believe it has. I'm often afraid of the dark, for no reason at all. But maybe that's something else again."

"Is there any way of knowing? There are so many strange things between heaven and earth, beautiful, inexplicable things, presentiments that can't be explained, terrors that make your blood freeze. Imagine hearing someone brushing against the walls on a dark night. You're wide awake, sitting at a table smoking a pipe, but aware that your senses are somewhat blurred. Your head is full of plans that you are anxious to sort out. Then you distinctly hear someone brushing against the outside wall —or in the room, over by the stove where you can see a shadow on the wall. You remove the lampshade to get more light, and approach the stove. You stand there facing the shadow and you are face to face with an unknown person—a man of medium height wearing a black-and-white woolen scarf around his neck, with incredibly blue lips. He looks like the jack of clubs in a Norwegian deck of cards. You're more curious than afraid and you walk right up to the fellow and give him a withering look. But he doesn't move, though you're so close to him you can see his eyes blink and know he's as alive as you are. Then you try to be friendly, and though you've never laid eyes on him before, you say: 'Your name isn't by any chance Homan, Bernt Homan?' When he doesn't answer, you decide to call him Homan, and say: 'And why the hell shouldn't you be Bernt Homan?' And you leer at him. But he still doesn't move and you don't know what to do next. Then you take a step back, poke at him with the stem of your pipe, and say: 'Bah!' Still his expression doesn't change. That's going too far! Your anger mounts, and you give him a good whack. The man is definitely there in the room, though he doesn't react to your whack. He doesn't keel over but sticks both hands deep down in his pockets, and shrugs his shoulders, as if to say: 'Well, what is that supposed to mean?' 'What is that supposed to mean?' you repeat, and by now furious, you give him another whack in the pit of the stomach. After this, the man begins to fade away. You watch him slowly vanish, his form becoming more and more blurred, until at last there is nothing left but his stomach, which also eventually disappears. All this time he has kept his hands in his pockets, looking at you with that same defiant, scornful expression, as if to say: 'What's that supposed to mean?' "

Again Dagny laughed. "You do have the most fantastic adventures! Then what happened? How did it all end?"

"Well, when you settle down at the table again to begin working out your plans, you notice that you have bruised your knuckles, banging them against the wall . . . But the point I wanted to make was: tell this to your friends, and their immediate reaction is that you must have been asleep—he he, asleep—although God and all his angels know you were wide awake. It is pedantry and prejudice to call it sleep when in fact you were standing by a stove, smoking a pipe and talking to a man. Then the doctor arrives. He is an excellent physician, the spokesman of science, tight-lipped and superior. 'This is nothing but a case of nerves,' he says. Oh, God, what a joke! Just nerves! A doctor's brain has fixed dimensions, so many inches high and so many inches broad, something you can hold in your fist, a lump of thick, grayish matter. And then he writes the words 'iron' and 'quinine' on a piece of paper and you are instantly cured. That's the way it's done. But what a bumpkin he is, and what a cloddish brain he has to force himself with his limited frame of reference and his quinine into an area of science whose infinite mystery has humbled the most brilliant minds!"

"You're losing a button," she said.

"A button?"

With a smile she pointed to one of the buttons on his jacket that was hanging by a thread.

"Why don't you pull it off? Otherwise, you'll surely lose it."

To please her, he pulled a knife out of his pocket and cut the button off. As he took the knife out, some coins and a medal with a frayed ribbon fell out. She watched him as he quickly bent down to pick them up.

"Is that a medal?" she asked. "But what a way to treat it! Just look at that ribbon! What kind of a medal is it?"

"It's a lifesaver's medal. It just happens to be in my pocket. I didn't earn it."

She looked at him. His expression was unruffled, and he looked her straight in the eyes, as if he were being completely sincere. She still held the medal in her hand.

"Are you going to start that all over again!" she said. "If you didn't earn it, why do you carry it on you?"

"I bought it!" he exclaimed, laughing. "It belongs to me; it's my property, as is this penknife, this button—why should I throw it away?"

"But what a strange idea to want to buy a medal!" she said.

"Yes, it's something of a hoax, I don't deny that. But why not? I wore it one day, just to show off, and someone, seeing it, even drank to my health. One kind of fraud is as good as another, isn't it?"

"The name has been scratched out," she remarked.

His expression suddenly changed as he reached out for the medal.

"The name scratched out? It couldn't be. Let me see. No, it's just worn because I've carried it in my pocket. It's been banging around with my coins—that's why."

Dagny looked at him incredulously. Then suddenly, with a snap of his fingers, he exclaimed: "Oh, I completely forgot! Yes, of course the name is scratched out. I did it myself! How could I have forgotten? It wasn't inscribed with my name but the owner's—the rescuer. I scratched it out as soon as I got it. I'm sorry, I should have told you right away; I didn't mean to lie. My mind was elsewhere. How come you suddenly became nervous about that loose button? So what if I had lost it? Was all that by way of answer to my remarks about nerves and science?"

Pause.

"You're always amazingly frank with me," she said, bypassing his question. "I don't know what's behind it. Your opinions are rather unorthodox. Now you are trying to make me believe that everything is false; that there is no such thing as nobility, purity, magnanimity. Is that the way you really feel? Doesn't it make a difference whether one acquires a medal for a few crowns or earns it for an act of valor?"

He didn't answer, and she continued, weighing her words slowly and deliberately: "I just don't understand you. Sometimes when you talk I wonder if you are rational. Forgive me, but every time I meet you I feel more disturbed, more confused. No matter what you happen to be talking about, I find that you upset my equilibrium. Why? I've never in my life met anyone who contradicts my basic beliefs as you do. Tell me, how much of what you say do you actually mean? What do you really believe in your heart?"

She spoke with such warmth and such sincerity that he was disconcerted.

By way of answer, he said: "If I had a god who to me was sacred and omniscient, I would swear by that god that I meant every word I said to you and that I always mean to be honest even when I succeed only in confusing you. The last time we talked, you said that my thoughts and opinions were diametrically opposed to everyone else's. I admit that; I'm a living contradiction, and I don't understand it myself. I just can't understand why other people don't share my beliefs and convictions. These basic concepts appear perfectly obvious to me, and the issues stemming from them seem to fall perfectly into place. This is truly what my heart tells me, Miss Kielland. How I wish I could make you believe that, now and for all time."

"Now and for all time! That's really more than I can promise."

"It would mean so terribly much to me," he said. They were now in the woods and were walking so close to each other that their arms often touched; there was no wind and they spoke softly. The only sound was the occasional chirping of a bird.

Then he stopped so abruptly that she too stopped.

"You have no idea how I've longed for you these past few days!" he exclaimed. "Don't look so frightened! I've scarcely said anything and I don't expect anything; no, I have absolutely no illusions. Maybe you misunderstood me. I started out by saying the wrong thing—what I didn't intend to say . . ."

When he fell silent, she remarked: "You're so strange today!"

She began walking again, but he stopped her a second time. "Please, Miss Kielland, wait a moment. Please be patient with me today. I'm afraid to say anything for fear that you will stop me and tell me to go away. But I have been turning this over in my mind during many sleepless hours."

With growing astonishment, she looked at him and asked: "What is all this leading up to?"

"What is it leading up to? Will you let me speak out? What it is leading up to is that I love you, Miss Kielland. That can hardly surprise you; I've met you, I'm made of flesh and blood, and I've fallen in love with you. There is nothing very strange about that, is there? Maybe I shouldn't have told you that either."

"No, you shouldn't have."

"But desperation often drives us to extremes. I have even said nasty things about you, out of love for you. I've called you a flirt and tried to demean you, in order to console myself and bolster my ego, because I knew that you were unattainable. This is our fifth meeting, and I haven't given myself away before this fifth time, though I could have done so at our first meeting. Besides, it's my birthday today; I'm twenty-nine, and I've been singing and feeling gay from the moment I opened my eyes this morning. Of course it's absurd, but I thought: 'If you meet her today and tell her, and it is your birthday, it won't do any harm. If you tell her that too, she may be more willing to forgive you.' You're amused—yes, I know how ridiculous it must sound, but I can't help it. I want to kneel before you as did all the others."

"All I can say is, it's unfortunate that this should be happening today," she said. "This wasn't a very happy birthday for you."

"I'm aware of that. God, what power you have over people! I can understand why a man can go mad over you. Even now as you spoke these unencouraging words, your voice was music. It thrilled me to the very core of my being. How strange it is. Do you known that I've been pacing up and down in front of your house at night, hoping to catch a glimpse of you at a window; that I've been kneeling here in the woods, praying to God for you, I with my feeble faith? Do you see that aspen? I had to stop at this spot now because of the many nights I have knelt under that tree, lost in frenzy and filled with silent despair, utterly dejected because I couldn't get you out of my mind. In this spot I've said good night to you every evening. I've knelt and begged the wind and the stars to bring you my message, and I'm sure you must have sensed it in your sleep."

"Why are you telling me all this? Don't you know that I'm . . ."

"Yes, yes!" he broke in violently. "You were going to say that you promised to marry someone else a long time ago, and that I am a scoundrel to try to force myself on you, now when it's too late. Of course I know that! Well, why have I told you this? To try to sway you, to impress you, to make you think about it. As God is my witness, I'm speaking from the heart; there is nothing else I can do. I know that you are engaged, that you are in love with your fiancé, and that I don't have a chance. But still I had to plead my cause; I just refuse to give up hope. Perhaps if you realize what it means to give up all hope, you'll understand how I feel. When I said just now that I expected nothing, I was lying. I only said it to put your mind at ease, so that you wouldn't panic, to gain time for myself. I seem to be making things worse, don't I? You've never given me any encouragement, nor did I even for a moment think that I could take someone else's place in your heart. But during these hours of anguish I've been thinking: 'She's engaged and she'll soon be gone, farewell; but all is not yet lost. She's still here, she isn't married, she isn't dead, so who knows? If I did my utmost, perhaps there's still time! You're an obsession with me; you're never out of my mind. I see you everywhere, and every blue stream I pass I call Dagny. I don't think there has been a single day during these past few weeks that I haven't thought of you. No matter what time I leave the hotel, as soon as I open the door and walk down the steps I'm filled with hope and elation: 'Maybe you'll run into her!' And I look for you everywhere. I don't understand it; I'm powerless. Believe me, I've struggled hard to keep this to myself. It's terribly frustrating to know that no word of mine can make the slightest impression on you, but even knowing this, I'm unable to give up; I shall hang on to the end. I know it's hopeless. Still, so many things race through my mind when I spend a sleepless night sitting by the window in my room! I have a book in front of me, but I can't read. I grit my teeth and read three lines, but I can't go on, and I put the book down. My heart is pounding, and I whisper tender, secret words, evoke a name, and caress it with my thoughts. The clock strikes: two, four, six. I decide to put an end to the agony and at the next opportunity confess all. If I dared ask anything of you now, it would be not to say anything. I love you, but don't say anything. Wait three minutes before you speak."

She had heard him out with growing consternation and seemed unable to utter a single word. They were both standing there motionless.

"But you must be out of your mind!" she said at last, shaking her head violently. Pale and shattered, with an icy glitter in her blue eyes, she added: "You know I'm engaged, you accept that fact, and yet . . ."

"I know it only too well! Do you think I'd be likely to forget his face and his uniform? He is an attractive man; there is nothing wrong with him, but I can't help wishing he were dead! I've told myself a hundred times that I don't stand a chance with you. But I try not to face facts, and hope against hope that there might be a way, so many things can happen, all isn't lost. And there still is hope, isn't there?"

"Stop it! Don't do this to me!" she cried. "What do you want from me? What can you be thinking of? Do you mean that I should . . . For God's sake, let's not talk about it any more, please! Now go! You've ruined everything with a few stupid remarks. You've spoiled everything—the talks we've had—and now we can't see each other again! Why did you do it? I've never heard of anything so insane! I beg you, don't mention this again, for your sake as well as mine. You know all too well that I can't be anything to you. I can't imagine how you could ever have gotten such an idea! Let's put an end to this conversation. You just have to go home and try to accept it. I feel very sorry for you, but there's nothing I can do."

"You mean that this is goodby—that I'm looking at you for the last time? No, that can't be! If I promise to be calm, to talk about anything but this, may I see you again? If I'm perfectly calm and never bring this up? Perhaps some day when you've gotten bored with all the others . . . anything, as long as this isn't the last time. You're shaking your head again—your lovely head. How hopeless everything is! Even if you won't have anything to do with me, if you would only lie and say yes—just to make me happy! This has turned out to be a sad day for me, though I woke up singing this morning. Let me see you just once more!"

"You can't ask that of me—I can't promise. Besides, what would be the point? Please go now! Maybe we'll meet again, I don't know, but it's possible. You must go now!" she cried in exasperation, adding: "That would be the kindest thing you could do."

Pause.

He stood staring at her, breathing heavily. Then he pulled himself together and bowed. He let his cap fall to the ground and took her hand, which she hadn't offered, and pressed it hard between both of his. She cried out, and he immediately let go, distressed at having caused her pain. As she walked away, he stood there staring at her. A few more steps and she would be out of sight. His face flushed; he bit his lip until it bled and turned his back on her in a fit of passion and fury. He was a man, after all; it was all right with him—goodby . . .

Abruptly she turned and said: "And you are not to hang around the parsonage at night. So it's you who made the dog bark so furiously the past few nights! One night you almost got my father out of bed. You must stop doing that, do you hear! I can only hope you won't make difficulties for both of us."

The sound of her voice dispelled his anger. He shook his head.

"And this was my birthday!" he said, covering his face with his arm as he walked away.

She watched him go, hesitated for a moment and then ran after him and took his arm.

"I'm sorry, but this is the way it has to be. I can mean nothing to you. But perhaps we'll meet again sometime. Don't you think so? Now I must go."

She turned her back on him and quickly walked away.

12

A VEILED lady came walking up from the dock, where she had just disembarked from the steamer. She headed straight for the Central Hotel.

Nagel happened to be standing at his window looking out. He had spent the whole afternoon pacing the floor, stopping now and then to drink a glass of water. His cheeks were feverish and flushed, his eyes bloodshot. For hours he had been obsessed with thoughts of his meeting with Dagny Kielland.

At one point he had the impulse to leave the town and put all this behind him. He opened his trunk, took out some papers, a couple of brass instruments, a flute, and some clothes, including a new bright yellow suit just like the one he was wearing, and various other things, which he spread all over the floor. Yes, he had to leave; he couldn't stay in this town any longer. The flags were gone and the streets were dead; why not clear out? And why the devil had he come here in the first place? It was a miserable hole with petty, snoopy people.

But in his heart he knew he couldn't bring himself to leave; he was just playing around with the idea to bolster his courage and keep deluding himself. Miserable and dejected, he packed all his things again and put his trunks back in their place. Then, frantic and distraught, he went on pacing from the door to the window, while the clock downstairs struck one hour after the other. Then it struck six.

As he stopped at the window, he caught a glimpse of the veiled woman just entering the hotel. His expression completely changed; he tapped his head several times. After all, why not? She had as much right to stay at this hotel as he. Anyway, it was no concern of his; he had other things to think about, and besides, he and she were through.

He made a great effort to control himself, sat down and picked up a newspaper from the floor, and pretended to read. After several moments Sara opened the door and handed him a card on which was written "Kamma" in pencil. That was all. He got up and went downstairs.

The lady was waiting in the hall. She still had her veil on.

"Hello, Simonsen," she said in a voice choked with emotion.

He started but then pulled himself together and asked Sara: "Is there somewhere we can talk for a moment?"

They were shown into a room next to the dining room, and as soon as the door closed, the lady collapsed into a chair. She was in a highly emotional state.

Their conversation was disconnected; they made many elliptical allusions to the past and used words and phrases that had meaning only for them. They obviously knew each other well. They talked for less than an hour; her speech was more Danish than Norwegian.

"Forgive me for calling you Simonsen still—my special pet name for you," she said. "Every time I say it to myself, it's as if you were right there beside me."

"When did you get here?" Nagel asked.

"Just now, a few minutes ago. I came on the steamer. But I'll be leaving shortly."

"So soon?"

"Look here, I know you're relieved; you're making that rather obvious, aren't you? But what should I do about the pain in my breast? Feel here—no, higher up. What do you think? It seems to me that it's gotten worse since we last saw each other, don't you think so? Well, it doesn't matter. Do I look a mess? Tell me frankly. How does my hair look? I'm filthy; I've been traveling for twenty-four hours. You haven't changed; you're just as cold as always. Do you have a comb?"

"No. What made you come here? What is it that . . ."

"I may ask you the same question. What made you hide away in a place like this? Did you think I wouldn't find you? It seems that you call yourself an agronomist here? I met some men on the dock who said that you had been tending currant bushes in the garden of a Mrs. Stenersen. It seems that you've been working there like mad for two days. What an odd idea! My hands are so icy cold; they always are when I'm upset, you know that, and I'm upset now. You don't seem to have very much feeling left for me, though I still call you Simonsen as in the old days and show such joy at seeing you. This morning while I was lying in my berth I wondered: How will he receive me? Will he talk to me as intimately as he used to, and pat me under the chin? I was almost certain you would, but I see I was mistaken. But now it's too late, so please don't try. Why do you sit there blinking your eyes that way? Are you thinking about something else while I'm talking to you?"

"I don't feel very well today, Kamma. Tell me honestly why you came here. I would appreciate a straight answer."

"Why did I come to see you? My God, how cruel you can be! Are you afraid that I've come to ask you for money—to pick your pocket? If you have such black thoughts in your heart, say so, please. Why did I come? Can't you guess? Don't you know what day it is today? Have you forgotten that it's your birthday?"

Sobbing, she threw herself on her knees before him, taking both his hands, which she held against her face and then pressed to her bosom.

Suddenly he was strangely moved by this outburst of tenderness which he hadn't expected. He drew her close to him and held her on his knees.

"I didn't forget your birthday," she said. "I never will. You've no idea how often I cry over you at night, when I can't sleep for thinking of you. My dearest, you still have the same red lips! I thought about so many things on board ship—I wondered whether your lips were still as red. How your eyes wander! You're annoyed, aren't you? You haven't changed at all. But your eyes are wandering, as if you were trying to think of some way to get rid of me as fast as possible. I think you'd be more comfortable if I sat next to you. I've got so many things to talk to you about, and I have to make it quick because the boat will be leaving very soon. But your air of indifference upsets me.

What can I say to make you listen to me? You don't appreciate my coming here, remembering your birthday. . . . Did you get a lot of flowers? I'm sure you did! Mrs. Stenersen must have remembered you! Tell me, this Mrs. Stenersen for whom you're playing agronomist—what does she look like? You haven't changed a bit! I would have bought you some flowers too, if I'd had the money, but I'm in a tight spot at the moment. For God's sake, won't you listen to me these few minutes? How changed everything is! Do you remember—but of course you don't —how you once recognized me from a distance by the feather in my hat and you came running to me? You must remember that! It happened one day on the Ramparts— but now I can't remember why I mentioned the feather. I've forgotten the point I was going to make, but I was going to use it against you. What's the matter? Why do you jump up like that?"

He had suddenly gotten to his feet, tiptoed across the room, and brusquely opened the door.

"They keep ringing for you in the dining room, Sara," he called from the door.

As he sat down again, he nodded, whispering to Kamma: "I had a feeling she was peeping through the keyhole."

Kamma showed her annoyance. "And so what?" she said. "Why is your mind on a thousand other things just now? I've been here for fifteen minutes and you haven't even asked me to remove my veil. But it's too late; don't you dare ask me now! It never occurred to you how uncomfortable a heavy veil is in this heat! Well, I guess I deserve it; why on earth did I come here? I heard you ask the maid if we might use this room for a moment—'just for a moment,' you said. That could only mean that you hoped to get rid of me quickly. I'm not reproaching you; only it makes me so terribly miserable. God help me! Why can't I let you go? I know you're crazy; your eyes are the eyes of a madman. So I've been told, and I can see it for myself. But still I can't let you go. Dr. Nissen said that you're mad, and God knows it must be true if you can bury yourself in a hole like this and call yourself an agronomist. I just can't get over that! And you still wear that iron ring and walk around in that loud yellow suit—no one else would be caught dead in that!"

"Did Dr. Nissen really say that I was mad?" he asked.

"Dr. Nissen made no bones about it. Would you like to know whom he said it to?"

Pause.

For a moment he was silent. Then he looked up and said: "Kamma, tell me frankly, couldn't I help you out with some money? I can easily do it, you know."

"No!" she cried. "Never! What makes you think you can hurl insult after insult to my face!"

Pause.

"I don't see any point in sitting here making bitter remarks to each other," he said.

She interrupted him, sobbing, apparently having lost all control over her emotions.

"Who's bitter? Am I? It's unbelievable how much you've changed in the past few months. I came here only to . . . I don't expect you to share my feelings any more, and you know I would never beg for your affection. But I had hoped that you would at least be kind. Good God, how miserable I am! I ought to tear you out of my heart, but I can't. Instead, I follow you around and throw myself at your feet. Do you remember the day on Drammen Road, you gave a dog a whack on the muzzle for jumping on me? It was all my fault; I screamed because I thought he was going to bite, but he only wanted to play. After you hit him, instead of running away, he lay down at our feet. And then you cried over the dog and petted him—I saw your tears, though you tried to hide them—but now there are none, though . . . I didn't mean to draw a parallel. You don't think I would compare myself to a dog, do you? God only knows what your incredible arrogance might lead you to think. I recognize that expression on your face. I saw that smile; yes, you're laughing at me! I just have to tell you straight out—no, forgive me—it's just that I'm so desperate. You're looking at a shattered woman. I've hit rock bottom. Give me your hand! Can't you forgive me for that minor indiscretion? If you would only stop to reflect, you'd know it didn't mean a thing. I should have come down to you that evening. You kept signaling, and still I didn't come—oh God, how I regret that! But he wasn't there, though you were convinced he was. He'd been there, but he'd left. I admit it and beg your forgiveness. I should have sent him away, I know, I admit it; I admit everything, and I shouldn't have . . . But I don't understand; I don't understand anything any more . . ."

Pause.

The silence was broken only by Kamma's sobs and the clatter of cutlery in the dining room. She went on crying and dabbing at her eyes with a handkerchief under her veil.

"He is so helpless," she said, "and a weakling too. Now and then he bangs his fist on the table and tells me to go to hell. He screams at me, tells me that I'm destroying him and that I'm vulgar. But the next minute he's miserable and he's unable to make the final break and let me go. He's spineless—what can I do? I put off leaving him from day to day, though it's an impossible situation. But don't you dare feel sorry for me; I don't want any of your contemptuous pity. At any rate, he's better than most men, and has made me happier than anyone—than you even. I want you to know that I love him; I didn't come here to complain. When I go home to him, I'll get down on my knees and beg his forgiveness for what I've just said about him—so help me, I will!"

"Please, Kamma, be sensible. Do let me help you! I know you need it. Won't you let me do something? It's unkind of you to refuse me when I want to do it and have the means."

With this he pulled out his wallet.

"Didn't you hear me say no?" she screamed.

"But then what *do* you want?" he said, exasperated.

She sat up and stopped crying, seeming to regret her outburst.

"Listen, Simonsen—do let me call you that once more. Don't be angry, but I'd like to ask you something: Whatever possessed you to come and live in a place like this? And then you wonder why people think you're crazy? You really have to know the country well to remember the location of this burg. It's a town of no importance, and still you go around play-acting and shocking people here with your crazy ideas. Can't you think of something better to do? Well, it's none of my business—I only said it out of old . . . But what do you think I ought to do about my breast? It feels as if it were about to burst. Don't you think I ought to see the doctor again? But how in God's name can I go to the doctor when I don't have a penny?"

"But I'll be only too happy to give you the money. You can repay me sometime if you want to."

"It doesn't really matter whether I go to the doctor or

not," she went on like a stubborn child. "Who would mourn for me if I died?"

Then suddenly, seeming to think it over, she changed her attitude and said: "On second thought, why shouldn't I accept your money? Since I did before, why not now? I'm not so rich that I can afford to . . . Time after time I've refused you, as you knew I would, when I was upset. You counted on that—yes, you did! You don't want to part with your money, though you seem to have a lot at the moment—don't you think I've noticed that? And even if you offer again to help me, you're doing it to humiliate me, to gloat over the fact that I just can't turn it down. But it can't be helped; humbly, I have to accept your money. I wish to God I didn't have to appeal to you! But you must believe me, that isn't why I came here today. You couldn't possibly be petty enough to think such a thing. But how much can you spare, Simonsen? Please don't mind my asking; I hope you won't mind my asking, and you must believe that I'm sincere . . ."

"How much do you need?"

"How much do I need? Good Lord, I won't miss the boat, will I? I need a lot . . . maybe several hundred crowns, but . . ."

"Listen. You mustn't feel humiliated if I give you this money. If you wanted, you could earn it. You could do me an enormous favor, if I only dared ask you . . ."

"If you dared ask me!" she exclaimed, overjoyed at this chance to save her honor. "What a question! What would you like me to do, Simonsen? You know I'll do anything for you, my dearest!"

"You still have forty-five minutes before the boat leaves . . ."

"What do you want me to do?"

"I would like you to call on a lady and transact a bit of business for me."

"A lady?"

"She lives in a one-story house down by the dock. There are no curtains on the windows, but there are usually white flowers on the windowsill. The lady's name is Martha Gude—Miss Gude."

"But is she the one—not Mrs. Stenersen?"

"No, you're on the wrong track. Miss Gude is a lady about forty. But she owns a chair, an old armchair I've made up my mind to have, and you must help me. Now, put your money away and I'll explain everything."

It was beginning to get dark. The hotel guests were coming out of the dining room as Nagel was giving her further details about the old armchair. She would have to be very tactful. Under no circumstances was she to reveal why she was there. Kamma was eager to get going; this clandestine mission obviously excited her. She laughed and kept asking if she oughtn't to wear some sort of disguise—at least she should wear glasses. Didn't he once have a red hat? She could wear that . . .

"No, I don't want any misrepresentation. All you have to do is bid on the chair in order to raise the price. You can go as far as two hundred crowns—let's say two hundred twenty. And don't worry, you won't get stuck with it—you won't get it."

"Good God, that's a lot of money! Why wouldn't I get it for two hundred twenty crowns?"

"Because it's already mine."

"But suppose she accepts my offer?"

"She won't. Now go and see what you can do."

She was self-conscious about her appearance and, before leaving, again asked him for a comb and showed concern over her wrinkled dress. "But I won't stand for your spending so much time with that Mrs. Stenersen," she said mischievously. "I just won't put up with it—it would break my heart." And she glanced quickly at the money, to make sure it was safe.

"How kind of you to give me all that money!" she exclaimed. Impetuously, she threw back her veil and kissed him on the mouth. But her mind was on her mysterious errand to Martha Gude. "How will I let you know all has gone well?" she wanted to know. "I can ask the captain to blow the whistle four or five times—wouldn't that be all right? You see, I'm not so stupid after all! You can depend on me. That's the least I can do for you when you . . . You do believe me when I say I didn't come here for money! Well, thank you again. Goodby!"

Again she made a quick movement to make sure the money was safely tucked away.

A half hour later Nagel heard the steamboat whistle sound five blasts.

13

A COUPLE of days went by.

Nagel stayed at the hotel, wandering around aimlessly, obviously worried and tormented. During these two days his eyes had become expressionless and listless. He didn't speak to anyone, not even the people in the hotel. One night when he had been out until the wee hours of the morning as usual, he came back with a handkerchief tied around his hand. He explained his two wounds by saying that he had tripped over some fishing tackle on the dock.

On Thursday morning it rained, which made him even more depressed. But after reading the papers and laughing over a stormy debate in the French Chamber of Deputies, he suddenly jumped out of bed and snapped his fingers. Why the blazes should he sit around and mope?

The world was big; the world was rich, gay, beautiful. Down with sorrow!

He rang for Sara before he was fully dressed and told her he was having a few people in that evening—six or seven, who would liven things up a bit—amusing fellows like Dr. Stenersen, Hansen the lawyer, the schoolmaster, and a few others.

He sat down immediately and began writing the invitations. The Midget accepted; Reinert was also asked, but he didn't come. At five o'clock they were all gathered in Nagel's room. It was dark and still raining, so the lamp was lit and the curtains drawn.

Then the revelry began: it was a boisterous, rowdy affair which gave the small town something to gossip about for many a day.

When The Midget arrived, Nagel walked up to him and apologized for having talked such a lot of nonsense the last time they met. He shook hands cordially with The Midget and introduced him to Øien, the student, the only one in the group whom he didn't know. The Midget whispered his thanks for the new trousers. Now everything he was wearing was new!

"You still don't have a vest!"

"But I don't need one! I'm not nobility, after all; I assure you I have no use for a vest!"

Dr. Stenersen had broken his glasses and was wearing a pince-nez without a chain; it was constantly falling off.

"This is an era of emancipation; there's no doubt about that," said Stenersen. "Just compare the elections we just had with the last ones."

Everyone was drinking a great deal. The schoolmaster, Holtan, was already talking in monosyllables, which was always an indication of his condition. Hansen, who ob-

viously had had a few drinks before he came, began as
usual to argue with the doctor and became quite abusive.

Hansen was a socialist—a progressive socialist, if he
might say so. He wasn't pleased with the elections. What
was so emancipating about them—could anyone tell him
that? The hell with all this emancipation! Didn't even a
man like Gladstone attack poor Parnell on moral grounds
—judging him by ridiculous bourgeois standards? To hell
with the whole rotten business!

"But you're talking like a damned fool!" the doctor
cried. "Are you against ethics in Parliament? If the voters
felt that there was no morality in parliaments, how many
do you think would go along?" You had to fool and cajole
people by continuously waving the standard of morality
and all that. Dr. Stenersen had a high opinion of Parnell,
but if Gladstone was so opposed to him, he must know
what he was about—with apologies to the host, Mr.
Nagel, who couldn't forgive Gladstone for being an honorable man. "By the way, Mr. Nagel, you don't seem to have
a very high opinion of Tolstoy either? Miss Kielland mentioned that you had some reservations about him."

Nagel was talking to Øien. He turned quickly and said:
"I don't remember having talked to Miss Kielland about
Tolstoy. I acknowledge him as a great novelist, but his
philosophy is naïve, to say the least . . ." After a moment
he went on: "I think we ought to speak freely tonight.
There are no ladies present, and these are a bachelor's
quarters, after all. Do we all agree? I'm in the mood for a
good argument! I'd like to get into a good fight . . ."

"Why don't you start," said the doctor in an offended
tone. "Tolstoy is a fool."

"Let's get everyone in on it," said Holtan. He had just
reached the state of drunkenness where all inhibitions are

shed. "The lid is off, doctor, or out you go. Everyone has to speak his mind. Stöcker, for example, is a bastard—and I can prove it!"

Everyone laughed, and it was a while before they got back to Tolstoy. He was a great writer and a great spiritual force.

Nagel suddenly flared up: "He is *not* a great intellect! He is a mediocrity, and his ideas are no more profound than the euphoric teachings of the Salvation Army. A Russian without his rank and title, and without his million rubles, would hardly have attained fame by teaching a few peasants how to repair shoes. But let's forget all that and have some fun. Your health, Mr. Grøgaard!"

From time to time Nagel went over to The Midget, clinked glasses with him, and was very solicitous. He repeatedly referred to his rambling at their previous meeting and asked The Midget's forgiveness.

"As far as I'm concerned, nothing you could say could possibly shock me," said the doctor, pulling himself up stiffly.

"I'm sometimes a bit argumentative," Nagel said, by way of reply, "and tonight I'm in the mood. It may be because of a few setbacks I had the day before yesterday, and also because of the weather, which depresses me no end. I'm sure you understand, Dr. Stenersen, and you will forgive me. To get back to Tolstoy, in my opinion his intellect is no greater than, say, General Booth's. They are both preachers, not thinkers but preachers. They deal with the status quo, popularize already accepted ideas, reduce them to the lowest common denominator, and then sit back and watch them take root. But if you're going to sell, you must do so at a profit, and Tolstoy's enterprises show a staggering loss. Once two friends made a wager; one bet the other twelve shillings that he could shoot a nut out of the other fellow's hand at a distance of twenty paces without grazing it. Well, he fired, missed, and blew the whole hand to shreds, but he did it with style. As he was about to faint, his injured friend moaned: 'You lost the bet—give me the twelve shillings. Give me twelve shillings,' he said! God, how Tolstoy labors to eliminate humanity's happy vices and make the world full of love of God and mankind! It just fills me with shame. Maybe it sounds impertinent to say that an agronomist is ashamed of a count, but that happens to be the case. It would be different if Tolstoy were a young man struggling against temptation or if he had a battle to fight and tried to win it by preaching virtue and clean living. But his sources have run dry; he has no more humanity left to struggle with. You may say: But this has nothing to do with his philosophy. But it has everything to do with it! Oh, just wait until old age has made you self-satisfied and callous! Then you go to the young man and say: 'Renounce all these superficial trappings.' The young man ponders, sleeps on it, and comes to the conclusion that this indeed is what the Bible preaches. But he doesn't 'renounce'; he goes on sinning happily for the next forty years. And so it is. When the forty years are up and the young man has grown old, he saddles his snow-white mare and rides off with his crusader's banner held high in his bony hand, calling out a pious message of renunciation to the youth of the world. It's a comedy that endlessly repeats itself. I get a kick out of Tolstoy. I'm glad the old boy is still capable of so much munificence. He will surely be rewarded by going to his Maker in the end! But, after all, he is only doing what so many old men have done before him, what many others will continue to do after he is gone. It's as simple as that."

"One more word," said the doctor, "and then we'll end the discussion. Don't forget that Tolstoy has been a true friend to needy and destitute human beings. Is that of no value? Show me an aristocrat in this country who has looked after the indigent the way he has! I can't help feeling that it's rather arrogant to claim that because Tolstoy's teachings aren't followed, he should therefore be considered a fool."

"Bravo, doctor!" roared Holtan, his face flushed. "Bravo! But you ought to express yourself a bit more sharply. Everyone is entitled to his own opinion. But you are being arrogant, Nagel. I can prove it!"

"Your health!" said Nagel. "We musn't forget why we're here. Do you mean to say, doctor, that a man deserves credit for giving away a ten-ruble note when he has a cool million left? I can't follow your thinking on this—or anyone else's, for that matter. I must have a different conception of things from the rest of you. For the life of me, I can't see why anyone—least of all, a wealthy man —should be commended for charitable deeds."

"I agree," said Hansen testily. "I'm a socialist and that is exactly the way I feel."

With a show of annoyance, the doctor turned to Nagel and exclaimed: "May I ask if you really have facts and figures on how much Tolstoy gives away to charity in the course of a year? There must be a limit to how far one can go, even at a stag party!"

"Tolstoy's position was this," replied Nagel, " 'I will give away a certain amount, and no more.' That is why he let his wife take the blame when he had reached what he considered to be his limit. Well, we'll let that go. But the point is this: do you give someone a crown out of the goodness of your heart, or because you must act according to your conscience and do a good deed? This seems like such simplistic thinking to me. There are people who are compulsive givers. Why? Because it satisfies their ego; it gives them real psychic pleasure. They don't do it in an obvious or calculated way; they do it quietly and unobtrusively. They would hate to give openly because that would rob them of a great deal of pleasure. No, it has to be done secretly, with a quick movement of the trembling hand, accompanied by sentimentality and a feeling of inner satisfaction that they themselves do not understand. Suddenly they have an impulse to give something away. It manifests itself by a strange sensation in the chest, a strange urge that suddenly comes upon them and makes their eyes water. They don't give out of kindness but by compulsion—for the sake of their peace of mind. That's what drives some people. You speak of generous people with such admiration. As I said, I must be different from the rest of you—but I don't admire them in the least. I'll be damned if there is a single human being who wouldn't rather give than receive! May I ask if there is a human being on earth who wouldn't rather alleviate suffering than inflict it? To use you as an example, doctor: I heard you say that you'd given five crowns to a man who rowed you over. Why did you give him five crowns? You certainly didn't do it to please God: I'm sure the thought never occurred to you. Maybe the man wasn't even hard up, but you still had to do it. At that moment you simply yielded to an impulse to dispose of something, which at the same time meant giving pleasure to someone else. In my opinion, it's nauseating to make such a fuss about charity. You're walking along the street one day—the weather, the kind of people you meet, everything contributes to putting you in a certain frame of mind. Suddenly you see a face, a child's face, the face of a beggar. Let's take the beggar's face—it shakes you. A strange feeling comes over you and you come to a dead stop. That face has touched a rare and sensitive spot in you. You lure the beggar into a doorway and press a ten-crown bill into his hand. 'If you say a single word about this to anyone, I'll kill you,' you hiss, and you are on the verge of gnashing your teeth and crying with suppressed emotion. After all, you can't afford to be caught doing this kind of thing! And this situation can come up day after day until you find yourself in the awkward position of not having a penny in your pocket. Mind you, this doesn't apply to me, but I know a man—as a matter of fact, two—who are compulsive givers. No one gives because he is forced to, and that's that—with the exception of misers and tightwads; they really make a sacrifice when they part with something—there's no doubt about that. Those people deserve much more praise for the øre they reluctantly part with, I think, than a man like you, him, or me, who indulge in emotionalism when handing out a crown. Tell Tolstoy from me that I don't give a damn about his disgusting show of generosity—not until he gives away all he owns, and not even then. But do forgive me if I've hurt anyone's feelings. Have another cigar, Mr. Grøgaard. Cheers, doctor!"

Pause.

"How many people do you think you'll manage to convert during the course of your life?" asked the doctor.

"Bravo!" cried the schoolmaster. "Holtan congratulates you!"

"I?" said Nagel, by way of reply to Dr. Stenersen's question. "No one. If I had to live by converting people, I'd soon be dead. But what I can't understand is that no one else seems to think the way I do. Therefore, I must be the one who is out of step. But I can't be completely wrong; I just can't believe that."

"But I've never yet heard you say anything constructive about any person or thing," said the doctor. "It would be interesting to know if there is anybody who meets with your approval."

"Let me explain—I can do it in a few words. What you really meant was: he respects no one; he is arrogance personified; no one can satisfy him. That's not true! My intelligence is only average, but I could name hundreds of run-of-the-mill characters who are thought of as great men and who run the world. Their names resound in my ears. But I would prefer to name two, four, or six really great spiritual leaders, demigods, molders of thought and values, who have achieved lasting fame. Then I'd like to mention a few who have never achieved fame, rare and exceptional geniuses who lived for a few short years and died unknown. I have a long list of them, but I'm certain that I wouldn't include Tolstoy."

"My dear man," said the doctor contemptuously with an impatient shrug of the shoulders, obviously wishing to put an end to the conversation, "do you think that a man could achieve universal acclaim, like Tolstoy, without being a man of great spiritual nobility? You're amusing to listen to, but you talk utter nonsense. As a matter of fact, your ranting makes me sick!"

"Bravo, doctor!" shouted Holtan again. "Don't let our host go too far . . ."

"Mr. Holtan reminds me that I'm not being a very good host," said Nagel, laughing. "But I promise to do better. Mr. Øien, your glass is empty. Why aren't you drinking?"

The young man had been sitting in his chair, erect and silent, listening to the conversation, obviously taking in every word. His eyes were wide open and alert; he was all ears and completely absorbed in the exchange of views. It was rumored that he, like other students, was working on a novel during the summer vacation.

Sara came and announced that supper was being served. Hansen, who had slumped down in his chair, suddenly came to and scrutinized her sharply. When she left the room, he jumped up, caught up with her as she was going down the stairs, and, devouring her with his eyes, he exclaimed: "Sara, you are really a delight!"

Then he came back and settled down in his chair, as somber as before. By this time he was really in his cups. When at last Dr. Stenersen got around to him and challenged him on his socialism, he was unable to defend his ideas. A fine socialist he was! He was a bloodsucker, a wretched middleman between power and incompetence— an attorney who makes his living from other people's miseries and who takes their money for championing rights which were theirs to begin with! And he had the nerve to call himself a socialist!

"But in principle I believe in socialism," Hansen interjected vehemently.

"Principle!" the doctor exclaimed scornfully. As they went down to the dining room, he made one snide remark after another, deprecated Hansen's abilities as a lawyer, and launched an attack on socialism. The doctor was a fervent liberal; he didn't go along with the doctrines of socialism. What was the basic philosophy of socialism anyway? To hell with the whole sophistry! The doctor was now riding his favorite hobbyhorse: socialism was the revenge of the lower classes. Just look at it as a political movement—masses of deaf and dumb creatures trotting after their leader, their tongues hanging out. Were they able to see beyond the tip of their noses? People just didn't think. If they did, they would join the Liberal Party and accomplish something useful and practical, something pragmatic, rather than driveling around in vague daydreams all their lives! The whole business was a farce! "Take any of the socialist leaders! What kind of people are they? Shabby, scrawny types who sit around on wooden stools in their garrets, writing essays on how to improve the world! No one can question their integrity —who can fault Karl Marx on that score? But there he is, this Marx fellow, trying to write poverty out of existence! In theory, that is. Intellectually, he has analyzed every level of poverty, every degree of misery; his brain is full of all the sufferings of mankind. He dips his pen in ink and, full of ardor, writes page after fiery page, covers large sheets with figures, takes from the rich and gives to the poor, redistributes the wealth of the world, revolutionizes world economy, flings millions at the poor, who look up in astonishment. Nothing but science and theory! And then it turns out that in his naïveté he has begun with a false premise—namely, that all men are equal. Bah! What could be a bigger lie! Instead of doing something practical and supporting the Liberal Party and its platform of reform to lay the groundwork for a working democracy . . ."

The doctor had worked himself up to a feverish pitch and come up with lots of figures of speech and personal opinions. At the table he became increasingly vociferous;

there was a lot of champagne, and the atmosphere became charged with emotion. The Midget, who was sitting next to Nagel and who had been silent up to now, joined in the melee, interjecting a few remarks. Holtan, the schoolmaster, sat stiff as a ramrod on his chair, fuming because he had gotten egg all over himself, which immobilized him. But when Sara came to help him clean up the mess, he seized the chance to grab her and take her in his arms, which caused an uproar around the table.

In the midst of the hubbub, Nagel ordered champagne brought up to his room, and shortly thereafter, everyone got up. Holtan and Hansen walked arm in arm, singing elatedly at the top of their voices, and Dr. Stenersen resumed his diatribe on the principles of socialism. But on the way upstairs he dropped his pince-nez again for about the tenth time, and this time both lenses broke. He put the frame in his pocket, and for the rest of the evening he could hardly see. This made him more irritable still, and sitting down next to Nagel, he said with a sneer: "Am I correct in assuming that you are a religious man?"

He meant it seriously and was waiting for an answer. After a brief silence he added that from their first encounter—the day of Karlsen's funeral—he had gotten the impression that he, Nagel, was a religious man.

"But I was defending the religious *spirit* in man," Nagel replied, "not Christianity in particular—as a matter of fact, not Christianity at all. I was talking about spiritual life in general. You said that all theologians ought to be hanged. I asked you why, and you said they were finished. I couldn't agree with you; religion is a fact. A Turk cries 'Allah is great,' and dies for his convictions; to this day, a Norwegian kneels at the altar and drinks the blood of Christ. There are even places where people believe they can attain salvation through cowbells! But what really matters is not *what* you believe but the faith and conviction with which you believe . . ."

"That kind of talk offends me!" exclaimed the doctor, scandalized. "I'm once more asking myself whether you aren't a conservative, masquerading as something else. You make one erudite pronouncement after another about theologians and books on religion. Any number of intellectuals make mincemeat out of that myth, and still you hold on to the fable of Christ's blood having meaning in our time. I can't follow your line of reasoning."

Nagel thought for a moment and said: "It's very simple: what are we gaining—excuse me if I'm repeating myself—what are we gaining by a pragmatism that robs our life of poetry, dreams, mysticism—are these all lies? What is truth? Can you tell me that? We can only struggle along by using symbols, and we change them as we alter our views. By the way, let's not neglect our drinks."

The doctor got up and strode across the room. The folds in the carpet near the door seemed to irritate him, and he got down on his knees to smooth them out.

"Hansen, you might as well let me borrow your glasses since you're only sitting there sleeping anyway," he said with ill-concealed fury.

But Hansen wouldn't part with his glasses, and Dr. Stenersen turned away from him in utter disgust. Again he sat down next to Nagel.

"In your opinion it's a lot of nonsense; words without meaning—maybe you're right, after all. Let's take Hansen here—sorry to use you as the butt of my joke, Hansen— lawyer and socialist. You aren't by any chance elated when two good burghers have a disagreement and drag each other into court? Of course not! You try to come to an amiable compromise, and of course you don't make a penny out of it! The following Sunday you'll go to the Labor Union and deliver a lecture on the socialist state to two workmen and a butcher's boy. Yes, according to you, everyone is to be rewarded according to his capacity to produce; everything is beautifully organized, and everyone will have his fair share. But then the butcher's boy gets up, and so help me, if he isn't smarter than all the rest of you. He says: 'I can consume on the same scale as the most affluent merchant, but when it comes to producing, I'm only a poor butcher's boy,' because that's my only talent.' I suppose that doesn't make any impression on you, you stupid fool? . . . Snore away, that's all you're good for . . . just keep on snoring away . . ." By this time the doctor was quite drunk; his tongue was thick and his eyes watery. After brooding for a while, he turned to Nagel and went on morosely: "I didn't mean that only the theologians ought to do away with themselves. Damn it, that's what we all ought to do. Get out of the world, and to hell with everything!"

Nagel clinked glasses with The Midget. The doctor, furious because his remarks went unanswered, cried: "Didn't you hear what I said? We all ought to do away with ourselves—and that includes you!" The doctor had blood in his eye as he uttered these words.

"Yes," said Nagel, "I've often thought about that. But I don't have the guts." Pause. "I'm far from saying that I would have the courage, but if I should one day, I'll have my pistol ready. I always have it on me, just in case."

He pulled a vial out of his vest pocket and held it up. It was marked "poison" and was only half full.

"Pure prussic acid—the purest water!" he said. "But I'll

never have the courage—I couldn't go through with it. Doctor, is there enough? I've used half of it on an animal, and it worked perfectly. Some spasms, a few contortions of the muzzle, two or three gasps, and that was that."

Dr. Stenersen picked up the vial, shook it, and said: "It's enough—more than enough. I really ought to take it away from you, but since you don't have the guts . . ."

"No, I don't have the guts . . ."

Pause.

Nagel put the vial back in his vest pocket. The doctor was gradually collapsing; he was taking sips from his glass, but his eyes were dull and lifeless and he spat on the floor. Suddenly he shouted at the schoolmaster: "How far have you gotten in your argument, Holtan? Can you still talk about the association of ideas? Because I can't any longer. Good night!"

The schoolmaster woke up, stretched, went toward the window, and stood there looking out. When the conversation resumed, he took the opportunity to slip away. He crept quietly along the wall, opened the door, and disappeared before anyone noticed. That was Holtan's usual way of leaving a party.

The Midget also got up and made a move to leave, but when he was asked to stay on for a while, he sat down again. Hansen, the lawyer, was sound asleep. The three who were still sober—Øien, The Midget, and Nagel—then began to talk about literature. The doctor listened with half-closed eyes but didn't utter another word. A few moments later he too was asleep.

Øien had read a lot and was an admirer of Maupassant. They surely must agree that he had penetrated the very soul of women and had no equal as the poet of love. What a genius for rendering a scene, and what insight into the human heart! At this Nagel flared up and, losing all control, banged his fists on the table, shouted, attacked one author after another—very few were left unscathed by his ire. His wrath seemed to come from deep within; he was breathing heavily and foam showed around his mouth.

Poets! Oh yes! One could say that they had penetrated the depths of the human heart. Who were these presumptuous creatures who had been cunning enough to acquire such influence in contemporary life? They were a rash, a scab on society, purulent pimples that must be constantly watched and carefully tended lest they break out. Yes, one had to make a big fuss over poets—especially the most stupid, the most insensitive oafs. If you didn't, they'd go off and sulk abroad! God, what a farce it was! "And I'd be willing to bet that if there were a poet or singer who was truly inspired from within, he would be rated way below that crude hack Maupassant. A man who has written reams about love and turns out books by the dozen— he gets the accolade! But a small bright star, Alfred de Musset, who within the scope of his work creates nothing but genuine art, a poet for whom love is not just a mating routine but a sensitive, ardent voice of spring, a poet so inspired that his every word emits a spark—this poet probably doesn't have half as many followers as that mediocrity, Maupassant, with his incredibly crude and soulless jigsaw verse."

Nagel could not stop. He even took the chance to attack Victor Hugo and to demolish the world's greatest writers. Would he be permitted to cite just one example of a so-called great poet's empty palaver? "Listen: 'Would that thy knife were as sharp as thy final no!' What do you think of that? Doesn't that sound just great? What is your opinion, Mr. Grøgaard?"

Nagel gave The Midget a penetrating look and stared fixedly at him while repeating this nonsensical line. The Midget didn't reply. His blue eyes opened wide with an expression of near panic, and in his confusion he took a large swallow from his glass.

"You mentioned Ibsen," Nagel continued, in the same state of agitation, though no one had mentioned the name. In Nagel's opinion there was only one poet in Norway, and it was *not* Ibsen! Ibsen was known as a philosopher—but wouldn't it be to the point to distinguish between *vox populi* thinking and philosophy? People were always talking about Ibsen's fame; his courage was always being drummed into you. But was there no difference between theoretical courage and courage put to the test? between an altruistic and passionate desire for reform and plain domestic upheaval? One is a source of inspiration; the other merely plays on our emotions as in the theater. The Norwegian writer who didn't give himself airs and wield a pen as if it were a lance was not a bona fide Norwegian writer. A true Norwegian must have issues and causes to pit himself against if he wanted to be thought of as having courage and guts. It was really very funny if one cared to look at it with detachment. The causes and issues engendered as much fanfare and manipulating as one of Napoleon's battles, but the element of risk was no greater than in a French duel! Ha ha! No, a man who wanted to revolt couldn't be a little scribbler with a literary penchant for the Germans; he had to be a vital being, caught up in the turmoil of life. Ibsen's spirit of revolution would certainly never bring a man onto thin ice! All that business about torpedoing the ark was a bureaucratic platitude compared to vigorous action. Well, when all was said and done, perhaps one was no worse than the other: we seem to venerate the kind of work best suited to women—just sitting around writing books for people. It was all empty and meaningless, but it had at least as much value as Leo Tolstoy's presumptuous philosophical ramblings. To hell with all of it!

"All of it?"

"Just about. We did have one poet—Bjørnson at his best. But he was the only one . . ."

But didn't most of his objections to Tolstoy also apply to Bjørnson? Wasn't he also preaching morality—wasn't he a mediocrity, a bore, a professional hack, and all the rest of it?

"No!" cried Nagel in a loud voice. He defended Bjørnson with violent words and violent gestures. Bjørnson and Tolstoy couldn't be compared: that would go against the sound, logical thinking of an agronomist; besides, one reacted against an invidious comparison like that with all one's instincts. In the first place, Bjørnson was at least on the same level as Tolstoy. Nagel had no regard for run-of-the-mill great, ordinary writers, so-called geniuses— God knows he didn't. Tolstoy had risen to their level, whereas Bjørnson had far surpassed them. This didn't mean that Tolstoy hadn't written books that were better than many of Bjørnson's, but what did that prove? Good books could be written just as well by Danish sea captains, Norwegian painters, English women. Secondly, Bjørnson was a human being, a great person, not just a public image. "He moves around the world making himself seen and heard, and needs a lot of elbow room. He doesn't sit like a sphinx or a mysterious sage, like Tolstoy on his steppe or Ibsen in his café. Bjørnson's spirit is like a forest in a storm. He's a fighter fighting everywhere, and wrecking his reputation with the clientele of the Grand Café. He is a man of great dimensions, a man with a commanding presence, a born leader. He can stand on a platform and with a gesture of his hand put a stop to the first signs of booing from the audience. His mind teems and seethes with new ideas. Whether he wins magnificently or fails abysmally, his spirit and personality are very much a part of it . . . Bjørnson is our only poet with soul, with a divine spark. His inspiration begins imperceptibly like a breeze rustling in a cornfield on a summer day; and when it ends, you hear nothing, nothing but his voice. His spirit gathers momentum until his true genius bursts forth. Compared with Bjørnson, Ibsen's poetry is hack work. Ibsen's poetry depends on finding the perfect rhyme; most of his plays are wood pulp in drama form. What the devil's happened to people? Oh, well, let's drop the subject. Cheers, everybody."

It was two o'clock; The Midget was yawning. He was tired after a hard day's work, tired and bored by Nagel's endless tirades. Again he got up to leave. But after he had said goodby and gone as far as the door, something happened which again kept him from leaving—a minor incident that was to have major consequences. The doctor woke up, made a sudden movement with his arm, and, being nearsighted, knocked over several glasses. Nagel, who was sitting next to him, was drenched with champagne. He jumped up, laughingly shaking his wet clothes, and gaily shouted: "Hurrah!"

The Midget immediately came to help, offering his services. He ran over to Nagel with towels and handkerchiefs to dry him off. His vest was soaked—if only he would remove it for a moment, it would be dry in no time. But Nagel wouldn't take it off. The noise woke Hansen, who also began to cheer, though he had no idea what was happening. The Midget again asked if he could have the vest for a moment, but Nagel only shook his head. Suddenly he looked straight at The Midget. Something seemed to have gone through his mind, because he immediately got up, removed his vest, and flung it at The Midget.

"Here!" he cried. "Dry it, and then you can keep it. Oh, yes, I insist! You don't own a vest. Please don't make a fuss. You're most welcome to it, my friend." And since The Midget still objected, Nagel stuck the vest under his arm, opened the door, and gave him a friendly shove.

The Midget left.

It all happened so quickly that the only one who witnessed the scene was Øien, who was sitting nearest the door.

Hansen, who had become quite reckless and had lost all inhibitions, suggested that they smash the rest of the glasses. Nagel made no objections, and the four men started amusing themselves hurling one glass after another against the wall. Then they drank straight from the bottles, roaring like drunken sailors and dancing around. It was four o'clock before the drinking bout ended. By then the doctor was extremely drunk. As he was leaving, Øien turned and remarked to Nagel: "What you said about Tolstoy also applies to Bjørnson. You're not consistent in your arguments . . ."

"Ha ha!" laughed the doctor savagely. "He wants consistency at this time of night . . . Are you still able to say 'Encyclopedists,' young man—or 'association of ideas'? Come, let me take you home. Ha ha, at this time of night!"

It had stopped raining. The sun still wasn't up, but there was no wind, and it looked as though it would be a pleasant day.

14

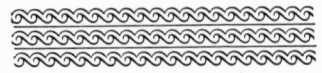

Early the following morning The Midget again appeared at the hotel. He tiptoed into Nagel's room and put his watch, some papers, a pencil stub, and the small vial containing poison on the table. He was just about to leave when Nagel woke up, and The Midget had to stay and explain his reason for being there.

"I found those things in your vest pocket," he said.

"In my vest pocket? Hell, yes, I had forgotten about them! What time is it?"

"Eight o'clock. But your watch stopped and I didn't want to wind it."

"You didn't drink my prussic acid, I hope?"

The Midget smiled and shook his head.

"No," he said.

"You didn't even taste it? The vial ought to be half full. Let me see!"

The Midget showed him the vial, which was indeed half full.

"Fine. And you say it's eight o'clock? Then it's time to get up. By the way, Grøgaard, can you borrow a violin for me from someone? I'd like to try to learn to—no, that's not what I mean. What I really want to do is *buy* a violin to give to a friend—I don't want it for myself. So you really have to get me a violin somehow."

The Midget said he would do his best.

"Thanks a lot. Stop by when you feel like it. You know where I am. Goodby."

An hour later Nagel was in the parsonage woods. The ground was still wet from the rain of the previous night, and the sun didn't give off much warmth. He sat down on a stone, his eyes glued to the road. He had spotted some familiar footprints in the wet gravel. He was sure they were Dagny's and that she had gone into town. He waited for a long time, but there was no sign of her, so he got up from the stone and decided to go meet her.

He was right, after all! Before he came out of the woods, he ran into her. She was carrying a book, *Gertrude Colbjørnsen*, by Skram.

For a while they talked about the book. Then she blurted out: "Our dog is dead. It just doesn't seem possible!"

"He is?" was all Nagel said.

"It happened a couple of days ago. We found him stiff and stone-cold. I can't imagine how it could have happened."

"I always had the feeling that the dog was a nasty

creature. I'm sorry, but he was one of those flat-nosed mastiffs whose faces look so appallingly human. When he looked at you, his jowls drooped as if he were carrying the woes of the world. I'm rather glad he's dead."

"How can you say such a thing!"

But he interrupted her; he seemed nervous and anxious to change the subject as quickly as possible. He launched into a long discourse about a man he had once known, who was one of the most hilarious characters in the world. "The man s-stuttered a bit and made no attempt to hide it; on the contrary, he seemed to exaggerate it to call attention to his affliction. He had the strangest notions about women. There was a story about Mexico that he told in a most amusing way. It seems that one winter it was terribly cold there—so cold that the thermometers kept cracking, and everyone stayed indoors. But one day he had to go to the neighboring town. He was walking through a more or less deserted area that only had a cabin here and there, the bitter wind lashing at his face. As he was struggling along in the icy cold, a woman—only half dressed—came dashing out of one of the cabins and ran after him, shouting: 'Your nose is frostbitten! Take care; you've got frostbite!' The woman had seen the stranger walk by with his nose all red and had run from her chores to warn him! Isn't that something? And there she stood in the biting wind with her arms bare and her right cheek turning white and becoming one huge blob from the cold! Can you believe it! Yet, in spite of that experience and many other instances he'd witnessed of feminine self-sacrifice, this stutterer was a confirmed misogynist. 'Woman is a strange, insatiable creature,' he'd say, without explaining why he thought her strange or insatiable. 'The things a woman imagines are beyond belief,' he'd add. This is how he told me another story: 'I had a friend who fell in love with a young lady by the name of Klara. He made great efforts to win her affection, but to no avail. Klara wouldn't have anything to do with him, though he was handsome and had an impeccable reputation. Klara had a sister, hunchbacked and terribly ugly—she was positively grotesque. One day my friend proposed to her; God only knows why he did it. Perhaps he had an ulterior motive, or it could be that he had fallen in love with her despite her ugliness. And what do you think Klara did? The female in her showed her claws. She screamed; she made dreadful scenes. "It was me he wanted all along," she cried. "But not for anything in the world would I accept his proposal." And do you think he was allowed to have the sister, with whom he had in fact fallen in love? Ah, there's the rub. Klara wouldn't let her sister have him either. Of course he wanted Klara, but having been rejected by her, he couldn't even have her hunchbacked sister, though no one else wanted her. And so my friend didn't get either girl.' This was one of the many stories the stutterer told me. His speech defect made them all the more amusing. He was a curious creature. Am I boring you?"

"No," said Dagny.

"He was certainly an odd character. He was a tightwad and a thief—so much so that he would remove the straps from a train compartment and take them home, where he would find some use for them. He stopped at nothing. As a matter of fact, I think he was once caught doing just that. Yet, when he was in a certain mood, he couldn't care less about money. Once he got it into his head to organize an excursion. He didn't have any companions, but he hired twenty-four carriages, which he dispatched one by one.

Twenty-three of them were empty, and in the last one, the twenty-fourth, he sat alone, looking down at the pedestrians, elated at the sensation he was creating."

Nagel embarked on one subject after another, but Dagny scarcely listened. Finally he stopped talking and was silent. Damn it, why was he always making a fool of himself, letting his tongue run away with him! To rant on to a young lady—one whom he loved—about frostbite and twenty-four carriages! Then he recalled that once before he had made a fool of himself with a stupid story about an Eskimo and a blotter. His cheeks flushed at the thought. He made an abrupt movement and almost stopped walking. Why the hell did he have to rattle on like that? God, he was ashamed of himself! These sudden streaks of rambling humiliated him, made him ridiculous, set him back weeks and months. What must she think of him!

"When is the bazaar?" he asked.

"Why do you make such an effort at conversation?" she replied, smiling. "Why are you so on edge?"

Her words were so unexpected that for a moment he looked at her in astonishment. In a hushed voice, his heart pounding, he said: "Miss Kielland, the last time we met I promised that I would talk about everything except the one subject you have forbidden me to mention. I'm trying to keep my promise, and so far, I have."

"Yes, we have to keep our promises—we mustn't break our word." She seemed to be talking more to herself than to him.

"Before I saw you, I made up my mind to try; I knew that I would meet you."

"How could you possibly know that?"

"I saw your footprints on the road."

She gave him a quick look but said nothing.

After a moment she said: "Your hand is bandaged. Did you hurt yourself?"

"Yes. Your dog bit me."

They both stopped and looked at each other. He wrung his hands and, beside himself, cried out: "I've been in these woods every night. Every evening before I go to bed, I come here to gaze up at your windows. Forgive me, but it's not a crime! You forbade me, but I just couldn't help it. The dog bit me, in self-defense. I killed him; I poisoned him because he always barked when I came to say good night at your window."

"So it was you who killed the dog!" she exclaimed.

"Yes."

Pause.

They stood there staring at each other. He was breathing heavily. "And I'm capable of even worse to get you to pay attention to me," he said. "You have no idea how I've suffered, how my thoughts are filled with you day and night. You couldn't possibly understand. I talk to people, I laugh, I even give splendid parties; last night I had one that lasted until four in the morning. We ended up smashing all the glasses. But even as I'm drinking and carousing, you are ever in my thoughts, and it's driving me out of my mind. I'm neglecting all my affairs, and I don't know how it will end. Please bear with me for two minutes; there is something I must tell you. But don't be afraid—I'm not trying to frighten you or seduce you, I just have to talk to you—I must!"

"But I thought you were going to stop this foolishness!" she said heatedly. "You promised."

"Yes, I guess I did; I'm not sure what I promised, but perhaps it was to be sensible. It's so difficult, but I'll behave myself; I promise. But how can I? Tell me! Teach me how! Do you know that one day I almost forced my way into the parsonage! I was ready to walk right in on you even if you had had visitors. I fought against that impulse with all my might, believe me. And all the while I have been saying unkind things about you, trying to break your spell over me by maligning you. I didn't do it out of a desire for vengeance; you must see that I'm close to breaking down. I did it to assert myself in the hope that I'd build up some self-respect and not lose face completely. That was my reason; but I'm not sure that I've succeeded. I've also tried to leave town; I started to pack but I couldn't finish, and I didn't leave. How could I go away! I would be more likely to pursue you if you weren't close by. And even if I never found you, I would go on searching for you, hoping to find you at last. But when it became futile, I'd gradually lose all hope, and then I'd be enormously grateful simply to meet someone who had been near you—a woman friend with whom you had laughed, whose hand you had touched. How could I possibly leave? Besides, summer is here; the forest is my place of worship and the birds know me. They greet me every morning; they cock their heads, look at me, and start to sing. I'll never forget the sight of the flags flying in your honor the evening I arrived. It made such a deep impression on me; I felt as if I, too, were being welcomed, and I walked around the ship in a daze, looking at the flags before I went ashore. I'll never forget that evening! But I've had many happy moments here. Every day I walk along the same roads as you, and sometimes I'm lucky enough to see your footprints, as I did today. Then, as I've done today, I wait for your return. I hide behind a rock in the woods and wait for you. I've seen you twice since our last meeting, and once I had to wait six hours before you came. I lay behind the rock all that time and didn't get up once, because I was afraid you'd come by and see me. God knows what kept you so long that day."

"I was at the Andresens'," she put in quickly.

"That may be. But when you finally walked by, I saw you. You weren't alone; I greeted you from behind my rock in a whisper. God knows what flashed through your mind at that moment—perhaps it was telepathy—but you turned and glanced at my rock."

"Oh, you look as horrified as if I had just pronounced your death sentence!"

"But you just did. I know that very well. Your eyes turned icy cold."

"There has to be an end to this, Mr. Nagel. If you think about it, you'll realize that you're not behaving in a proper manner toward my fiancé. Put yourself in his place—to say nothing of the pain and embarrassment you are causing me. What do you want of me! Once and for all, I love my fiancé, and I have no intention of breaking off my engagement. I hope I have made myself clear. But please, no more outbursts of this kind. I can't walk with you unless you respect my feelings. I mean that."

She was very upset; her lips trembled and she was obviously trying to hold back her tears. When Nagel didn't answer, she said: "You may walk me all the way home if you like—that is, if you won't make us both miserable. I would like you to tell me a story. I enjoy hearing you talk."

"Of course!" he almost shouted, overjoyed that he'd been allowed to keep talking. "Anything, as long as I can be with you! When you're so angry and give me one of those icy stares, you make my blood run cold."

For a time their conversation was casual; they walked

at such a slow pace that they scarcely covered any ground at all.

"What a wonderful smell!" he exclaimed. "You can almost see the grass and flowers sprouting after the rain. Are you fond of trees? It may sound strange, but I feel as if I had a secret bond with every tree in the forest. It's almost as if I had been part of them at one time. As I look around, a flood of memory seems to surge through me. Let's stop for a moment. Listen! How joyously the birds greet the sun! They are so ecstatic that they almost fly into our faces in delirium."

They walked on.

"I find myself still thinking of the lovely image you painted of the boat and the blue-silk, crescent-shaped sail," she said. "It was so beautiful, and when the sky seems very far away, I imagine myself floating up there fishing with a silver hook."

He was delighted that she still remembered his Midsummer Eve fantasy. Deeply touched, tears in his eyes, he answered: "Yes, and you would be the one sitting in the boat."

When they were about half way into the woods, she cast caution aside and asked him how long he would be staying in town. She immediately regretted the question and would have tried to rephrase it but was put at ease when he smiled and evaded it. She was grateful for his sensitivity; he surely must have noticed her embarrassment.

"I want to stay here near you," he said. "I'll stay as long as my funds last—but that won't be too long," he added.

She smiled at him and said: "You say it won't be too long? But I've heard that you're rich!"

His expression again became inscrutable as he answered: "Am I rich? Yes, there seems to be a story going around town that I have money and property of some value. It just isn't true. I don't have any property to speak of, except for a small piece of land that I own jointly with my sister. But that's a total loss because of debts and mortgages. That's the truth."

Her laugh had undertones of disbelief. "Well, you usually tell the truth about yourself, don't you?" she said.

"You don't believe me? Let me tell you the facts, although it's very embarrassing. You may have heard that the first day I was here I walked five miles to the next town. From there I sent myself three telegrams referring to a large sum of money and an estate in Finland. Then I left the telegrams open on the table in my room for everyone to see. Do you believe me now? Now do you see what started the rumor about my having money?"

"Assuming of course that you're not putting yourself down again."

"Again, Miss Kielland? I swear by all that's holy that I'm telling the truth!"

Pause.

"But why did you do it? Why did you send those telegrams to yourself?"

"It's a long story. But to make it short, I wanted to create an impression—make myself look important. That was the reason."

"Now you're lying!"

"I swear to you that I'm not!"

Pause.

"You're a strange man. God only knows what you expect to achieve by that. One minute you're bold enough to talk passionately about love. Then when I try to reason with you, you turn around and assume the role of a charlatan, a liar, a cheat. Why don't you stop it? Neither pose makes any impression on me. You see, I'm just an average human being; all these flights of fancy are lost on me."

All of a sudden she seemed to have taken offense.

"I wasn't trying to be clever. Since all is lost in any case, why should I make any effort?"

"But why do you persist in telling all these terrible things about yourself?" she cried vehemently.

Slowly, and completely in control of himself, he answered: "To make an impression on you, Miss Kielland."

Again they came to a halt and stared at each other. He went on: "Once before, you were kind enough to listen to me when I told you what my aims were. You ask why I still make confessions that put me in a bad light, confessions I could easily have kept to myself? My answer is that it's part of the scheme—I'm doing it deliberately. I'm hoping, despite your remarks to the contrary, that my complete frankness will make some impression on you. Anyway, perhaps you'll feel a certain respect for my utter honesty. Maybe I'm wrong, but I couldn't have acted otherwise. Even if I could, you're beyond reach and I've got nothing to lose. I am taking a last desperate chance. I provide you with strong arguments against me and so help you in your determination to send me away. Why do I do it? Because my wretched soul won't let me plead my own case and profit by such cheap means. I just couldn't do it. But perhaps you feel that I'm trying to achieve by guileful and devious means something that others gain by being bold and straightforward? No, I won't even bother to defend myself. Call it fraud if you like. Why not? That's the word for it. To put it stronger still, it's the lowest kind of deception. All right, I don't deny it. I am a phony.

But we're all phony to a greater or lesser extent; since that is a fact, one form of deceit is no worse than another.

"I'm feeling in the mood to talk—I'd like to speak frankly for a moment. On second thought, no. Good God, how sick I am of everything! If only there were a way of getting out! Incidentally, who would ever have supposed that there's anything wrong with the Stenersen marriage? I'm not saying that there is anything wrong in that respectable household, you understand; I'm just wondering if the thought would ever occur to anyone. There are only the two of them, no children, no major problems, but there may be a third person involved—who knows? Perhaps a young man who's become too intimate a friend— I'm speaking of Reinert, the deputy. Who are we to judge? There are probably faults on both sides. Maybe the doctor is aware of the situation but powerless to do anything about it. Anyway, he drank a great deal last night and was so fed up with everything and everybody that he prescribed prussic acid for the whole human race and to hell with everything! Poor man! But he isn't the only one who's knee-deep in hypocrisy, even if I exclude myself— Nagel—because I'm up to my waist in it. And what about The Midget—a kind and just man, a martyr! He is a good soul, but I'm keeping an eye on him—I'm watching him. I'm telling you, I have my eye on him! You seem surprised. Did I shock you? I didn't mean to. Let me reassure you; The Midget can't be corrupted. He is a completely honest man. Then why don't I let him out of my sight? Why do I spy on him from around a corner at two o'clock in the morning when he comes home from an innocent walk—at 2 A.M.? And why do I keep my eyes peeled when he carries his sacks of coal around, greeting people in the street? No reason whatever. He just happens to interest me, that's all. I like him, and at the moment he represents truth and righteousness in the midst of all this phoniness. That's why I mentioned him, and I'm sure you understand what I mean. But to come back to myself—no, I don't want to come back to myself, anything but that!"

This last remark was so filled with anguish that her heart went out to him. She was suddenly struck by the realization that this was a tortured, shattered human being. But when he immediately tried to mitigate the reaction his outcry had produced in her by suddenly laughing harshly at nothing at all, and repeating that life was nothing but a hollow mockery, her compassion quickly vanished.

"You made some remarks about Mrs. Stenersen which were not only in bad taste but extremely crude besides," she said angrily. "And then you try to make yourself important at the expense of a poor cripple like The Midget. It was a mean and shabby thing to do." She walked on and he kept pace with her. He made no reply but kept his eyes to the ground. His shoulders trembled, and to her astonishment she saw tears running down his cheeks. To hide his emotion, he turned and whistled at a bird.

They walked on for a few minutes, neither of them saying anything. Again she was filled with compassion and regretted her outburst. Perhaps what he said was true—how was she to know? Wasn't it possible that this man had seen as much in a few weeks as she had in as many years?

They continued walking in silence. He had regained his composure and was toying with his handkerchief. In a few minutes they would be in sight of the parsonage.

She broke the silence, saying: "Is your hand badly hurt? Let me see."

She stopped. Whether she wanted to show concern or had weakened momentarily was hard to tell, but her words were sincere, almost affectionate.

Now he lost control of his emotions. She stood so close to him, with her head bending over his hand so that he caught the scent of her hair and neck, and without a word spoken between them, his passion overwhelmed him. With one arm around her, he pressed her close to him, and when she resisted, he held her tight against him with both arms, almost lifting her off her feet. He felt her back grow limp as she succumbed to his embrace. She didn't move away but looked up at him with misty eyes. He murmured words of endearment and said that he would love her until the day he died. One man had already given his life for her, and he would do the same at only a nod, a word from her. He loved her to distraction! As he held her tighter still, he whispered tenderly: "I love you, I love you!"

She no longer resisted. Her head rested on his left arm as he kissed her passionately, between words of love. He felt her cling to him, and her eyes closed even more as he kissed her.

"Meet me tomorrow by the tree—you remember the one—the aspen. Meet me! I love you, Dagny. Will you come? Come when you can—come at seven."

She didn't answer but said quietly: "Let me go now." Slowly she freed herself from his embrace. For a moment she stood there looking around, bewildered and confused. Then her lips began to tremble. She made her way to a stone by the roadside and sank down, sobbing. He leaned over her, speaking in a low voice. After a minute or so, she leaped up, her face white with rage, and pressing her clenched fists against her breasts, she cried: "You're rotten through and through. My God, what a low creature you are—though I'm sure not in *your* opinion! How could you—oh, how could you!"

And she began crying again.

Again he tried to soothe her, but to no avail. For a half hour they stood there by the roadside without moving.

"After what's happened, you dare ask me to meet you again? Never! I don't ever want to lay eyes on you again! You're a scoundrel!"

He pleaded with her, got on his knees and kissed her dress, but she only repeated what a scoundrel he was, how outrageous his behavior had been. What had he done to her! She ordered him to leave and forbade him to follow her one step further.

And she started to walk toward the parsonage.

He still tried to follow her, but she stopped him with a gesture of her hand, crying: "Don't come near me!"

He stood there watching her until she had walked twenty paces or so, and then he too clenched his fists, ran after her, and forced her to stop.

"I don't want to hurt you," he said. "But have pity on me! I'm willing to kill myself right here, on the spot, just to rid you of my presence. All you have to do is say the word. And I would repeat this tomorrow if I met you. But in the name of humanity, you must give me a chance. Listen to me, in the name of justice! You have such power over me that I am putty in your hands. And it isn't entirely my fault that you came into my life. I hope to God that you may never suffer as I am suffering now."

With that he turned and walked away.

The broad shoulders on his short, sturdy body were shaking as he disappeared down the road. He looked straight through the people he met, not recognizing anyone. Only after he had walked through the town and reached the hotel did he regain control of himself.

15

FOR the next three days Nagel was not to be seen in the town. He had locked the door to his room at the hotel and left by the steamer. No one knew where he had gone, except that it was somewhere up north. Perhaps he had taken a brief holiday.

He returned very early one morning, looking pale and tired. He didn't go directly to the hotel but paced up and down the dock and then took the new road along the fjord, where the smoke was just beginning to rise from the mill chimney.

He ambled around, obviously trying to while away a few hours. When the town came to life, he stationed himself at the post office by the marketplace. His eyes carefully scrutinized the passers-by, and when he caught sight of Martha Gude's green skirt, he immediately walked up to her.

Perhaps she didn't remember him? His name was Nagel—he was the one who had made a bid on her chair. Was it sold already?

No, she hadn't sold it.

That was good news. And no one else had been there to bid on it in excess of what he had offered? There had been no visits from collectors of antique furniture?

"Yes, someone came, but . . ."

"You had a client? A lady, did you say? Those darned women, always poking their noses into everything! This one probably got wind of the rare piece and immediately felt that she had to have it. That's the way these women operate! How much did she bid? How high did she go? But remember, I won't relinquish my option on that chair for anything!"

He was obviously so upset that Martha answered quickly: "It's yours, of course."

"Then may I call on you this evening so that we can settle everything?"

"Yes, but wouldn't it be better if I sent the chair to the hotel?"

"Out of the question. An object like that should be handled by experienced hands. As a matter of fact, I should prefer that no one see it. I'll be back around eight o'clock. Incidentally, please don't try to dust or clean it— and for heaven's sake don't even think of using water on it!"

Nagel went back to the hotel and without removing his clothes lay down and slept until evening.

When he finished dinner, he walked down to Martha Gude's cottage on the dock. It was then eight o'clock. He knocked and walked in.

The room was freshly cleaned; the floor was spotless and the windows sparkled. Martha was even wearing a necklace. He was obviously expected.

After greetings and some small talk, he sat down and started to talk business. She wouldn't give in but insisted more tenaciously than ever on making him a gift of the chair. Finally he became furious and threatened to throw five hundred crowns in her face and make off with the chair. She had asked for it! Banging his fist on the table, he told her that she was out of her mind and that he had never met anyone like her.

His eyes fixed on her, he remarked: "You know, your stubbornness is really giving me second thoughts about that chair. I wonder if the price we have agreed on is a fair one, after all? In my business I deal with all kinds of people and one can never be too careful. If you have acquired the chair in a dishonest way, I won't touch it. But if I have misinterpreted your reluctance to sell it, please forgive me."

He implored her to tell him the truth.

Bewildered, frightened, and offended by his suspicions, she spoke up in her own defense. The chair had been bought by her grandfather and had been in the possession of her family for a hundred years. There was nothing to hide. As she talked, her eyes filled with tears.

He wanted to settle the matter once and for all, he said, taking out his wallet.

She took a step toward him as if to stop him, but he placed two bills on the table and snapped his wallet shut.

"Now that's all settled," he said.

"Please don't give me more than fifty crowns," she begged, and in her confusion she touched his hair in a pleading gesture. She didn't seem to be aware of what she was doing and went on stroking his hair, imploring him to settle for fifty crowns. The silly woman still had tears in her eyes.

He looked at her intently. This penniless, white-haired spinster of forty had fire in her eyes, but still there was something about her that made him think of a nun. Her strange, exotic beauty touched something in him, and for a moment he, too, was confused. He took her hand and said: "What an odd creature you are!" Yet the next moment he got up, abruptly letting go of her hand.

"I hope you have no objection to my taking the chair with me now," he said, laying hands on it.

She was, obviously, no longer afraid of him. Noticing that his hands were getting dirty from touching the chair, she pulled out a handkerchief from her pocket and gave it to him to wipe his hands on.

The money was still lying on the table.

"By the way," he said, "don't you think it would be wiser not to mention our little transaction? There's no reason for the whole town to know about it, is there?"

"No," she said quietly.

"I think you ought to put the money away at once," he said. "But first you'd better hang something in front of the window—take that skirt."

"But it will make the room so dark, won't it?" Nevertheless, with his help she fastened the skirt in front of the window.

"We should have done this right away," he said. "I shouldn't be seen here."

She didn't answer but picked up the money from the table. She took his hand and her lips moved, but she didn't utter a word.

Holding her hand, he said impulsively: "Excuse me for

asking, but are you having trouble making ends meet? I mean, without some assistance. —Or perhaps you are receiving assistance of some kind?"

"Yes."

"Do forgive me for asking, but it just occurred to me that if it becomes known that you have some money, your benefits may stop. That's why it's important to keep our little business deal a secret. You do agree, don't you? I'm a practical man and I do hope that you'll take my advice; don't tell anyone about this. While I think of it, I'd better give you smaller notes, so that you won't have to get change."

He had carefully thought out every move. He sat down again and began counting out bills of smaller denomination. He counted them perfunctorily, gathered them together, and handed them to her.

"Now hide these carefully," he said.

She turned away from him, loosened her bodice, and tucked the notes inside.

When this was done, he still made no move to get up but went on sitting there. After a moment or so, he said casually: "By the way, do you know The Midget?"

He noticed that she blushed.

"I've had occasion to meet him several times," Nagel remarked. "I'm quite fond of him. He seems to be a fine fellow. I've just asked him to find me a violin. I'm sure he'll manage that all right, don't you think? But perhaps you don't know him?"

"Yes, I do."

"Of course. Now I remember him telling me that he had bought some flowers from you for a funeral—Karlsen's funeral. Maybe you even know him quite well? What do you think of him? Do you think that he'll be able to find me that violin? When one must deal with as many people as I do, one must take certain precautions. I once lost a sum of money because I trusted a man blindly and didn't bother to find out anything about him; that was in Hamburg."

And Nagel proceeded to tell the story of the man who had caused him to lose money.

Martha stood facing him, leaning against the table. She seemed nervous and finally blurted out abruptly: "Don't talk about him!"

"About whom?"

"About Johannes—The Midget."

"Is his name really Johannes?"

"Yes, Johannes."

Nagel didn't say anything, but the expression on his face indicated that he was startled by this bit of information. For a while he sat there speechless and then he said: "And how come *you* call him Johannes, not Grøgaard or The Midget?"

Embarrassed, she looked down and mumbled: "We've known each other since childhood."

Pause.

Then casually, and in a jocular tone, he said: "Do you know, I have the feeling that The Midget is deeply in love with you? That's how it strikes me. I must say I'm not surprised, though I think it's pretty bold of him. Don't you agree? In the first place, he is no longer young, and besides, he is a bit deformed. But God knows, women are strange creatures! If something catches their fancy, they are capable of throwing themselves away with joyful abandon. That's the way they are.

"I saw an instance of this once in 1886 when a girl I knew up and married her father's errand boy—that was really something! He was an apprentice, about sixteen or seventeen, with a face as smooth as a girl's, good-looking, and with a great deal of charm—that couldn't be denied. Well, she threw herself at this kid and they went abroad together. After about six months she came back—alone, disillusioned with love. Sad, isn't it? For the next few months she was bored to death. Since she was a married woman, she was out of circulation. Then one day she made up her mind—kicked over the traces, began running around with students and salesmen, and ended up being called 'La Glu.' It was pathetic. But once again she surprised everyone. After she lived this wild life for a couple of years, she suddenly began to write novels and was generally considered to be quite talented. Her two years with students and salesmen had given her experience and maturity which she was able to translate into her novels—and she wrote some that were very good! She turned out to be a remarkable woman! Well, that's the way you women are. You laugh, but you can't deny it! An errand boy of seventeen can make you all lose your heads! I'm sure The Midget doesn't have to go through life alone either, if he makes an effort and shapes up. There is something about him that impresses even a man—even me. He is pure at heart, and there isn't a trace of deceit in him. You know him intimately and you know that I'm right, don't you? But what about his uncle, the coal merchant? I have the feeling that he's a sly old rascal—a disagreeable character. It's obvious to me that it's The Midget who keeps the business going and I ask myself why he shouldn't be capable of running a business of his own. In any case, The Midget is perfectly able to support a family . . . You shake your head?"

"No, I didn't."

"Well, I understand. You're getting bored and annoyed by all this talk about a man who doesn't concern you, and I don't blame you. By the way, don't be angry, I'm only thinking of you, but you ought to lock your door at night. You look so frightened! Please don't be, and especially not of me. I just wanted to warn you now that you have money around. I've never heard any talk that this town isn't safe, but one can never be too careful. At two o'clock in the morning it's pretty dark around here, and sometimes I hear the oddest noises outside my window. I hope you aren't angry with me for giving you this bit of advice? I'm glad that I was finally able to persuade you to part with the chair.

"Well, goodby, my dear," he said, taking her hand. "On second thought, you'd better say that I gave you a couple of crowns for the chair, but not a shilling more, remember. I can rely on you, can't I?"

"Yes," she said.

Once outside, he chuckled to himself, laughing aloud as though he had pulled off a clever trick. "God, how happy she is now," he said to himself, obviously relishing the thought. "She won't be able to sleep tonight because of all that money!"

When he got back to the hotel, The Midget was waiting for him. He had come from a rehearsal and had a bundle of posters under one arm. Yes, the tableaux would certainly be a success. They consisted of various historical scenes and would be spotlighted in different colors. He, The Midget, had a walk-on part.

When was the opening of the bazaar?

On Thursday, July 9—the Queen's birthday. That evening The Midget was going to start putting up posters all over. They even had permission to put one up by the cemetery gate. But his reason for coming was to report on the violin. He hadn't been able to find one anywhere. The only decent violin in town wasn't for sale. It belonged to the organist, who needed it for the bazaar; he was going to play a few selections.

Well, it couldn't be helped.

The Midget was standing there, cap in hand, just about to leave, when Nagel said: "How about a drink? I've had a stroke of luck and I'm in a very good mood this evening. After a great deal of trouble I've acquired a chair that no collector in this country can match. Have a look at it! Do you know a treasure when you see one? It's Dutch—the workmanship is unique. I wouldn't sell it for anything! I would like to celebrate by having a drink with you. Shall I ring? No? But you can put up those posters tomorrow! I can't stop thinking how lucky I was today. Perhaps you didn't know that I'm something of a collector and that I'm here to see what I can find. Have I told you about my cowbells? Well, I see you don't know anything about me. I'm an agronomist, of course, but I have other interests as well. Thus far I've collected two hundred and sixty-seven cowbells. I began ten years ago and now, I'm happy to say, I have a very fine collection. And do you know how I came upon this chair? It was pure luck. One day when I was walking along the street, I happened to pass a small house down by the docks, and as I went by, I looked in the window without thinking. What I saw made me stop in my tracks. The chair was there and I immediately realized its value. I knocked at the door and a white-haired lady of a certain age answered—what was her name? I've forgotten. Well, it doesn't matter. You probably don't know her. Miss Gude, I think it was—Martha Gude, or something like that . . . anyway, she didn't want to part with the chair. But I worked on her until I got her to promise to let me have it, and today I went to fetch it. But, can you imagine, I got it for nothing—she *gave* it to me! Of course I put a couple of crowns on the table to keep her from having any regrets, but the chair is worth hundreds. Please don't mention this to anybody; I don't want to get a bad reputation around here—not that I have anything to reproach myself for. The lady didn't understand the value of the piece, and since I'm a connoisseur and a buyer, I didn't feel it was up to me to look out for her interests. One must use one's head, take advantage of every opportunity—the age-old struggle for survival, you know . . . But surely you can't refuse to drink a glass of wine with me, now that you know the story?"

The Midget insisted that he had to leave.

"I'm sorry," said Nagel. "I had been looking forward to having a talk with you. You're the only man around here who interests me—the only one worth keeping an eye on—keeping an eye on, I said, ha ha. And your name is Johannes? My dear friend, I've known it all along, though no one had told me until tonight. But don't let me frighten you. Unfortunately, I always seem to scare people. You looked terrified just now, though you tried to hide it."

The Midget had gotten as far as the door. He obviously wanted to end the conversation and get out as fast as possible. Things were getting more unpleasant by the minute.

"Is today July 6?" Nagel asked abruptly.

"Why, yes," said The Midget. "It's the sixth of July." He now had his hand on the door handle.

Nagel slowly walked up to him until they almost touched, staring him straight in the eyes, his hands behind his back. Without moving a muscle, he whispered: "And where were you on June 6?"

The Midget was dumbstruck. Those staring eyes and that mysterious whisper filled him with terror, and unable to grasp the insistent query about a date a month earlier, he hastily opened the door and stumbled out into the hallway. As he was trying to pull himself together and find the stairs, Nagel called to him from the door: "It was all a mistake. Please forget it. I'll explain some other time!"

But The Midget neither saw nor heard. By the time Nagel finished speaking, he was already downstairs. Looking neither right nor left, he dashed into the street, across the marketplace, and over to the big pump, where he took the first turn and disappeared.

An hour later—at ten o'clock—Nagel lit a cigar and went out. The town was still full of life. People were strolling along the road that led to the parsonage, and the streets echoed with the laughter of children playing. On this pleasant summer evening, men and women were sitting on the steps of their houses, chatting in subdued voices. Now and then someone would call out to a neighbor on the other side of the street, who would send back a jovial rejoinder.

Nagel strolled down toward the dock. He saw The Midget putting up posters on the walls of the post office, the bank, the school, and the jail. How carefully and conscientiously he was doing his job! He put all of himself into what he was doing and didn't seem concerned about the time, though it was late and he must be tired. Nagel greeted him as he walked by, but didn't stop.

When he was almost at the dock, someone stopped

him: it was Martha Gude, and quite out of breath she exclaimed: "Excuse me, but you gave me far too much money."

"Good evening," he said by way of reply. "Are you also taking a walk?"

"No, I've been to town; I was waiting for you outside your hotel. You gave me too much money."

"Are we going to start that all over again?"

"But you made a mistake!" she cried in dismay. "There were more than two hundred crowns in small notes."

"So there were a few crowns over and above the two hundred? Well, in that case, you can return them to me."

She began to undo her bodice but then checked herself and looked around, confused. Again she apologized; there were so many people around. Maybe she couldn't take out the money right here; she had it so well hidden.

"No," he said quickly. "I can come along and get it." And together they walked back to her house. On the way they met several people, who looked at them curiously.

When Nagel came into her room, he went over and sat down by the window where he had been sitting before; the skirt was still hanging there. While Martha was busy getting out the money, he said nothing. Not until she had handed him the worn and faded ten-crown notes, which were still warm from her bosom, and which her honesty wouldn't permit her to have even overnight, did he ask her to keep the money.

But, now as before, she seemed to suspect his intentions. Giving him a bewildered look, she said: "I don't understand you . . ."

He got up abruptly.

"But I understand you perfectly," he said. "That is why I am heading for the door. Does that reassure you?"

"Yes—no, please don't stand at the door," she said, stretching both arms out toward him. This singular spinster was much too afraid of offending anyone.

"I have a favor to ask of you," Nagel said, still standing. "You'd give me great pleasure if you would . . . I would find some way of repaying you—that is, I would like you to come to the bazaar on Thursday evening. Will you? It would amuse you—there will be lots of people, lights, music, and of course the tableaux. Please come—you won't regret it. Why are you laughing? My God, how white your teeth are!"

"I don't go out," she said. "What makes you think that I could go there—and why should I? Why would you want me to go?"

He talked to her in an open and straightforward manner. He had been thinking about it for a long time. The idea had come to him a couple of weeks ago, but it had slipped his mind until now. She had only to show up and mingle with the crowd; he would like her to come. If she wished, he wouldn't even speak to her; he didn't want to embarrass her—that wasn't his intention. But it would give him pleasure to see her with other people and hear her laugh, see her looking young. She simply had to come!

He looked at her closely. Her hair was snowy white—and those dark eyes! One hand was fumbling with the buttons of her dress. It was a delicate hand with long fingers—not very white; perhaps it wasn't quite clean, but it made a strangely chaste impression. Along the wrist, two blue veins protruded slightly.

Yes, she said, it might be amusing. But she didn't have any clothes—no dress to wear on an occasion like that.

He cut her short. Thursday was still three days off. That would give her enough time. Was it settled then?

Gradually she gave in.

One mustn't isolate oneself completely, he said. There was nothing to be gained by that. And besides, with her eyes, her teeth—it would be a shame. Those bills on the table were for the dress—no nonsense now! Besides, the whole thing was his idea and she was doing it to please him.

He said good night quickly, so that she wouldn't have the slightest cause to feel uneasy. But as she saw him to the door it was she who held out her hand to thank him for inviting her to the bazaar. Nothing like this had happened to her for years. She wasn't used to going out, but he would see—she would behave very well.

What a child she was, offering to behave though he hadn't even asked her to!

16

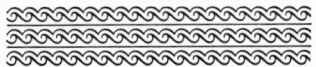

THURSDAY. It rained a bit, but in spite of that the bazaar opened with a band and crowds of people. The whole town had turned out, and people had come in from the country to take part in this unusual event.

When Johan Nagel arrived at nine o'clock, the hall was packed. He found a place near the door where he stood for a few minutes listening to a speech. He was pale, and as usual he was wearing his yellow suit. He had removed the bandage from his hand: the two punctures were almost healed.

Dr. and Mrs. Stenersen were on the stage; to the right of them was The Midget with the other participants in the tableaux. But Dagny was not to be seen. The heat from the lamps and the crush of people soon made Nagel leave the hall. At the door he met Deputy Reinert and bowed, but his greeting was barely acknowledged by a nod. He remained standing at the entrance.

Then he happened to see something which totally absorbed his attention and aroused his curiosity. To his left there was an open door leading to a cloakroom, and by the light of the lamp he clearly saw Dagny Kielland standing there touching his coat, which he had hung on a peg. He couldn't possibly be mistaken. No one in town had a coat like that. It was definitely his—besides, he remembered exactly where he had hung it. She could have no reason for being there, yet she seemed to be looking for something and was apparently taking the opportunity to run her hands along his coat. He quickly turned away so as not to catch her in the act.

The incident troubled him. What was she looking for and why was she interested in his coat? He kept thinking about it, he couldn't dismiss it from his mind. Who knows, perhaps she was only looking to see if he had a pistol in his pocket. She probably thought him mad enough to do anything. But maybe she had slipped a letter into his pocket? He actually began to daydream about this happy impossibility. No, she had probably been looking for her cloak; it was only a coincidence. How could he allow himself to indulge in such fantasies! But a few minutes later, on seeing Dagny making her way through the hall, he slipped out and went through his coat pockets, his heart pounding. No letter, nothing except his gloves and his handkerchief.

Suddenly there was a round of applause in the hall. The mayor had just finished his opening speech. The audience was spilling out into the corridors, the cloakrooms, anywhere where they could get a breath of air. Then they settled down at the tables along the wall and ordered refreshments. Several of the young girls from town, dressed as waitresses, with napkins on their arms, ran around with trays and glasses.

Nagel went looking for Dagny but didn't see her anywhere. He greeted Miss Andresen, who also had a white apron on; he ordered wine but she brought him champagne.

He looked at her in surprise.

"But you never drink anything else," she said with a smile.

This somewhat impudent remark brought him to life. He asked her to join him and she sat down, though she was very busy. He was appreciative when she accepted, complimented her on her dress, and was fascinated by an old filigree brooch she was wearing. She was a handsome girl; her long, aristocratic face with its prominent nose was delicately chiseled—it looked almost fragile—and there was no mobility in her face, no change of expression. She spoke quietly and with reserve. One felt comfortable in her presence. She was a woman and a lady.

When she got up, he said: "There is someone coming here this evening whom I should like to do something for. Her name is Miss Gude, Martha Gude—perhaps you know her. I'd like to show her a little kindness. She is so lonely—The Midget has told me something about her. Would it be all right if I asked her to join us? That is, of course, if you have no objection."

"Not at all," Miss Andresen replied. "I'll be glad to go and look for her. I know where she is sitting."

"You will come back too, won't you?"

"Yes, thank you."

While Nagel was waiting, Reinert, Holtan, and Dagny came in. Dagny was as pale as himself, despite the heat.

She was wearing a yellow dress with short sleeves, and a heavy gold chain around her neck which was most unbecoming. She stopped for a moment in the doorway and, with one hand behind her, toyed with her braid.

Nagel went up to her. Urgently and passionately he asked her to forgive him for his behavior last Friday. It would never happen again; she would never again have any cause to forgive him for anything. His voice was subdued, and after having said these few words, he paused.

She listened; she even looked at him as he spoke, and when he finished, she said: "I'm not sure I know what you're talking about; I've forgotten it; I *want* to forget it."

Then she walked away with an air of complete indifference.

One could hear the mingled sound of voices, the clinking of china and glasses, the popping of corks, laughter, shouting; from the hall came the echoes of the town brass band, which played very badly.

Miss Andresen and Martha came in, accompanied by The Midget. For about fifteen minutes they sat at Nagel's table. Miss Andresen kept getting up to serve coffee. Finally she got so many orders that she disappeared altogether.

Then the program began: a quartet sang, Øien recited one of his poems in a stentorian voice, two ladies played the piano, and the organist gave his first violin solo. Dagny was still sitting there with Reinert and Holtan. Then someone came for The Midget. There were things for him to do; more glasses and cups were needed, and more sandwiches. They had underestimated the turnout of a small town like this.

When Martha found herself alone with Nagel, she also

got up to leave. She couldn't stay, especially since she had noticed Mr. Reinert making remarks which made Miss Kielland laugh. She'd better go.

But Nagel persuaded her to have one more glass. Her new dress fitted very well but didn't suit her. It made this curious woman look older and contrasted harshly with her white hair. But her eyes were full of fire, and when she laughed, her expressive face became quite animated.

"Are you having a good time?" he asked.

"Yes, thank you. I'm enjoying the evening very much."

He focused all his attention on her, choosing topics of conversation that would interest her. He told her a story that made her burst into laughter—the story of how he had acquired one of his most valuable cowbells. It was a gem—a priceless antique. On it was engraved the name of a cow—Øystein, no less, which seemed to indicate that it was a bull . . .

She laughed, no longer self-conscious. She was oblivious of her surroundings and shook her head and laughed like a child at his bad joke. She was absolutely radiant.

"You know, I think The Midget was jealous," he said.

"No," she said, flustered.

"I had that impression. But I do prefer to sit here alone with you. I love to hear you laugh."

She lowered her eyes and didn't answer.

They went on talking. He was sitting so that he could observe Dagny's table.

A few minutes went by. Miss Andresen returned, chatted for a minute or so, took a sip from her glass, and went off again.

Suddenly Dagny left her table and walked over to Nagel.

"You seem to be having a good time," she said with a

slight tremor in her voice. "Hello, Martha. What are you both laughing about?"

"Oh, everything and anything," Nagel replied. "I keep on talking away and I've made Miss Gude laugh several times. May we offer you a glass?"

Dagny sat down.

A round of applause from the hall gave Martha a pretext to get up and see what was happening. She edged farther and farther away, until finally she called over to them: "It's a magician! This I have to see!" And she moved out of sight.

Pause.

"You've deserted your party," said Nagel, and he would have continued, but Dagny cut him short: "And your party has deserted you."

"Oh, she'll be back. Isn't there something strange about Miss Gude? Tonight she is as happy as a child."

Dagny made no reply but asked: "Have you been away?"

"Yes."

Pause.

"Are you enjoying yourself this evening?"

"I don't even know what's going on," he replied. "I didn't exactly come here to enjoy myself."

"But then what did you come here for?"

"To see you again, naturally. But only from afar, without speaking . . ."

"Oh. And that is why you brought a lady along?"

He didn't understand what she meant and looked at her for a long moment.

"Do you mean Miss Gude? I don't know how to answer that. I've heard so much about her. She is always alone, never goes out. Her life is empty. I didn't bring her here; I only wanted to show her a little attention so that she wouldn't be bored, that's all. Miss Andresen brought her over here. God, how that woman has suffered! It's turned her hair completely white."

"You couldn't possibly think—I mean, you don't imagine that I'm jealous? You couldn't be more mistaken! I remember the story you told about a madman who went out driving with twenty-four carriages. He s-stammered, you said, and fell in love with a girl named Klara. Oh, I remember it very well. And although Klara wouldn't have anything to do with him, she couldn't stand the idea of her hunchbacked sister having him either. I don't know why you told me that; you must have had your reasons, but it's got nothing to do with me. You certainly won't succeed in making me jealous, if that's what you're trying to do tonight. Neither you nor your s-stammerer!"

"Good God! You can't possibly mean what you're saying."

"Yes, I do," she exclaimed.

"Do you think I would do a thing like that if I wanted to make you jealous? That I would invite a forty-year-old woman to join me, allow her to leave, drop her as soon as you appear on the scene. You must think me a complete fool!"

"I don't know what you are. I only know that you've forced yourself on me and caused me the most miserable hours of my life, and that I no longer understand myself. I don't know whether you're a fool or a madman, but I'm not going to bother to find out. I don't care what you are!"

"I fully realize that," he said.

"And why should I care," she said, irritated by his humility. "Why on earth should you be any concern of mine? You've behaved badly toward me, and after that, you can hardly expect me to care what happens to you. But you take the trouble to tell me a story filled with allusions and insinuations. I'm convinced that you had a reason for telling me about Klara and her sister—yes, you did! But why are you persecuting me? I don't mean now—it was I who came to you—but why can't you leave me alone? You will probably interpret the fact that I've stopped to talk for a minute as a sign that I'm worried and concerned."

"My dear Miss Kielland, I have no illusions."

"No? But I never have any way of knowing whether you're telling the truth. I have a deep distrust of you and I believe you capable of just about anything. It's possible that I'm being unfair to you now, but I feel I have the right to retaliate—you have it coming to you. I'm sick to death of all your insinuations and your scheming . . ."

He said nothing but just sat there turning his glass. When she repeated that she didn't believe a word that came out of his mouth, his only answer was: "I deserve that."

"As a matter of fact, there is hardly anything about you that I do believe," she went on. "I've even suspected your big, broad shoulders of being padded. A while ago, I confess, I went into the cloakroom to check the shoulders of your coat. But though I was wrong, I still doubt everything about you. I'm sure that you'd be capable of making yourself a few inches taller, for instance, since you could certainly use the additional height. Good God! Who could possibly believe you! Who are you, anyway, and why did you come here? You're even using a pseudonym—your real name is Simonsen—just plain Simonsen! I heard it at the hotel. You had a visit from a lady who called you Simonsen before you could stop her. That, too, is cheap and vulgar beyond belief. They say in town that you pass out cigars to little boys and that you commit one indiscretion after another in the streets. I've heard that you made advances to a servant girl in the presence of several people. But, in spite of that, you have the nerve to come and talk to me of love and to keep on pursuing me! Your incredible audacity—that is what hurts and offends me so terribly."

She stopped. Her lips trembled, betraying her emotion. Every word had come straight from the heart—each had made a direct hit, as was her intention.

After a short silence, he replied: "Yes, I know. I've caused you a lot of anguish. But it goes without saying that if you carefully observe a man for a month and make a point of remembering everything he says and does, you can always find something to find fault with. You may be a bit unfair in your judgment of me, but that's not important. This is a small town. I'm rather conspicuous, and everywhere I go, people recognize me and watch my every move. And besides, I am a bit odd."

"Of course," she retorted sarcastically, "it's because of the size of the town that you create a sensation. In a larger town you wouldn't be the only one to attract attention."

Despite this icy remark, he couldn't help but admire her. He was about to acknowledge it with a compliment, but changed his mind. She was too upset, too angry with him, and she was belittling him. That was what really hurt. How did he appear to her, in truth—perhaps as just a run-of-the-mill stranger in a small town, a man who attracted attention simply because he was a stranger and wore a yellow suit.

With a touch of bitterness he said: "But aren't they also

saying that I wrote an obscene verse on a tombstone—Mina Meek's tombstone? Didn't anyone see it? I assure you it's true. It's also true that I've been to the pharmacy in town to get some medication for a loathsome disease, the name of which I had written on a piece of paper, but I couldn't get the medication because I didn't have a prescription. And, incidentally, didn't The Midget tell you that I once offered him two hundred crowns to recognize a child of mine as his? The Midget himself can testify to that.

"I'm sure I could find lots of other things . . ."

"That's not necessary; I've heard quite enough," she said contemptuously. And with an icy expression in her eyes she brought up the bogus telegrams, the large sum of money he had bequeathed to himself, and the violin case he was carting around though he didn't own a violin and couldn't play. One thing after another she flung in his face, his posturing, his fraud, deception, his charlatanism, and the medal that, by his own admission, he hadn't acquired honorably. She was merciless and spared him nothing. Every detail suddenly took on enormous significance for her, and she told him that though at first she had believed that all these execrable deeds were pure fiction, she was now convinced they had indeed been committed by him. He certainly had a vile and shiftless character! "And although you know what you are," she continued, "you still try to catch me off guard, upset me, even seduce me. You have no shame, no feeling for anyone but yourself. All you do is explain, explain . . ."

She was interrupted by Dr. Stenersen, who emerged from the hall, obviously very much engrossed in his responsibilities. He was one of the sponsors of the bazaar and was working very hard at it.

"Good evening, Mr. Nagel!" he cried. "That was certainly a blast we had the other night! Miss Kielland, it's about time to get ready for the tableaux," he said, and disappeared.

There was another musical number and the crowd was growing very restless. Dagny leaned forward, looked through the door, and turning to Nagel, said: "Martha is coming back."

Pause.

"Didn't you hear what I said?"

"Yes," he answered absentmindedly. He didn't look up but continued to turn his glass around without drinking from it. His head was bent so low that it almost touched the table.

"Come on," she said mockingly. "Now they're playing again. To listen to that kind of music, one ought to be some distance away—in an adjoining room, say, holding the hand of one's beloved—isn't that what you said once? I think it's the very same Lanner waltz, and now when Martha comes . . ."

Suddenly she seemed to regret her malicious remarks. She lapsed into silence, her expression changed, and she fidgeted nervously in her chair. He was still sitting there with his head bowed. She could see his chest heaving; his breathing was short and irregular.

She picked up her glass, got up, and started to say something, a few conciliatory words to end the conversation. "I have to go now," she began.

He glanced up at her, rose, and lifted his glass. They drank in silence. He made an effort to keep his hand from shaking; she could see that he was struggling to appear composed. Suddenly this man, whom she thought she had crushed and destroyed with her contempt, said in an offhand manner: "Miss Kielland, I don't suppose I'll see you again, but when you write to your fiancé, would you remind him of the shirts he promised The Midget once, a couple of years ago? Please forgive me for meddling in something that doesn't concern me; I'm only doing it for The Midget's sake. Do excuse my presumptuousness, but tell him that it was two wool shirts and then he'll probably remember."

For a moment she was stunned. She stared at him with her mouth open, unable to utter a word—she even forgot to put down her glass—and she stood there for a full minute as if frozen.

But then she regained her composure, looked at him with all the exasperation and anger that had built up within her—a look she meant to annihilate him with—and turned and walked away. When she reached the door, she slammed her glass down on a nearby table and went back into the hall.

She seemed to have forgotten about Reinert and Holtan, who were still sitting at the same table waiting for her.

Nagel sat down again. His shoulders shook, and several times he raised his hands to his head in an agonized gesture. He was leaning over the table seemingly in a state of collapse, but when Martha came he jumped up and with a look of gratitude pulled out a chair for her.

"How kind of you to come back!" he exclaimed. "Sit here. I want to talk to you alone and tell you all kinds of stories, if you like. I promise to amuse you if you'll sit down. Please! You may leave whenever you wish, and you will let me see you home, won't you? You do trust me, don't you? You'll have a small glass of wine with me now, won't you? I'm going to tell you a story that will make you laugh again. I'm so glad you came back. God, how wonderful it is to hear you laugh—you who are always so serious! There wasn't anything too interesting going on in the hall, was there? Let's rather stay here for a while. It's too hot in there. Do sit down."

Martha hesitated for a moment, but sat down.

Then Nagel began talking incessantly, keeping up a steady flow of funny stories and anecdotes. He chatted away, covering every imaginable topic, speaking at an intense, feverish pace, terrified at the thought that she might leave if he stopped. The strain of it made him flush, he became confused and tapped his head in desperation, trying to pick up the thread of his story. Martha thought this was part of the fun and laughed like a child. She was far from bored. Her spinster's heart leaped with joy, she lost her inhibitions, she even joined in the talk. There was such a warm glow about her, and how naïve she was! When he remarked that life was an unfathomable misery —didn't she agree?—this woman, who had lived for years in poverty and had sustained herself by selling eggs at the marketplace, retorted that life wasn't at all bad, often it was even quite good!

Often life was good, she said!

"You may be right," he said. "Well, we should have a look at the tableaux. Let's stand here in the doorway; then we can sit down again if you wish. Can you see from there? If not, I'll lift you up."

She laughed and shook her head reproachfully.

As soon as he saw Dagny on the stage, he became somber. He fixed his gaze on her and saw nothing else. He followed the direction of her eyes, scrutinized her intently from top to toe, avidly watched the expression on her face, and noted that the rose pinned to her bosom moved gently with her breathing. She was standing farthest back in the group of participants but was easily recognizable despite her elaborate make-up. Miss Andresen played the queen and sat in the center of the stage. This tableau was spotlighted in red, and the mise en scène had been worked out with great care by Dr. Stenersen.

"It's lovely!" Martha whispered.

"What is?" he asked.

"Up on the stage. Can't you see from where you're standing? What are you looking at?"

"Yes, it's lovely."

And to get her attention away from the single spot on which his eyes were focused, he began to ask her who the performers were, but scarcely heard her answers. They remained standing there until the red light faded and the curtain came down.

There was a few minutes' interval between the five tableaux. By now it was midnight and Nagel and Martha were watching the last tableau. When it was over and the band started up again, they went back to their table and resumed their conversation. She became increasingly relaxed and no longer made any move to leave.

Two young ladies came around selling raffle tickets for dolls, rocking chairs, embroideries, a tea set, and a clock. There was a general hubbub; the crowd became animated and noisy; the hall and the adjoining rooms resounded with a babble of voices like the floor of a stock exchange. Closing time was not until two.

Miss Andresen again sat down at Nagel's table. She was absolutely exhausted. Yes, thank you, she would like to have a glass—half a glass. Shouldn't she go and look for Dagny?

She returned with Dagny, who had The Midget in tow.

At that moment a table was upset near them and cups and glasses shattered on the floor. Dagny gave a little cry and nervously grabbed Martha's arm. The next moment she was laughing at herself and apologizing. But she was obviously in an emotional state; her face was flushed. She uttered shrill little laughs and her eyes had a feverish brightness. She was ready to leave and had put on her cloak but was waiting for Holtan, who was her escort, as usual.

Holtan, however, was still sitting at the table with Reinert. He hadn't moved from his chair for over an hour and was in fact quite drunk.

"I'm sure Mr. Nagel will see you home, Dagny," Miss Andresen said.

Dagny burst into laughter and Miss Andresen gave her a startled look.

"No, I don't dare walk with Mr. Nagel any more. One never knows what he'll do next. This is strictly between you and me, but once he actually asked me to meet him in secret! It's true—under a tree—a big aspen at a certain spot in the woods. No, Mr. Nagel is too unpredictable. Just now he actually asked me in all seriousness about a couple of shirts my fiancé once promised Grøgaard. Grøgaard doesn't know a thing about it, do you, Grøgaard? It's all very odd!"

Still laughing, she quickly got up, walked over to Holtan, and said a few words to him. She was obviously trying to get him to leave.

The Midget was ill at ease. He tried to explain about the shirts, became increasingly confused, and gave up. Anxiously, he looked from one person at the table to another.

Even Martha looked puzzled and embarrassed. Nagel whispered a few reassuring words to her and started to refill the glasses. Miss Andresen quickly changed the subject and began talking about the bazaar—what a turnout, in spite of the weather! It must have brought in a lot of money that would more than cover expenses . . .

"Who was the attractive lady who played the harp?" Nagel wanted to know. "The one with the Byronic mouth and the silver arrow in her hair?"

She was a stranger here on a visit. Was she really so attractive?

He thought she was. And he went on asking questions about her, though it was obvious that his thoughts were elsewhere. What was he thinking about? Why was he frowning so angrily all of a sudden? Slowly, he twirled his glass.

Dagny came back to the table. Standing behind Miss Andresen's chair buttoning her gloves, she asked in her clear and beautiful voice: "What did you have in mind when you asked me for that rendezvous, Mr. Nagel? Please, do tell me!"

"Dagny!" whispered Miss Andresen, getting to her feet. Everyone felt awkward. Nagel looked up. His face showed no emotion, but they all noticed that he put down his glass and began wringing his hands. He was breathing heavily. What would he do? What was behind that faint smile which immediately vanished?

To everyone's surprise he answered calmly: "Why did I ask you to meet me? Miss Kielland, wouldn't you really prefer me not to explain? I've already caused you so much unpleasantness, and believe me, I would do anything to have it undone. But you are well aware of my reason for asking you to meet me. I've made no attempt to hide it, though perhaps I should have. Please forgive me—there is nothing else I can say . . ."

He stopped; and she made no reply. Evidently she had expected something else from him. Finally Holtan appeared, just in time to put an end to this painful scene. His face was flushed, and he wasn't very steady on his feet.

Dagny took his arm and they left.

The relief of the small group was almost audible. The festive mood returned; Martha laughed at nothing at all, and clapped her hands gaily. When she felt she was laughing too much, she blushed and checked herself, furtively looking around to see if anyone had noticed. Nagel found her confusion charming and purposely played the clown to keep her in high spirits. He even played "Old Man Noah" on a cork that he held between his teeth.

Mrs. Stenersen joined the group, declaring that she had no intention of leaving until the very end. There was still one more act—a couple of acrobats that she simply had to see. She was always the last to leave: the night was endless, and it was so depressing to come home to an empty house. Why didn't they all go in and watch the acrobats? And they all filed into the hall.

Shortly after they were seated, a tall bearded man walked down the center aisle carrying a violin case. It was the organist; he had finished his part in the program and was leaving. He stopped and bowed and launched into a conversation with Nagel about the violin. The Midget had come to see him and offered to buy it. But he couldn't possibly sell it; it was an heirloom. He loved it as if it were

on a good show and give it all you've got! Why don't we have another glass of wine? Do ask Miss Gude to join us!"

All together, they went back to the adjoining room, still excited about this mysterious man who had caused such a sensation. Even Reinert stopped in passing and said: "Thank you for inviting me to your stag party the other night. I couldn't come, because I had another engagement. But I do appreciate it!"

"Why on earth did you end your performance with those discordant notes?" Miss Andresen asked.

"I don't know," said Nagel. "It just happened. I wanted to pull the devil by the tail, I guess."

Once more, Dr. Stenersen came up to offer his congratulations, and again Nagel insisted that his playing was superficial and full of cheap effects. If they only knew! His double fingering was phony, his notes were flat—he was well aware of it, but he was quite out of practice.

People were crowding around the table, and the group remained seated until the lights began to go out. It was then two-thirty.

Nagel leaned over and whispered to Martha: "You did say I might walk you home, didn't you? There is something I want to tell you."

He quickly paid the bill, said good night to Miss Andresen, and followed Martha to the exit. She had no coat but was carrying an umbrella, which she tried to hide because it was full of holes. As they left, Nagel noticed The Midget watching them with a pained expression. His face was even more distorted than usual.

They went straight to Martha's house. Nagel looked around but there was no one in sight.

"If you would let me come in for a little while, I would be so grateful," he said.

"It's so late," she said hesitantly.

"You know you have my word that I will never give you the slightest cause for concern. I *must* speak to you!"

She opened the door.

When they entered, Martha went to light a candle and he hung something in front of the window as before. He waited until she had finished, and said: "Did you enjoy the evening?"

"Yes, I did, thank you," she replied.

"However, that wasn't what I wanted to talk to you about. Come and sit a little closer. You mustn't be afraid of me. Promise? Let's shake hands on it."

She gave him her hand and he held on to it.

"You don't believe that I'm a liar—that I would tell you a lie—do you? There's something I want to say to you—you won't doubt my sincerity?"

"No."

"I'll explain everything afterwards. But how far do you trust me? I mean, how much faith do you have in me? I'm not making any sense, but it's so hard to begin. Would you believe me if, for instance, I told you I was very fond of you? You must be aware of that. But if I should go a step further—I mean, if I should ask you to be my wife. My wife—there, I've said it! Not just my mistress but my wife. Good God, what's the matter? No, please let me hold your hand. I'll be able to explain myself so much better, and I'm sure you'll understand. Now, try to accept the fact that your ears do not deceive you, that I've proposed to you, that I've come straight to the point and mean every word. First of all, you must accept this possibility, and then allow me to continue. Now! How old are you? I didn't mean to ask you that, but I'm twenty-nine, I'm past the irresponsible and reckless years. You're perhaps four, five, six years older, but that makes no . . ."

"I'm twelve years older," she said.

"Twelve years older!" he exclaimed, terribly pleased that she had been paying attention to him and hadn't panicked. "That's splendid—as a matter of fact, it's marvelous! Do you think that twelve years make any difference? You can't really mean that! Even if you were three times twelve years older—if I care deeply for you, and I mean it, what would that matter? I've been thinking about this for a long time—well, for a couple of days, anyway—and I'm telling you the truth. I implore you to believe me! For several days and nights I've had this on my mind and haven't been able to sleep. You have such mysterious eyes; they captivated me from the first moment I saw you. Eyes have a particular fascination for me; they could entice me to the ends of the earth. Once an old man lured me around a forest for the better part of the night by the magic of his eyes alone. The man was obsessed. Well, that's another story. —Your eyes have a strange effect on me. Do you remember the day you were standing here in the middle of the room looking at me as I passed by? I'll never forget that moment—you didn't turn your head, but your eyes followed me. And once I'd met you and had a chance to talk to you, your smile went straight to my heart. I don't think I've ever met anyone with a warmer and more genuine laugh than yours. But you are completely oblivious of it—therein lies the magic and the charm. I know I'm talking a lot of nonsense. But I feel I must go on talking; otherwise, you won't believe me, and the mere thought makes me desperate. If only you wouldn't sit there so rigid, as if you were about to get up and go away, it would be easier for me to gather my thoughts. Please let me hold your hand; it would be so much easier for me to say what is in my heart. Bless you! I'm not asking any more of you than what I've just said. I'm hiding nothing. What have I said that shocks you so? You think it's an insane idea, you can't understand that I want to marry you—and you refuse to believe that I mean it. That's what you're thinking, isn't it?"

"Yes—no, for heaven's sake stop this!"

"But listen to me! I surely don't deserve that you should still suspect me of underhandedness . . ."

"I don't suspect you of anything," said Martha, suddenly stricken with remorse. "But it's impossible."

"Why? Is there someone else?"

"No, no."

"Honestly? Because if there were someone—let's say The Midget, for example . . ."

"No!" she cried vehemently, and he felt her tighten her grip on his hand.

"No? Well then there's no obstacle. Let me go on. You mustn't think that I'm so far above you socially that it's impossible on those grounds. I'm being perfectly candid; in many ways I probably don't live up to what is considered standard behavior. You heard yourself what Miss Kielland said this evening. And you must have heard from other people in town how badly I've behaved on several occasions. Sometimes I think they are not being quite fair, but on the whole they're right. I have many faults. And you with your fine character and your purity of heart are infinitely superior to me—not the other way around. I can promise to be good to you always—believe me, that wouldn't be hard. My greatest joy would be to make you happy . . . One more thing: maybe you're concerned about what the town might say? Well, in the first place, the town would have to accept your marrying me—in the town church, if you like. In the second place, people already seem to have found enough to talk about. I'm sure they've noticed that we've met a couple of times and that this evening you gave me the pleasure of your company at the bazaar. So it couldn't possibly make things any worse. And good God, so what? Why should you care what people think? You're crying? Have I hurt you by exposing you to more gossip this evening?"

"No, it isn't that."

"What is it, then?"

She didn't answer.

Suddenly something occurred to him and he said: "Am I perhaps being too hard on you? You didn't drink very much champagne—I don't believe you even drank two glasses. Maybe you think I want to take advantage of your having had a few sips of wine to put you in a more receptive mood. Is that why you're crying?"

"No, not at all."

"Then why *are* you crying?"

"I don't know."

"But you can't possibly still harbor the idea that I came here with any ulterior motives. If I'm anything at all, I'm honest; you must believe that!"

"I do believe you, but I don't understand. It's all so confusing . . . You can't—you couldn't mean it!"

Yes, he did mean it! And he went on talking and explaining, holding her delicate hand in his, while the rain beat down on the windowpanes. He talked away quietly, trying to follow her train of thought, from time to time lapsing into senseless prattle. It would work out beautifully! They would go far away—God knows where—but they would disappear and no one would be able to find them. Wouldn't that be wonderful! They would buy a cottage and a small plot of land somewhere in the woods, and they would call it Eden. It would be a beautiful place—their very own. He would till the ground and make it yield its fruits—how he would work! But he had a tendency to get depressed at times; it could happen—a memory of an incident in the past might suddenly emerge to haunt him, it could come over him for no apparent reason. But she'd be patient with him, wouldn't she? He would promise never to worry her. He would ask only to be left alone to work it out, or to go into the forest for a while. No harsh word would ever be spoken in their cottage. And they would fill it with the most beautiful wildflowers, stones, and moss. The floor would be covered with juniper branches that he would gather, and at Christmas time they would not forget to put a sheaf out for the birds. How quickly time would pass and how happy they would be! They would spend their days in and around their cottage, and never be far apart from each other. In the summer they would take long walks and note how the bushes and trees grew from year to year. And they would always welcome strangers who happened to be passing by. They would have cattle, a couple of big, sleek animals that they would train to eat out of their hands. While he was hoeing and tilling the ground, she would look after them . . .

"Yes," said Martha. She said it unconsciously, and it didn't escape him.

He went on. Then of course they would have a day or two for hunting and fishing every week. They would walk hand in hand: she in a belted short skirt, and he in a sports jacket and buckled shoes. How the woods would echo with their shouting and singing! They would be holding hands, wouldn't they?

"Yes," she said again.

Little by little, she let herself be carried away. He had thought of everything, down to the minutest detail. He even said that they'd have to find a place with water nearby. He would take care of that; he would take care of everything—she could rely on him. He was strong; he would make a clearing for their home in the middle of the forest. He had a pair of strong hands—she could see for herself! Smiling, he put her slender, childlike hand next to his.

She allowed him to touch her, and when he caressed her cheek, she looked at him without moving. Then, with his mouth close to her ear, he asked her if she dared, if she would want to. Again she said yes, a dreamy, whispered yes. But after a few moments she began again to hesitate. On second thought, she couldn't. How could he expect it of her? What did he think she was?

And again he convinced her that he wanted her, that he meant every word he said, that he wanted her more than he had ever wanted anything. He would always take good care of her, but of course they would need some time to get on their feet; she mustn't worry—he would work for both of them. He talked for an hour, and little by little he broke down her resistance. Twice she backed down, hid her face in her hands, and cried, "No, no!" But in the end she surrendered. She looked into his eyes and convinced herself that it wasn't a momentary triumph he was after. Could it be possible that he really wanted her! She yielded; she couldn't fight it any more. Finally she said yes to him.

The candle in the bottle had almost burned down, and

they were still talking and holding hands. She was quite overcome by emotion; tears welled up in her eyes, but she was smiling.

"To come back to The Midget," he said, "I'm absolutely certain that he was jealous at the bazaar."

"Well, perhaps he was," she said, "but it can't be helped."

"No, that's right, it can't be helped. Look Martha, I would so much like to do something to make you happy this evening. I would like to give you something that would make you gasp with pleasure. Tell me what you would like! You're much too modest, my darling, you never ask for anything! Martha, always remember what I'm saying to you now: I will protect you, I will try to anticipate your every wish and care for you for the rest of my life. You'll always remember that, my dearest, won't you? You'll never be able to say that I didn't live up to my promise."

It was now four o'clock.

They got up. She took a step toward him and he put his arms around her. She circled his neck in her arms, and for a moment they embraced. Her pure, shy nun's heart beat against his hand, and he gently caressed her hair. They were as one.

She was the first to speak: "I shall lie awake for the rest of the night, thinking. Maybe we'll see each other tomorrow—if you want to?"

"If I want to! Yes, tomorrow. What time? May I come at eight?"

"Yes—would you like me to wear this dress?"

The naïve question, her trembling lips, her big eyes looking up at him, moved him deeply.

"Dearest child, wear anything you like! How good you

are! But you mustn't stay awake tonight! Say good night, think of me, and go to sleep. You're not afraid to be here alone?"

"No—now you'll get wet going home."

She was concerned that he'd get wet!

"Be happy and sleep well," he said.

He was already outside when he remembered something, and turning toward her, he said: "One more thing: I'm not a wealthy man. Did you think I had money?"

"I don't know," she said, shaking her head.

"No, I don't have money, but I have enough to buy a home and to take care of our needs. And after that, I'll see to everything; I'll provide for us—that's what I have hands for. I hope you're not disappointed because I'm not wealthy?"

"No," she said, taking his hands in hers once more. In parting, he told her to bolt the door, and stepped out into the street.

It was very dark and raining heavily. He didn't head toward the hotel but took the road through the woods which led to the parsonage. He walked for about a quarter of an hour. It was pitch black and he couldn't see a thing. Then he began walking at a slower pace, left the road, and groped his way to a huge tree. It was an aspen, and there he stopped.

Except for the wind rustling through the trees and the torrential rain, all was deathly silent. He whispered: Dagny, Dagny, to himself, stopped, and then repeated it in a loud voice, standing against the tree. She had hurt him deeply this evening, poured all her wrath and contempt on him. Every word had been like a dagger, yet he stood there saying her name. He knelt down by the tree and in the inky blackness carved her name on the trunk. He was at this for several minutes, feeling his way with his fingers, carving and touching until it was done . . .

While he was carving, he had removed his cap.

When he again came out on the road, he stopped, hesitated for a moment, and then retraced his steps. He groped his way back to the tree, ran his fingers over the trunk, and found the letters. Once more he knelt down and kissed this name, these letters, as if for the last time. Then he got up and quickly walked away.

It was five o'clock when he got to the hotel.

17

THE next day the same downpour, the same dark, heavy atmosphere. There seemed to be no end to the water that flooded the gutters and streamed down the windowpanes. Hour after hour it poured, and by noon the sky was overcast still. The small garden behind the hotel was awash with bent and broken trees and floating leaves —covered with mud and water.

Nagel spent the day in his room, reading and pacing the floor as he usually did, continually looking at the clock. The day seemed endless. He waited impatiently for evening to come.

At eight o'clock he went down to Martha's cottage. He hadn't the faintest idea that anything had gone wrong, but she greeted him in tears and was obviously very much upset. When he tried to talk to her, she answered evasively and in monosyllables, without looking at him. Time after time she asked him to forgive her and not be offended.

When he took her hand, she trembled and tried to pull back. But finally she sat down next to him, not stirring until he left an hour later. What had happened? He plied her with questions and asked for an explanation, which she was unable to give. No, there was nothing wrong with her, but she had been doing a lot of thinking . . .

Was she going back on her promise? Perhaps she didn't care for him, after all?

Yes, perhaps, but she implored him to forgive her and asked him not to be angry. She had been thinking about it all night and had come to the conclusion that it was impossible. She had searched her soul and she knew she couldn't love him the way he should be loved.

So that was it! Pause . . . But didn't she think she might come to love him in time? He had so looked forward to this chance to begin a new life! He would be so good to her!

She was obviously moved and pressed her hand against her bosom, but looked down and said nothing.

Didn't she think that he could bring her to love him in time, if they were always together?

There was a no, scarcely audible, and two tears rolled down from her long eyelashes.

Pause. He began to tremble, and the blue veins in his forehead throbbed.

Well then, there was nothing to be done about it. She mustn't cry any more. He had forced his way into her life, and he hoped she would forgive him. His intentions had been the best . . .

She took his hand and held it.

He was startled by this show of emotion and asked if he had offended her in any way. He wanted to make amends, if he could. Perhaps she didn't like that he . . .

She interrupted him: "No, it's nothing like that! It's just that the whole thing is so fantastic! I don't even know who you are! I know that you want the best for me. Please don't misunderstand . . ."

"Who I am?" he repeated, looking straight at her.

Suddenly he was struck by the thought that something had come between them, a hostile force that had shattered her confidence in him. "Have you had any visitors today?" he asked.

She didn't answer.

"I don't want to pry; it really doesn't matter. I have no right to ask you any questions."

"I was so happy last night!" she exclaimed. "How I longed for morning to come, and for you! Now I'm all confused!"

"Please tell me just one thing. Don't you believe I've been completely honest with you? You still have no faith in me, in spite of everything?"

"Not always. Please don't be offended, but you're a complete stranger here. I only know what you tell me. Perhaps you do mean it now but will change your mind later. How can I know what is in your mind?"

Pause.

He put his hand under her chin, lifted her head slightly, and said: "What else did Miss Kielland say?"

Completely taken aback, she gave him a quick, timid glance that betrayed her confusion. "But I didn't say so, did I? I didn't say that!"

"No, no, you didn't," he said, lost in thought, his eyes staring into space. "You didn't say it was she; you didn't even mention her name—you've got nothing to worry about. But Miss Kielland has been here. She came in through that door, and when she had accomplished what she came for, she left again the same way. Her mission was so important that she had to come out today, in this weather . . . Dearest Martha, I kneel before you because you are so good. Have confidence in me, just for tonight, and I'll prove to you later that nothing was further from my mind than deceiving you. Don't take back your promise! Will you think it over till tomorrow and let me see you then . . ."

"I don't know."

"You don't know? Does that mean that you would prefer to be rid of me once and for all?"

"I would rather come to you one day when—well, when you're married and you've finished it—the house, I mean . . . I would rather come as your maid . . . I would much prefer that."

Pause.

Her suspicion of him was already deep-rooted. He was no longer able to sway her, put her at ease as before. His heart sank when he saw that the more he talked, the more she withdrew from him. But why was she crying? What was tormenting her? Why was she still holding his hand? His thoughts went back to The Midget. He would put her to the test; he would force her to see him again tomorrow when she had had a chance to think it over.

"Forgive me for mentioning The Midget once more. Now don't get upset, but I have my reasons. I'm not going to say anything to discredit him; on the contrary. You remember how I spoke of his good qualities to you. I thought that he might possibly be a rival, and that's why I brought him up. I even said I thought him capable of supporting a family if he had some help in getting started. But you vehemently denied it; you swore you had nothing to do with him, you even stopped me from talking about him. But I'm not entirely convinced that what you said is the truth; you haven't allayed my suspicions, and I'm asking you again if there isn't something between the two of you. If there is, I'll immediately back out. You shake your head. But then I can't understand why you refuse to think things over until tomorrow and give me your answer then. That would only be fair, after all. And you who are kindness personified!"

At that, she gave in. She got up and, overcome with emotion, her eyes filled with tears, she smiled and stroked his hair as she had done the previous evening. She would gladly see him tomorrow, but he must come a bit earlier, four or five o'clock, while it was still light, so that no one would make any comments. But he must leave now—it would be better if he left at once. Then he could come back tomorrow; she would be waiting for him . . .

What a strange blending of a child's soul with that of a spinster! A single remark, a single word made her heart leap with joy, made her smile, moved her to tenderness. She held his hand until he got up to leave, and walked him to the door, still holding his hand. On the doorstep she said good night loudly, as if to defy anyone who might be within earshot.

The rain had almost stopped. Here and there a blue patch of sky showed through between the lowering clouds, and a few last raindrops fell intermittently on the sodden ground.

Nagel breathed a sigh of relief. He would regain her confidence now—why not? He didn't go back to the hotel but went down to the docks, walked along the shore, passed the houses at the edge of town, and came to the road leading to the parsonage. There was not a soul anywhere.

When he had walked a few paces, a figure suddenly darted out from the side of the road and started to walk ahead of him; it was Dagny. Her blond braid hung down her back over her raincoat.

An intense feeling of elation surged through him, and he almost came to a standstill at this astonishing sight. So she hadn't gone to the bazaar this evening—or perhaps she was only taking a stroll before the tableaux went on? She walked very slowly, even stopping to look up at the birds that were beginning to stir among the trees. Had she seen him? Did she want to test him? Was she deliberately walking in front of him to see whether he would dare approach her?

She didn't have to worry, he would never bother her again.

And suddenly a blind rage flared up inside him against this creature who was perhaps once more trying to tempt him to make a fool of himself, only to have the satisfaction of humiliating him afterwards. She was quite capable of telling people at the bazaar that he had again attempted to meet her. Hadn't she just been to Martha's to try to ruin his chances there too? Couldn't she stop her campaign to hurt him? She was out for revenge, but she was going too far!

They were both walking slowly, one behind the other, about fifty steps apart. They kept this up for several minutes. Then suddenly she dropped her handkerchief. He saw it flutter from her raincoat and down to the ground. Was she aware that she had dropped it?

He was convinced that this was a test of some kind. She

was still angry and bitter; she wanted him to pick up the handkerchief and hand it to her. Then she would have a chance of looking him in the face and gloating over Martha's rejection of him.

His fury had risen to a feverish pitch. He pressed his lips tight together, and agonized lines appeared on his forehead. That's what she wanted! She wanted him to come before her, so she could look him in the face and laugh her scornful laugh!

There was the dainty white lace handkerchief lying in the middle of the road; he might just pick it up . . .

He walked at the same slow pace, and when he got to the handkerchief, he stepped on it and kept walking.

The game continued a few minutes longer. He saw her suddenly look at her watch. Then she turned abruptly and walked toward him. Had she noticed that she had lost her handkerchief? He also made an about-face and walked slowly ahead of her. When he reached the handkerchief, he stepped on it again, right before her eyes, and walked on. He sensed that she was right behind him, but he didn't increase his pace. They kept this up until they reached town.

He had guessed right; she turned off in the direction of the bazaar. He went straight to his room.

He opened the window and leaned on the windowsill, crushed and defeated. His anger was gone; he collapsed, sobbing convulsively; his whole body shook. So this was the end! How he regretted it—how he wished none of it had ever happened! She had dropped her handkerchief, most likely on purpose, most likely to humiliate him, but what did that matter? He could have picked it up, pocketed it, and carried it next to his heart for the rest of his life. It was snow-white and he had trampled it into the mud! Maybe she wouldn't have taken it away from him once he held it in his hands; maybe she would have let him keep it! But had she reached for it, he would have gone down on his knees and begged her to let him keep it, a token of her charity. And would it really have mattered if she had scorned and ridiculed him once more?

Suddenly he got to his feet, leaped down the stairs and into the street, raced through the town, and in a few moments was back on the road leading to the parsonage. Perhaps he could still find the handkerchief! His guess had been right; she had left it lying there, though he was sure she had seen him trample it into the ground the second time. Luck was with him in spite of everything! Thank God! He slipped it into his pocket, his heart beating violently, ran back to the hotel, and carefully rinsed it and smoothed it out. It was a bit frayed; he had torn one corner with his heel. But that didn't matter. He was so happy to have found it!

When he sat down again at the window, he realized that he had walked through the town bareheaded. He must be mad—yes, he was mad! Suppose she had seen him! She had wanted to put him to the test, and again he had made a fool of himself! He would have to put an end to this—the sooner, the better! He had to force himself to look at her calmly, head high—with no show of emotion! He would make a supreme effort. He would leave town and take Martha with him. She was much too good for him, but he would make himself worthy of her!

It was getting warmer, milder. Gentle winds carried the scent of earth and fresh grass to his window, and it had a stimulating effect on him. Tomorrow he would go back to Martha and plead with her.

But by next morning all his hopes were shattered.

18

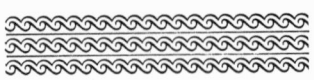

D<small>R. STENERSEN</small> arrived before Nagel had gotten up. He excused himself for coming unannounced, but this blasted bazaar kept him busy night and day. He had come on a mission—he had been asked to persuade Nagel to perform at the bazaar again that evening. His playing had set the town buzzing. The whole town had spent a sleepless night—everybody's curiosity was aroused; it was true! "I see you read the newspapers—the political situation is certainly a mess! Did you read about the latest appointments? The elections went the wrong way—the Swedes didn't get the dressing down they deserved. You seem to be a late riser—it's ten o'clock. The weather is marvelous! You ought to go out for a walk."

Yes, he was about to get up.

Well, what should he tell the bazaar committee?

No, Nagel wouldn't play.

He wouldn't? But it would mean so much to the town. How could he possibly refuse such a small favor?

He just couldn't; that's all he had to say.

What a shame! Just when everyone was so worked up about it! The ladies had insisted last night that the doctor must not come back until the arrangements had been made. Miss Andresen had been very insistent, and Miss Kielland had taken him aside and begged him to keep at Nagel until he promised.

But Miss Kielland didn't have any idea how he played; she had never even heard him.

Nevertheless, she was the most eager of them all. She had even offered to accompany him! In the end she had said: "Tell him that we all beg him to come!" —"Won't you play just a few bars to please us?"

He couldn't, he just couldn't.

That was just an excuse; he had played on Thursday night, hadn't he?

Nagel began to feel awkward. What if he said he couldn't play anything except that miserable medley of tunes that he had learned just to make an impression that evening? Besides, he played so out of tune that he couldn't even bear listening to himself!

"Yes, but . . ."

"Dr. Stenersen, I won't do it!"

"But if not tonight, how about tomorrow night? It's Sunday, the last day, and we're expecting a lot of people."

"No, please excuse me, but I won't play tomorrow either. I feel like an idiot even touching a violin when I play as I do. I would have thought that you were more musical!"

This appeal had an effect.

"Yes," he said, "I noticed that you were a bit off key at times, but what does that matter? We're not all connoisseurs."

But the doctor had to give up and take his leave.

Nagel began to dress. So Dagny had been in on this—she had even offered to accompany him! Was that another trap? Since her ruse had failed last night, she was trying to get back at him this way. Perhaps he was misjudging her, after all; maybe she didn't hate him any more and would stop persecuting him! In his heart he begged her to forgive him for distrusting her. He looked out at the square; there wasn't a cloud in the sky, and the sun was brilliant. He began humming to himself.

As he was about to go downstairs, Sara handed him a letter. It hadn't come through the mail; a messenger had brought it. The letter was from Martha and contained only a few lines: he mustn't come this evening—she had already left. He must forgive her for everything and not come to see her any more. She couldn't bear to see him again. Goodby. In a postscript she added: "I'll never forget you." These few words were filled with sadness; even the lettering looked melancholy and pathetic.

He sank down on a chair. He had reached bottom. Even that door had been shut on him! How strange that everything and everyone was conspiring against him! Never in his life had he been more open, more sincere! And again he had failed! For several minutes he sat there in a kind of stupor.

Suddenly he looked at the clock: it was eleven. He leaped off his chair. Perhaps if he went right away he could still catch Martha before she left. He set out immediately for her cottage, but when he got there it was locked; he peered through the windows, but both rooms were empty.

Stunned, he retraced his steps to the hotel, not knowing where he was going, not taking his eyes off the ground. How could she do this to him! How could she! At least she could have allowed him to say goodby to her and wish her every happiness wherever she was going. He would have wanted to get on his knees before her, she was so good and so pure. And she had denied him that! Well, it was all over now.

When he met Sara in the hall, he learned that the letter had been brought by a messenger from the parsonage. So Dagny was behind this too! She had planned the whole thing, carefully calculated every detail, and acted quickly. No, she would never forgive him!

All day he paced the streets, the woods, his room, never stopping for a moment. He walked with his head bowed, and with open, unseeing eyes.

He spent the next day the same way. It was Sunday. Crowds of people had come in from the country to attend the bazaar and see the final presentation of the tableaux. Again, Nagel was pressed to play just one piece. This time the request came from another member of the committee, Consul Andresen, Fredrikke's father, but again he declined. For four days he wandered around like a demented man, withdrawn, barely in touch with reality, totally absorbed by one obsessive thought. Several times a day he went down to Martha's house to see whether she had returned. But even if he did find her, what good would that do? Everything was lost, hopeless.

One evening he almost ran into Dagny. She was just leaving a shop and was so close to him that she practically touched his elbow. Her lips moved as if she were about to speak, but suddenly she blushed and said nothing. Flustered as he was, he didn't recognize her at first and stared at her for a moment before turning abruptly and walking away. She followed him; he could hear by her footsteps that she was walking faster, and he had the feeling that she was trying to overtake him. He tried to get away from her, to hide. He was afraid of her. She was obviously going to take every opportunity to make life miserable for him. Finally he fled into the hotel and, terror-stricken, made a dash for his room.

Thank God, he was safe!

This was on July 14, a Tuesday.

The next morning he seemed to have come to some kind of decision. In the past few days his face had undergone a complete change. It was rigid and ashen, and his eyes were lifeless. He would often be way down the street before he'd realize that he had forgotten his cap. Then, clenching his fists, he would tell himself that there just had to be an end to this!

When he got up on Wednesday morning, the first thing he did was examine the vial in his vest pocket, shake it, smell it, and put it away again. As usual, while he was getting dressed, he became immersed in an endless chain of confused thoughts that obsessed him, plaguing his weary mind, which churned away frantically. He was in a state of extreme agitation and so despondent that he had difficulty holding back his tears. A myriad of thoughts forced themselves on him.

Thank God, he still had the vial! The liquid was as clear as water and smelled of almonds. He might need it after all, and very soon if there was to be no other solution. That would be it—and why not? And what dreams he had

had of accomplishing something in this world—something meaningful that would make the carnivores all sit up and take notice! But everything had gone wrong; he had fallen far short of his mark. Why shouldn't he make use of that vial—all he had to do was swallow it, without grimacing too much! Well, he would do it when the time came, when the clock struck.

And Dagny would have her victory . . .

What power that girl wielded, though there was nothing striking or unusual about her—that is, unless one considered her long braid and her common sense! He sympathized with the poor man who couldn't live without her, the one with the knife and the final no. He had given up—what else was there for him to do?

How her velvety blue eyes will sparkle when I go the same way! But I love you for your wickedness too, not merely for your virtues, though you torture me to the breaking point with your condescending air. You can't seem to stand the fact that I have more than one eye. You ought to gouge the other one out—take both of them. You won't let me walk along the street in peace, you begrudge me a roof over my head. You've managed to wrest Martha from me, and I love you in spite of it. You know it, and it makes you laugh, but I love you for that too. Your scornful laugh! Can you ask for more? Isn't that enough? Your slender white hands, your voice, your blond hair, your very breath, your soul—I love all of you as I've never loved anything before. I can't help it—it's beyond my control—God save me! You may despise and ridicule me, but, Dagny, what does it matter? I love you! I know it makes no difference. You can do anything you like with me, and you'll still be just as beloved and just as beautiful; I gladly make this confession. I have disappointed you in some way. I'm thoroughly corrupt in your eyes—you think me capable of anything. If there were some means by which I could make myself taller, I would even resort to that. Whatever you say I accept with my whole heart; my love wells up within me as you say it. Even when you give me a scathing look, or turn your back on me without speaking, or try to overtake me in the street to humiliate me, my heart sings with love for you. I'm not trying to delude you or myself, and even if you laugh again it doesn't matter. Nothing can change my feeling for you. If I should happen to find a diamond one day, I would call it Dagny, because the very sound of your name thrills me. I only wish that I could forever hear your name, hear it spoken by all men and beasts, by every mountain and every star. I wish I were deaf to every sound except your name ringing in my ears day and night for the rest of my life. I would like to introduce a new oath that would invoke your name—an oath that all the peoples on this earth would swear by. If this were blasphemy and God admonished me for it, I would say: "Inscribe it in my ledger, I'll pay for it with my soul when the time comes, when the clock strikes . . ."

The irony of it all! Everywhere I turn, my path is blocked, and yet nothing is changed; physically and mentally I am the same as before. The same opportunities are open to me; my potential is the same. Why then am I thwarted at every turn? Is it my fault? If I only knew what I had done to deserve this! I'm in possession of all my faculties. I have no bad habits; I don't have a single vice, and I'm cautious by nature. My thinking and my feelings are the same, I'm in control of my life as I've always been, and the standards by which I judge people are unchanged. I befriend Martha; in her, I know, is my salvation; she's my rescuing angel, a pure spirit. At first she is afraid of me, but we end up understanding each other and are in complete harmony. I begin to look forward to a life of peace and happiness, to retreating, to living with her alone in a cottage by a spring, wandering around in the woods—she in a short skirt, and I in buckled shoes—just the life her kind and sensitive nature craves. What's wrong with that? Mohammed went to the mountain. And Martha is by my side. She fills my days with goodness and my nights with rest, and God watches over us. But now the world breaks in on us, the world is shocked, the world looks upon our idyl as madness. The world maintains that no rational man or woman would have chosen this way of life—therefore, it *is* madness. Alone I confront them and tell them that nothing could be saner or truer! What do people really know about life? We fall in line, follow the pattern established by our mentors. Everything is based on assumptions; even time, space, motion, matter are nothing but supposition. The world has no new knowledge to impart; it merely accepts what is there.

Standing in the middle of the room, Nagel put his hands to his eyes and moved his head from side to side as if he were dizzy.

What was I thinking about? Oh, yes, she is afraid of me; but there is understanding between us, and I know deep down that I'll always be good to her. I want to break with the world; I'm returning the ring. I've stumbled around like a fool among fools; I've done idiotic things. I've even played the violin and been received with tumultuous applause. Being acclaimed by the carnivores—what a cheap triumph, and how it sickens me! I'm no longer competing with a telegraph operator from Kabelvåg. I'm bound for the valley of peace, and I shall become the most peaceful creature in the woods. I shall worship my god and hum joyful melodies; I'll become superstitious, shave only at high tide, and listen for the sounds of certain birds before sowing my seeds. And when I'm weary from work, my wife will stand in the doorway waving at me and I will bless her, so grateful for her loving smile. Martha, we were so close, weren't we? And your promise was so definite! You agreed so completely with me when I explained everything. Then it all turned to dust. You were abducted, caught unawares and whisked away, not to your downfall but to mine . . .

Dagny, I don't love you. You have blocked my every move. I don't love your name; it throws me into turmoil. I twist it around, call you Dangni, and stick my tongue out at you. Listen to me, for Christ's sake! I'll come to you when the clock has struck and I am dead. I'll appear before you on the wall as the jack of clubs, haunt you as a skeleton, dance around you on one leg, and paralyze your arms with my grip. I'll do it—you'll see! God protect me from you now and forever! I fervently pray the devil take you . . .

But I'm asking myself for the last time: What good would it do? I would still love you; I'll always love you, Dagny—you know that, and that I regret my bitter words. What is the good of anything? Besides, who knows if it isn't better this way? If you say so, that is the way it will be. My wandering is at an end. But suppose you had wanted me—that you had broken off with the others and bound yourself to me—something I didn't deserve, but let's suppose for a moment—what would it have led to? Your aim would probably have been to help me perform great deeds, accomplish something in the world. I feel so ashamed, so utterly humiliated, when I think about it. I would do as you wish because I love you, but it would devastate my soul . . . What is the use of making all these conjectures, of setting up imaginary premises? You would never break with the world, and you would never accept me. You say no, thank you, scorn me, laugh at me—why then should I concern myself with you? Period.

After a short pause, he continued as vehemently: Now I'm going to drink this water and you can go straight to hell! You're stupid and vain to think that I love you, that I would even entertain the thought of loving you, now that the end is so near. I loathe your bourgeois life—phony, orderly, meaningless. I loathe it with a vengeance, and I feel the wrath rising within me, like the wrath of the Holy Spirit, when I think of you. What would you have done with me? I'm willing to bet anything that you'd have turned me into a great man and then gone around bragging to the preachers. My heart bleeds with shame over your great men . . .

A truly great man! How many of them are there in the world? First, there are the great men of Norway—they are the greatest. Then there are the leading lights of France, land of Hugo and the poets. And someone emerges now and then in Barnum's realm. All these geniuses have to try to keep their balance on a globe which, when compared to Sirius, is no bigger than the back of a louse. But a great man does things on a large scale! He doesn't just live in Paris; he occupies Paris. A great man looms so big that he can look over the top of his own head. Lavoisier asked to have his execution postponed until he had completed a chemical experiment. "Don't tread on my circles," he said. What a farce! Not even Euclid with his axioms contributed more than a snippet to the fundamental conception of science! What a miserable and confining mold we have made of God's earth, and how little we have accomplished!

And here we go creating great men out of artisans who happened to have stumbled on a way to improve electrical apparatus or had the brawn to pedal through Sweden on a bicycle! And we solicit great men to write books promoting the cult of other great men! It's really very funny, and worth the price of admission! It will all end up with every village having its own great man—a lawyer, a novelist, and a polar explorer of immense stature! And the world will become wonderfully flat and simple and easy to master . . .

Dagny, now it's my turn; I'm saying no to you; I'm laughing at you, sneering at you, so why don't you let go of me? I will never join the ranks of great men . . .

But if there is around us a plethora of geniuses of varying greatness, what of it? Am I supposed to be impressed? The more of them there are, the worse it is. Or should I follow the precepts of a world which never changes, a world which kneels before the past and blindly accepts it, a world which is in awe of what it has created and treads on the heels of its great men, shouting bravo. And you would want me to join the pack? What a farce! The so-called genius walks along the street and one citizen nudges the other in the ribs and says: There is so and so—a great man! He goes to the theater and one school-marm pinches the other's sexless thigh and whispers: There he is—in that box! And the great man himself? Why, of course, he enjoys every moment of it. These people are right, after all, and he accepts their accolades as his due. He doesn't brush aside their adulation, and he doesn't blush. Why should he? He is a great man, after all!

But young Øien would object. He is going to be a great man himself. He's working on a novel during his summer holiday. He would challenge me: I'm being inconsistent; would I please explain?

And I would proceed to explain.

But my explanation wouldn't satisfy Øien. He would continue putting questions to me: "Then, in your opinion, there are no great men?"

Unable to grasp what I'm saying, he would keep on questioning me. And again I would try to explain. I'd get into the spirit of things and answer him: "On the contrary, there are hordes of great men, do you hear? Hordes of them! But of the *very great* there aren't many. That's the point. The day will come when every village will produce a great man; but a *very great* one we may see only once in a thousand years. What the world understands by a great man is simply someone with talent, someone who excels in something—good God, genius is a democratic conception! An X number of pounds of beef a day will produce a genius in the third, fourth, fifth, tenth generation. Genius in the popular sense has become common. Imagine being in an observatory on a clear night looking through a telescope at the Orion constellation. Then Fearnley the astronomer says good evening. You turn; Fearnley makes a deep bow. A great man has just come in, a genius, the gentleman from the theater box. Don't you then smile to yourself and once again focus your attention on the Orion constellation? I once had this experience. Do you understand what I'm trying to say? Rather than admire the mediocre great men over whom passersby nudge each other in awe, I venerate the young, unknown geniuses who die in their teens, their souls shattered—delicate, phosphorescent glowworms that one must see to know they really did exist. That's how I feel.

fallen into place this moment, right in this room! Everything was solved, and I had a flash of eternal wisdom. It was radiant; it was glorious!"

Pause.

"Well, here I am a stranger among my fellow men, and soon the clock will strike! But what do I have to do with the great anyway? Nothing whatsoever, except I find greatness a farce—all phoniness and fraud. But then isn't everything? Kamma and The Midget, people in general, love, life—all a hoax. Everything I see and hear and feel is a delusion; even the blue of the sky is ozone, poison oozing down on us . . . And when the sky is really clear and blue, I sail leisurely up there, letting my boat glide through the treacherous blue ozone. The boat is made, of wood that has a wonderful fragrance, and the sail . . .

"Even Dagny said that it was a beautiful image. Dagny you did say it, and I thank you. It made me deliriously happy. I remember every word. I think about it as I walk along the road. I'll never forget it. And when the clock strikes, you shall have your triumph! I won't pursue you any more. I won't haunt you by materializing on the wall either. Forgive me; I said that because I wanted revenge. No, I will hover over you on white wings while you sleep, and when you're awake, I'll follow you and whisper beautiful words in your ear. Perhaps you'll even smile at me. And if I'm not accorded white wings—if they don't happen to be so very white—I'll ask one of God's angels to do it for me. I won't come near you, I'll hide in a corner to see if you smile at him. I want to do this to atone, if possible, for some of the worst things I've done to you. Just the thought of it makes me happy, and I can't wait. Perhaps I can give you pleasure in other, ineffable ways. I would love to sing above your head on Sunday morning as you are going to church, and I'll ask the angel to do that for me too. And if I can't persuade him, I'll prostrate myself before him and beseech him so humbly that he won't be able to refuse my plea. I'll offer him anything in return. I'll do all kinds of things for him if he will grant me this. I'm sure I can arrange it speedily, I can't wait! I'm thrilled at the thought. Just think, when the mists have vanished, la, la, la . . ."

In an exalted state, he ran downstairs and into the dining room, still singing. But a minor incident dampened his spirit and threw him into a black mood that lasted several hours. Though he wasn't alone, he went on singing while standing at the table, hurriedly downing his breakfast. When he saw that the two other guests looked annoyed, he quickly apologized: Had he noticed them before, he would have been quieter. On days like this he was oblivious to everything! Wasn't it a glorious morning? The flies were already buzzing.

But there was no response to his remarks. The two strangers looked as forbidding as before and continued their political discussion. Nagel's spirits fell. He said no more and quietly left the dining room. He went down the street to get some cigars and then as usual headed for the woods. It was then eleven-thirty.

People were all alike, weren't they! There they sat, these lawyers, salesmen, landowners, or what have you, talking politics, and looking sour and grim just because he happened to be humming cheerfully. They solemnly chewed away at their breakfast, refusing to be side-tracked. They both had paunches and puffy, fat fingers; their napkins were tucked under their chins. He ought to go back to the hotel and taunt them a little. Who did they think they were, anyway? Probably grain merchants, dealers in American hides, or perhaps in ordinary crockery. Important men, were they? And still, with one look they had managed to deflate his high spirits! They weren't particularly impressive either. One wasn't too bad, but the other one—the hide merchant—had a crooked mouth that opened on one side of his face only, so that it looked like a buttonhole. He also had a lot of gray hair growing out of his ears. God, he was a repulsive sight! But no joyful sounds allowed while this man had his nose in the trough!

Yes, they were all alike. The gentlemen talk politics, the gentlemen comment on the latest official appointments. Thank God, Buskerud may still be saved from the clutches of the conservatives! Oh, the look on those mine owners' faces as they talked away! As if Norwegian politics were anything but bar gossip and peasant palaver! I, Ola Olsen, domiciled at Lister, will vote for a compensation, not exceeding 175 crowns, to a widow in Nordland, provided I get three hundred crowns for a road in Fjaere parish, Ryfylke. That's what you call a horse trade!

But for heaven's sake don't make any joyful sounds that might disturb Ola in his parliamentary duties! You would really live to regret that! Silence! Ola is thinking, Ola is weighing the issues. What is going on in his head? What political move will he propose tomorrow? He is a man of distinction in Norway's minuscule universe, chosen by his people to speak his line in the national farce, dressed in the sanctified national frieze, puffing away at his short-stemmed pipe, his paper collar soaked with the sweat of honest endeavor. Get out of the way, damn you, stand aside for the people's representative—give him elbow room!

When it comes down to it, isn't it always the big fat zeros that make the difference in the total?

To hell with your zeros. Period. You get fed up to the teeth with the phoniness of it all, and you can't stand it any longer. You go to the woods and lie down under an open sky, where there is more room for those who are strangers among men and for birds in flight. And you find a bed in a damp patch, you lie on your stomach on the marshy ground and take pleasure in getting thoroughly soaked. And you bury your head in the reeds and soggy leaves and crawling things, and soft little lizards crawl on your clothes and onto your face and look at you with their green velvety eyes; you are surrounded by the gentle rustlings of the wind and the trees, while God on high sits looking down on you—you, the most fixed of all his fixed ideas! Your spirits begin to soar and you feel a strange diabolic joy which you've never felt before. You go to every extreme of madness—scramble right and wrong, turn the world upside down; you are as elated as if you had just done a noble deed. And why not? You yield to powers beyond you; you yield to them and let yourself be carried away by whimsy, by ruthless indulgence in pleasure. Everything you once reviled you now have an irresistible urge to glorify: you exult at the thought of decreeing universal peace; you would like to appoint a committee to improve the footwear of mailmen; you would put in a good word for Pontus Wikner and take it upon yourself to defend God and the universe. To hell with the idea of the interrelation of all things; that's no longer any concern of yours. You boo and jeer, and that ends it. Hi, hi and deia, the sun is shining on heia! Let yourself go, tune your harp and sing psalms and psongs as they've never been sung before!

And the next minute you let yourself float idly on winds and waves, becoming prey to idiotic streams of thought. Let the mind drift; it feels so good to give in, to stop struggling. And why struggle? Shouldn't a wanderer who has ceased wandering be permitted to dispose of his last moments as he sees fit? Yes or no? Period. And you do what your spirit tells you.

There is something you could do, though; you could promote evangelical missions, Japanese art, the Hallingdal Railroad—anything, as long as you help a project get started. Out of the blue you think about J. Hansen, the tailor with a fine reputation in town from whom you once ordered a coat for The Midget; he is a good citizen and a fine human being; you begin by respecting him and end up loving him. Why? Is it impetuousness, is it defiance, or perhaps some perverse emotion stemming from the strange influences you are yielding to? You whisper a few flattering remarks in his ear. You wish him wealth and success in all things, great and small, and when you take leave of him, you slip your lifesaver's medal into his hand. Why not, since you are already yielding to these mysterious powers? But you haven't gone far enough still; you regret that you once said some very disrespectful things about Parliament-Ola. Now you're really giving way to the most delicious madness—all the barriers are coming down!

Hasn't Parliament-Ola given his all for Ryfylke and his country? Gradually you begin to appreciate his faithful, honest efforts, and you mellow. Your compassion gets the upper hand; you weep for him and swear by all that's in you to pay double, triple indemnity. The mere thought of this old fellow, a product of the striving, suffering proletariat, this man in the homespun coat, fills you with a wild, ecstatic desire to put things right. In your ardor to elevate Ola, you vilify the whole world, and every soul in it; you gloat in destroying everything and everyone for his sake; you search for words worthy to praise and glorify him. You actually insist that Ola has accomplished most of the worthwhile things in this world, that he has written the definitive dissertation on spectral analysis, that he, in 1719, was the one who plowed all of America's prairies, that he invented telegraphy, that he has even visited Saturn and talked to God five times. You know very well that Ola didn't accomplish all this, but in your desperate desire to be noble you claim that he did, and you cry, and curse and swear by the devil that it was Ola and Ola alone who did all this. Why? From generosity of spirit, and to make it up to Ola. And you begin to sing his praises exuberantly; you sing a bawdy and blasphemous song of praise to Ola, who has created the world and put the sun and the stars in the firmament, and managed to keep everything in its place ever since. And to this you append a long line of imprecations as testimony to the truth of what you're saying. You abandon yourself to the most frantic soul-searching, only to swing back to a licentious, impelling desire to mouth oaths and profanity. And every time you hit upon something really unique, you pull up your knees and chuckle with glee over the amends that will be due Ola. Yes, Ola has it all coming to him; Ola deserves it because you once spoke disrespectfully of him, and now your conscience plagues you.

Pause.

I once made a stupid remark about a body—wait a minute—it was the body of a young girl who, as she was dying, thanked God for the use of her body which had never been touched. Now I remember! It was Mina Meek, and it makes me burn with shame. We toss off without thinking so many remarks that afterwards cause us to groan with anguish and regret! Only The Midget heard it, but I am ashamed to the very core. I once made an even more egregious gaffe that haunts me still. It was about an Eskimo and a blotter. Good God, it makes me cringe with shame! Come now, pull yourself together—the hell with scruples! Think of the day when you will be in the presence of the Almighty, in glory—are you sure you'll be among the chosen? Good God, how dreary it all is! How empty, dreary, hopeless!

When Nagel got some way into the woods, he threw himself down on the first patch of heather he saw and covered his face with his hands. His mind was in turmoil, the wildest thoughts assailed him. After a time he fell asleep. It was only four hours since he had gotten out of bed, yet he fell into a deep, exhausted sleep.

When he awoke, it was evening. The sun was sinking behind the mill on the fjord, and from the trees came the singing of birds. His head was clear, his spirit serene. His bitterness and confusion had vanished; he was at peace. He leaned against a tree, and thoughts came surging in on him. Was this the time? It would be as good as any. No, first he had to put several things in order. He had to write a letter to his sister, and a note to Martha with a small token of his affection. He couldn't die tonight. Besides, he hadn't paid his hotel bill, and he would like to do something for The Midget too . . .

Slowly, he walked back to the hotel. But tomorrow night all would be over—at midnight, without any fuss, neat and clean!

At three o'clock in the morning he was still standing at the window of his room, looking out on the square.

19

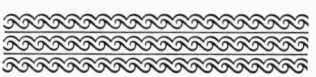

Around midnight the following night, Nagel left the hotel. He had made no preparations except for writing to his sister and putting some money in an envelope for Martha. But his trunks, his violin case, and the chair he had bought were in their usual place, and several books were lying on his table. He still hadn't paid his bill; it had completely slipped his mind. On his way out he had asked Sara to clean the windows before he returned, and she had agreed, although it was midnight. Then he carefully washed his hands and face and left the room.

He was calm, almost in a stupor. Good Lord, why make a fuss about it? A year earlier or later wouldn't make the slightest bit of difference; besides, it had been in the back of his mind for a long time. And now he had had his fill of disappointments, shattered hopes, hypocrisy and deceit.

Again he thought of The Midget, whom he had also remembered with an envelope and an enclosure, though his suspicion of the wretched, crippled dwarf was as strong as ever. He thought of Mrs. Stenersen, who, though sickly and asthmatic, deceived her husband right before his eyes without batting an eyelash; of Kamma, the greedy little golddigger who followed him around with her deceitful arms outstretched wherever he went and was always turning his pockets inside out for more, never satisfied. East and west, at home and abroad, he had always found people to be the same; the same vulgarity, the same hypocrisy—from the beggar who bandaged up a perfectly good hand, to the blue, ozone-filled sky. And he, Nagel, was he any better than the rest? No better, but this was the end.

He walked down to the docks to have a last look at the ships, and when he got to the farthest pier, he suddenly took the iron ring from his finger, threw it into the sea, and watched it sink far off from the pier. Well, at least in the last moments of his life he was doing his best to rid himself of hyprocrisy.

He stopped at Martha Gude's house and for the last time peered through her windows. Everything was the same: quiet and peaceful and empty.

"Goodby," he said and walked on.

Without knowing where he was going, he found himself on the road to the parsonage. He didn't realize how far he had come until he saw the garden through a clearing in the woods. He stopped. Where was he going? What was he doing on this road? He glanced for the last time at the upper-story windows in the vain hope of seeing a face that never appeared! No, that wasn't the way to do it!

He had meant to do it for a long time, but that's as far as he had gotten. For a while he stood looking at the parsonage with eyes full of longing; he swayed slightly and uttered a silent prayer.

"Goodby," he said once again.

Then he turned abruptly and took a path that led farther into the woods.

He walked straight ahead, looking for a place to stop. This was going to be done without deliberation, without sentimentality. What a fool Karlsen had made of himself in his desperation! As if a trifling love affair warranted such melodrama! He noticed that one of his shoelaces had come undone and he stopped, set his foot on a tuft, and tied it. Shortly afterwards he sat down. He looked around in a daze. He was surrounded by tall fir trees. Some juniper bushes were scattered about, and the ground was covered with heather. It was a perfect spot!

Then he took out his wallet, which contained the letters to Martha and The Midget. In a separate pocket he carried Dagny's handkerchief wrapped in paper. He pulled it out, kissed it over and over, knelt and kissed it again, after which he slowly tore it into tiny shreds. This occupied him for a long time. One o'clock, one-thirty, and he went on tearing at it until it was only thread. He got up and put it under a stone, hiding it well so that no one would find it, and then sat down again. That was about all, wasn't it? He went over everything and, convinced that he had forgotten nothing, wound his watch as he usually did before going to bed.

Again he looked around. The woods were now quite dark; there wasn't a soul around. He listened, held his breath, and listened again. Even the birds were silent, and the night was warm and still. It seemed as if life had stopped. He reached into his vest pocket and took out the vial.

The vial had a glass stopper that was covered by a paper cap sealed closed with a blue pharmacist's string. He undid the string and pulled out the stopper. The liquid was clear as water, with a faint smell of almonds. He held the bottle up and looked at it; it was only half full. In the distance he heard the sound of the church clock striking two. He whispered to himself: The clock has struck! Quickly he put the bottle to his mouth and emptied it.

For a few moments he sat upright still, with his eyes closed, holding the vial in one hand and the stopper in the other. It had been so effortless that he didn't quite realize what had happened. Now thoughts gradually suffused his conscious mind. He opened his eyes and looked around in a daze. These trees, this sky, this earth, he was seeing all this for the last time. How strange that seemed! The poison was already spreading through his body, penetrating the tissues, forcing a blue path through his veins. In a while the cramps would come, and then he would be lying there rigid and still.

He felt a bitter taste in his mouth and had the sensation that his tongue was shriveling. He moved his arms to see how far along in death he was. He began counting the trees around him, got as far as ten, and gave it up. Was he really going to die tonight? No, surely not tonight! What a strange sensation!

Yes, the hour had come. He clearly felt the acid burning his entrails. But why now, why this minute? In the name of God, he couldn't die just yet! How dark it was getting! The wind was rustling through the trees, though there was no wind. And why were red clouds forming above the trees? No, not just now, not right away! What shall I do? Good God, I don't want to die, what shall I do?

And suddenly a torrent of thoughts assailed him with overwhelming impact. He wasn't ready yet; he had a thousand things to do, his mind was aflame with all that remained to be done. He hadn't paid his hotel bill; it had completely slipped his mind, and he just had to straighten that out. He had to live through the night! God grant him an hour, or a little longer! There was another letter he had forgotten to write—a few lines to a man in Finland about his sister and her property; that was something that simply had to be done. His mind was so lucid and was functioning at such a feverish pace that he even thought of his subscriptions to various newspapers. No, he hadn't canceled his subscriptions either, and the papers would continue to arrive, piling up from floor to ceiling. What could he do? And now the end had practically come!

He ripped up tufts of heather with both hands, threw himself on his stomach, and tried to bring up the poison by sticking his fingers down his throat, but to no avail. No, he wasn't going to die, not today, not tomorrow; he would never die; he wanted to live, to see the sun for all eternity. He had to get rid of the poison within him; damn it all, he had to expel it!

Beside himself with terror, he scrambled to his feet and staggered through the woods, looking for water. He shouted: "Water! Water!" and only an echo answered from afar. In his delirium he screamed, stumbled in all directions, ran into tree trunks, jumped over juniper bushes, groaning in agony. But he didn't find any water. Finally he tripped and fell. His hands dug into the earth and he felt a spasm of pain on one side of his face. Dazed, he tried to get to his feet but sank back, growing weaker and weaker until he was no longer able to move.

Well, this was it! Dear God, he was going to die after all! Maybe if he had had the strength to go on looking for water he might have been saved! But what a horrible end; he had imagined something quite different. And now he was going to die poisoned under the open sky! But why hadn't the paralysis set in? He could still move his fingers and open his eyes. God, what an endless time it was taking!

He put his hand to his face; it was cold and drenched with perspiration. He was lying on his stomach facing the bottom of the slope and made no effort to get up. His limbs were trembling and the cut on his cheek was bleeding. How long it was taking! It was endless! And he lay there, waiting patiently. Again he heard the church clock —three strokes this time. He suddenly rallied: could he have had the poison in him for a whole hour and still be alive? He raised himself on his elbow and looked at his watch. Yes, it was three o'clock! My God, what a long time it was taking!

Well, maybe it would be better if he died right now. Suddenly he thought of Dagny, for whom he was going to sing Sunday mornings, for whom he wanted to do so much, and he became resigned to his fate. Tears welled to his eyes; in an upsurge of emotion that overwhelmed him in the midst of his tears and his prayers, he began thinking about all the things he would do for Dagny. He would protect her from all harm—perhaps even tomorrow he would fly to her and be near her! Dear God, if he could be at her side by tomorrow and make her wake up radiantly happy! He regretted having fought death a moment before; that was mean and selfish, when he might ensure her happiness. He repented and begged her forgiveness—what had made him do it? But now she could rely on him. He hardly had the patience to wait until he could float into her bedroom and stand at the foot of her bed. In a few hours, perhaps within the hour, he would be there. And he was sure he would get one of God's angels to do it for him if he couldn't be there himself. He would promise the angel anything in return. And he would say: "I'm not white, but you are; you can do me this favor, and I'll be yours to command. You are surprised because I'm black? Of course I am—what's so strange about that? But I'd gladly promise to stay black for a long, long time if you would do what I ask. I can stay black for a million years, and much blacker than I am, if you insist. And if you like, we can add another million years for every Sunday you sing to her. Believe me, I mean it. I'll think of all kinds of things to gratify you; there won't be any limits to what I'll do! And you won't fly alone; I'll be at your side. I'll gladly support your wings and fly for both of us, and I won't besmirch you even though I'm black. I'll carry us both and all you'll have to do is rest. Perhaps I could give you something you want, something you need. I'll keep it in mind, should anyone give me something. Perhaps I might be lucky and earn a lot of things that would give you pleasure . . . One never knows . . ."

Yes, he was sure he would be able to persuade an angel to do this for him. Again the church clock struck. Absentmindedly he registered the four strokes, but thought no more of it. He folded his hands and prayed to God to be allowed to die quickly, within the next few minutes; then perhaps he'd be able to see Dagny before she wakened. He would give thanks and praise everything and everyone if this great mercy were bestowed on him—that was his one fervent desire.

He closed his eyes and fell asleep.

He slept for three hours. When he awoke, the sun was shining down on him and the woods were alive with the sound of birds. He sat up and looked around. In a flash, all that had happened during the night came back to him. The vial was lying beside him, and he recalled how passionately he had begged God to be allowed to die quickly. And here he was, still alive!

Once more an evil force had crossed his path! He couldn't grasp it. Painstakingly he went over every detail. The only thing he was sure of was that he wasn't dead.

He picked up the vial, got to his feet, and walked a few steps. Why was there always an obstacle when he tried to do something? What had gone wrong with the poison? It was prussic acid; a doctor had assured him that it was more than enough, and in fact, he had killed the parson's dog with a single drop of it. And he was positive that it was the same vial; it had been half full. He remembered having noted that before he swallowed the contents. The vial had never changed hands, either; he always carried it in his vest pocket. What were these evil forces that dogged his every step?

Then it struck him like a thunderbolt that the vial had been in other hands after all! Almost involuntarily, he stopped and snapped his fingers. There was no question: The Midget had had the vial in his possession for a whole night. It was the evening of the stag party in the hotel that he had given The Midget his vest; the vial, his watch, and some papers were in the pockets. Early the next morning The Midget had returned the things. That old half-witted cripple had been at it again with his diabolic do-goodism! What a shrewd, calculated bit of filthy deception!

Nagel ground his teeth in fury and frustration. What was it he said that night in his room? Hadn't he made a point of saying that he didn't have the courage to use the poison on himself? And that misshapen rotten hypocritical creature had sat next to him, doubting his word all the time! That sneaky, dirty dog! He had gone straight home, emptied the vial, probably rinsed it several times, and then filled it half full of water. And after this noble deed he had gone to bed and slept peacefully!

Nagel began walking toward town. He was more or less rested and his thinking was clear, but his thoughts were bitter beyond words. The experience he had just gone through made him feel humiliated, and utterly foolish. To think that he had actually smelled the essence of almonds in this water, felt his tongue shrivel from it, and had sensed the approach of death after drinking it! And because he had swallowed a few drops of innocuous, baptismal spring water, he had hurtled over stumps and stones! Furious and flushed with shame, he stopped and screamed at the top of his lungs. He caught himself, looked around quickly, and afraid that someone might have heard him, began singing, to cover up the outcry.

As he walked along, he calmed down; the gentle morning air and the singing of birds restored his spirit. A horse-drawn cart approached him; the driver saluted and Nagel returned the greeting. A dog in tow looked at him and wagged his tail. But why hadn't he been allowed to die during the night, honestly and without complications? He was still fretting and was terribly confused. He had lain down with a feeling of infinite relief that the end was near. A sense of peace had enveloped him and he had closed his eyes and fallen asleep. By this time Dagny was up—perhaps she had already gone out—and he hadn't been able to do a single thing to make her happy! He felt empty and betrayed; everything had been taken from him! The Midget had done one more good deed, he and his heart overflowing with kindness! The Midget had saved his life—the same service he himself had once rendered a stranger who for some reason didn't want to arrive in Hamburg! That was the time he had earned the medal, and he hadn't really deserved it—*earned* it, indeed! You save people instinctively, not to do a noble deed, it's just reflex action!

He managed to get to his room without being seen, completely crushed. The room was clean and cheerful; the windows had been washed and clean curtains had been put up. On the table was a vase of wildflowers. He was pleased and surprised—this had never happened before, and today of all days! What a charming gesture on the part of a poor servant girl! Sara was a kind soul. It was a glorious morning. Even the people in the market-place looked happy. The man with the plaster figurines sat at his table, complacently smoking his pipe, though apparently he hadn't made any sales. Perhaps, after all, it had been a stroke of good luck that his previous night's plans had misfired! He shuddered at the terror he had experienced as he stumbled through the woods in search of water. He still trembled at the thought of it, sitting here comfortably in his chair in this pleasant, bright room drenched in sunlight, with a marvelous feeling of having been snatched from the jaws of death at the last moment. There was still a way out, though, that he hadn't yet explored. The first attempt might meet with failure; you didn't die, you got up again. But how would it be with a six-shooter, available at the nearest gunsmith's whenever you wanted it? It was something to think about.

Sara knocked at the door. She had heard him come in and wanted to tell him that breakfast was served. As she was about to leave, he called her back and asked if the flowers were from her.

Yes, she had put them there, but it was nothing.

But he took her hand and thanked her.

"Where have you been all night? You just came home," she said, and smiled.

"I very much appreciate the flowers you put in my room. Since yesterday you've also washed the windows and changed the curtains. It pleased me very much and I'm very grateful to you."

Suddenly he was overtaken by one of those mad moments when his mind unexpectedly wandered in all directions, quite beyond his control. "I had a fur coat with me when I came here," he said. "God knows what's happened to it, but I did have it with me, and I would like to give it to you. I would like to show my gratitude to you. Yes, it's yours."

Sara burst into laughter. What on earth would she do with a fur coat?

That was up to her, of course, if she would only do him the favor of accepting it—it would give him such pleasure. Her gay laughter was infectious; he found himself joining in. He even began teasing her. What lovely shoulders she had! But he had seen even more of her than she realized! It was in the dining room: she was standing on a table washing the ceiling when he caught a glimpse of her through the door. Her skirt was tucked up and he spotted a foot, part of a leg—as a matter of fact, he had seen quite a bit of lovely leg! That evening, in an hour or so, he would like to present her with a bracelet. That was a promise, but she mustn't forget that the fur coat was hers too.

This madman—had he completely lost his mind? Sara laughed, but she was beginning to feel a little apprehensive at all these strange goings-on. The day before yesterday he had given the laundress far more money than he owed her, and today he insisted on giving away his fur coat! All sorts of stories were circulating about him in town.

20

Yes, he was stark raving mad. There could be no other explanation; she offered him coffee, tea, milk, beer, everything she could think of, but still he got up from the breakfast table a moment after he sat down, leaving his food untouched.

He had suddenly remembered that about this time Martha used to bring her eggs to the market. Maybe she had returned—what a stroke of luck if he could see her today, of all days!

He went up to his room and settled down by the window.

He could see the whole square from where he sat, but Martha wasn't there. He waited half an hour, an hour, with his eyes fixed on the spot, but no Martha.

Then his attention was diverted to a scene taking place

at the steps of the post office, where a crowd had gathered. There was The Midget, jumping up and down in a kind of dance. He had removed his coat and also his shoes. He kept dancing frantically, wiping his face all the time, and when he finished, he collected coins from the spectators.

So The Midget had gone back to his old profession; he had started dancing again.

Nagel waited until he had finished and the crowd had dispersed. Then he sent for him.

The Midget came, respectful as always, hat in hand, with downcast eyes.

"I have a letter for you," said Nagel, producing the letter and putting it into The Midget's pocket. Then he said: "You've put me in an extremely awkward position, my friend. You have made a fool of me, deceived me with a deviousness I can't help but admire, though it was devastating to me. Do you have a few minutes to spare? Do you remember that I once said I would explain something to you? Well, the time has come. Incidentally, have you heard any rumors in town to the effect that I'm mad? As you can see for yourself, that is not the case. I do admit that I've been overwrought the past few days. Many things have happened, and not all of them pleasant. Fate, I guess! But now everything is fine, I'm quite all right—I'm sure you can see that for yourself. I suppose there's no point in offering you something to drink?"

The Midget declined.

"Well, I expected that. But to come to the point: I don't trust you, Grøgaard. I'm sure you know full well what I mean. You pulled the wool over my eyes so completely that I can no longer pretend that I'm not aware of it. You tried to dupe me in a matter of utmost importance to

me—for humanitarian reasons, to be sure, out of kindness of heart, if you will, but nevertheless you've done it.
You had this vial in your possession?"

The Midget looked furtively at the vial but didn't
answer.

"It contained poison, but water was substituted for it.
Last night there was nothing but water in it."

The Midget still said nothing.

"No crime was committed. It was done perhaps out of
kindness, out of a desire to prevent harm. But it was you
who did it!"

Pause.

"Well, didn't you?"

"Yes," said The Midget at last.

"From your point of view, it was the right thing to do,
but from mine it was quite wrong. Why did you do it?"

"I was afraid you would . . ."

Pause.

"But you see how wrong you were, Grøgaard. Your
kindness misled you. Didn't I make a point of saying the
night you walked off with the vial that I would never have
the courage to use it myself?"

"But I was still afraid you might do it, and now you
have."

"What do you mean? I'm afraid you're mistaken, my
good man. I did empty the vial last night, but I certainly
didn't drink its contents."

The Midget looked at him in astonishment.

"Now you see, you're the one who was thoroughly
fooled. I happened to take a walk during the night along
the docks and came across a cat writhing in the most
horrible agony. I stopped and looked at it; there was something stuck in its throat. It had swallowed a fishhook and

choked on it; despite frantic contortions, it could get it neither up nor down and the blood was streaming out of its mouth. I grabbed it to try to pull the fishhook out. But the cat, writhing in pain, rolled over on its back and savagely clawed at the air and ripped my cheek—you can see the gash. Now the cat is on the point of suffocating, the blood gushing from its throat. What could be done about it? While you sit there trying to decide, the church clock strikes two. It's too late to get help; it's two o'clock in the morning. Then you suddenly remember the magic vial in your vest pocket. You want to put an end to the poor beast's misery, and you empty the vial down its throat. Having swallowed the terrible liquid, it crouches low and looks desperately around. Its eyes filled with terror, the animal breaks away, springs up, wrenches itself loose, takes a couple of high leaps, and again begins its violent contortions along the dock. How could that be? Why, there was nothing but water in the vial! It couldn't put the poor creature out of its misery but only prolong its agony; it still had the hook in its throat and was bleeding and gasping for breath. Sooner or later it will bleed to death, or crawl into a corner and die in mute terror."

"I had only your best interests at heart," said The Midget.

"Of course you did! Everything you do is underlaid with good intentions. You just won't be caught doing something dishonorable, and your noble and honorable cheating with my poison is nothing new. Just now, for instance, when you were dancing down on the square, I was standing here at the window watching you. I'm not reproaching you—I'm just asking you—why did you take your shoes off? You are wearing them now. Why did you take them off to dance?"

"So that I wouldn't wear them out."

"That's what I thought your answer would be, and that's why I asked you. You're purity personified and the most irreproachable soul in town. Everything about you is noble and unselfish; you're without stain or blame. Once I wanted to test you and offered to pay you to assume the paternity of a child that wasn't yours. Although you're poor and could have used the money, you rejected the offer without a moment's hesitation. Your very soul revolted at the idea of such an infamous transaction, and I was unable to persuade you, though I offered you as much as two hundred crowns. Had I known you better, I wouldn't have offended you so crudely. Now I know that in dealing with you one has to spur one's horse on, yet hold the reins tight at the same time. Well, let's go back to what we were talking about. It is quite like you to take your shoes off and dance barefoot, displaying your disregard for pain. You don't complain; you don't say: 'I'm taking my shoes off so as not to wear them out. I have to, because I'm so poor!' No, you seek to impress by your silence, if you'll permit me to say so. It's against your principles to ask a favor of anyone. But you manage to get what you want without opening your mouth. You are above reproach in your dealings with other people as well as in your personal ethics. I'm making a point of this character trait of yours, but to go on—don't be impatient—I'm about to explain. You once said something about Miss Gude which has stuck in my mind. You said that if one went about it the right way, she wasn't so unapproachable after all; at any rate, you had gotten somewhere with her."

"No, but . . ."

"I remember it very well. It was the evening you and I

were sitting here drinking together; that is, I was doing
the drinking, and you were watching. You said that Martha—yes, you called her Martha—called you Johannes.
Isn't that so? She does call you Johannes, doesn't she? I
distinctly remember your telling me that. You said that
Martha had allowed you all kinds of liberties, and as you
said it, you made an obscene gesture with your forefinger . . ."

The Midget jumped to his feet, his face flushed, and
protested vehemently: "I never said such a thing! I never
said that!"

"You never said it? What do you mean? Suppose I were
to send for Sara and ask her to swear that during the
conversation she was in the next room and heard every
word through these thin walls? I'm astounded at your
denial, but if you say so, that's the end of it. Yet I really
would like to go into this with you a little further; it intrigued me, and I've thought about it often, but if you deny
having said it, there's no point in pursuing the subject.
Please sit down, and don't bolt the way you did last time.
By the way, the door is locked—I locked it!"

Nagel lit a cigar and suddenly changed his tone.

"Good God! What have I said? Mr. Grøgaard, I've made
a terrible mistake—please forgive me! Of course you
never said that! Forget it, my friend. Someone else said
that, not you! Now I remember—I heard it a couple of
weeks ago. How could I possibly think you'd compromise a
lady, and more than that, give yourself away so fla-
grantly! I can't understand how I could have gotten that
into my head. I must be mad, after all! But when I've
made a mistake I admit it, and apologize immediately, so I
can't be mad, can I? If my thoughts are a bit confused and
rambling, you mustn't think it's intentional; I'm not trying

to befuddle you; you mustn't think that. Besides, it would be impossible, since you hardly open your mouth and there is no way of knowing what you're thinking. I'm rattling on like this because I happen to be in a talkative mood at the moment—that's the only reason. Excuse this digression; you must be anxious to hear my explanation?"

The Midget didn't answer. Nagel got up and began to pace nervously between the door and the window. Suddenly he stopped and with an air of complete resignation exclaimed: "I can't be bothered playing games with you any longer; I want to make a clean breast of it. I've probably been confusing you with my erratic talk, and up until now I've been doing it deliberately. I wanted to get something out of you. I've tried all kinds of ways and got nowhere, and now I'm sick and tired of it. So here, Grøgaard, is the explanation you wanted. I have come to the conclusion that you are a scoundrel—that you have a secret vice."

As The Midget had started to tremble, his eyes terrified, darting wildly in every direction, Nagel continued: "You don't open your mouth; you're still playing the part. Nothing will make you budge; your silence is a powerful weapon. I admire you; you intrigue me. Do you remember the time I talked to you for a whole evening, staring intently at you several times and then implying that you had reacted with alarm? I did that to try to get something out of you. I've kept my eye on you and tried all sorts of ways to get at you, but I've been unsuccessful, because you're inscrutable. I've never doubted for a moment that in your piousness you had a secret vice of some kind. I can't prove it; unfortunately I have no evidence whatever against you, so you don't have to worry. It will remain our secret. I suppose you can't understand how I can be so sure when I have no proof. No, you can't. And yet you have a way of looking down when we talk about certain things; your eyes assume an odd expression. They flinch at certain words, certain subjects. And a strange tone comes over your voice—I can still hear it. But to come to the point: you arouse a strong feeling of antipathy in me; I feel it the moment you approach me; my very soul is repulsed by your presence. You don't understand it? Neither do I, but that's the way it is. I'm convinced that I'm right, but I can't do anything about it because I don't have any proof. The last time you were here, I asked you where you were on June 6. Would you like to know the reason I asked? That was the day Karlsen died, and up to that time I believed you had murdered him."

Almost speechless with horror, The Midget repeated: "*I killed Karlsen?*" Then he lapsed into a stunned silence.

"Yes, I was convinced up to that moment. My certainty that you were a scoundrel had brought me that far. I no longer believe it; I admit I was mistaken. I went too far, and I ask your pardon. Whether you believe me or not, I'm immensely distressed that I've done you this injustice, and many times at night when I'm alone, I ask your forgiveness. But though I was wrong in this instance, I'm convinced that you are a corrupt and insidious person. And by God I know that's true! I feel it deep inside me as I stand here looking at you, as God is my witness! And why am I so sure? From the very beginning I've had no reason to think ill of you, and everything you've said and done has been correct and proper, even noble. Too, I've had an odd and beautiful dream about you. I dreamed that you were in the middle of a swamp, that I had been torturing you and bullying you, and that you kept thanking me. You threw yourself down and thanked me for not having bullied you and tortured you even more. It was a lovely dream. There isn't a soul in town who thinks you capable of wrongdoing. They all respect you and think kindly of you—that is how well you have hidden your true self. And yet my instinct tells me that you're a cringing, cowardly God's angel with a kind word for everyone and a good deed every day. Now, haven't you talked about me behind my back, made trouble for me, broadcast my secrets? No, you haven't—and that is the way you operate; you never argue with anyone, you never step out of line, you are pious, above reproach, incapable of doing anyone any harm. The world accepts that image of you, but I don't. I distrust you profoundly. The first time I laid eyes on you, I had the most curious sensation. One morning a couple of days after I had come here, I saw you outside Martha Gude's house down by the dock—it was about two in the morning. You suddenly appeared in the middle of the street and I had no idea where you had come from. You stood still as I passed, and I felt you looking at me from the corner of your eye. That was before I'd ever spoken to you, but an alarm rang inside me, told me your name was Johannes. If it's the last word I ever utter, I swear an inner voice told me your name was Johannes and I was to watch out for you. Not until long afterwards did I learn that Johannes was indeed your name. But since that day I've had my eyes on you, and you've always avoided me. I've never been able to corner you. And finally you substitute water for a few drops of poison, out of kindness, and because you fear in your soul—so full of integrity—that I might want to use it. How can I explain my reaction to all this? Your virtue brings out the brute in me. Your superficial words and deeds won't distract me from my goal, which is to destroy you. I want to rip your mask off and make you show yourself for what you really are. My blood turns cold with loathing every time I see your blue, hypocritical eyes; I recoil at the sight of you. You are a lie, down to the very bottom of your soul! Despite your anguish and terror at this moment, I have the feeling that you are sitting there laughing gleefully to yourself, because you are well aware that I can't get you for lack of proof."

The Midget still did not utter a word. Nagel went on: "Naturally, you think me brutal and despicable for hurling these accusations at you. But that makes no difference to me; you may think what you like. You know in your soul that I'm right, that I've exposed you for what you are, and that is enough as far as I'm concerned. But how can you tolerate my treating you like this? Why don't you get up, spit in my face, and walk out?"

The Midget seemed to have regained his senses. "But you locked the door," he said.

"So you're waking up!" Nagel said. "Are you saying that you actually believe the door is locked? The door is unlocked, and look, now it's wide open. I told you it was locked to test you, to trap you. You knew all along that the door was unlocked, but you pretended not to know it so you could sit here looking innocent and virtuous as always, and allow me to abuse you. You didn't even make a move to leave the room. As soon as I let on that I had my suspicions about you, you were on the alert; you wanted to find out how much I knew, what kind of threat I might be to you. So help me God, that's the way it is; you can deny it all you want—it doesn't matter to me. And why have this showdown now? You might well ask—you might say it's no concern of mine. But, my friend, it does concern me. In the first place, I would like to warn you. Just now

I'm being completely sincere. You are leading some kind of surreptitious, low life, and sooner or later you'll be caught. One day you'll be exposed for everyone to trample on. In the second place, I'm convinced that despite your denials, Miss Gude is more to you than you care to admit. And why should I be concerned with Miss Gude? Again you have a point. I can't answer that question, because Miss Gude couldn't concern me less. But on purely human grounds it distresses me if you associate with her and corrupt her with your sanctimonious depravity. That is why I confronted you with this."

Nagel relit his cigar and went on: "Now I'm through and the door isn't locked. Can you claim that you've been mistreated?

"You may answer or not as you please, but if you do, let your conscience speak. My friend, before you leave, let me assure you that I wish you no harm."

Pause.

The Midget got up, took Nagel's letter from his coat pocket, and said: "After this, it's impossible for me to accept it."

Nagel had not expected this; he had forgotten all about the letter. "You can't accept it—and why not?"

"I just can't."

The Midget put the letter on the table and walked toward the door. Nagel went after him, with the letter in his hand. There were tears in his eyes and his voice was unsteady.

"Take it just the same, Grøgaard," he said.

"No," said The Midget, opening the door.

Nagel shut the door and repeated: "Take it, take it! I'd rather have you think that I'm mad than have you remember any of the things I've said today. As a matter of fact,

I'm quite mad; you must ignore my ramblings of the past hour. You realize that if I'm not in my right mind I can't be responsible for what I say? But do take the letter! I don't want to do you any harm, even though I'm not myself. For God's sake, accept it; it isn't much, believe me; it's only a token, and I did want to write you a letter; it's been constantly on my mind; I wanted to give you a letter even if it hardly had anything in it, just as long as it was a letter. It's only a greeting. There—I'm very grateful to you."

He thrust the letter into The Midget's hand and ran toward the window to avoid having to take it back. But The Midget didn't give in. Shaking his head, he put the letter on the table and left.

21

EVERYTHING was going from bad to worse. Whether he remained in his room or roamed the streets, he didn't have a moment's peace. A thousand thoughts surged through his mind, and each brought its own piercing pain. Why did everything turn against him? It was beyond him; everything was closing in on him. Things had gone so far that he hadn't even been able to persuade The Midget to accept his letter!

Everything was hopeless and he was depressed beyond belief. And to add to his anguish, he felt a dread, oppressive threat hanging over him. He would recoil in terror at the sight of a curtain fluttering in the breeze. What new torments were in store for him? His rather austere features, which had never been handsome, were even less so with the dark stubble growing on his face. And he noticed that his hair had become grayer at the temples.

Well, what of it? The sun was shining, and he was happy to be alive and free to go wherever he liked. The whole world seemed to be at his feet. The sun beamed down on the square and on the water, and the birds were singing in the charming little gardens in front of the houses. Everything was flooded with golden sunshine; the gravel on the roads glistened in it, and the silver globe at the top of the church spire glittered in the sky like an enormous diamond.

He suddenly felt ecstatically happy and so elated that he impulsively leaned out of the window and threw a handful of silver coins to some children who were playing by the hotel steps.

"Now be good," he cried, and could scarcely get the words out because of the emotion that overcame him. What was there to fear? He didn't look any worse than usual, and he could always get a shave and clean up a little. That was no problem. And he set off for the barber's.

Suddenly he remembered a few things he had to buy, including the bracelet he had promised Sara. Singing to himself, he went about his shopping, carefree as a child and content with the world. There was nothing to be afraid of; fear was a delusion.

His jubilant mood didn't leave him, and his mind wandered off in a myriad of happy thoughts. The scene he had had with The Midget was blurred and almost erased from his memory. The Midget had refused to accept his letter, but he had one for Martha also. In his desire to share his elation, he looked about for someone to deliver it to her. But how? He opened his wallet and found the letter. Couldn't he send it to Dagny, marked confidential?

No, that wouldn't do. He kept turning it over in his mind. He was determined to get the letter off immediately. Actually, it wasn't really a letter; it was just an envelope containing some money—no note, no word. Perhaps he could ask Dr. Stenersen to take care of it? And convinced that that was the best way, he went to see Dr. Stenersen.

It was six o'clock.

He knocked at the office door, but there was no answer. Then he went around the back to the kitchen, and at that moment Mrs. Stenersen called to him from the garden.

A group of people were sitting at a large stone table drinking coffee. It was quite a large party, and Dagny Kielland was among them. She was wearing a white hat trimmed with tiny pastel-colored flowers.

Nagel tried to retreat, stammering: "The doctor . . . it was the doctor . . ."

Good God, was something wrong?

No, nothing was wrong.

Well then, he had to join them.

Mrs. Stenersen took him by the arm. Dagny got up and offered him her seat. He looked at her—their eyes met. She had gotten to her feet and said in a low voice: "Please, won't you sit here?" But he found a place next to Dr. Stenersen and sat down.

The gathering made him ill at ease—but Dagny had given him a kind look, she had actually offered him her seat. His heart was pounding violently—perhaps, after all, he could entrust Martha's letter to her?

After a few moments he regained his composure. The conversation was animated. Once again his happy frame of mind returned, making his voice unsteady. He was alive, not dead, and not about to die! A gay, lively group of people were sitting around this table with its snowy table-cloth, bright-eyed and laughing. How could he possibly feel dejected?

"If you really wanted to please us, you would fetch your violin and play for us," said the doctor's wife.

How could she have such an absurd idea!

As the others chimed in, pleading with him, he laughed aloud, and exclaimed: "But I don't even own a violin!"

They would send for the organist's violin. It wouldn't take a minute!

No, he just couldn't. Besides, the organist's violin was worthless, with those tiny rubies encrusted in the finger-board. They made the instrument sound tinny. They should never have been put there; they spoiled the tone completely. Besides, he was out of practice; for that matter, he had never played well, and after all, he was the best judge of that, wasn't he?

Then he told them about the first and last time his playing had been accorded official mention; one might almost say the experience had been symbolic. That evening he had bought the newspaper and was reading it in bed; he was very young and was living at home at the time. The local paper had reviewed his performance—the review had made him so happy! He had read it over and over, till he finally fell asleep with the candles still burning. In the middle of the night he woke up, exhausted. The candles had burned out. The room was in total darkness, but he could discern something white on the floor, and as he knew there was a white spittoon in the room, he thought that must be it. He was embarrassed to say it, but he spat, and his aim was true. Pleased, he tried again and again hit the target, whereupon he fell asleep. In the morning he discovered that it had been the precious review he had spat on. It had upset him very much!

They all laughed; the conversation grew more animated. Then Mrs. Stenersen remarked: "But it seems to me you're paler than usual?"

"Oh, there's nothing wrong with me," Nagel replied, laughing aloud at the idea that something might be wrong with him.

But suddenly his face flushed, he got up from his chair and said there was something wrong with him after all. He had a strange feeling that something was about to befall him, and he felt apprehensive. Wasn't that absurd? It certainly was mere fantasy, wasn't it? Yet, all the same, something had happened to him.

They insisted that he tell them what it was.

No, what would be the point? It was of no consequence; it was ridiculous; why waste everyone's time with such nonsense? It was only a bore and absolutely of no importance.

On the contrary.

But it was such a long story. It started in San Francisco once when he had smoked opium . . .

"Opium? How amusing!"

"No, Mrs. Stenersen, hardly amusing, as I still find myself haunted by strange fears in broad daylight. Don't think I'm an addict; I've only smoked it once or twice, and the second time it did absolutely nothing to me. But the first time I had a strange experience. All of a sudden I found myself in an opium den. How had I gotten there? It was all quite by chance. I have a habit of roaming the streets, looking at people; sometimes I choose an individual to follow from afar to see where he ends up. At night in a large city it can be fascinating and lead to fantastic encounters. Well, that's getting away from the point. But there I was, roaming the streets of San Francisco. It was late; a tall, slender woman was walking in front of me. I was keeping her well in sight. In the gaslight I could see that she was wearing very light clothing, and around her neck she wore a cross of green stones. Where was she headed? She walked on, turned several corners—with me right behind her. At last we found ourselves in the Chinese quarter. The woman disappeared into an underground passage and I followed her. She walked through a long corridor, with me just behind. On the right was a wall, and on the left, cafés, barbershops, and laundries. She stopped at a door and knocked; a pair of slanting eyes looked through a peephole and she was let in. I waited for a few moments, keeping perfectly still, and then I too knocked. The door opened again, and I was admitted.

"The room was filled with smoke and noisy conversation. The woman was standing at the counter talking to a Chinese whose blue shirt was hanging outside his trousers. As I approached them, I gathered that she was trying to pawn her cross but didn't want to relinquish it; she wanted to hold on to it. It was a matter of a couple of dollars, and it seemed that she owed them something already, so that in all it came to three dollars. She wrung her hands, haggled, and cried a little, and she intrigued me. The Chinese in the blue shirt was also fascinating to watch. He wouldn't make a deal unless the cross was handed over. No cross, no money!

" 'I'll sit here and think it over,' said the woman, 'though in the end I'll probably give in. But I shouldn't do it!' Then she began to sob and, looking straight at the Chinese, wrung her hands over and over.

" 'What shouldn't you do?' I asked her.

"She sensed that I was a stranger and didn't answer.

"There was something beguiling about her, and I decided to lend her the money and see what happened. I thought it might prove amusing; I even slipped an extra dollar into her hand, just to get her reaction.

"She thanked me, giving me a penetrating look, but added nothing. She nodded and looked at me with eyes filled with tears—and I had done it out of curiosity! She paid up at the bar and asked for a room, handing over all the money.

"Thereupon she left, and I followed her. We walked through another long corridor, with numbered rooms on either side. The woman slipped into one of them and shut the door. I waited for a while, but she didn't reappear. I even tried the door, but it was locked.

"Then I went into the adjoining sitting room and settled down to wait. There was a red sofa and a service bell. The room was lit by a fixture attached to the wall. I lay down on the sofa, and after a while I began to get bored. So as to do something, I rang the bell. I didn't want anything, but I rang just the same.

"A Chinese boy appeared, looked at me, and vanished. Several minutes went by. 'Come back; let's have another look at you,' I said, to pass the time. 'Why don't you come back?' And I rang again.

"The boy came back, wearing felt slippers and moving without a sound. Neither of us said anything, but he handed me a small porcelain pipe with a long stem, which I accepted. Then he put what looked like a glowing charcoal into it and I proceeded to smoke. I hadn't asked for it, but I smoked nevertheless. Soon afterwards I felt a buzzing sensation in my ears . . .

"After that I remember nothing except a feeling of floating on air. I was soaring in space. Everything around me was bathed in light, and the clouds were blinding-white. Who was I, and where was I going? I tried to think, but my mind was a blank, and I was soaring. I saw distant green fields, blue lakes, mountains and valleys basking in golden light. I heard music from the stars, and the room swayed with the melody. The white clouds had an indescribable effect: they floated right through me, and I thought I would die of pure joy. This went on and on; I had no conception of time and no idea who I was. Then a feeling of reality flashed through me and I began sinking, falling through space. The light faded; everything around me grew dark; I saw the earth below and I knew where I was; I saw towns, and there was wind and smoke. Then I stopped. I looked around and found myself surrounded by a sea. My feeling of euphoria was gone. I bashed against the rocks, and felt cold. There was a white sandy bottom at my feet, and above me only water. I swam a few strokes; around me were exotic plants, luscious green leafy plants, and flowers of the sea which swayed on their stems—a world of utter silence, but where everything lived and moved. I swam on and reached a coral reef. It had been plundered; all the coral was gone. I said to myself: 'Somebody has been here before me,' and I no longer felt so lonely. I started to swim toward the shore but stopped almost instantly. There was a body lying on the bottom right in front of me. It was a tall, slender woman. She was lying across a rock, her body badly mangled. I turned her over and realized that I had seen her before. I couldn't understand how she could be dead; I recognized her by the cross with the green stones. It was the same woman I had followed through the long corridor with the numbered rooms. I wanted to swim on, but I felt I had to stop to straighten out her body; the way she was sprawled over that stone made a most ghastly impression on me. Her eyes were wide open. I dragged her to a sandy spot. I tucked the cross at her throat into her dress so that the fish wouldn't get at it. Then I swam away . . .

"The next morning I was told that the woman had died during the night. She had jumped into the sea by the Chinese quarter; they found her in the morning. I couldn't believe that she was dead. Perhaps I could see her once more if I tried. So again I smoked opium, but it didn't work.

"Wasn't that uncanny? And sometime after that I had another adventure. I had come back home to Europe. One balmy night I was walking around and I came to the harbor and stopped for a while by the dredging pumps, listening to the talk on board the ships. The pumps weren't operating and everything was still. I felt tired but didn't want to go home because it was very hot, so I climbed up onto the framework of one of the pumps and sat down; but the night was so warm and still that I couldn't stay awake. I fell sound asleep.

"I was awakened by a voice calling me. I looked down and saw a woman standing on the cobbles below. She was tall and slender, and in the flicker of the gaslight I could see that she was wearing very light clothing.

"I greeted her.

" 'It's raining,' she said.

"I hadn't been aware of it but thought it best to seek shelter. I climbed down from the framework. At that moment the dredging pumps went into operation, a shovel came swinging in the air and disappeared, followed by a second one. I realized that if I hadn't gotten away just then, I would have been smashed to bits.

"I looked around and saw that it was raining a little. The woman was walking in front of me and I had no doubt who she was; she was still wearing the cross. I had recognized her from the beginning, though I pretended not to. Now I wanted to overtake her and I walked as fast as I could, but I couldn't reach her. She didn't touch the ground but seemed to glide along without moving her feet. She went around a corner and disappeared.

"That was four years ago."

Nagel stopped talking. The doctor seemed on the point of bursting into laughter but assumed a serious expression and said: "And you haven't seen her since?"

"Yes, I saw her again today. That's why I can't seem to shake this uneasiness. I was standing at the window of my room looking out, and there she was, heading straight toward me across the square, as if she were coming from the harbor and the sea. She stopped beneath my windows and looked up. I wasn't sure that she was looking at me, so I moved to the other window, but her eyes followed me. Then I bowed to her, whereupon she quickly turned and floated back across the square in the direction of the docks. The puppy Jacobsen bristled and darted out of the hotel, barking furiously. This struck me as rather odd. I had almost forgotten her after all this time, but here she was again. Perhaps she wanted to warn me about something."

The doctor burst into laughter. "She only wanted to warn you about coming to see us," he said.

"Well, this time she made a mistake. There's nothing to

be afraid of, I know that. But the last time there were those shovels that would have torn me to pieces. That's why I've been a little uneasy. So you don't think it means anything? How ridiculous to find oneself caught up in something like that. It really makes me laugh."

"Only superstition and nerves," said the doctor tartly.

The others began telling stories, and the clock struck again and again. It was almost evening. Nagel was silent throughout the conversation. He was beginning to feel cold. At last he got up to say goodby. He couldn't give Dagny that letter; it would have to wait. Perhaps he could call on the doctor tomorrow and give it to him then. His happy mood had completely disappeared.

He was astonished to see Dagny also getting up as he was about to leave.

"You've all been telling such horrible stories that I feel all shaken. I must be on my way home before it gets any darker."

And they left the garden together. Nagel was delighted; a flush of color rose to his cheeks. Now he would be able to give her the letter. He would never have a better opportunity.

"Did you want to see me about something?" the doctor called after him.

"Not really," he replied, somewhat confused. "I just thought I'd stop by . . . It had been such a long time since I saw you last. Good night."

As they walked down the street, they were both ill at ease. Dagny was obviously embarrassed—all she could talk about was the weather. What a lovely warm evening!

Yes, wasn't it?

He couldn't find anything to say either but just walked along looking at her. Her velvety eyes were the same as ever, and her long, blond braid hung down her back. All his tenderness for her came back to life. Her nearness made him dizzy, and for a moment he covered his eyes with his hands. Each time he saw her, she was more beautiful! He forgot everything—her scorn, her taking Martha away from him, her cruel taunting with the handkerchief. He turned away to keep from making another passionate declaration. No, he simply had to control himself. Twice before, she had driven him wild—he was a man, after all! He held his breath and steeled himself against her.

They had reached the main street; the hotel was on the right. She looked as if she were about to say something. He walked alongside her in silence. Perhaps he would be allowed to walk through the woods with her?

Suddenly she looked at him and said: "I appreciated hearing your story. Do you still feel anxious? There is nothing to worry about!"

She was being gentle and kind this evening—he would bring up the subject of the letter.

"I would like to ask you to do me a favor," he said. "But I hardly dare—I don't suppose you would do it for me?"

"I would be glad to," she replied.

She would be glad to! He took the letter from his pocket.

"I would like you to deliver this letter. It's only a few lines—nothing important, but . . . it's for Miss Gude. She has gone away—perhaps you know where she is?"

Dagny stopped. A strange, indefinable expression suddenly appeared in her blue eyes, and for a moment she stood as if transfixed.

"For Miss Gude?" she said.

"Yes, I would appreciate your kindness very much, but it can wait—there's no hurry . . ."

"Yes, of course," she said quickly. "Give it to me and I'll see that she gets it." When she had pocketed the letter, she nodded and said: "Well, thanks for your company. Now I have to go."

She looked at him again and walked away.

He was left standing there. Why had she gone so abruptly? Yet she hadn't seemed angry; on the contrary. But she had left him so suddenly! She turned off onto the parsonage road and was gone. When she was no longer in sight, he turned and went back to the hotel. She was wearing a snow-white hat, and she had given him such a strange look . . .

22

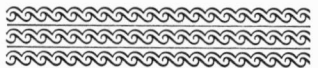

THE look she had given him—he just couldn't make it out. If he had offended her again, he would make it up to her the next time they met. His head felt so strange, but there was nothing to worry about—he felt reassured, thank God!

He sat down on the sofa and began leafing through a book but couldn't read. Feeling restless, he got up and walked to the window. He didn't dare admit it to himself, but he was actually afraid to look out the window for fear of seeing another strange vision. His knees began to tremble—what was wrong with him? He went back to the sofa and let the book fall to the floor. His head was pounding and he felt ill. There was no doubt that he had a fever. The two nights of exposure in the woods had affected him. He had felt a chill coming on in the doctor's garden.

Well, it would pass. He was not in the habit of letting a common cold get the better of him. Tomorrow he would be all right. He rang for some brandy, but it had no effect on him, and he didn't feel high, though he drank several glasses. What really alarmed him was that something seemed to be wrong inside his head; he couldn't collect his thoughts.

This had happened very suddenly—within the last hour! But why were the curtains fluttering like that; there was no wind. What could that mean? He got up and looked at himself in the mirror. He looked distraught and ill; his hair had turned grayer and his eyes were red-rimmed. "Do you still feel anxious? You mustn't be afraid!" Lovely Dagny in her snow-white hat!

There was a knock at the door and the hotelkeeper entered. He was finally presenting Nagel with the bill. It was itemized and covered two pages. But the proprietor was smiling and being extremely polite.

Nagel pulled out his wallet and began going through it; trembling with apprehension, he asked how much he owed. The hotelkeeper told him. But it could wait until tomorrow or another day; there was no hurry.

Well, God knows if he could pay; he wasn't sure if he had enough money. His wallet was empty! He threw it on the table and began turning his coat pockets inside out. He was desperate and looked everywhere. Finally he went through his trouser pockets, pulled out some change, and said: "Here is some money, but I don't suppose that's enough; count it yourself."

"No, it isn't enough," said the hotelkeeper.

Perspiration broke out on Nagel's forehead; he was anxious to give the hotelkeeper these few crowns to begin with, and kept searching his vest pockets, hoping that they also might contain some small change. They, too, were empty. But of course he could always borrow some! Surely someone would do him that favor! He was sure that someone would come to his rescue!

The smile had vanished from the hotelkeeper's face; even his air of politeness was gone, and he picked up Nagel's wallet, which was still lying on the table, and began going through it.

"Go right ahead!" said Nagel. "You can see for yourself that it contains only identification papers. I just can't understand it!"

Then the hotelkeeper opened the center compartment and dropped the wallet on the table. On his face was one great smile of surprise.

"Well, there it is! There must be thousands! You were joking! You wanted to see if I could take a joke."

Nagel, childishly happy, went along with this. Breathing a sigh of relief, he said: "Yes, I was only joking. I thought I would have some fun with you. Thank God I still have lots of money left. Look here!"

There were many large notes—a lot of thousand-crown bills; the hotelkeeper had to go out and get change before he could take what was due him. But long after he had left, Nagel's forehead was still covered with perspiration and he was trembling with emotion. This had really shaken him—and what a strange roar in his head!

A while later, he fell into a fitful sleep on the sofa, writhing in nightmare, talking aloud, singing, calling for brandy, which he drank, feverish and only half awake. Sara came in repeatedly, and although he kept up a stream of conversation, she understood very little of what he was saying. He lay there, his eyes closed.

No, he didn't want to undress. What was the matter

with her—it was the middle of the day, wasn't it? He distinctly heard the birds singing. She was not to get the doctor either. The doctor would only give him a yellow salve and a white salve; then they would make a fatal mistake, get them all mixed up, and he would be dead in no time. That's how Karlsen had died; did she remember Karlsen? Yes, that was the way he died. Well, at any rate, Karlsen had gotten a fishhook in his throat, and when the doctor arrived with his medicines, it turned out to be a glass of pure, baptismal spring water that had choked him. But that was nothing to laugh at. "Sara, you mustn't think I'm drunk. I'm just stringing ideas together—you know what I mean. The Encyclopedists, and so on. Count the buttons, Sara, and see if I'm drunk! Listen! The town mills are in motion! What a god-forsaken hole you live in, Sara! I'd like to deliver you from the hands of your enemies, as it says in the Bible. Oh, go to hell! Who are you, anyway? You're hypocrites, every last one of you, and I'm going to call you to task for it, all of you! Don't you believe me? I've been keeping my eye on you! I know that Lieutenant Hansen promised The Midget two wool shirts, but do you think he delivered them? And do you think The Midget would dare to admit that he hadn't? Let me assure you that he would never dare! He squirms and avoids the subject, doesn't he? If I'm not mistaken, Grøgaard, you're sitting there grinning your swinish grin behind that newspaper. You're not? Well, it makes no difference to me. Are you still here, Sara? Fine! If you'll sit here five minutes longer, I'll tell you a story—all right? But first try to imagine a man whose eyebrows are gradually falling out. You've got that? The man is losing his eyebrows. Next, may I ask you if you've ever slept in a bed that creaked? Count your buttons and see if you have. I've been most suspicious of you. I've been watching everyone in town, for that matter. And I think I've fulfilled a function. I've given all of you a dozen juicy topics of conversation, and no end of distraction in your dull lives. I've created one scandal after another in your dreary, conformist lives! What a terrible noise those mills are making—what a deafening roar! Therefore I advise you, respectable spinster, Sara Barmaid, daughter of Josef, to drink the clear meat broth while it's hot, because if you let it get cold, you'll have nothing left but water. More cognac, Sara; my head hurts on both sides and up the middle. It's an odd kind of pain . . ."

"Can't I get you something warm?"

Something warm? What kind of a crazy idea was that? In a matter of minutes it would be all over town that he had been drinking something warm. She must understand that he didn't want to create a scandal. He wanted to behave like a taxpayer in good standing, take regular walks along the parsonage road, and never be so bold as to profess opinions that differed from other people's. That he would swear to—three fingers in the air. She needn't worry. But he was really in terrible pain, that's why he wouldn't get undressed. It would go away faster that way. One had to fight this kind of thing . . .

He was getting worse and Sara became alarmed. She would have liked nothing better than to get away, but the minute she tried to get up he asked if she was leaving him. She was waiting for him to talk himself into exhaustion and fall asleep. But he kept rambling on, his eyes shut and his face flushed with fever. He had thought of a new way of ridding Mrs. Stenersen's currant bushes of lice. This was the idea: one day he'd go into a shop on the square and buy a can of kerosene, and then he'd go out on the square, fill his shoes with it, and set fire to both of them, one after the other. Then he would sing and dance around them in his socks. He was planning to do this one morning when he was well again. He would make a real circus of it, a real horse opera, and he would walk around cracking a whip.

He also thought up odd, funny names and titles for his acquaintances. For instance, he called Deputy Reinert "Bilge," and claimed that it was a title. "Mr. Reinert, the honored town bilge," he mused. Finally he began to rant about how high the ceilings might be in Consul Andresen's house. "Seven feet! Seven feet!" he shouted over and over. "That's my guess. Am I not right?" But seriously, he was really lying there with a fishhook in his throat—he wasn't making that up, and it was bleeding terribly, and was terribly painful . . .

Finally he fell into a deep sleep.

About ten o'clock he woke up. He was still lying on the sofa. The blanket that Sara had put on him had slipped down on the floor, but he wasn't cold. Sara had also closed the windows, and he opened them. His head seemed to have cleared, but he felt faint and was trembling. Once more he was seized with terror and apprehension. When the walls creaked, or when there was a shout from the street, he felt the noise going through the very marrow of his bones. Maybe if he went to bed and slept until morning it would go away. He undressed.

But he was unable to sleep. He lay there going over everything that had happened to him in the last twenty-four hours, from the moment he went into the woods and emptied the vial of water until now, when he lay here raging and racked with fever. How endless the day had seemed! And he was still possessed by that vague, mysterious fear that he was approaching a catastrophe. What had he done? Why was there so much whispering around his bed? The room was filled with murmurs. He folded his hands and had the sensation of dropping off to sleep.

Suddenly he looked at his hands and saw that his ring was missing. His heart beat faster and he looked again. There was a faint dark mark around his finger, but no ring! Good God, the ring was gone! Yes, he remembered—he had thrown it into the sea; he didn't think he would need it any more, since he was about to die. But now it was gone—his ring was gone.

He jumped out of bed, quickly got into some clothes, dashing around the room like a madman. It was ten o'clock—by midnight he had to find that ring; that would be the last possible instant—the ring, the ring!

He ran downstairs, out into the street and down toward the docks. People in the hotel stared at him, but he didn't care. He felt faint again, his knees were giving way under him, but he wasn't conscious of it. Now he knew why he had been uneasy all day—his iron ring was gone! And the woman with the cross had appeared to him!

Panic-stricken, he jumped into the first boat he came to. It was moored to the dock and he couldn't loosen the rope. He called out to a man and asked him to help him cast off. But the man said he didn't dare, because the boat wasn't his. Nagel would take all responsibility; he had to find the ring—he would buy the boat. But the boat was padlocked. Didn't he see the chain? Well, then, he would take another boat.

And Nagel jumped into another boat.

"Where are you headed for?" asked the man.

"I'm looking for the ring. You may know who I am. I

had the ring on this finger. You can see the mark for yourself—I'm telling the truth. And now I've thrown it away; it's lying out there somewhere."

The man didn't seem to understand.

"You are going to look for a ring at the bottom of the sea?" he asked.

"That's it," said Nagel. "You do understand. I must have my ring, you realize that. And now come and row me."

Again the man asked: "You're going to look for a ring you threw into the sea?"

"Yes, come. I'll pay you well."

"Good God, give it up! Are you planning to fish it out with your fingers?"

"Yes, it doesn't matter how—and I can swim like a fish. Maybe we can think of some other way of getting it."

The stranger actually got into the boat, began making plans how to go about it, all the while keeping his face averted. It was madness to attempt it! If it were an anchor or a cable, it might have been possible—but a ring! And he didn't even know the exact spot!

Nagel himself began to see the futility of the undertaking. But he refused to admit it, because it meant that all was lost! His eyes stared vacantly into space and he was shaking with fever and terror. He made a movement as if to jump overboard, but the man grabbed him. Nagel collapsed. He was faint, exhausted, and far too weak to put up a struggle. Good God, it was hopeless! The ring was gone; it would soon be midnight and the ring would be forever lost to him! And he had been given the warning!

Suddenly his mind was clear; countless thoughts raced through it during these two, three minutes. He remembered something that had slipped his mind: the evening before, he had written a farewell note to his sister and mailed it. He wasn't dead yet, but the letter was gone; it couldn't be stopped. It would have to follow its course, and it was well on its way now. When his sister received it, he just had to be dead! Besides, the ring was gone; life was no longer possible.

His teeth were chattering. He looked around in desperation. The sea was only a short leap away. He stole a glance at the man on the rower's seat in front of him, who had his face averted but was watching, ready to grab him if necessary. But why did the man keep his face turned away like that?

"Let me help you ashore," said the man, lifting him under the arms.

"Good night," said Nagel, walking away.

But the man followed him warily, watching his movements discreetly from a distance. Furious, Nagel turned and said good night again, and tried to jump off the dock.

But again the man grabbed him.

"You can't pull it off," he whispered into Nagel's ear. "You're too good a swimmer. You'll come up again."

Nagel was startled and then collected his thoughts. Yes, he was a good swimmer; he would probably come up again and would be saved. He glanced at the man; then he stared at him; a hideous face leered back at him—it was The Midget!

Again The Midget, always The Midget.

"May the devil take you, you filthy, crawling snake!" Nagel screamed, and began to run. He staggered along the road like a drunk, tripped, fell, got to his feet again. Everything was blurred, and he went on running and stumbling along in the direction of town. For the second time The Midget had wrecked his plans. In the name of

God, what would he think of next? Everything swayed, and a strange roaring sound was coming from town— what was it? He fell again.

He got to his knees and began rocking his head from side to side. Listen! There was a cry from the sea! It was almost midnight and the ring was still missing. Something was coming after him; he heard the sound of a scaly beast with a scrawny belly dragging itself along the ground, leaving a damp trail behind, a gruesome monster with arms growing out of its head and a yellow claw protruding from its nose. Get away! Get away! Again there was a cry from the sea, and he put his hands to his ears so as not to hear it.

He leaped up. There was still hope; there was still the six-shooter, the last recourse, the sure way out! He wept, overcome with gratitude, running as fast as he could, shedding tears of joy and relief at having thought of this solution. Suddenly he realized that it was late; there was no way of getting a pistol—all the shops were closed. At that instant he gave up, fell forward without a sound, his forehead sinking to the ground.

The hotelkeeper and several of the guests came out to see what had happened to him.

He came to and looked around. It had all been a nightmare—he had been asleep. Thank God it was all a dream; he hadn't even left his bed.

He lay there for a moment, thinking. He looked at his hand; the ring was gone. He looked at his watch; it was almost midnight—only a few minutes left. Maybe it was finished—maybe he would be saved in the end! But his heart was beating violently and he was shaking all over. Maybe midnight would come and nothing would happen?

He took the watch in his trembling hand, counted the minutes, the seconds . . .

The watch fell to the floor and he leaped out of bed. "Someone is calling," he whispered, and looked out the window with eyes bursting out of their sockets. He quickly put some clothes on, threw the door open, and ran out into the street. He looked around, but there was no one watching him. He started to run toward the docks, his white vest catching the light.

He reached the docks, ran to the farthest pier, and leaped into the sea.

Some bubbles came up to the surface.

23

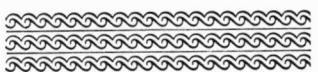

L ATE one night the following April, Dagny and Martha
were walking through town; they were on their way
home from a party. They were walking slowly because it
was dark and there were icy patches on the road.

"I was just thinking about all the things that were said
about Nagel this evening," said Dagny. "A lot of it was
new to me."

"I didn't hear any of it," said Martha. "I left the room."

"But there was one thing they didn't know," Dagny
reflected. "Nagel told me last summer that The Midget
would come to a bad end. I don't understand how he could
have known. He said it a long time before you told me
what The Midget had done to you."

"He did?"

"Yes."

They had turned onto the parsonage road. The woods around them were dark and silent. There wasn't a sound except for their footsteps on the frozen ground . . .

After a long silence, Dagny said thoughtfully: "This was the road he always took."

"Who?" said Martha. "It's slippery. Don't you want to take my arm?"

"Yes, but you had better hold on to mine."

And silently they walked on, arms linked, holding each other tightly.